The
INHERITANCE

Annabel Dilke is a novelist, journalist and screenwriter. She lives in South London.

Annabel Dilke

The INHERITANCE

POCKET
BOOKS

LONDON • SYDNEY • NEW YORK • TORONTO

First published in Great Britain by Pocket Books, 2004
An imprint of Simon & Schuster UK Ltd
A Viacom Company

1 3 5 7 9 10 8 6 4 2

Simon & Schuster UK Ltd
Africa House
64–78 Kingsway
London WC2B 6AH

www.simonsays.co.uk

Simon & Schuster Australia Sydney

A CIP catalogue record for this book is available from the British
Library

ISBN 0-7434-8963-2

Typeset by M Rules
Printed and bound in Great Britain by
Bookmarque Ltd, Croydon, Surrey

Acknowledgements

Thanks to my late father, Christopher Dilke, author and teacher of English to the world, who first encouraged me to become a writer, and my daughter Sasha for her wonderful support and advice, and my mother, Mary Dilke, who is the best-read person I know; to Bill Hamilton and Sara Fisher at A.M. Heath, and Suzanne Baboneau and Melissa Weatherill at Simon & Schuster; to Katharine Begg, Michael Calder, Kate Hamilton and Max Southwell for advising on various subjects; and Cilla and Gareth van den Bogaerde, David Roberts and other marvellously supportive friends.

No villain need be! Passions spin the plot;
We are betrayed by what is false within.

George Meredith
– *Modern Love*

For Caroline and John, with love

Foreword

'Next to Alice,' Felicity told the grandchildren with dreamy pride, 'all the other girls looked like black beetles.'

'Mum's not a beetle!' protested the smallest anxiously.

'Of course not, darling!' she reassured him. 'It's a figure of speech! Your mother had other gifts. Anyway . . . it was Grandpa who said it, not me.'

She told them solemnly, as always, 'Your grandfather had all the virtues that mattered,' but added, almost as an afterthought, 'though he could be unkind sometimes.'

Then her mood darkened as she remembered a blatant destructive beauty that had rendered even Alice's creamy perfection less remarkable. There was no record of it here in the old photograph albums, of course; just as there was none of that other outsider who'd brought such disaster to the family. 'Sex!' thought Felicity a little tartly, in her eightieth year. 'Thank goodness it's not my business to explain it to the grandchildren.'

It was always Alice's wedding they wanted to know

about, and Edgerton. In the uneasy world of their growing up, they sought comfort from tales of servants and parties and ghosts – and of course they knew that, though she might not be able to remember where she'd last left her pills or handbag, the flavours of nearly four decades ago were fresh as anything in her mind.

Strange how, all these years later, the memory of an intercepted glance could return the same strength of anguish: 'Not her too! I can't bear it!' Oh, she was glad she'd done what she did! Revenge had been very sweet. When you were old, it was *not* having seized the chance of happiness that seemed the crime.

'How many servants did you have, Grammy?'

Cuddling her smallest grandchild on her lap, relishing their easy intimacy as they crowded around her, fidgeting, she turned the pages: guiding them through the family's glorious past, providing a familiar commentary alongside her own faltering internal one, her attempt – even now – to understand what it had all meant.

'We were never so . . .' she began, as they looked at the backdrop to Alice's wedding: a sixteenth-century honey-stoned palace set in a lush valley where horses had roamed. The exquisite harmony of it stood out, even in these old black and white pictures. 'Never ever again . . .'

'Did she love him?' They always asked.

'Of course! But it was very quick.' Then, with tremulous sincerity: 'Your grandfather and I did urge her to wait until she was quite quite sure . . .'

Felicity shivered. The grandchildren didn't know it, but she was seeing a beautiful eighteen-year-old girl who believed she was alone, on the night before her wedding.

Alice was prone on her bed, sobbing her heart out, shoulders shaking, hands clutching at the pillow. Even now the memory caused Felicity pain. She longed to remember that she'd rushed in and taken her daughter in her arms. 'It's not too late to back out, my darling!' she'd have said. If she'd failed Alice, how was it that – all these years later – she could feel the shape of Alice's shoulders, her long hair tickling her cheek, the strength of her bare arms as she returned the embrace? She could even hear her own soothing voice!

But Alice had chosen to go ahead. Felicity's lips twitched with her own private justifications. Alice, who'd been brought up to marry young, had wasted ten clandestine months on the wrong man. Great houses mattered; ironically, it was Alice who'd appreciated that. 'And maybe it's better *not* to be in love with your husband . . .'

Out loud, she assured the grandchildren with an innocent troubled look, 'The planning was an absolute nightmare, but I couldn't leave it to anyone else, could I?'

There, in the photographs, was the result of her careful plans – perfection, just as everyone had learnt to expect.

'See her beautiful dress? Bellville Sassoon. It cost a fortune. There she is, against the lilies! Just like a Madonna . . .'

One of the grandchildren suddenly looked surprised and interested – as if she'd said something new – but Felicity carried straight on, as if she were really speaking to herself.

'I was very pleased with that particular flower arrangement. See her beautiful pearls . . .' Felicity's voice faltered a little as she said this, but the grandchildren didn't notice. As always, they pored over Alice as if she were an exquisite stranger.

'See the marquee; it took half a dozen of Stevens' men to put that up . . . See the cake! It was the most beautiful cake you've ever seen – I designed it all – and it had white doves, just like Edgerton. Here – if you look hard, you can just see them. Each one was made of sugar . . . See Great Gran's diamond and emerald tiara! I wept when that went. Can you imagine, she was wearing green rubber beach sandals on Alice's wedding day!

'Oh, we were all so rich! It was August the seventh nineteen sixty-five, darlings, and we were so so rich . . .'

Then Felicity sighed deeply, because she wasn't only thinking of the money.

Chapter One

Alice awoke early on her wedding day and, through her flimsy curtains, sensed stillness and brilliance, and knew that her mother's prayers had been answered.

From the depths of the house she could hear the grumpy roar of hoovers sucking exhaustedly at already clean floors, and, outside her window, the discreet crunch of wheels over gravel as food and drink were delivered in enormous quantities. The dogs barked frantically each time, as if it were a novelty for them to see a van come down the drive. All eleven would have to be locked in the stables once guests started to appear.

'This is the last time I'll ever sleep in this room on my own,' Alice thought, and immediately pulled the quilt over her head.

She loved her room. Set directly above the house's turreted porch, looking on to the long drive, it was like sleeping in the prow of a ship. It was also like being enclosed in a nest: a very cluttered one at present.

After a moment she peeped out from under the quilt, as if she could scarcely believe what she was seeing. On every surface lay neatly folded piles of marvellous new clothes, layered with white tissue paper, to be packed at the last minute in her suitcases (which already contained jigsaw bases of unworn shoes). There were fresh cotton and lawn dresses for sunny days of expeditions and lunches, formal gowns for smart evenings in grand restaurants, confections of satin and lace for night. Alice was marrying well, and her trousseau reflected it.

Her two outfits for today – her wedding dress and her pink going-away suit – hung, shrouded in more swags of wispy tissue, from padded hangers.

'As if they've had a chance to gather dust!' thought Alice with a nervous smile.

She hadn't stood still and contemplated her life for three months. She'd lost a stone and a half and her wedding dress had had to be taken in twice. The first time she'd tried it on in the shop that was filled with dreams, she'd spilt over its bodice. In the mirror she'd seen a flushed and disbelieving self: a girl who'd lit a fuse.

'We wore ostrich feathers in our hair,' Felicity would tell her daughters, 'and trains. And, when my time came to curtsey, one of the gurkhas standing guard winked at me . . .' But by the time Alice left school at sixteen, the young monarch had done away with presentations at court, so, after her launch in virginal white at Queen Charlotte's Ball, she just went to all the parties. Though it was never spelt out for her, the idea, of course, was to find a husband. Neither parent encouraged her to have a career, whereas Eve easily got her wish to try for university. Alice was the pretty one, Eve the clever one. For them, it had always seemed as uncomplicated as that.

Every young man Alice brought home was assessed as marriage material. Her father was unfailingly courteous, believing he hid his contempt for the boring ones; her mother watched her covertly, trying to divine her feelings. She never brought Marcus, but might as well have. She conveyed anguish and obsession mingled with a strange inner peace. She was more easily upset and even sweeter. Meanwhile her childhood friend Edward held her hand and listened, and waited for his moment.

It was odd that nobody had anticipated he would carry off the prize of Alice, because, as heir to Mossbury Park (and a title), he was very eligible. He was amiable, too. His hair was always a little too short. He was the sort of man who arranged romantic evenings for beautiful girls, only to have them weep on his shoulder over someone else.

One evening – unhappier than she'd ever been – Alice sought out her father for guidance.

'Pa . . .'

'Yes, my turtledove?' Exclusively for her: his look of doting delight, a special name. How handsome he was, how youthful: how wonderfully different from everyone else's father.

It was just before dinner and, having had his bath, Harry Chandler was sitting in his green velvet chair in his study, wavy dark-blond hair sleeked with brilliantine, wearing his favourite mole-coloured corduroy jacket and sipping an Amontillado. A log fire crackled in the grate, warming his tiger skin rug with its glassy glare and lockjaw snarl. This was where he kept his books and sporting trophies (he was an excellent horseman and tennis player), and personal heirlooms like his father's ivory paper knife and a framed note signed by Nelson. There was an exquisite arrangement of purple irises by his wife, Felicity, like a discreet signature, in a Lalique vase on a small inlaid Sheraton table by the window.

He'd already removed his hated new spectacles and laid his book aside. He'd been re-reading *Barchester Towers*.

His daughter's misery was affecting him deeply but, as usual, he shied away from addressing anything painful or difficult. For all Alice knew, he'd noticed nothing.

She allowed him to pour her a glass of sherry with his usual ceremony and took the beige tapestry chair opposite. Suddenly all she wanted to do was sit in silence, basking in his company. But he was clearly waiting for her to begin.

She said nervously, 'Um, it's about Edward,' and stared at him mutely, willing him to read her mind: anxious, as always, to please.

'Edward.' At first he knitted his brows, went through an elaborate charade. Which one of her legion of admirers could she possibly be referring to? 'That's the one with the chestnut quiff, is it? Or the feller who keeps clearing his throat?'

'Oh, Pa!'

He gave his lazy smile that always made her want to smile too (though not today). Finally he pronounced, 'A decent enough sort of feller, on balance.' He raised his eyebrows, still amused for some reason. 'Knows his wine, too . . .'

'Decent?'

'I think so. Don't you?'

Alice shrugged miserably. Was decent sufficient? Was knowledge of wine relevant? She whispered, 'He's been jolly kind.'

Her father wasn't helping at all.

'Actually, Pa, he's asked me to marry him.' She couldn't help showing her pride. Being proposed to was a feather in one's cap, whoever had done it.

'Ah!' He looked taken by surprise, oddly thoughtful all of a sudden.

Alice said, 'He wants to know – and, um, maybe it would be *good* to decide quickly.' Her voice rose to a squeak that threatened tears. It wasn't Edward she really wanted to talk about. Couldn't Pa guess?

Another quizzical charming smile. Another ruminative sip of sherry. Then, in his teasing sentimental way, 'All turtledoves should be married.'

'Yes, but, Pa – Edward?'

What she wanted him to tell her, of course, was 'Never marry without love. Never never never. Don't marry out of gratitude. Don't marry for escape. Don't even *think* of marrying for revenge.' She knew him as a romantic: a soft-hearted lover of beauty. She knew how greatly he cherished her (though it was never his style to spell it out). So why couldn't he, for once, stop fencing with his own feelings and everyone else's? Stop finding everything so *amusing*?

He was the only person who could have prevented the marriage – and he did nothing.

The next day Alice astonished Edward (who professed himself the happiest man alive), and generated madness and true contentment.

Totally occupied, obsessed with detail, Ma was in her element.

Suddenly Alice was required to draw up lists of people she didn't think of as friends, whom she was assured would feel mortified if they weren't invited. She had to make more lists of things it was suggested she couldn't do without (like silver grape scissors), which guests would be nudged into buying. The plus was being given a licence to buy clothes – almost everything she liked, including an exquisite dress and its accessories, which she'd only ever wear once on what everyone started calling 'the great day'.

Yesterday evening – the night before her great day – the family had enjoyed a quiet supper. As usual, they'd eaten with all formality, in the dark-green dining room lit by silver candelabra, shadows alternately shrinking and looming in its corners, dull painted eyes observing them contemplatively from above. Pa had opened a special bottle and Mrs Briggs had made Alice's favourite: roast chicken with all the trimmings. There was a tacit ban on teasing, and Pa had shown his gentle, thoughtful side. Even Ma had put aside her ubiquitous pencil and notebook to concentrate on her – that admiring but cautionary look in her eyes, as always: that 'make sure you use your great gift while it lasts' expression. The parents had presented a peaceful united front. Alice had been urged to keep up her strength, made to feel more invalid than bride.

'This time tomorrow you'll be in one of the most beautiful places in the world!' said Ma. She smiled at Mrs Briggs, who was bending over her offering roast parsnips and a robust personal mix of cooking fat and sweat. 'This looks nice.' There were more hot dishes on the sideboard, but there was still plenty for the staff to do before tomorrow, and the weather had been very warm. She said kindly, 'I *think* we can manage on our own, Briggs.'

'You must tell Edward to order the calves' liver with onions,' Pa told Alice solemnly, as he helped himself to more bacon. '*Fegato alla Veneziana.*'

'Ugh, liver!' cried ten-year-old Kathy.

'You must be sure to visit the glass factories on the islands,' said Ma, 'and bring home some of those charming coloured beads that look like sweets.'

'And shoes,' said Eve, who was bored, but trying. 'Isn't leather the thing in Italy?'

'*More* shoes?' commented Hugo with heavy irony and his adolescent's smirk like a rictus of pain.

Trying to swallow her food and engage in the conversation, Alice concentrated on postcard views of canals and gondolas and piazzas. She thought of staying in the Danieli Hotel and being pampered. She thought of quiet days with Edward and the relaxation and companionship that would follow the one-off performance of tomorrow.

She put down her knife and fork, rose from the table, murmured, 'Sorry,' and fled the room.

Running up the long, dark staircase that had held so many terrors in childhood, breath catching in her throat as she clattered past family portraits, she expected to be followed. But Pa must have ordered everyone to stay where they were. He'd probably decided that, if nobody reacted, they could pretend this was nothing more than pre-wedding nerves. And Ma would go along with that, of course. Nobody would come.

In her little blue and white nest, Alice flung herself face down on her bed and inhaled its smell of lavender. She thought, 'I've been over this a million times. I know what I'm doing. I'm sure we can be happy.' She repeated like a mantra, 'Edward's my friend. Pa's right – he's decent, and kind. He wants the same things out of life as I do.' So far, it had worked: like pushing shut a door and twisting a key. But, to Alice's dismay, the door had burst open. 'I never ever want to suffer again,' she told herself desperately. (What sane girl would wish for that?) But along with the torment had gone passion; and now the memory flooded back, unbearable in its intensity.

Since news of her engagement had been broken in *The Times*, she and Edward had received nearly a thousand messages of congratulation. But there'd been silence from the one person she'd been convinced would make contact. It was only on the eve of her wedding that she understood it was permanent.

It was pretty ghastly being the elder unmarried sister of the bride.

'I'm only twenty,' thought Eve indignantly, 'and my real life has just begun. In two months I'll be back in Oxford. Oh, I can't wait! I can't wait!' And yet she must have been kindly reassured at least half a dozen times so far, 'You'll be next.'

In her role as chief bridesmaid, she'd been coerced into wearing a pastel frilled dress that looked more like a nightgown, forced (by her mother) to abandon her spectacles. But she'd put her foot down about allowing Alice's hairdresser to do anything special with her hair.

Scraped into an unflattering French pleat, it was her only rebellion. 'I know I look awful,' thought Eve, trying to avoid her mother's troubled gaze. 'Doesn't she understand I'll never try and compete with Alice?'

Yesterday evening, when Alice had rushed from the dining room, Eve had immediately tried to follow. But both parents stopped her. It was Ma who went to check on Alice, so that was sort of all right. Pa would have called her his turtledove and stroked her hand, but otherwise been useless.

He adored pretty women, Eve thought bleakly. It made him a legendary flirt. (All show, though, she told herself with the blind confidence – and natural revulsion – of the young.)

Ma was absent for only about ten minutes – roughly the time it would have taken her to climb the succession of staircases to Alice's room at the top of the house and make an immediate descent. But she'd assured them quietly and firmly as she resumed her dinner, 'Everything's fine.' 'All right?' Pa had enquired unnecessarily, not sounding particularly concerned. And then they'd started discussing the weather for tomorrow (set fair, according to the barometer, which Pa kept tapping obsessively), and Ma spoke of her intricate plans for the sheaves of waxy white lilies resting in cool buckets in the pantry.

When the last table napkin had been refolded and replaced in its engraved silver ring, Eve was liberated.

She'd found Alice sitting at her dressing table brushing her blond hair a hundred times, like their old nanny had taught them. ('Fifty's enough,' said Ma, 'and never use soap or water on your face or sit in the sun.') She was wearing her cotton pyjamas, probably for the last time. She looked pale but composed, and all she said, with a brittle laugh, in response to Eve's anxious enquiry, was, 'I just felt sick. It's funny, isn't it? I hate chicken, actually!' And then, 'I'm going to bed now.' That mirthless smile again. 'I'm s'posed to look my best tomorrow, aren't I?'

In the chapel striped with dusty sunlight, all Eve could make out of her sister was a blurry meringue of satin and net, the occasional glint of jewels. As the vows were exchanged, she anxiously listened for tremors or hesitations; but Alice's little voice rang out clear and certain. She must have looked all right, too, because all round her Eve could hear muted exclamations of 'angelic!' and 'exquisite!'

And now she had jovial old Edward for a brother-in-law – a man who'd never been heard to say anything malicious or surprising. 'Rather her than me,' thought Eve, who had no plans whatsoever to marry, at that moment. But she and Alice were so different it scarcely seemed possible they were sisters, let alone friends. Alice saw nothing wrong in being rich and having servants. She'd no desire to pursue a career or even learn about the world. From an early age all she'd wanted – she said it again and again – was four children and a continuing life in the country with horses and dogs.

It was her tragedy that, before she was safely married, she'd met Marcus, in the coffee bar in the town, where he'd stared at her from under his heavy black fringe ('Honestly, Eve, no one's *ever* looked at me like that before!'). Then he'd turned abruptly away. Handsome faithless Marcus had shifted her aspirations as carelessly as a child shaking a kaleidoscope.

Eve had been in on it from the start.

'*You* don't think I'm ignorant, do you?' Alice had asked, coming into Eve's bedroom just before two o'clock in the morning. It was thoughtless, but couldn't wait.

Once she'd woken up properly, Eve said, 'Well, you could read the newspapers a bit more.' She could smell Alice's scent, Carven's Ma Griffe. She heard a light clatter as Alice kicked off her shoes, and felt the horsehair mattress flinch as she flung herself down on the end of it. Then the chiming started up. First the bell in the clocktower outside, pompously bonging out the hours; then hollow, repressed confirmation from the big grandfather clock in the hall; and finally, joyous, crystalline pinging from the clover leaf-shaped gold timepiece on the mantelpiece in the grand drawing room.

'I read the *Express*!' giggled Alice.

'William Hickey and the fashion page!'

Alice laughed again. Then she asked, in the same interested cheerful way, '*You* don't think I'm spoilt, do you?'

Puzzled, Eve fumbled for the switch on her bedside light and felt around for her spectacles.

Alice looked rumpled and gorgeous – skin glowing like a lamp, sleepy happy eyes shedding grainy rings of mascara. She was wearing a skirt so short it was more like a band and a grey skinny rib sweater (inside out, Eve noticed) that showed off her voluptuous bosom.

'Who's been saying you are?'

'Well, not *exactly*!' Alice smiled in a satisfied way, as if none of this should be taken too seriously. Then she opened her big blue eyes wide as if she couldn't quite believe what had just happened to her, and smiled again, and bit her bruised lips as if trying to stifle a secret. 'Guess what?' she said. But Eve already had.

Marcus's family was gentry too; but impoverished, tainted by ancient scandal. It made him very resentful even though, at twenty-two, he was a successful horse dealer.

He was an outstanding rider also. It wasn't so surprising Alice found him more interesting than any of the young men in her circle. The point was, he had the gift. ('Oh, Eve, he can take the worst horse in the world and make it good!') What she didn't know was how adept he was at manipulating buyers, too – selling them a lame horse for jumping, a young one for hunting. ('Feller's no better than a second-hand car salesman,' said Harry when he finally found out about Marcus.)

Alice loved to watch Marcus operate. He would bring a new horse into the manège, let it off the head collar and allow it to behave as it wanted. Some would dash around; others would stand, lashing their tails, searching vainly for escape. He'd plant himself squarely in front of the horse, staring into its eyes. Then he'd turn his back and walk away. After a moment the horse would almost invariably follow, and the process of mastery had begun.

Alice had gone back to the coffee bar the next day, hoping to see Marcus again, and the day after that he was there. It was she who'd had to start a conversation, though, and begged to see his horses. Marcus said little. When he spoke, it was mockingly, as if he already knew her.

As it turned out, he was the most lethal of lovers: casually caressing with one hand, abusing with the other. But even as Alice was reprimanded (uneducated, vapid, took her privileged life for granted), she was made to feel interesting as never before. For such an unkind person, Marcus could be extraordinarily tender.

Later on, as he tested his power, the harshness encompassed real humiliation – but, by that miserable bewildered time, Alice was hooked. She'd never have been the one to break off the affair. It was cruel she hadn't been given time to get over it.

Eve thought, 'It's so unfair I'm not allowed to wear my specs.'

Standing to make his speech, impatient to shush his chattering guests, Harry tapped a glass with a heavy silver knife, whereupon a shard of leaded crystal crashed on to the table and crimson claret spattered the white tablecloth. ('The first omen,' Felicity called it, much later.)

There was an exclamation of alarm from the nearest guests but, because Harry never lost control, he used the accident to his advantage. He knew the power of his slow wolfish grin, his lazy drawl.

'Hope you're all enjoying my Lafite?' he enquired innocently, and waves of tipsy laughter rollicked round the marquee. He flashed his teeth again at one of the servants, and was instantly provided with a filled new glass. Then genuine emotion snagged his voice, viscous with excellent food and drink, and the audience settled back to enjoy the spectacle of Harry the doting father forced to make a graceful surrender.

Blonde Alice, parcelled in ivory satin, glowed exquisitely

under all the attention, and Harry thought, relishing her:
'She'll be all right . . .'

It wasn't surprising that Harry had few romantic notions
about marriage. When you knew from childhood that you
would inherit a great house, you understood you must
search for the most suitable partner to share the burden.
And when you found that you passionately loved that
house, there was no way you'd consider something as
destructive as divorce. Besides which, it would unsettle the
children and he was very fond of Felicity, who was a good
wife. He believed that he manifested his fondness in loyalty.
To Harry's way of thinking, loyalty meant public support,
discretion, and refusing to discuss your wife with another
woman. By contrast, infidelity was unimportant unless it
involved love or commitment – which it never had and
(Harry was certain) never would.

He was a man moved to tears by beautiful music, who
prayed in church, and was fair to those he employed, and
rose to his feet unfailingly each time a woman entered or left
a room, and doted on his favourite dog, Champion, and
believed he would give his life for any of his children. He
had also had sex with half a dozen of the guests at Alice's
wedding. He could count them now at his leisure – wives of
his friends dotted throughout the marquee – even as he
paused with a smile to allow for a storm of appreciative
laughter.

As he finished his speech (with an elegantly phrased
threat concerning what he would do to Edward if he didn't
make Alice happy), Harry caught the eye of Priscilla
Copeland on the fifth table to his left and both

immediately looked away. Demure in high-necked cream and a wide-brimmed cream hat with a veil, she looked as if butter wouldn't melt in her mouth. 'And that's just what I like,' thought Harry.

Last Tuesday afternoon replayed in his mind as he basked in his guests' applause and, under cover of the tablecloth, lightly touched his crotch. Pink sunlight sieving through the crimson curtains in Priscilla's bedroom; an unrestrained but tender frolic among tangled cotton sheets; her white body with its red hair enmeshed with his athletic one, his head and arms burnt mahogany by the sun. On her wireless, by sublime chance, the second of Strauss's four last songs; staring blurrily up at the damask belly of her four-poster, her soft breasts against his chest; a shared (though not disloyal) joke about her husband Ian's predilection for books on the First World War, several of which lay on the small table on Harry's side (the right-hand, whichever bed he was occupying). A fifteen-minute recuperative zizz; a civilized cup of Earl Grey downstairs; a last kiss, like a fierce promise, before leaving. 'The very best thing in life,' thought Harry, 'and no one's getting hurt.'

As the guests rose to drink a toast to Alice and Edward, Harry looked to Felicity, as usual, for approval. But she was staring straight ahead with that familiar cool set look of hers.

'Speech all right?' he murmured unnecessarily.

But Felicity did not respond, and Harry was genuinely taken aback and wounded.

On Alice's wedding day you could see the wealth everywhere. It nestled in the dense emerald springiness of the lawn sloping down to the sparkling lake with its pattern of water lilies. It was evident in the symmetry and colouring of the herbaceous borders, where each flower and leaf had been coaxed to its perfect prime; the ribbon-swagged green-striped heavy canvas marquee, and the five-piece band tuning up to flood it with music; the scores of poached salmon with cucumber slice scales lapped with waves of mayonnaise, and crystal bowls piled with hay-scented home-grown strawberries; the barrels of ice where champagne magnums lay cooling; the dozens of scurrying servants.

It wasn't really done, in that circle, to discuss personal prosperity. But a mixture of family tradition and mutual recommendation meant that Harry and many of his friends belonged to the same exclusive club and, on that perfect day, its benefits seemed so magical and limitless that the feeling of being smiled on by the gods was bound to burst out, like song. So, after the ceremony, the lunch and the speeches, and much excellent drink, they found themselves discreetly comparing notes. It had been a good year, they said. They didn't mean there'd been less war or famine or disaster in the world. What they meant was that they'd become even richer. One of them was using the extra money to build a swimming pool, he boasted; another had bought a holiday house in Majorca. As for Harry, he'd barely noticed the cost of this wedding. His latest plan was to take flying lessons and buy himself an aeroplane. He led a charmed life. They all did. They raised their glasses of Moët and Chandon and toasted family life and friendship and England and everlasting contentment.

*

The band started up with that catchy tune, 'Love', by the phenomenal Beatles, and the guests followed the bridal couple on to the floor.

Hugo thought how ridiculous the old ones looked, jerking around like stick insects. Why couldn't they be dignified and keep to their own stuff?

To be fair, his father was doing some such thing. Moving silky smooth as oil in a sea of frantically bobbing heads, he was doing a slow waltz. Hugo nudged his friend Simon Copeland.

The boys studied their respective parents. They were very close. Harry's hands were clasped round Simon's mother's waist; her head rested against his shoulder. With her sharp features and brush of auburn hair, she looked like a pretty fox.

'Let's go to the rope,' said Simon. Like most of the children at the wedding, he was bored and looking for adventure. He also felt very uncomfortable watching his mother – especially as he could see his father sitting on his own, drinking solemnly, bleak and rubicund.

Hugo considered. He'd been specifically forbidden to take his friends to play on the rope because they'd mess up their clothes and their parents might not like the danger; but now the wedding bit was over, there was a feeling of abandonment in the air.

'I'm going,' said Simon, and suddenly he was off, whooping wildly as he leapt across the lawn. After only a moment's hesitation, Hugo followed.

Harry murmured: 'She'll be all right . . .'

Priscilla opened her eyes. She saw that Alice had hitched

her train over one arm and was jiving gracefully with Edward. She looked flushed and happy. But then, what girl wouldn't adore being given a wedding like this?

'She doesn't want another engaging ruffian who'll break her heart,' Harry continued in Priscilla's ear. He sounded as if he were holding the conversation with himself. His body felt very fit and lithe and his thick wavy hair smelt of the Bronnley lemon soap he used for shampoo. 'What she needs is someone to take care of her.'

It was the first Priscilla had heard of an unhappy love affair. She pulled her head back and looked at him questioningly. She said, 'You're not worried, are you?'

'Of course not.' Harry sounded smooth and amused. 'Excellent man, Edward.' His eyes were blank as a shark's as he flashed the smile that made her heart turn over. But he'd broken his cardinal rule of never discussing family, so she knew it was an untruth. She also realized, to her satisfaction, that he'd grown closer to her than he'd like.

True to form, he changed the subject. 'Guess what I'd like to be doing,' he crooned in her ear along with the music, and briefly and very indiscreetly ground his hips against hers.

Priscilla gave her deceptive shy smile – then caught sight of her friend Felicity staring at them from across the marquee. Her expression was cold and unsurprised as if she already knew (which was impossible). With her usual presence of mind, Priscilla maintained the smile and rolled her eyes as if to say, 'Only flirting with your delicious husband!'

But Felicity looked away and, being quite drunk, Priscilla made the fatal mistake of confiding her concern to Harry.

Her cheek was still close to his (though no longer pressed against it for Felicity's sake) and she didn't see his reaction: first alarmed, then thoughtful and increasingly remote.

She longed for the following afternoon, when they'd arranged to meet in private.

It never occurred to her that they'd made love for the last time.

Eve jived with one well-scrubbed young man in tails after another, high on champagne and energy and the music and yet, at the same time, oddly aloof.

It was her sister and all the other girls who danced with the future.

'I'm different!' thought Eve, thinking of the world outside the marquee. 'I will marry. Of course. I want children, don't I? But not just yet, and never to one of these . . .' And she beamed ecstatically at her partner, as if apologizing.

'Excuse me,' said Edward, appearing at her side.

'Bridegroom's privilege,' he explained with a smile, as he swept her into an expert foxtrot. He was good at dancing, in an old-fashioned way.

'Lovely wedding,' said Eve, because she couldn't think what else to say.

But Edward wasn't listening. He was watching Alice dancing with his best man.

Eve had never felt she had anything in common with predictable conventional Edward. But as his dreamy eyes — just inches away — swam into focus, she saw reflected her own exact mix of triumph and wonder. Edward had transcended himself too. For one fleeting moment they shared something intimate and rare.

'Did you say something, Eve?' he enquired without interest as he twirled her round so he had an even clearer view of Alice.

Harry's mother, Beatrice, sat on the sidelines with the other ancient ones. Such a dearth of men, when you got to seventy. But how they enjoyed watching the young girls dance! You'd think that hungry goggling would keep them alive. They leant, trembling, on their sticks and stared at all the taut young flesh and God only knew what flickering scratchy scenes of love and lust replayed themselves in their minds. She'd danced with Ivor Barker, the rarity on her right, when she was a girl.

'You never change.' She meant every word – even though he'd lost most of his hair and all his spring and never stopped fiddling with his flesh-coloured hearing aid.

'Nor you, Beatrice, not one bit,' he roared back, accompanied by a piercing whistle of static. She was exactly the same autocratic eccentric he remembered from his youth.

Beatrice's granddaughter, Kathy, who'd overheard this exchange, stared at them in blank wonderment.

Beatrice was wearing her only dress. It was maroon velvet, covered in white spaniel hair and very creased. It was kept rolled up at the bottom of her wardrobe while mothballed lines of jodhpurs and jackets commandeered the hangers above. She disliked dressing up, but would rise to the occasional necessity (though refuse to give up her comfortable sandals). Her dandelion flower hair was crowned with her favourite tiara (kept in a disused bread oven in her dower house, together with other heirlooms).

'Be a love,' she said to Kathy, 'and hand me my shooting stick.' She refused to use a walking stick. That really would mark one down as an old crock. Besides, a shooting stick was far more practical.

She'd rested her creaking back on it in the churchyard as Alice and Edward posed. She hated being photographed. It was only because of Alice's pleas that she'd agreed to join the family group. She'd stared resolutely down at her naked toes with their curving yellow nails as the photographer clicked away beneath his black cloth.

On this stillest of hot days, a breeze from nowhere had whipped Alice's white veil above her head like ectoplasm, and Beatrice felt a sudden presentiment. She knew about bad luck. It lurked in the shadows, snapping at random like a nasty-tempered terrier. The husband's parents looked like healthy stock, but that was no guarantee. Alice was a love, with more common sense than her parents gave her credit for. Even so, she was probably wise to marry young.

Family was everything. Beatrice's husband and a still-born son were boxed up beneath the turf just a few yards away. Maybe in less than a year a new bud on the tree might be celebrated in this very place. This mingling of extremes gave perspective, made the losses easier.

Sitting next to Ivor in the marquee, feeling his bony knee jab her padded one, Beatrice did not miss her son dancing too closely with Priscilla Copeland, nor her daughter-in-law's cool comprehension. Naughty boy. It was the humilation she abhorred more than the infidelity (his father had been much the same). Felicity might be chilly and meticulous, but she deserved discretion. Bad behaviour ruffled the surface of family life. Beatrice would say nothing specific to her son, of course, but nevertheless make her displeasure felt.

Kathy said, 'Gran?'

'Yes, my treasure?' This little one looked sweet in her bridesmaid's dress. Not like her clever Eve. Might even be a beauty, though you never could tell at this age.

'Why's it called a honeymoon?'

'D'you know,' said Beatrice, crinkling her eyebrows, 'I really don't know . . .' Kathy was always asking questions like this nowadays – in an important, serious way, as if striving to prove she'd crossed the dividing line between child and woman.

'Because she's his honey,' pronounced Ivor triumphantly (his hearing aid was behaving, for a change), 'and he's mooning!'

They all stared at Edward and Alice, now dancing as slow and close as Harry and Priscilla. Edward was bathing Alice in a doting new possessiveness: he dared to blow kisses into her ear; he moved his hands down her shapely back like a cello player feeling the wood; he narrowed his eyes in ecstasy as he breathed in her scent. Alice had her own eyes tight shut. It was impossible to guess her thoughts.

'Used to look at her like a chocolate he was frightened someone else was going to gobble up,' pronounced Beatrice gruffly, and Ivor cackled with lascivious pleasure.

Kathy's eyes widened with fright. She backed away from them, surreptitiously put her thumb in her mouth and looked round for the smaller bridesmaids. It was she, not Eve, who'd kept this distracted group in order in the chapel:

hissing when they trod on Alice's train and nudging them into correct formation. Now nothing would make her feel more secure than to play baby games with them – if they'd let her.

The wedding was a triumph. 'How do you do it?' the guests asked Felicity over and over again, but it was only what they'd come to expect. And so was Felicity's response, a faint dismissive smile implying that it had been the merest of efforts to orchestrate all this – the flowers, the music, the food, the whole performance of Edgerton at its finest. Actually, one whole salmon had gone missing (a greasy tail was found, a week later, tucked into a dog basket) and the beef was slightly overcooked (though nobody except Felicity noticed).

The cake was her *pièce de résistance*. Small enough to encapsulate absolute perfection, it had a round table with a long white lace cloth all to itself in a corner of the marquee. It had taken one month to plan, two to create. Six pillar-separated fruit-loaded layers sheathed in snowy icing (five for slicing now, one to keep for the first christening); heavy white flowers entwined over every edge; the family crest embroidered in sugar, and 'E and A' enclosed in a sweet lover's knot. The plan was to cut it at five o'clock, when tea would be served; then Alice and Edward could get changed and everyone would see them off to the station.

Hysterical shrieking floated across the grass from the lake. Hugo and Simon were taking turns to swing on the rope strung up by the head gardener. It was fixed from the highest branch of a pine that leant over one corner. It afforded a thrillingly long swoop over water, pale lilies piercing the dark surface.

'Let me! Let me! You've had it for ages!'

Reluctantly, Simon relinquished the rope to Hugo. After all, he was the son of the house. Hugo was spoilt: didn't enjoy sharing. Sometimes Simon didn't think he liked him that much.

Hugo took a run from the bank, at the last possible moment wedging his right foot in the loop of the rope. He felt his heavy fringe part over his forehead as he flew through the air, and saw below him the tiny island where coot and moorhen nested. It might be possible to land on it if he let go now – at the highest point of his trajectory – and allowed the momentum to carry him. But before he could even consider the idea, he was on his way back to the bank. He went on swinging in shorter and shorter arcs. It was important to judge exactly when to leap off, otherwise you ended up dangling over three feet of water with no option but to splash in. It would not be a good idea, when he was wearing a tailcoat that had once belonged to his father.

'Just one more . . .' he insisted.

'It's not fair! You had two goes last time, too.'

'Okay . . .' Then something possessed Hugo to suggest, 'Why don't we both try?' He added kindly, 'You can have the loop. I can easily hang on by my arms . . .'

It was cake-cutting time, and – though nothing had been said about music – the bandleader made a snap unilateral decision. After all, it was his fifth wedding in a week. (He was as indispensable as an undertaker, he told himself, in the legendary years of the early sixties.) So he bounced on his heels, jabbed his baton like it were a needle doing petit point, and the band struck up with 'If you were the only girl in the world'. It wasn't until the last sugary notes had died away, and he glanced triumphantly at the bride's mother, that he realized his mistake.

Harry and Felicity stood next to the groom's parents, Lord and Lady Farquhar, who radiated nonchalant superiority. They were roughly the same age, but Farquhar's hair had sloped away to a rim of fading fuzz above his ears and – unlike Felicity – Edward's mother had let herself go.

'We'll be grandparents before we know it,' chuckled Lady Farquhar.

Harry flashed his wonderful smile, appeared only enchanted to have been shoved a little further towards old age by this salt and pepper helmeted frump. The sight of her puffy veiny legs in beige tights offended him. He'd welcomed the advent of the miniskirt – what healthy man wouldn't? But when even a woman like Lady Farquhar took to showing her knees . . .

Felicity murmured, looking round, 'Where's Hugo?'

Harry frowned. 'He ought to be here.' There was growing tension in his relationship with his thirteen-year-old son.

'Should we send someone to find him?' She didn't look at her husband as she spoke. As usual she appeared very composed and aloof. But, inside, she felt beyond hurt: as if she'd never been a trusting innocent bride herself. The pale castle-like cake gleamed in filtered sunlight. Thank God it was possible to impose beauty and order somewhere.

Harry pulled his father's gold fob watch out of his waistcoat. 'We're running late.'

'I don't want him to miss this,' said Felicity, who doted on Hugo.

'Anybody seen my son?' Harry's mellifluous bellow, with its threatening undertones of impatience and irritation, carried across the great lawn, and two shivering dripping wet boys cowered behind the trunk of the copper beech. At that moment they were bonded by panic, though each would subsequently blame the other. In fact, only Hugo would be punished – for the great sin of breaking a billiards cue.

There was no way they could return to the marquee in their present state. It would be best to creep up to the house and find some dry clothes. Then, perhaps, they could discreetly rejoin the wedding party and, if necessary, make up a story about feeling uncomfortable in their suits. Nobody would notice anyway. Hugo, who'd inherited his father's charm, was growing more confident by the moment. In the meantime, they'd filch some strawberries and trifle from the kitchen. They could let the dogs out. They might take advantage of the empty billiards room.

In the end, Harry and Felicity forgot about Hugo, who missed the ceremony of cutting the cake (but, in time to come, would tell the story exactly as if he'd been there.)

It was Mrs Briggs who'd made the cake, under Felicity's meticulous instruction. She beamed with pride as she carefully handed over Harry's father's silver sword, polished till it shone and specially sharpened. There were beads of perspiration on her dark moustache and, as usual, wet patches under the armpits of her cotton dress.

The young couple had been assured their task was

simple. Each layer of cake had the hidden support of stiff cardboard in foil, and the pillars were sturdy as anything. Just one gentle steady cut through the topmost layer – and Mrs Briggs and her team of helpers would do the rest.

The photographer assumed his position. The bridegroom clasped his hand over the bride's, which held the sword. They exerted gentle pressure and aimed more fixed joyous smiles at the camera.

It might not have been anybody's fault, but straight afterwards Edward made a terrible error. He muttered, 'Sorry,' but it was down to pure good manners. Anyone with his sort of background would have done the same. 'Sorry' was what men like him said when strangers trod on their foot. He might also have been trying to protect his new wife.

One glance from Felicity was all it took and the servants swung into action. In a matter of minutes the cake had been scooped from the floor. Moments later, it seemed, it was returned in dark sticky little oblongs bordered with marzipan and arranged on porcelain.

'Delicious!' the guests enthused, before they even tasted it.

If it hadn't been for Harry, the accident (or second omen) might have been forgotten.

Harry said in his amused drawl, 'Plenty of plates to smash, too. Please! Feel free!'

It didn't take much to make his guests laugh, in their inebriated state. Even the groom's parents raised an uneasy smile. But Edward turned dark red, like the beef should have been, and Alice couldn't look at him.

Beatrice said sharply to Harry, 'That's not fair!' She added, 'Could easily have been a mouse.'

Harry's smile faded. He couldn't bear dominating women, and how dare his mother speak to him like that in public? But – though pale with rage – he managed a fine mix of joviality and ridicule as he repeated, 'A mouse, Mama?'

Ivor was straining forward on his stick, striving to follow the mouthings of a suddenly mute cast.

'They like sugar, don't they?' Beatrice demanded. 'How long was that cake kept in the pantry?'

Felicity said with quiet control, 'Of course, it had a cover.'

Ivor was almost certain she'd said 'lover'. A house and a lover? Deafness was a bugger: forcing you into a choice between blind incomprehension and making a fool of yourself.

'Take a good look at those pillars,' said Beatrice. 'Think you'll find a mouse had a good gnaw at one of them. Lots of them about at this time of year. Only possible explanation, if you ask me.'

'Honestly, I nearly died,' said Alice, as her sister followed her upstairs to help her change. Her train hissed softly as it swept along the first landing, ruffling its ancient rugs and gathering dust. Someone had released the dogs from the stables and Kaiser and Tinker had managed to infiltrate the house. They bounded alongside with their tongues hanging out.

'It's probably good luck,' said Eve, 'in some cultures.' She'd been able to put on her spectacles at last and the relief was indescribable. She added, 'Poor Edward,' and waited for

Alice to leap to his defence. She continued encouragingly, 'It was dreadful of Pa to say that, wasn't it?'

'He was only trying to be funny.' Alice was already pulling the pins out of her hair. She'd be wearing it down, as usual, to go off.

'He can be cruel,' said Eve with feeling. 'Good old Gran, not letting him get away with it.'

They'd reached Alice's room by now.

'Stay!' Eve ordered the dogs, and they stopped dead in their tracks, looking foolish and offended, as the door was shut in their faces.

Alice's trousseau had all been packed. Her pink suit hung, stripped of tissue paper, ready for her to put on. Fresh underwear had been laid out on a chair. Alice turned her back on Eve, so she could unzip her, then started easing her dress up over her head.

Muffled by layers of satin, she said: 'Guess what?'

'I can't hear you.'

Alice struggled out of her Bellville Sassoon dress and dropped the mass of heavy material, all tangled up and inside out, on the floor. She had an odd expression that Eve couldn't pin down. 'I've got the curse!'

'You haven't!'

'I felt it come on in the chapel. Honestly, I nearly died.' Sheer terror it had been, kneeling at the altar with her back to a packed congregation, imagining a scarlet stain spreading over white satin. She couldn't remember a single thing about the ceremony. All she'd been able to think of was getting to a bathroom.

'It's a joke! You're going off on honeymoon!'

'I know.' Alice peeled off the long silk petticoat she'd worn under her dress and unhooked her strapless bra. She looked all round and pink and innocent, her shiny hair tumbling over her shoulders. She slotted herself into one of the new bras – white broderie Anglaise – and its matching half-slip. 'I expect they've packed some S.T.s. Can you check?'

Eve said slowly, 'You weren't *meant* to get it now, were you?'

'Of course not!' Alice sounded very prim. 'Everything's gone haywire. I've been like that for weeks.'

'You're lucky Edward's a nice man . . .'

'Mmm . . .' She started brushing her hair as if that were the only thing on her mind. She seemed suddenly sober, as if the champagne jollity had been removed along with the wedding dress.

'. . . and you *are* going away for a whole month.'

'Well,' responded Alice, with an odd new sharpness to her voice, 'he always said he'd wait, didn't he?'

Eve said anxiously, 'Alice?'

'Well, he did!'

At last her sister met her eyes, and Eve thought with dreadful clarity: 'She's relieved. That's what it is. And she knows I know why. Oh, Alice, how could you possibly have been so stupid?'

Chapter Two

Only on the iciest of days was it warmer inside Edgerton than without. The thick walls never absorbed much heat, even during the most scorching of summers; the stone-flagged floors exuded a profound and eternal chill.

As winter approached and the temperature plummeted, tons of coal were decanted into copper scuttles, and it was one servant's job to split logs all day long. It made little difference. Edgerton had always been cold, and it was considered feeble to complain. Anyway, few people in the countryside went in for central heating. It was ruinous to the skin, cautioned Felicity. More to the point, it might warp the ancient panelling.

By early September the Chandlers were already anticipating pulling on overcoats to scurry along draughty corridors, Turkish rugs rippling above bare boards like underpowered magic carpets. The stone hot water bottles would come out, and gin steeped with sloes and sugar over the summer. Woollen garments laced with fresh moth-holes would be tugged out of drawers. Ice patterns of feathers and ferns would line the insides of the mullioned windows. Meals would become ever more stodgy and substantial. And nakedness would be dreaded and hasty, with any lovemaking confined to beds loaded with quilts and heavy blankets.

As Felicity pottered in the flowerbeds under the terrace, she savoured the last rays of sun, thinking, 'How lucky we are to have had this beautiful summer.' She looked uncharacteristically unkempt in faded old trousers and ragged straw hat, as if rehearsing for the Beatrice-like figure she might one day become. Her hands were soiled, because she chose never to wear gloves for gardening. It was surprising, for such a fastidious woman.

She'd been chatelaine of Edgerton for almost two decades. Four years into her marriage, her father-in-law had broken his neck in a hunting accident. The estate had passed to Beatrice. But Harry had longed to take over while still a young man, and Beatrice was tired of being ruled by an estate, and – after token grumbling – quite happy to swap places and move into the small mansion nearby known as the dower house. She liked to remind Harry that, technically, she could take back Edgerton at any time. It gave her unusual rights, as an old person, though none of the responsibility.

Felicity had come to love Edgerton as passionately as Harry did and, with her eye for beauty, had made it even more remarkable. It was she who'd planned the backdrop of dark purple buddleia to the clumps of gold potentilla edging a border; a bed of blue delphiniums entwined with velvety crimson irises to catch the eye near the lake. Her subtle brush strokes were everywhere, like the touches of a dedicated pupil following a master.

As she worked she glanced up at the empty sky as if anticipating Harry circling the house in the aeroplane he dreamed of buying, dipping the wings in salute before landing in the meadow on the far side of the lake. Flickering hope overlaid the personal humiliation that had marred Alice's wedding. Perhaps fantasizing about flying would prove enough this time. Besides, Alice was back.

A delicious smell had been building up all day: a mixture of caramelized sugar and overcooked chocolate cake. Wisps of it escaped each time the green baize door separating the kitchen quarters swung back and forth, and drifts wafted out of the open kitchen windows. Mrs Briggs had been baking to celebrate Alice's return from Italy. Eve's new term didn't start for a week and the younger children weren't going back to their schools until tomorrow so the whole family would be there to greet the newlyweds when they arrived at teatime.

Felicity heard the popping exhaust of Harry's Daimler chugging up the long drive. For her he'd gone in search of a rose: a purple gallica to adorn the kitchen garden. He'd been very attentive lately. He always was, when an affair ended.

Last week they'd bumped into the Copelands at a local cocktail party. Felicity had been scrupulously civil to Priscilla and watched Harry closely; she had even discovered a measure of pity in her new dislike, for nothing in Harry's relaxed, urbane demeanour indicated that Priscilla had ever been more to him than the wife of an old friend. It almost made Felicity doubt what she'd seen for herself. It was having a violent effect on Priscilla, who was drinking too much and displaying her white bosom like a last throw of the dice. 'We must have dinner,' said Ian Copeland, and Priscilla seemed to catch her breath as she waited for Harry's response. But Harry had turned deferentially to his wife, ready to approve whatever she chose to reply. 'We're awfully busy just now, Ian,' said Felicity. 'And – as you know – Alice is back on Friday. We'll telephone.'

Harry had missed Alice dreadfully. It had been painful to watch him each morning as he tried to concentrate on finishing yesterday's *Times* crossword while waiting for the frenzied barking of the dogs that heralded the postman toiling up the drive on his bicycle. But Alice was a bad correspondent. There'd been only two cards in a month, and she might as well have copied them from a travel guide. 'The churches are divine . . . Lake Como is magnificent . . . The Trevi Fountain is spectacular . . .' Edward had signed the cards too. It was maddening to be told so little.

He hated the idea of Alice coming to Edgerton as a visitor. But, as a newly married woman, she had her own house now: a pleasant farm on the Mossbury Park estate that had been done up whilst they'd been away.

At four o'clock the dogs started barking again. Alice had driven herself over in her little silver Mini. She was wearing a pale-blue shift from her trousseau and was a little plumper than she'd been at her wedding and deeply tanned. She seemed pleased to see them all again, but it was she who pulled away first from Harry's embrace.

'Turtledove.' His voice trembled a little as he stared at her beautiful face; and Alice brushed her long blond hair back with a brown hand and looked anywhere except into his eyes.

The dogs were trying to leap up at her too, with much the same moist soppy expressions. 'Hey!' she told them sternly. 'Leave me in peace, you pathetic old things. Okay?' She looked curiously at the Ham stone façade of the house as if she'd forgotten how it would glow in the sun then dull when a cloud passed over; the way the leaves on its tracery of Virginia creeper became rimmed with scarlet as summer expired.

'No Edward?' enquired Felicity, who'd changed into a neat shirtwaister and put on fresh lipstick and scent – as much for her husband as for her daughter.

'He's really sorry. His pa needed to talk to him about something. He said he'd be here for drinks.'

'So sorry,' said Harry, grinning uncontrollably. When everyone had calmed down, he asked casually, 'And how is the cake-wrecker?'

'Edward's fine.' Alice picked at a speck of mud one of the dogs had left on her dress. 'Italy was wonderful. But I'm glad to be home.'

'She looks well, doesn't she?' said Harry triumphantly, as if he'd been proved right. 'She looks very well.'

'Very well,' Felicity agreed. 'But she's a naughty girl, sitting in the sun. She'll ruin her skin.' And Alice rolled her eyes heavenwards (because this was so predictable from Ma) and smiled and said, 'I've got some stuff for everyone,' and automatically shrugged on a cardigan as they went into the house.

She'd brought a pair of hand-blown crimson glass goblets from Venice for her parents, a leather belt from Rome for Eve, Bacci chocolates for the children, even a packet of dried porcini mushrooms for Mrs Briggs.

'Don't ask me what you do with them,' said Alice airily, and Mrs Briggs kept her delighted smile as she puzzled over mysterious Italian instructions.

'I hope you're hungry,' said Felicity. 'Briggs has made a feast.'

'Don't!' said Alice, patting her flat stomach. 'Honestly, all that spaghetti, I've got to stop.'

Alice answered every question dutifully. 'The house is an absolute nightmare,' she told them with a bright laugh. Apparently, the plumber had let them down with the new taps, so the second bathroom couldn't be used yet, and the decorator had made the magnolia paint too dark in the morning room and the curtains for the drawing room hadn't been hung right. 'Nightmare!' she repeated.

She talked about 'we' as in 'We visited the Colosseum, gosh it was hot!' and 'Guess what, we saw smoke coming out of Etna.'

After tea, she produced stout packets of photographs. But because they'd all been taken either by her or Edward, there was no record of them as a couple. Edward looked contented enough posing on the beach or at the wheel of the car they'd hired; Alice smiled sweetly in different items from her trousseau against dramatic and famous backdrops. It was very unsatisfactory for the family. They wondered if Edward had been exasperated by her legendary inability to map-read, but teasing seemed suddenly inappropriate. Sitting in a half-circle dictated by the sofas surrounding the fireplace in the grand drawing room, they passed around each photograph too quickly because they kept hoping the next would provide more information.

Eve suggested a walk to Alice, but she replied with an apologetic smile that all she felt like doing for the moment was sitting down. Then Eve said, more cunningly, that she wanted to show Alice a new top she'd bought (which would mean taking her upstairs to her bedroom) but Alice told her, 'In a minute, I promise.'

And then Edward arrived and it was too late, and at last the family could see them as a married couple.

Alice used to tell the dogs as they coated her face with wet and smelly kisses, 'You're my darling animals and I love you more than anything in the whole world.' She used the same endearment for Edward now but might as well have been using his Christian name. ('Did you have a good meeting with your father, darling? ... Pa's going to buy a plane, darling ... They adored the glasses, darling.') They had become a unit. They touched hands occasionally as they sat on the sofa side by side and instantly smiled as if it had been a mistake. They listened to each other politely and didn't interrupt. But they didn't exchange adoring glances or try to finish each other's sentences. Alice responded to the family's curiosity as sweetly and enigmatically as the girl in the photographs; Edward played the attentive amiable young husband. They were framed in their separate spaces: unreadable.

At seven o'clock, Beatrice hobbled up from the dower house on her shooting stick to join them all for dinner. She hadn't changed out of the baggy skirt and food-spotted pullover she'd been wearing all day, and an elderly spaniel accompanied her in place of a husband. As the true owner of the house, she was – of course – entitled to behave as she pleased.

She was delighted with her present from Italy – a natural sponge. 'It's not a hint, is it, treasure?' She gripped Alice in an impossible to break free from hug, scraping her soft cheeks with her prickly skin, and the others saw Alice bite her lip and look suddenly serious.

'Cheeky young bugger!' Beatrice exploded as soon as she'd relinquished Alice. It startled Edward, who'd been anticipating an embrace too.

'Champagne?' Harry asked with his lazy smile.

'Hopped right over the netting!' Beatrice went on. 'Wouldn't have believed it if I hadn't've seen it with my own eyes.'

Harry placed a full glass by Beatrice's side.

'As close as you are now!' she went on. ' Cool as a cucumber! Cheeky bugger!'

It seemed that, earlier that day, a fox had carried off two of her ducks. He'd been far too quick for Beatrice. 'This damned arthritis! Oh he was crowing! If only I'd had my gun!'

'Not again, Gran!' sighed Alice.

And Edward agreed. 'Rotten business. But we'll get him when we meet this weekend, Lady C., don't you worry.'

'I won't,' said Beatrice grimly. She'd be there herself. She'd taken to skipping meets lately, what with her crippled old limbs. Wouldn't dream of doing so now.

These late summer evenings, they'd sit out on the terrace before dinner. As they sipped their champagne, they watched Hugo on the lawn below. Seemingly in slow motion, he bowled a ball gracefully over and over again for eleven scurrying competitive dogs. His hair flopped across his forehead. In the last few weeks a shadow of down had smudged his upper lip.

Beatrice said, 'That boy's shot up like a beanstalk.'

'His feet are a whole size bigger than at the beginning of the holidays,' said Felicity with a proud smile.

'Going to be a real looker,' said Beatrice. 'Oh, *he*'ll leave a trail of broken hearts!'

Immediately Harry shouted at Hugo, 'You're not following through!' And he told the others testily, 'That boy never makes an effort at anything.'

Beyond the lawn, the lake lay dark as treacle, criss-crossed by the silvery wakes of coot, moorhen and duck hastening in V-formations. Nearer at hand they could hear the murmurings of doves in the cote in the clocktower, rustling flurries as wanderers returned for the night. The long sweep of the southern façade of the house reared up behind them, lights springing on one after another in the line of reception rooms on the ground floor as the servants prepared them for the evening ahead. They'd be putting flaming tapers to big fires laid that morning; and, upstairs, would be picking up dirty clothes dropped thoughtlessly on floors, tidying books and papers into neat piles, turning down beds.

It made Eve uneasy now. For all its comparable beauty and exclusiveness, Oxford had changed her – though not as much as the man she'd met during her last term.

She loved her family but found herself critical of them in a new way. Their knowledge was so limited, their horizons so narrow. They couldn't conceive of the conversations she'd soon be resuming – rambling sometimes shocking talk that stretched into the early hours, reclining on big cushions in front of a wonderfully warm hissing gas fire in a fug of cigarette smoke, surrounded by half-empty bottles of cider and Nicolas and overflowing ashtrays.

'Pa . . .'

'Mmm.'

As always, Eve hoped against hope that she, the less beautiful daughter, might enchant Pa with her own distinction; that, one day, he'd turn to her with that delighted proprietorial look Alice had always known. But, even when – trembling with her own accomplishment – she'd shown him the letter about winning a place at Oxford, all he'd said was, 'St Anne's? A Chandler should be at Somerville.'

As dusk crept in from the direction of the lake, neutralizing the bright green of the grass, escorting a drop in temperature, Harry was still watching his son bowling for the dogs. Their ears were pricked to painful attention, their eyes fixed unblinkingly on the ball.

'What do you think about Marx?'

Harry shouted: 'Lift that arm up! No! Higher!' Then he said, 'Marks? What for? He's not even trying. Oh well *caught*, Champion! Ten out of ten.'

'No, Pa, Karl Marx.'

'You mean Groucho, don't you?' said Alice in a lifeless voice. 'Or Harpo.'

Edward repeated slowly for her: 'She said Karl, darling.'

'Who?'

'Karl Marx?' There was a wealth of scorn in Harry's voice and he turned to face his eldest daughter with that familiar dismissive impatience.

'Have you read him?' asked Eve, keeping her nerve.

'Have I read him?' Harry missed a beat, then his expression became first astonished and after that amused; and, with a sinking heart, Eve remembered his talent for ridicule, his perfect timing.

He turned to Beatrice with elaborate courtesy. 'Mama, did you educate me? Can you remember?'

But Beatrice was distracted: munching at nothing, grappling with some unvoiced problem.

Harry crinkled his forehead. 'I *think* I read the odd book. I could be wrong.' He tapped his head. 'Not much up here, you see.'

'I could always get a man to urinate round the duckpen,' mused Beatrice out loud. 'They do say that puts 'em off.'

It was one of Harry's affectations to paint himself as a pampered fool. How could Eve, of all people, have forgotten? Just because he didn't need to work, nobody should assume he wasn't clever. In between managing his finances and hunting and all kinds of other adventures, he somehow found time to read almost everything of note. It was one of the qualities she appreciated in him. Though mortified, she believed it would be an error to appear repentant. Pa was always claiming he liked women who stood up to him. What Eve never appreciated was that it had to be done in a flirtatious manner quite beyond her.

There was an interruption.

Kathy had found a baby rabbit trembling beneath one of the grand stone urns on the terrace. 'Oh, the poor thing! I'm going to take it straight up to my room and make a little bed for it.'

'No, Kathy!' protested Felicity.

'Let me take a look,' said Beatrice, with all the tenderness that had been reserved for the grandchildren. She hobbled over to where Kathy was squatting and, with the help of her shooting stick, lowered herself on to the stones of the terrace. She didn't touch the rabbit, but spoke to it gently, as she might have to Kathy: 'It's all right, little one.'

'It's going to be okay, isn't it?'

''Fraid not.'

'But we can take it to the vet!'

'Look, my treasure.' With a shaky old finger, Beatrice pointed to a patch of dark blood dried into soft fur (and forgot about all the rabbits she'd enjoyed shooting – like the one from the window of her bedroom). 'Something's attacked him. And if you try and move him, that'll upset him more.'

'Oh, but—' Kathy was very agitated. As usual, she found herself confused and emotional on her last night at Edgerton before returning to boarding school.

'For heaven's sake, Kathy,' said Harry impatiently. He seemed far angrier than the situation warranted. 'I seem to remember you tucking into rabbit pie a few days ago. You even had a second helping.'

And Alice – whom they all knew to be even more soppy about animals – said briskly and to their amazement, 'Pa's right, Kath. It's only a rabbit.'

They heard the plastic click of Mrs Briggs' stout black shoes on stone. 'Dinner is served, Your Ladyship.'

'Thank you, Briggs,' said Felicity.

Beatrice said, 'Why don't you go into dinner with the others, darling, and I'll come in a minute.' She seemed to debate for a moment. 'Hugo can stay and help me up.'

'Why? Why?'

'You wouldn't want Champion and the others to find him like this, would you? Or my Charlie? That would be really cruel. So lucky it was you that happened on him.'

Felicity said without expression, 'The food will get cold, Mama,' as if it wasn't already cooled by the journey on Briggs' rattling wooden trolley from the warm kitchen to the icy dining room. Meals at Edgerton were always tepid.

Kathy was sobbing – raging against being a child. She knew very well why Beatrice wanted her to leave and Hugo had been asked to stay. She hated grown-ups for the casual power they wielded. She hated her father for his appalling joke, and Alice, too (who'd changed beyond recognition); and she'd never ever eat rabbit again.

The rabbit's demise hung over the dinner table. Harry had carved Kathy breast of chicken, just as she liked, but every so often she slid a piece off her plate and dropped it into the mouth of Beatrice's dog crouching below. It was a small gesture of support for the rights of animals – even though Charlie would not have been kind to the rabbit. It was obvious her sulking was irritating Harry but, because he was so delighted to have Alice home, he was trying to ignore it. One more loud sniff or mournful sigh, however, and he might explode – if not in her direction, then in another.

'Hugo!' he said sharply. 'You have revolting table manners.' And Hugo started, outraged. It was a free country, wasn't it? All he'd done was eat his food. He hadn't held his fork in his right hand or made a noise. It wasn't he who'd been feeding Gran's dog under the table. And he was going back to Eton tomorrow. He pouted under his heavy fringe.

Edward saw a way of pleasing his new father-in-law. He tilted his glass back and forth against a candle to assess the colour, sniffed the bouquet with half-closed eyes, rolled the wine lasciviously across his tongue.

Eve wondered if Alice was required to witness the same performance each evening.

'Burgundy all right for you?' asked Harry mildly. He pushed the bottle towards Edward so he could read the label.

'Could have sworn it was claret,' said Beatrice, who'd disagree with her son for the sake of it.

'Fleshy,' Edward ventured solemnly. He glanced at Alice for approval but she was absorbed in cutting a roast potato into tiny pieces.

Eve thought, 'Poor Alice. Now she must listen to him.'

'Fleshy?' Harry sounded as if the word was foreign to him.

'Fleshy,' Edward confirmed. 'And, erm, fragrant . . .'

'Oh yes?'

'. . . with a nice hint of blackcurrant.'

'Blackcurrant, eh?'

'Very senior, sir.'

Edward looked pleased with himself, but Eve had seen her father's lips twitch. She had the strong suspicion that he'd been leading Edward on for his own amusement. She'd never understand him. Scoring points off Edward wasn't going to help this marriage succeed.

But then, her parents' own marriage mystified her. They seemed to be getting on all right at present. However, Eve had observed that warm patches seldom lasted more than a few weeks. Then her father would become progressively tetchy and difficult to please. He'd become obsessed with his tennis. Then, one day, he'd turn maddeningly jolly and spruce and give up the tennis and, for some reason, go and visit his old friend Bill Manners a lot; but by that time, conversely, her mother would be cool and withdrawn. Silences would stretch at the dinner table. Ma would become involved in some intricate project concerning the house that irritated Pa by taking up all her time and energy. Then, all of a sudden, as if in response to some unseen threat, her parents would draw close again and start calling each other 'my love' and 'darling'. And then, after a short period of peace, the whole cycle would repeat itself.

Harry had turned to another subject: the newly elected leader of the Conservative party. 'Got a face looks as if it's been carved out of pink plasticine.'

Edward cleared his throat. 'Heow neow breown ceow!' He giggled.

Alice's face was like a mask as she dabbed at a corner of her mouth with her napkin.

'Have to be careful,' said Beatrice.

'Sorry?' said Edward.

'Man's a queer, isn't he? Tories can't afford any more scandals.'

Felicity protested. 'Just because he hasn't got a wife doesn't mean—' As usual, she avoided using words she disliked or disapproved of.

Edward said, 'That other one was all right.'

'He was just a silly ass,' said Eve confidently.

'Well, hardly,' said Harry. He paused. 'But don't let's forget you're the world authority.'

As the family sat at the table listening to Harry

discoursing on Sir Alec Douglas-Home's fine academic record – every so often glancing sharply at his eldest daughter to make sure she was listening – dusk gave way to night, the pools of shadow deepened around the silver candlelabra, and Eve remembered so many times in her childhood when her father had told them all what to think. For years and years she'd accepted his pronouncements without question.

From her father she'd learnt that she must never ask questions about his war. Also, that it was tedious to pay too much attention to security (even though it was unnecessary at Edgerton because there were always servants around). And it was interfering with nature to neuter domestic pets – with the result that there were far too many dogs. He maintained it was boring to mend things (but knew Felicity would arrange for all necessary repairs), and not done to flash around money (which didn't prohibit him from planning to buy an aeroplane, but meant it was a virtue for him to wear his much darned old cardigan year after year). Thinking and talking about money too much was 'mere'. Courage was admirable, like style. Pretentiousness was unforgivable, and so was being boring. The greatest of all distinctions was to have been born a Chandler – a pedigree, of course, and not one of the pretenders.

There was a fresh tradition at Edgerton. After dinner, the whole family was required to watch the news on television. Rather later than his friends, Harry had purchased a set. But because he regarded television as a basically vulgar – though interesting – invention, he insisted the set be housed in a distant room reached by a narrow spiral stone staircase.

It was the only place in the house where Felicity had not laid her stylish imprint, and was known as the keeping room because it was where things were put that were considered too good to throw away but for which there was no real use. The room was like the answer to one of those silly questions: what do a chaise longue in severe need of upholstery, a stuffed squirrel in a cracked glass case, an enormous moulded papier maché map of Europe pre-World War II, a broken card table and an ancient gramophone have in common?

A collection of uncomfortable old chairs, including a couple of good ladderbacks, faced the television set. Balding rugs banned from the rest of the house inadequately covered the stone floor. Harry didn't consider it worth installing a paraffin stove since the room was only used for half an hour a day, so the news was watched in a chill which, as winter advanced, would become almost intolerable. Nobody was encouraged to watch any other programmes, and nor would they have wanted to. The whole experience was counter-productive, in that the younger children developed a lifelong aversion to current affairs.

It was the first time Edward had been put through this ritual and his expression was bemused but game. At his parents' home, Mossbury Park, a much bigger television was kept in his father's study, where his parents regularly enjoyed comedy programmes and dramas in front of a crackling log fire. He and Alice had placed their brand new set in their drawing room and yesterday evening, after their first dinner in their new home, he'd switched it on and watched indiscriminately until the screen went fuzzy and started humming.

Harry always hurried everyone up to the keeping room in good time and, once the television set had warmed up and black and white pictures appeared, they caught an advertisement for tinned peas accompanied by a catchy jingle. Hugo and Kathy looked suddenly alert and interested, but Felicity raised her eyebrows at Harry and he shrugged and twisted the switch to the other channel, the BBC. Since the news was all the family ever watched, it meant one of the servants must have been up there.

Beatrice said, 'Waste of money, if you ask me. I know what I like and nobody's going to change my mind for me.' She added chattily, 'Your father used to tin his peas.'

At this time of year there was seldom any real news. It was as if the whole world were still on holiday. Perhaps that was why an item about a hurricane that had begun thousands of miles away in the Caribbean was accorded any attention at all. It had involved winds of 135 miles an hour, said the announcer. In the early hours of yesterday the hurricane had crossed Florida and slammed into the Gulf of Mexico. There was a grainy shot of trees bowing under pressure, enormous whipped-up waves, whole roofs being torn off, houses staggering to their knees.

'Nothing much,' Harry pronounced as he switched off the set.

And with that the whole family trooped down to the enormous drawing room where, in their absence, the log fire had been coaxed into flaming life so they could play Consequences.

Chapter Three

Arthur Stevens had been the head gardener at Edgerton for fifteen years. He was a handsome rosy-cheeked man of forty-five – the same age as Harry.

He arrived early one grey rain-lashed morning, as Harry was still sitting over breakfast, yesterday's *Times* folded into a bulky square beside him.

Felicity put her head round the dining room door and said, 'Sorry, darling, can you see Stevens?' She was dressed to go out in a brown tweed suit with a scarf in autumnal colours loosely tied over the point of her chin. 'I'm late for the dentist as it is.'

Harry looked up from his crossword. His expression was vulnerable, pleading: a man who disliked being interrupted so early in the day, and was used to his wife sorting out servant problems. 'What does he want, my love?'

'Something about a leak . . .' The keys to Felicity's Morris Minor jangled in her hand as she blew him an awkward kiss. 'Listen to that wind!' she said, just before she left.

Arthur Stevens had put on a suit and tie to come up to the big house. After being admitted at the servants' entrance by Mrs Briggs, he'd given his good shoes an ostentatious wipe on the mat. He'd left his oilskins and his wet cloth cap to drip on to stone from a wooden peg.

He stood in the great hall talking to Harry who, as usual, wore his much-darned cardigan and a pair of old corduroy trousers blobbed with mud from the dogs' paws, with woollen combinations hidden beneath. Arthur Stevens spoke quietly, deferentially; and Harry thought of the bellowing he often heard coming from the garden as Stevens communicated with the dozen boys who worked under him.

'We've had that much coming in, sir, and there's no holding off,' Stevens explained. He sounded very apologetic for having interrupted his employer doing his crossword. As he spoke he glanced briefly and without expression at the plain whitewashed walls with dead antlered heads looming out of them, the seldom-lit, hanging iron candelabra, the big amphora of faded honesty and corn set in the empty fireplace – and tried not to react obviously to the damp chill he felt eating into his bones. He smiled anxiously as he informed his employer, 'The wife's threatening us with no dinner.'

'We certainly can't have that,' said Harry pleasantly, showing none of the irritation he felt at having his morning interrupted.

The Stevens family inhabited one of the dozen or so tied cottages on the Edgerton estate. As befitted a senior employee, it was a bigger property, with a little more land.

But, to Harry's surprise, the grass needed mowing and the rose bushes were very unkempt.

The front door was unlocked, and suffocating warmth enfolded Harry as he stepped out of the teeming rain on to a spotless mat with 'Home Sweet Home' picked out in black lettering. There was a similar sentiment in blues and greens, 'Home is where the Heart is', expressed in a fake tapestry picture decorating the tiny hall. The warm air smelt pleasantly of boiling apples and he could hear hoovering going on upstairs.

'Please, sir,' said Stevens, as he took Harry's mackintosh. Then he ushered him into the front parlour. He gestured at the ceiling. As if that sight weren't shocking enough for his employer, he added in a low worried voice: 'And it's coming in that bad in our girl's room.'

'Ah,' said Harry. He registered a small neat space: busy wallpaper, similar carpeting, an upright piano bearing a few framed photographs he didn't bother with, no books to speak of, a small television set. In a corner of the ceiling, which was sodden and stained, pear- shaped drops were forming every minute before falling with metallic pings into a frying pan arranged beneath.

As usual, Harry was carrying a stick (not, of course, because he was anything less than fit, but for whacking nettles and similar obstacles out of his path). He advanced a few steps, raised his stick to the ceiling and prodded, and immediately a chunk of wet plaster crashed into the frying pan, splashing water over the floral carpet.

Arthur Stevens looked interested rather than reproachful. The matter was out of his hands now. If his employer wished to further damage his own property, then that was his affair.

'Ah well,' said Harry, raising his eyebrows and smiling slightly. Maintaining Edgerton's roof was a never-ending business, involving regular large injections of money and much labour. He was pretty sure that, at this very moment, raindrops were tunnelling through cracks in ancient leading and slates blowing awry. Unlike Stevens, he was quite relaxed about it. As a matter of fact, he was rather fond of the small stain on the ceiling of his bedroom that no amount of repainting could obliterate. Sometimes he thought it resembled a naked woman, at others a cantering horse.

'No real harm done,' he went on, and Stevens nodded solemnly. He seemed very passive in his own home.

The hoovering ceased and, after a moment, a small pretty blonde woman appeared in the doorway wearing a mauve floral apron.

As she took in this new disaster she looked horrified. She glanced quickly at her husband but, before she could utter a word (which looked as if it would be sharp), Harry gave her his charming lazy smile.

'*Mea culpa*,' he drawled.

'Beg pardon, sir?'

Harry smiled again. 'Never fear, Mrs Stevens, we'll sort this out.' He paused. 'Obviously, erm, the primary leak lies above.'

Mrs Stevens looked baffled, as if Harry spoke in a foreign tongue.

'If I may, I'll take a look upstairs.'

As he climbed the cramped staircase behind Mrs Stevens he couldn't help noticing her shapely bottom and neat ankles. Lucky Stevens. He'd no idea his head gardener had such an attractive wife. Harry thought, 'There's a lot I don't know and Felicity never tells me.' Mrs S. was out of bounds, of course. He went for married women of his own class.

Harry found himself more than ever appreciating Edgerton. It beat him how it was possible to exist at all in rooms this size. He thought of the dreadful pressure of low ceilings and a whole lifetime spent pressed into a box, and silently hunched his shoulders in his leather-patched tweed jacket. More than anything, he loved the space at Edgerton: the procession of huge stately rooms where grand pieces of furniture became almost unobtrusive; the freedom of choice. He believed he would rather die than have to live in a house like this.

There was more floral carpet upstairs, and prints of cute children, and Harry found himself silently blessing Felicity's austere and perfect eye. The charming thing was, sweet little Mrs S. was patently so proud of the house. She smiled as she gestured at a throng of rabbits and daffodils and explained: 'Arthur done the wallpapering for me this Easter.' What she wanted to show him, though, was the devastation the leak had wrought in her daughter's room. Harry hadn't even known Stevens had a daughter, though, of course, it was more than likely the couple had children.

There was busy wallpaper there too, but it was scarcely noticeable because every inch was plastered with posters of pop stars. There was shaggy pink carpet on the floor, and pink brushed-nylon sheets tumbled on the unmade bed; clothes and underwear were strewn everywhere and a guitar was propped up by the fireplace. Mrs S. shook her head with a smile as she hastily gathered up a pair of knickers. There was no daughter to be seen. There was, however, a steady stream of drops falling from another sodden ceiling and pinging into more saucepans. The rain was coming in very steadily. Obviously at least one tile had been blown off. Harry was starting to feel irritated and put upon. Why hadn't Stevens – a highly competent man – climbed on to his own roof and fixed the damage? After all, he'd done it often enough at Edgerton.

His lips were already forming platitudes, he was calculating how quickly he might leave, when there was a commotion somewhere nearby: a door opening and banging shut, a steamy blast of synthetic strawberries, a thundering of bare feet. Suddenly a young woman wearing only a pink bath towel appeared. Long wet blond hair streamed over her shoulders and drops of water clung to her dark lashes. She looked as if she'd come in from outside, like some sort of freshwater mermaid, rather than straight out of a hot bath. She was even younger than Alice. But Harry absorbed a half innocent, half knowing face like that of the girl in one of his favourite paintings, Clouet's 'The Billet-Doux', skin like the cream topping the milk in the big steel vats in Edgerton's dairy.

'Oh my gawd!' said the girl in the same sweet, soft voice as her mother.

Afterwards, Harry decided that if she'd immediately retreated, overcome by embarrassment, matters would have turned out differently. But instead, she started giggling. She stood there in her skimpy little towel and shook with laughter. She put one hand to her mouth and the towel nearly came off, and she laughed even more. And, instead of ticking her off for her shamelessness, and maybe her lack of respect also, Mrs S. joined in, glancing at Harry every so often – who'd cautiously started grinning by now, as if to confirm that he, too, thought her daughter completely adorable.

The post had arrived by the time Harry returned, and *The Times*, but for some reason he felt none of the usual compulsion to check yesterday's solutions. There was no immediate desire to open the post either. There was nothing special anyway, apart from a letter from Kathy he pocketed to share with Felicity later. There was a seed catalogue for her. A dividend cheque – good. A bill from Berry Brothers – not quite so good. A familiar stiff white envelope – very good. He left them fanned out on the table in the great hall. He decided to go up to Monkton Beacon. He might even pop into the chapel first and kneel for a few moments on one of the rock-like maroon cassocks.

When Felicity came home, it had stopped raining. There was no sign of Harry. She noticed the unopened sheaf of letters, the folded uncreased copy of *The Times*, and looked momentarily thoughtful as she untied her silk scarf. She decided to ask Mrs Briggs to cook up some of the pheasant pâté Harry loved. But first she would get her daily phone call to Beatrice over with.

'Mama?' Her lips were still numb from the anaesthetic.

'Yes? Who is it?' Each morning Beatrice reacted in exactly the same curt impatient way.

'Felicity, Mama! How are you?'

She was sure she knew very well how Beatrice was, and her fastidious nature recoiled as she imagined the damp meaty odour of dog, spoilt overfed animals slumped on sofas laced with their hair. Beatrice would probably be in a rage about her fox, too. Felicity couldn't help wondering if the majority of the raids they were told about were invented. Perhaps it was part of the natural process of decay: a feeling of growing powerlessness, terror that death would slip in one day.

But Beatrice surprised her. She said brusquely: 'She's worrying me.'

'Sorry, Mama?' It was another of Beatrice's irritating habits to continue with conversations begun in solitude, then act surprised when nobody understood what she was talking about.

'Peaky,' said Beatrice. 'Looks as if she needs a tonic.'

'Sorry, Mama?' Felicity repeated.

'I'll bet my life she's not pregnant.'

'Alice?' Felicity sounded as if she'd taken a wild guess. She told Beatrice: 'I spoke to Alice yesterday on the telephone.' Her tone was cool and measured, as if the same thoughts had not been troubling her, too. 'She said she was fine.'

'Hmm. You've obviously not noticed her hair and skin.'

'She looks beautiful.'

'Beautiful girl – always has been – but coat's a giveaway, isn't it, my lovelies?' Felicity heard a plump slapping sound from the other end, a faint ecstatic moan from one of the spaniels.

'Harry's not here at the moment,' said Felicity, 'and I have to do the flowers for the chapel this afternoon. But I'll try and get over to see her soon.'

'You do that,' said Beatrice. 'And tell Harry to get himself over there too – if he's not too busy.'

*

Harry was, at that moment, standing at the top of Monkton Beacon, staring at the comb shapes receding foam had daubed in zigzags along the beaches far below. It was one of the local beauty spots: a purple crag jutting over a vast bay, with views across most of the county, and an uninterrupted horizon beyond the sea. It was cold and very windy at that great height and Edgerton was a golden speck in the distance. The heather rippled and bowed around Harry's feet and his hair flapped about his ears, and he wondered why he'd been so forgetful as to leave his cap behind. Usually the experience was cleansing. Faced with all this grandeur and permanence, who could continue to believe that problems or faults were of any real consequence? He'd return home humbled and soothed, and be affable to his family and grateful for small miracles like buttered crumpets.

But this time when he blinked through streaming eyes at the almost imperceptible line where the sea joined the sky, all he could think of was Stevens' daughter's rich milky skin and that brazen joyous laugh.

Felicity opened the newly painted door of Alice's house, and called: 'Anyone there?'

After the conversation with Beatrice, she'd had a brief solitary lunch in the dining room and then she'd gathered up a sheaf of cut white chrysanthemums intended for the chapel, climbed into her car and driven over.

But the house seemed quite empty. It smelt of whitewash and wallpaper glue and fresh rubber, and the new grey wool carpet on the stairs was still shedding rolls of fluff, which Alice's cleaner was quite correctly allowing to settle. Felicity had advised on the wallpaper – pale grey and white Regency stripes – and thought how successfully it had turned out. Just right for their first house: a charming perch to sit and wait for the prize of Mossbury Park. She opened a door to the right, looked into the newlyweds' neat drawing room and admired her own choice of pale-blue carpeting and pale-blue and cream William Morris paper. She'd seen it before, of course, but always gained pleasure from symmetry of colour and design, a small dream well executed.

It struck her that there were no flowers anywhere. How strange. What luck she'd brought the chrysanthemums. She'd surprise Alice with an exquisite arrangement. It would be something to occupy herself with; and she thought she remembered a silver lacquered vase amongst Alice's cache of wedding presents.

Priscilla said, 'Well well, fancy meeting you!' All wrapped up in a dark-green overcoat, she'd parked her estate car behind Harry's distinctive Daimler at the end of the narrow lane that became a track that eventually led up to Monkton Beacon. She must have seen it turn in there; possibly she'd been following him for some time.

His heart sank, but he said with a courteous smile, 'Ah, Priscilla!'

'Oh, you remember me,' she said with the sly smile he'd once adored. Now he felt only impatience. The wind had matted her red hair and blotched her pale complexion. He noticed creases in her tissue paper skin, and thought for the first time, 'Why does she wear so much lipstick?'

However, he responded (as she expected) in his slow drawl resonant with hidden meaning: 'How could I possibly forget?' But it was a mistake, and he realized it straight away.

'Oh, Harry,' she said in a rush, 'why does it have to be like this?'

'Like what?' He appeared flippant, as always when he felt himself encroached upon.

'Don't!' She came closer and he secretly clenched his hands in his pockets whilst managing to maintain what he believed to be a friendly though distant expression. 'We were so good together. So good.' She put a white freckled hand on his sleeve, and he took an involuntary step backwards. Another mistake. Immediately she accused him: 'You think you can just . . . pretend it never happened?'

'Come on,' he said in an encouraging sort of tone. 'We both knew the score.'

'I'm not asking for much,' said Priscilla, and he flinched at her shameful lack of pride. 'I don't see why—' she began.

'I can't hurt Felicity.' It was exactly what he'd said dozens of times before, to other women, when the time came, as it always did.

'It's a bit late for that, isn't it?'

Harry's expression was like stone. 'I'm very fond of my wife.'

'You've a strange way of expressing it!'

'Come on,' said Harry reasonably, 'we're both civilized people. You're pretty fond of old Ian, aren't you?' He paused. 'Good man, Ian.' He gave his toothy wolfish grin. 'Very fond of him myself.'

To his astonishment, Priscilla lunged at him and tried to slap his face. But Harry easily restrained her. Fury turned to triumph as she felt him holding her close. She had the measure of his sensuality and amorality, and her confidence was absolute. Separated by only a few inches they looked into each other's eyes and Priscilla gave her demure smile as she patted the bonnet of her car and suggested, 'Why don't we get out of the wind for a minute?'

But, to her dismay, Harry detached himself while somehow managing to give the unpleasant impression of removing a stained garment. 'I must be getting back,' he said. And then he pulled his chin down as if composing himself – putting on another face for his return to Felicity and Edgerton.

'I'll tell you something about yourself,' she shrieked above the wind, and he thought how much he hated shrillness in women. 'You think that because beautiful music makes you cry and you love art and nature, you have a heart.'

Harry put up a hand as if to protest. His expression was pleading, starting to be alarmed.

'Coward,' thought Priscilla. She knew enough about him to understand that he loathed messiness. But there was no way she was going to stop now.

'Oh, you might sleep with everything that moves so long as it doesn't make trouble for you,' she ranted on. 'You might betray your precious wife every day! But deep down you think it doesn't really count because you, Harry Chandler, can appreciate what's fine and beautiful.' She paused to draw breath. 'Well, I'll tell you something – you're cold as ice, Harry. You have no heart. None. You can't feel. You're unable to care about anything and always will be. And from the bottom of my heart I pity you!'

Alice came in just as Felicity was admiring the little patch of beauty she'd created. She'd put the vase in the hall, in a

Regency-striped niche where it fitted perfectly, the densely petalled white blooms entwined with sprays of jasmine she'd cut from the garden.

'Ma! What are *you* doing here?' She was dressed in riding clothes and, to Felicity's great relief, looked healthy and glowing. Her hair seemed fine – just a bit blown about – as did her skin, which was pink with exercise. In fact, she looked beautiful. What had Beatrice been up to, frightening her like that?

'I thought I'd pay you a visit,' smiled Felicity with her usual composure. As always, she was neatly dressed and perfectly groomed, making Alice feel untidy and sweaty.

Alice said quickly, 'I've just been out on Bailiff!' She put a hand on her chest and beamed, as if she might be reliving the wonderful exhilaration of cantering through woodland on her beloved horse brought from Edgerton. Then, to her mother's puzzlement, she looked suddenly apprehensive, almost guilty.

Felicity was alarmed too, but she asked very coolly: 'Is he settling in all right?'

'Fine,' said Alice with another sunburst smile.

'I expect he misses everyone.'

Alice nodded. 'He was dreadfully homesick at first, miz actually, but he'll be okay now. Yup.' Then she bit her lip as if she'd revealed more than she'd meant to. 'I'd better go and get changed.'

Felicity wanted to say warmly, 'No darling. It doesn't matter,' but found herself physically unable to. So much the better if Alice put on something pretty and brushed her hair. Then they could have a nice cup of tea in her elegant new drawing room.

'Where's Edward?' she asked, almost as an afterthought.

'Dunno,' said Alice vaguely. 'Didn't say. I think he's with his pa.'

Felicity said nothing, but went into the kitchen to put the big heavy kettle on the Aga. She wasn't used to dealing with kettles or even kitchens. Mrs Briggs came to the morning room after breakfast to take her instructions for the day.

Everything looked very neat and clean. She opened the refrigerator to take out milk, and was shocked at the emptiness of it. There was a bottle of champagne, a bottle of Chablis, a packet of pork sausages, half a packet of butter, a greasy block of hard cheddar and a tired half of a green cabbage. As part of her preparation for marriage, Alice (unlike Eve) had been sent on a cookery course. It was considered an asset now. So where were the makings of Edward's dinner? Felicity decided to ask, in a teasing uncritical sort of way.

'There you are.'

Alice had put on a skirt and a jumper and a dab of lipstick and, as usual, Felicity felt a swell of pride in her daughter's looks. It occurred to her that Alice's beauty had acquired a different quality. She looked so glowing and vibrant that Felicity even began to wonder if Beatrice was wrong and she could be pregnant.

'No need to do that, Ma.'

'All done.' Felicity had found the tea caddy with Earl Grey and the cupboard where the silver teapot engraved with Edward's family crest (a unicorn and a bear) was kept. 'Cake?' she asked.

'Sorry,' said Alice, biting her lip with a smile.

'Doesn't Edward eat tea?'

'I think there might be some shortbread.' Alice sounded awfully casual.

'And what are you giving him for dinner tonight?'

'Dunno.' Alice sounded as if the thought hadn't even occurred to her.

In the drawing room, Alice poured tea and offered her mother soggy fingers of shortbread arranged on one of her new Minton plates. Then she asked about her father. Then she asked about her sisters. And then she asked about her brother. And after Felicity had given bright surface answers to all her questions, silence fell.

But Felicity looked as if she hadn't even noticed it. She sat on her daughter's plump new sofa with its scattering of bright cushions and smiled pleasantly at her neatly painted surroundings and said, 'Well, all this is very nice.'

'It's been a nightmare,' said Alice, and – just for a second – her mother's smile froze. She went on blithely, 'They forgot to put gloss on the window sill in the morning room, and then it was days and days before they fixed it. Honestly, builders!'

'And how is Edward?' As she asked the question in the same brittle way, sitting side by side with her daughter, Felicity thought how deeply she loved all her children, and cursed her own profound terror of rejection, and even longed for a fraction of Beatrice's brutal directness.

'How was my turtledove?' asked Harry.

'Very well,' said Felicity. Edward had come home at about four o'clock and told them about his day, and Alice had listened dutifully but without interest, with a dreamy inward-looking smile. They'd waved her off at the door, and Felicity had looked at their amiable bland faces and driven home with a quite different fear from the one she'd arrived with.

'Being good to her, is he?'

'He seems to be,' she said slowly.

'Smashed a cake for you, did he?'

'Darling!' She didn't share her anxiety with Harry. Besides, it had become second nature to concentrate on the practical matters that made up the fabric of their life, rather than examine the stitching.

They'd happened to arrive home, in their respective cars, almost simultaneously. As always, they stood in the drive for a moment while the dogs gambolled and yelped round them. The beauty and grandeur of their house never failed to impress them each time they saw it afresh. It was extraordinary to reflect that Edgerton had scarcely changed in four hundred years. Throughout those centuries, other Chandler couples had probably stood more or less exactly where they were now. Felicity suddenly had a picture of a husband and wife – linked, talking intently to each other – and felt acute loneliness.

There was a big black bird of some sort perched on one of the turrets above. It cawed every so often: a harsh disturbing sound. Then the bell in the clocktower bonged the quarter hour and, as usual, the cretinous inhabitants of the dovecote reacted in momentary fluttering panic.

The heartfelt though seldom expressed sentiment hung in the air: 'How lucky we are.'

'Mmm,' said Harry. 'Quite.' He paused. 'Time for a hot bath.' He looked momentarily thoughtful as he contemplated removing his clothes in the bathroom, which faced north, before climbing into the claw-footed cast-iron bath and immersing his body in steaming water that would cool in minutes. He said, as if the idea were quite novel, 'Think I'll take a whisky in with me.'

In the great hall Felicity decided to keep on her overcoat for the time being. She said, breath white in the still, beeswax-scented air, 'Your post!'

'Ah yes.' He produced the unopened letter from his youngest child from his inside pocket where he'd kept it like a talisman. 'Here you are.' Then he rubbed his hands together very briskly and stamped his feet hard to help get his circulation going. And after that he finally got round to concentrating on his other letters.

'Oh good,' said Felicity. She was on her way up the long staircase, trying to open the envelope with her leather gloves still on, when she heard Harry exclaim, 'What the devil?'

She pulled out a sheet of lined blue paper and started to read the first few words in Kathy's round script. 'Dear Ma and Pa, I hope you're well and so is Champion and Bingo and Tinker and Humbug and Kaiser and Bracken and Freckle and Trigger . . .'

She could still hear him because he was shouting. 'This is ridiculous!'

'Mmm?' It was probably the bill from Berry Brothers. He'd ordered a lot of Madeira this winter. She went on reading the letter, smiling fondly, looking forward to sharing it.

'Felicity!'

Something in his tone made her turn round and go back to the great hall.

He was still standing by the big table, holding a stiff white sheet of paper.

'This is ridiculous, Felicity!' He put his hand over his face and pulled the folds of it downwards – a man trying to alter his expression. But it was no good. He looked utterly shocked.

Chapter Four

Darling Eve,

Pa and I much hope you're working hard. You're a lucky girl, and you must make the most of all this. I long to see Oxford again. I had hoped to drive over and see you before your end of term but, with one thing and another, it's been impossible to leave Edgerton.

Time goes so quickly and I can't believe Christmas will be upon us in only a week. But I'm looking forward to having everyone at home. I told Hugo he could invite Carson minor (whose brother unfortunately drowned, a boating accident), so if you want to bring your friend, then that will be fine.

Briggs made the puddings last week and we had a good stir for luck and Pa dropped in the silver threepenny pieces as usual. Alice and Edward will be coming for dinner on Christmas

Eve, but spending the day with his parents, which will feel strange. A. seems happy with her little house, which is looking very pretty. Hugo and Kathy will both arrive on the 18th. K. has become senior pet monitor, looking after the school hamsters, and is delighted. Our boy has been selected for his house cricket team!

I'm afraid Champion has had a bit of an accident. He must have chased a deer onto the road and got hit by a car. Poor old chap. Pa is upset, of course, but says it's nothing much to worry about and should be left to heal naturally . . .

Felicity laid aside her pen at her desk in the window of the morning room looking on to the terrace and, beyond, the frosty lawn sloping down to the lake dulled by ice. Blue flames danced over the glowing coals in the grate, but nothing could counteract the deadly chill of December. Even a spare arrangement of holly in a Bernard Leach bowl failed to comfort.

Stoicism and pretence had become the bricks and mortar of her marriage. But surely the children – particularly Eve – would discover the truth when they arrived for Christmas? Unless, of course, she filled the house with so many people there'd be no opportunity to notice anything.

Felicity put her head in her hands. 'Darling Eve, Pa has gone mad. We might lose everything we possess, but I don't think he'd even notice. I am terrified for Alice, who will not talk to me. My only shred of cheer is that yesterday I met an old friend . . .'

*

She'd been coming out of the bank in Nether Taunton, square leather handbag strung over one stiff arm, other hand anchoring the knot in her Hermès scarf, thoughts in a loop of despair, when a loud voice had hailed her.

'Flicky!'

It had been so long since anybody had called her by her old nickname that she almost failed to react.

'Flicky Wapshott, as ever was!'

The hailer was wearing a nice camel-hair coat and a dark-brown Homburg, immediately swept off. Thinning gingery hair, a pleasant rather chubby face: oddly familiar.

Felicity stared at him dumbly.

'Johnny Tyson!' he said, as if he couldn't imagine that she, of all people, might have passed him by.

Felicity recovered herself. 'Johnny!' How dreadful not to have recognized him! More discourteous still because he'd written a nice note – oh, at least a month ago – informing her he'd moved to the area, and, very unusually, she hadn't responded. Because she felt so guilty, Felicity reacted with uncharacteristic effusiveness. 'How nice!'

His wife had died of cancer a year ago, he told her matter-of-factly to forestall the dreaded pity. There were no children, he added, with even less expression. He'd moved to the area to be near his elderly father, who lived in Milton Saunter.

After that, Felicity noticed his string bag containing a small Fray Bentos tinned steak and kidney pie, a packet of Oxo cubes and a half-bottle of Glenfiddich. He was very clean shaven, and his shoes shone.

'What are you doing now?' he asked.

'Now?' she echoed dully.

'I happen to know that the George does a very decent cup of coffee.'

In the gabled George Hotel, with its comforting smells of Brasso and pickled onions, its scorching gas fire, Felicity was bathed in the affectionate reminiscences of a stranger. 'The Bartlett dance at the Dorchester with that magic grotto caper and those wonderful steel band fellas . . . You lost your earring in that nightclub, didn't you? . . . Lord, we had fun!'

Beyond his name, she didn't remember him at all. There'd been so many young men, all of them treating her like precious china, ignorant of the brutal discourteous world they would shortly be plunged into. Then he leant forward to light her cigarette and she caught a whiff of exactly the same aftershave he'd used and the past came surging back – that carefree past, all the sweeter in retrospect. She and Johnny had danced cheek-to-cheek. He'd nibbled at her ear – it was all very innocent – and dislodged a diamond star (later found undamaged). He'd crooned the words, 'Bewitched, Bothered and Bewildered' – she could hear his jolly tuneless droning now. He'd had lots of fine red hair. He'd been thin, too.

'We did,' she agreed wholeheartedly. It had been before Harry rendered all other men invisible. She felt seventeen again: eager and trusting. So she enquired about Johnny's wife's illness with unusual warmth; and he responded gratefully, revealing misery beneath the armour of stoicism. It had been terrible to watch the suffering, he told her. If only he could have taken over the pain himself.

'Worst thing was,' he said slowly, 'people acting as if

nothing had happened.' Felicity shook her head in disbelief, as if she couldn't comprehend those who shied away from others' pain. 'That was another reason I moved, Flicky. You live in a place for twenty years, then your wife dies and your friends cross the road to avoid speaking to you.'

She surprised herself. 'Not *real* friends, Johnny.'

'Dear girl,' he said affectionately. 'You haven't changed a bit.'

'Oh I have, I have!' she responded before she could stop herself; then, to her horror, felt tears welling up. She never cried. She rose abruptly and said coldly: 'I must go.'

'Flicky?' he asked with real concern.

'I'm fine,' she insisted. She struggled to gather up her things: a well-to-do upper-class woman in early middle age, battling distress.

'What you need,' said Johnny with brisk decisiveness, 'is lunch. And a proper drink.' He put up a dismissive hand. 'No, I insist! Not here, though. There's a little bistro tucked away behind the cathedral . . . D'you know it? Good French food – and it's nice and quiet.'

Harry might or might not be home by now, and expecting her. Mrs Briggs most certainly was (last night's lamb, cold, with boiled potatoes and leeks, followed by apple purée and cream). It was an indication of her anguish and confusion that Felicity let Johnny open the door for her and lead her out of the George.

They sat in the dark back of the restaurant, either side of a red and white checked table-cloth bearing a white candle encased in drips of melted white wax, and Johnny ordered large gin and tonics.

'First things first.'

Felicity murmured faintly, like a girl, 'Gosh, I never have alcohol at lunch!' She took a sip of the drink, which tasted delicious, and almost immediately started feeling light-headed.

Johnny was studying the menu. 'What d'you fancy?'

She smiled at him. 'Would you choose for me?'

'D'you like mussels?'

'I don't know!'

He smiled. 'Mary and I used to catch the boat train to *la belle* France. We'd take it in turn to pick places out of the Michelin. Mary adored moules marinières . . . And then . . . mmm hmm hmm . . . What about a nice Châteaubriand steak with Béarnaise?'

'That sounds wonderful.'

'Spinach?'

'Yes please.'

'Mary was always nagging me to eat my greens.' He beamed at the memory, before turning to the wine list.

'Have you decided, Major?' asked the waitress, all plump and smiley, pencil and pad at the ready.

'So, Flicky Wapshott, what have *you* been doing with yourself this last quarter of a century?'

'The usual things.'

As she forked plump mussels from cream-bathed navy shells, she told him about marrying Harry a year after war broke out, but skated over the years at Edgerton with her in-laws while he was away fighting. She told him about Alice's grand wedding and Eve winning a place at Oxford, and Hugo and Kathy. She made her life sound special and fulfilled.

It took until the steak was almost finished for her to tell him about the shocking letter Harry had received from Lloyds. After all, there had to be some sort of explanation for her embarrassing loss of control.

Johnny was impressed. 'It's that hurricane, isn't it? Betsy. Matter of fact, I'd heard it was going to cost a packet. Got a few friends who are names.' He cupped a hand around his clean-shaven chin. '£6,000, you say?'

Felicity nodded.

Johnny whistled. 'That's more than double what I just paid for my house! I trust he's with a reliable syndicate?'

Felicity shrugged helplessly. 'It's the same one he's been with for years and years. The family's always belonged to Lloyds – Harry's father and his grandfather before him.'

'D'you know,' said Johnny, 'I've never quite dared.' He made a pantomime out of crossing himself.

'Nothing like this has ever happened before,' said Felicity. 'Oh, there've been not such good years, but we've relied on it.' She paused. 'There'll be even more to pay next year. He's been warned it's going to cost Lloyds millions.'

Johnny looked suitably serious. Then he said, 'Harry's a rich man, isn't he? Edgerton must be worth a fortune.'

'Well, yes,' Felicity agreed. 'But that's beside the point really.'

'So it is.' Johnny came from much the same social background. He understood that money tied up in great houses was just that – untouchable.

Then he said, 'But look here, dear girl, it's only money in the end.' He paused. 'If there's one thing I've learnt from my own trouble it's that, compared with good health, nothing much matters. It really doesn't.' He smiled at her encouragingly. 'It's certainly not worth getting yourself into a stew over.'

Felicity didn't dare look at him. The good food, the alcohol, and, above all, the kindness were making her perilously emotional. He'd endured a war in his youth, like Harry, and must have believed he'd earned the right to peace and happiness. Yet he'd emerged from the suffering with none of Harry's brutal self-protectiveness. It had made more of a person of him, not less.

He leant across the table and put his hand over hers. 'But that's not all, is it, Flicky?'

'I'm fine,' said Felicity in the clipped dismissive way that warned most people off.

'You can't be sure,' said Johnny. He was still holding her hand over the table. 'I don't usually like being touched,' thought Felicity – but curiously, as if thinking about another woman.

It had been strangely easy, in the end, to confide the truth, though she'd studied the checked table-cloth intently as she did so.

'My dear girl . . .' How long had she been married? Twenty-five years? 'It happens,' he said cautiously, because of course he'd seen this sort of caper before.

'You don't understand . . .'

'Sit tight,' he urged her gently, with his sweet bracing smile. 'Keep your nerve. A blip.'

The waitress brought coffee and chocolate cake. She was curious about the Major's new friend: though glad that, for once, he had company. She'd seen him holding her hand, of course, before she pulled it away, and noticed it wore a wedding ring. 'I hate to see a gentleman eat on his own,' she told the other waitress.

'You were saying . . .'

Felicity looked at Johnny sadly. She was about to destroy his innocence. 'You wouldn't believe how many times this has happened before.'

He stared at her with his concerned, slightly protruberant brown eyes. He'd be regretting his impulsive invitation, she knew: filled with distaste that a civilized lunch had become an emotional abattoir.

But now it was impossible for Felicity to stop, because the relief outweighed the shame. 'I always know. Usually it's the wife of a friend. This time it's different, I can tell. What frightens me is I have absolutely no idea who she is . . .'

All the same, something crucial had been gathered about Harry's latest affair. He'd been boasting, without uttering a word, because he longed to brag, and there was no one closer than she.

Usually, when their marriage went through one of its cyclical downturns, he'd wear a sleek, shuttered air. But this time he seemed in the grip of uncontrollable impatience and joy. It was all the more suspicious, given his financial worries.

She could tell there was no room in his mind for anything beyond the wonder of what he was experiencing – certainly none for kindness or tact. Yesterday he'd come into the bathroom as she was getting out of the bath. She'd reached for a towel – though not before she'd caught his half critical half preening look.

'He's comparing us,' she thought, and knew with miserable certainty that, this time, the woman was younger.

'This is—' Johnny began, but could not find the word.

'Atrocious,' thought Felicity. 'Cruel. Unbearable.' But she raised her eyebrows, gave her painful little smile and the impression that nothing could impinge on so cold a woman.

'Shouldn't happen to someone like you.'

Felicity shrugged.

'You're such a stunner. Always were. Haven't changed an iota.'

But Felicity's self-esteem had sunk so low that she couldn't endure a compliment. She murmured fearfully, 'I shouldn't have said anything, Johnny.' Already she was regretting her loss of control. 'You won't tell anyone?'

'Dear girl,' he said – but this time as if she'd wounded him.

'Well, it's been lovely,' she informed him in her old tight-lipped way. He couldn't cope, of course. She'd embarrassed him horribly. If they should meet again, she'd pretend it had never happened. It would come very naturally.

'The pleasure was all mine,' he responded formally.

Felicity started to gather up her bits of shopping: a pretty antique lace runner for one of the bedrooms, twisted silver candles for the next dinner party, pot pourri to scent Edgerton's musty air.

'*I* think,' he went on, 'we should make this a regular thing. I'll be your comfort and your escape. How are you fixed for next week? Same time, same place?'

*

'Silly,' Felicity told herself with a grim little smile, as she sat over her unfinished letter to Eve. The cell door had slammed shut again. She was back at Edgerton, and Harry had come down to breakfast in clean jodhpurs, and hummed as he looked over his post, and laughed for no reason, and told her he might call in on his old friend Bill Manners.

Even so, something impelled her to go to the oval mirror above the fireplace. She hadn't properly looked at her reflection for days. She'd brushed her hair and powdered her nose with her eyes averted, like a woman with a deformity.

But now – the fire scorching her tweed-clad knees – she dared to assess herself. She wasn't young or dazzling. But she had nice wide-set dark-brown eyes, an excellent pale skin and plenty of glossy hair. 'Not an iota,' she whispered and made an appalled amused face. Then she frowned at a strand of grey. She'd make an appointment with the hairdresser. She might even treat herself to a perm.

In the misty depths of the mirror, she noticed the beige and grey bowl laden with spiky leaves and dotted with scarlet berries. Soon it would be spring and then she could fill it with cascading snowdrops.

Chapter Five

When Eve turned the battered little Austin Beatrice had given her off the main road, snow was falling in dizzying net curtains and Seb was talking and so the enormous stone gateway went unremarked.

It was the briefest of reprieves. If only, thought Eve, the fuggy companionable journey could continue for ever: the jokes, the shared cigarettes, the occasional longed for kiss, the heart-stopping secret anticipation. Whilst it did so they remained equals in spirit, if not intellect. But in roughly five minutes Seb would understand that he'd been deceived. He would know that his new girlfriend belonged to the section of society he professed to abominate most. 'But,' she thought, anguished, 'if I'd told him, he'd never have come!' Staying in Seb's orbit had been her whole objective: setting up a situation where he could at last make love to her. It had obscured all sense and logic. Too late she appreciated that taking him to Edgerton would almost certainly end the relationship.

She became very silent as the drive rounded a bend, to reveal an endless vista of more drive. The car whined as its tyres struggled with the icy surface that usually sported a central toothbrush of grass, and beech trunks marched slowly past under a lofty canopy of snow-laden branches.

'This isn't yours, is it?' he asked suddenly. He didn't really mean it. Crazy! Eve was so approachable and sweet: it was what had first attracted him.

Eve managed to sound vague and unconcerned. 'Oh, it just goes with the house.'

'*I* geddit.' A sardonic little half-smile that was quite new to her. Now he'd retreated into the fashionable beat-speak that was a mask for insecurity: his own way of ironing out differences that became horribly apparent in a place like Oxford.

'It's been in our family for four hundred years. It's just one of those things.'

'*I* geddit.'

Eve wished he wouldn't keep on saying that. He was coming for family Christmas, wasn't he? Hadn't he confessed, like handing her a gift, 'I hate Christmas now. I only want it to be over.'

He pounced. 'You haven't got a title, have you?'

'The blindest Eng. Lit. student?'

'You'd better tell me!'

'Pa's a baronet, that's all. It doesn't make *me* anything.'

'*I* geddit it!' She'd never seen Seb sneer before. 'So how should I – a lowly commoner – address him?'

Eve put her foot on the brake, managed to control a skid, and switched off the engine. Flurries of icing-sugar snow shook themselves down through the cathedral-like space. It felt very quiet and lonely and, now the heater was off, the temperature was falling rapidly. In the gloomy light he looked like a sulking blond eagle – and he hadn't even seen the house yet.

He shook a Camel out of a crushed packet and lit it with a crack of his Zippo against his denimed knee as if re-establishing his virility. As an afterthought, he passed it to her and lit another for himself.

Eve put a hand on his leg. 'Seb? They're not like that! Hey, it's Christmas Eve!'

Silence. He blew a perfect smoke ring, and followed it up with another.

'What difference does it make? It wouldn't make any difference to *me*!'

'It wouldn't make any difference to you,' he said slowly, 'that I was brought up above a pub in the East End of London?' He sneered. 'My dad was a lord, too – a landlord.'

'You silly thing! Your parents were lovely – I know they were.'

She was learning, day by day, how to handle him. Just as the nonchalant slang masked a cleverness that had lifted him out of his background, so the defensive resentment hid a loving heart. He took away her half-smoked cigarette, opened the door and threw it out as a blast of icy air rushed in. Then he carefully unhooked her spectacles and parked them under the windscreen.

'Sorry,' he muttered.

As usual, Eve was overwhelmed by his attraction: humbly astonished he'd chosen to be with her. 'Oh, Seb,' she said, her lips against his, 'I wish we could just stay here.'

'Me too, chick.' He shrank into his sheepskin jerkin. 'But

could do with a big fire right now. Hot cuppa'd be cool, too.'

She smiled at him, was about to say, 'I'll ask Briggs to make you one right away,' and luckily thought the better of it.

Every Christmas, an enormous fir tree – the biggest Stevens' boys could hew from the estate – was erected in the great hall. Then Felicity would unpack the decorations shrouded in tissue paper for the past twelve months: like the gilded wooden doves, the hand-blown glass balls and, the last exquisite touch, the angel in gold brocade and Chantilly lace that had graced at least a hundred Edgerton Christmases. The ritual was unchanging. As strings of coloured lights were switched on in miniature trees in cottage windows all over the estate, the Chandlers would light candles clipped to the lower branches of their felled giant (and detail the younger children for firewatch duty). The great hall was lit by candlelight and firelight, just as it had been for centuries.

As the house loomed into view through a veil of scurrying snowflakes, the size and splendour of the tree, its bright candles flaming, could be glimpsed through shimmering mullioned windows, and the great iron candelabra burning aloft. Edgerton looked half magic castle, half fairy palace and Eve silently cursed it for never failing to live up to expectations – and also her mother, for staging the performance. If its grandeur and beauty moved her every single time she came back to it, how on earth would it affect Seb? What reaction could possibly sum up the impact?

'Fuck me!'

Elizabethan, thought Seb. But the porch was clearly a Gothic addition: an extravagant confection of battlements and buttresses with carved angels standing guard each side. He guessed this approach was not the principal façade of the house: already visualizing a grand sweep in the style of the Old Ashmolean, large symmetrical windows surmounted by ornate pediments looking on to a wide terrace, a roof hidden by a balustrade. He couldn't see the colour of the house clearly in this light, but it seemed like a soft biscuit.

An enormous pack of dogs dashed out and surrounded the car, barking madly. One of them – large, with a patchwork coat of black and ginger – was dragging a limp back leg behind it like a suitcase it couldn't put down.

'They're not savage, are they?'

'Never!' Eve felt her spirits rise at the sight of her parents, two black shapes dwarfed by the huge open oak door, with the glowing flickering great hall as a backcloth. Both put great store by courtesy; they wouldn't let her down there. She prayed that her father wouldn't tease her, and her mother would be warm and welcoming.

If he'd thought about it at all, Seb had envisaged Eve's father as about sixty – a lord of the manor in heavy tweeds with a moustache and possibly even a monocle. He was surprised when a slim good-looking man in his forties wearing a very old cardigan appeared. He darted an anxious look at Eve. He still didn't know how to address him. Then he thought, setting his jaw: 'Why the fuck should I care?'

Eve's mother wasn't bad looking either. But there was something glacial and off-putting about her, and Seb sensed an abyss between husband and wife. She appeared to permit her daughter to kiss her. 'How nice,' she conceded through thin lips, and Seb ached for his own loving embarrassing mother who'd died in a car crash, together with his father, two years before.

'Down!' roared Eve's father with terrifying force. Then he said, very pleasantly, as he shook Seb's hand: 'Welcome. We were beginning to wonder if Eve *had* any friends.'

Inside the great hall, two adolescent boys were sitting on a stone-flagged floor in front of a big log fire in an enormous fireplace with a quatrefoil frieze, absorbed in some sort of card game. There was a strong smell of scorching fir.

'Hugo!' Another petrifying sound from Eve's father, which made Seb nearly drop his suitcase.

Eve's father rushed at the tree with a blackened blanket he produced from somewhere, and the smell of burning fir needles was overlaid by a stench of toasted dog. Then he smiled at Seb, a high-voltage beam Seb couldn't help responding to. 'That wretched boy,' he told him, as one of the children looked blank and furious and the other continued to flip over cards like a zombie.

'We'd better blow them out now,' said Eve's mother, sounding very abrupt and unsurprised, as if almost causing an inferno was part of the Christmas ritual.

By now Seb had noticed the extreme chill, but nobody else seemed to – not even Eve who, like him, had a gas heater in her room at Oxford. He tried to edge closer to the fire, but a mound of dog was in the way – the big black and ginger job with the wonky leg. He noticed it was the only animal allowed anywhere near the heat, though the others kept trying – wave upon wave of them, like a well-organized army. Eve's father was giving it affectionate slaps on its rump that made the dog wheeze with pleasure and open a doleful eye whenever he paused. 'Dear old Champers,' he heard him say. 'Good old chap!' Then, to the other dogs, at top volume: 'Out, you devils! Back to the stables!'

'I've put Sebastian in the Chinese room,' said Eve's mother, and Eve said eagerly, 'I'll show you, Seb, shall I?'

The other side of the great hall was a grand stairwell with a very long straight uncarpeted polished wooden staircase. As they humped their luggage up, Seb thought he'd never been so cold in his life. It seemed to eat into his marrow, the ache spreading through his bones. He couldn't believe people would choose to live like this. But, even so, as a classicist, he appreciated the paintings and statues on the way. There was a Sargent at the top of the stairs, he noted; an Epstein in an alcove. ('Foreplay!' he thought bitterly, long afterwards.)

His room was a poem of green and gold. He noticed that although the curtains were in perfect accord with the lacquered furniture – rampant blue and green dragons entwined amid golden pagodas – they were quite old. There was a very clean but obviously ancient lace runner on the dressing table; an old-fashioned green china jug and ewer; and, to his amusement, a china potty tucked under the single bed.

There was a small selection of orange and white Penguin paperbacks beside it – he noticed one of P. G. Wodehouse's Blandings novels, Dodie Smith's *I Capture the Castle*, something by Nevil Shute and a Book Society Choice edition of Daphne du Maurier's *My Cousin Rachel* – but the bedside lamp had a very dim bulb, as if to discourage reading at night. There was a silver box containing Bath Oliver biscuits that had long since lost their crispness, and a small bottle of tomato juice with a rusty cap but no suitable implement to lever it off with. The room was at the back of the house, and looked on to a bleak lake.

Eve was gazing at him with a mixture of affection and trepidation. 'You don't mind about everything?'

'It's cool,' Seb conceded. For her sake, he'd reserve judgement.

'You can say that again! It's freezing!'

He wrapped his arms round her. A long and tender kiss.

Nothing had been said yet, though there'd been many such kisses. 'I can be here at night . . .' she began very hesitantly.

'Yeah?'

'. . . if you want me to, that is.'

'Cool.'

It was settled, then.

'I'll be your extra hot water bottle.'

Seb didn't realize, until everyone convened in the drawing room at a quarter past seven, that he was expected to dress for dinner. But, even if Eve had thought (or dared) to warn him, it wouldn't have been any help. All he possessed was his uniform: a few pairs of jeans, a number of jerseys (he wished he'd brought more), his leather boots, his sheepskin jerkin.

He looked at the grandeur surrounding him – the long sweep of honey silk curtains, the Oriental lamps, the fine rugs, the exquisite flower displays, the enormous family portraits marching through the centuries (with echoes of

Harry but none of his allure) – and all his chippiness came to the surface. 'I'm as good as them,' thought Seb, the scholarship boy. But to Eve he whispered: 'I feel a prat.' He'd caught a glance from her mother, too; and interpreted it as tight-lipped disapproval.

'It's okay, Seb – really.' To her credit, she wore the same very short woollen skirt over heavy black wool tights and black polo-neck sweater she'd arrived in.

'Yeah?' To his further mortification, he'd seen a couple appear through the double doors, he, penguin-like in dinner jacket and black tie, she in a long velvet skirt with a cashmere shawl draped round her top.

Then Eve's father approached him with his all-embracing smile. 'My dear chap!' He was wearing a burgundy silk cravat and a dark-grey corduroy jacket that, together with the brilliantine on his hair, made him look sleek as a mole. 'Come and join us! Have some champagne!' And, to his astonishment, Seb felt a king in his Levi's and heavy wool sweater covered in bobbles. 'Now who have you met?'

He'd met the kid sister, who was lying beside the big dog in front of the fire, holding its damaged paw and crooning something into its ear. He'd met the grandmother, a pleasantly batty old girl in a shapeless purple garment covered with white hairs who'd nagged away at Eve's pa to get the big dog's leg set properly. (Eve had raised the question with him too, but he'd refused even to discuss it.) He was about to be introduced to the blonde married to the penguin.

'This is my sister Alice,' said Eve.

She was a Bardot lookalike – not a bit like Eve, who was pretty much okay in her own right. Seb looked at her very ordinary companion and thought there must be more to him than met the eye. But then he noticed they didn't seem much like a couple. She laughed and joked with her family, but whenever her husband uttered the animation fell away.

She started arguing with her father, in a sweet gentle voice like a caress. 'Honestly, Pa, his leg looks perfectly dreadful!'

'Don't have a go at me, turtledove.' He sounded pained but doting: more like a lover than a father. In fact, crazy though it might seem, if Seb hadn't known better, he'd have thought *they* were the couple. Both extraordinarily attractive, they radiated the same creamy sense of well-being. They gave the impression of holding a quite different conversation, even of sharing a secret.

'Poor poor Champion,' sighed Alice. 'It's not fair.'

'*He* doesn't want to be tortured. What *he* needs is peace and quiet in his own home so he can recover naturally.'

Alice pouted deliciously. 'Oh, Pa, you know that stuff's just nonsense! I'm going to take him home with me tonight – I will! – and I'll drive him in to the vet tomorrow. There's bound to be someone on duty.'

Her father shrugged and gave his lazy smile, the impression that to capitulate to her was only delight. 'Whatever you say, turtledove.'

'It's Christmas Day, darling!' the husband chimed in.

'Yes,' said Alice in her soft little voice that, for him alone, seemed to acquire a base of steel.

The family decided to open presents before dinner, as Alice and Edward would not be with them the following day.

It was a revelation for Seb, who'd spent money he could

ill afford on whisky for his host, perfume for his hostess, and books and chocolates for the children. He hadn't consulted with Eve (for whom he'd purchased a silver bracelet). He'd selected the same sort of presents he wished he could still give his own family.

But the Chandlers' gifts to each other were very cheap and mostly useless and not even wrapped properly. Extraordinarily, nobody seemed disappointed. 'How wonderful!' they enthused as they ripped open newspaper packages stuck together with tape, minus ribbons or cards. 'How did you *know* I wanted a plastic shoe horn/pair of knitting needles (when I don't even knit)/yet another handkerchief?' If insufficient gusto was displayed, the giver of the present was entitled to nag gently: 'You do like it, don't you?'

Kathy gave her father a plastic dog's bone and giggled when she received, in return, a cheap print of a rabbit. Harry gave his son Hugo a paperback on manners and his new son-in-law a layman's guide to wine with simple helpful drawings. For some reason, Felicity gave Harry a plastic compass, and her present to her mother-in-law was a clothes brush. Beatrice retaliated with a set of bright-blue plastic coasters. 'How very useful,' Felicity responded with her dry smile.

Seb kept glancing at Eve for enlightenment. This must be an upper-class joke – a ritual tease that preceded the giving of the real presents. But no, it seemed this pile of rubbish was all the Chandlers would be getting for Christmas.

He could tell that he'd embarrassed them with his expensive gifts. When Eve gave him her present, he attempted to play the game. 'Cool! Can't have too many socks!' But it had a desolate ring. He and Alice's husband and Hugo's friend Carson minor were on the edge of a bizarre family circle: made to feel welcome, but very uneasy.

By contrast, dinner was lavish and generous, with tender well-hung beef from the estate and the finest of wines. The room was poorly lit and, capitalizing on the inky pools of shadow, the crippled dog launched a triumphant raid on the trolley.

'Clever boy!' crooned Alice. 'He's not feeling so bad, is he?'

Harry laughed delightedly. 'He needs his strength.'

Kathy seized the opportunity. 'Can I give him the rest of the beef then?'

Felicity consented with a cool nod, though she added, to Seb's puzzlement, 'I expect Briggs will want to put it in a stew.'

It was at that moment the telephone started ringing. It was the only one in the house: kept in the great hall, where the aching chill was severe, to discourage lengthy chatting. They all heard it, tinny and insistent in the distance. It must have rung about four times before anyone reacted. Probably Harry and Alice had no idea how similar they suddenly looked. The candlelight played sadistically with their emotions – surprise, excitement, alarm.

'That's your telephone.' Despite her eccentricity, Beatrice could be relied upon to state the obvious.

'So it is, Mama,' said Harry smoothly.

'I'll go, I'll go!' squeaked Kathy, who loved answering the telephone.

'Shall I?' faltered Alice, with a glance at her husband.

'No, no, I'll see to it,' insisted Harry, and, pushing back his chair, he set off into the icy darkness at a brisk pace.

Beatrice said: 'Who on earth's going to telephone on Christmas Eve, when they know everyone's eating their supper?'

'Exactly!' Edward looked as triumphant as if he'd said something perceptive.

'Can't be a family emergency. Everyone's here!'

'We'll soon find out,' said Felicity.

When Harry came back, he couldn't stop smiling. It was odd, because what he told them was not amusing. Apparently, the call had come from the head gamekeeper – a most conscientious man, Harry said, passing a hand over the lower part of his face to mask inappropriate delight. It seemed, he told them all gravely, that a shot had been heard in the lower copse and the servant had taken it upon himself to interrupt his own festive supper and investigate. 'I'm afraid it very much looks as if the poacher has returned.'

'Oh, the poacher always returns,' said Felicity, and laughed too. But there was no merriment in it – none at all.

After dinner, the family played Charades – another Christmas Eve ritual. By this time, the fire in the drawing room had burnt low and – as Harry threw enormous logs on to it and ordered the two boys to puff away with bellows – Alice and Eve fetched a pile of heavy overcoats and a variety of hats.

The company divided itself into two teams: one headed by Eve, the other by Hugo. Beatrice was the last to be selected and she sat on one of the big sofas, looking bemused and dishevelled and feeling a little tipsy.

'Gran,' said Hugo reluctantly.

'Oh, is that me, my precious?'

Hugo's family so terrified Carson minor that he'd become Hugo's shadow. If anybody asked Hugo to do something, Carson minor would mutely echo his response in an attempt to become invisible. Accordingly, he simmered because their team had been landed with Alice as well as the old granny. Somehow or other, Eve had managed to scoop up Harry (who was sure to be brilliant) as well as her friend Seb, who she'd told them all proudly was on a scholarship. True, they'd also been lumbered with Edward. But it wasn't fair.

Eve and Hugo tossed a coin for who could stay in the now freezing drawing room and think of their word; who must go into the sub-zero corridor and wait. Eve's team lost, and the pile of clothes disappeared from the floor. The team in the drawing room heard stamping and laughing and squabbling in the distance. There was the sound of glass shattering on stone, too, and Felicity started nervously, before settling back into apathy as if it no longer mattered to her. 'Let's think,' she said in a lifeless voice, and Beatrice knitted her caterpillar brows and fixed her daughter-in-law with a glare. She'd caught the whiff of trouble all evening. No prizes for guessing what. But this time seemed different. 'Silly girl,' thought Beatrice. 'Hasn't she learnt by now they never leave?' She sensed secrets everywhere: shafts of intense happiness, gleaming against the despair. Oh, they burdened you with anxieties that kept you awake at night – like the atrocious bill from Lloyds, which would affect her too – but otherwise left you out. She brooded. And now she was being bullied to think of words – all of which were scornfully dismissed by Hugo, who'd entered the tiresome adolescent phase she termed 'the tunnel'.

'Cataclysm!'

'What's *that*?'

'Doom,' said Beatrice.

'And how would you do "clysm", Gran?' How handsome and mocking he was: his father's son in character, with his mother's dark looks. Born long after his paternal grandfather's untimely death, Hugo was his namesake.

'Well, I don't know, do I? I'm only trying to help.'

Alice said triumphantly: 'Existentialism!'

'Same!' exclaimed Hugo, continuing his maddening impersonation of a patronizing schoolmaster.

'Ex. Is. Tent. Shall. And they'll have guessed it by then, won't they?' She glowed with the pleasure of astounding them.

'What's it mean?' mumbled Carson minor, momentarily so dazzled by Alice that he forgot his vow of silence.

'Long word for you, darling,' said Felicity wryly. There was no intention to be cruel: there could be no contest, for her, between beauty and intellect.

Beatrice moved in smartly to protect her granddaughter. 'It's a philosophical term. Isn't it, my treasure?'

'Um . . .' Alice blushed with confusion.

But Hugo rejected the word, as usual. And nobody thought of asking Alice where she'd come across it.

Eve put her head round the door. She was wearing a Russian army general's hat with fur flaps Harry had picked up in the course of his secret war, and a long mink coat that had once belonged to Beatrice, which the moths had ruined. As always, Felicity's hand twitched involuntarily, as if she longed to remove her daughter's unsightly spectacles. (*How* many times had she warned her, as a child, not to read in bed?)

'We've got a word.'

'So've we!' said Hugo immediately.

'We want to come back in.'

'Oh, let them, poor lambs,' said Beatrice.

Eve said: 'We've picked Alice,' and Alice sighed and rolled her eyes. She was hopeless at Charades. She was famous for it. It was mean of them to choose her straight away.

The others watched as she rose gracefully from the sofa, looking like a thirties film star, and approached her sister. It was the first opportunity they'd had since dinner to speak intimately – but this was of little significance for anyone else.

Eve bent forward and whispered in Alice's ear, and they all saw Alice pull back and stare at Eve, shock and dismay on her pretty face.

Eve nodded, very stern in her spectacles and army general's cap.

Alice looked as if she were pleading with her sister. She opened her blue eyes wide, stared at her mutely.

Then they seemed to remember they were being watched.

Eve bent forward and whispered again.

'What?' asked Alice loudly. It sounded as if her courage had, all of a sudden, returned. 'Never even heard of it!' she declared. Then she did a strange thing: she put a finger to her lips, and Eve nodded gravely.

*

Eve had expected her first experience of sex to be painful. But, as it turned out, one tiny moment of natural resistance was almost immediately overtaken by fierce excitement. Feeling him drive deeper and deeper inside her, already knowing how to rise to meet him, she thought: 'I was made for this!'

'I love you,' she whispered as it was ending – for wasn't love what this was all about?

But Seb said nothing. Not for a moment, anyway. And Eve waited, feeling bruised and vulnerable. Her chin tingled from all the rough kissing. She hoped it wouldn't start peeling next morning. Her mother would be sure to notice, even if she said nothing.

Seb lit them both cigarettes, then: 'They're all crazy!'

But he held her very close. Perhaps it was for warmth – even though he was wearing a vest and two sweaters and, over that, his sheepskin jerkin.

'Really?'

'Crazy, yeah!' he confirmed. It was a compliment then. *Talk to me*, she pleaded silently. *Talk to me as you did before I revealed all this to you*! After all, hadn't he spoken to Pa in his true voice at dinner? For there was nobody on earth who could resist Pa, when he was exercising all his charm. Seb had spoken eloquently, passionately, honestly. It was beauty they'd talked about, of course: beauty, the great leveller. And Pa, who revered excellence, had perceived Seb's quality. Surely he had?

The bell in the tower bonged ear-shatteringly outside.

'Fucking Big Ben!' Then, as other clocks chimed support, one after the other, from the depths of the house: 'Fucking orchestra!' He hadn't forgiven her yet, then.

'Sorry about tonight . . .' Even as she said it, Eve thought: 'I shouldn't be apologizing for them.' It was the beginning of understanding that for him – for the sake of this – all betrayals might become possible.

'Your dad's a gas!' Another grudging compliment.

So it was going to be all right, then. 'I'm glad you think so.'

'When he did "plenipotentiary"!'

'Pa loves Charades.'

Eve thought of spending all night in his arms. She knew already that she wouldn't sleep. She'd listen to him breathe, and draw pictures of his face in the dark, and re-live every single detail of what had just happened. *Talk to me . . .*

'Your sister's a doll!'

'Now she really is crazy!' Eve didn't mean to sound judgmental, but it was hard to hear Seb praise another woman, even Alice.

'You mean, for marrying that berk?'

'He's kind,' said Eve immediately.

'Yeah?'

'And decent.' As Eve said it, she thought, 'Why am I defending Edward like this?'

'Boring.'

'Perhaps that's what she needs,' said Eve, managing to sound both prudish and wise.

'Nah! I know what she needs! Trust me.'

Eve hated the way he said it: the rough stranger he'd become; the implication that he himself could tackle the problem, if so minded. Love made her afraid. She'd no confidence in her own powers of attraction; without really intending to, both parents had seen to that.

So she broke a solemn (though unspoken) promise to Alice.

All she meant to convey to Seb was that her sister was unavailable, not to mention out of bounds.

But, of course, in portraying Alice as a passionate woman of mystery, she did herself no favours – and realized it almost immediately.

Chapter Six

On Boxing Day, Eve telephoned Alice. 'I thought I'd come over.'

The smell of breakfast kippers lingered on the formal air of the great hall like the memory of a shameful *faux pas*. Through distorting ice flowers decorating the inside of the mullioned panes she could see blurry shapes moving aimlessly around an expanse of white, occasionally joining up. Then there was a cacophony of ferocious barking and all the shapes streamed off in the same direction and Eve knew the postman had wobbled into view.

'Isn't your friend there?'

'He has to write an essay.'

'I've got to go out,' Alice responded.

'Alice!'

'Well, okay,' she conceded, 'I s'pose it can wait.'

As usual, Eve wondered how the postman could be so cheerful after his mile-long bicycle ride up the rutted drive, knowing what was in store.

The dogs sniffed and muttered round him as he sorted out a pile of letters. 'Three for Sir Harry, one for Her Ladyship, and there's his paper.'

He straightened at the sight of Eve's father, touched his cap. 'Morning, sir!'

'Morning, Woodhouse!' Harry sounded as relentlessly positive as the postman. 'Lovely day!'

The postman beamed indulgently. 'Parky.'

'Kill the bugs. I trust these idiotic fellows haven't been pestering you over much?'

'No, sir!'

'Good, good! Full of beans, that's all it is.'

'Just the ten of them today, sir?' He didn't even show his relief at being terrorized by one dog fewer.

'Yes, yes, yes!' As usual, Harry distanced himself from anything that upset him. He'd already dismissed the postman. He glanced at his letters – 'Damn vampires!' – and slung them on the table, unopened. He was humming an aria from *Rigoletto*, reviewing his plans for the day.

Alice said indignantly, 'It needn't have happened.'

Eve looked at Champion on his blanket in front of Alice's Aga: a mound of traumatized dog with a bandaged stump he nuzzled in miserable disbelief.

'If Ma had taken him to the vet straight away . . .'

'Don't blame Ma,' said Eve. 'Pa wouldn't let her.' She went on bitterly, 'He likes to think he's kind.'

Predictably, Alice sprang to her father's defence. 'He doesn't mean it.'

'That's immaterial.' Eve stroked the dog's dull fur, his limp ears hanging like pieces of cloth, but he shut his eyes as if he couldn't stand pity. 'Poor poor old chap.'

'He'll be all right,' said Alice, her voice full of tender promise. 'He'll be hopping around in no time, you'll see. I'm going to give him the best life.'

'Even if you weren't going to,' said Eve slowly, 'Pa wouldn't want him back. He couldn't bear the guilt.'

'Don't be hard on him.'

'Yes, but . . .' Eve wanted to say: 'It's all very well for you.'

It was the first time she'd visited Alice's new house and she liked the way that the kitchen had a status of its own. But then, unlike their mother, Alice was familiar with a kitchen. She'd been sent to the Cordon Bleu School in London for a three-month course; and, after that, she'd gone to Constance Spry.

'It's so nice and warm in here and I don't want to leave Champion and you don't really want to be in the drawing room, do you?' wheedled Alice. So they sat at the wooden table scrubbed pale by Alice's new daily, Mrs Baldwin, drinking coffee made in Alice's new percolator.

Eve remembered Seb's admiring comment – 'Your sister's a doll!' – and thought she'd never seen Alice look so pretty. Wary, too.

But it was Alice who brought up the subject. 'How did you guess?'

'When the telephone rang on Christmas night,' said Eve, 'you thought it was him, didn't you?'

Alice nodded, biting her lip. 'It was dreadful . . . He wouldn't promise not to . . .'

'You must have been scared stiff.'

Alice got up from her chair and shut the door. 'Swear you won't breathe a word?'

Eve nodded, trying to forget about Seb.

Alice sat on the floor beside Champion and kissed his big passive head. 'I love you so so much, my darling,' she told him.

'How *could* it have happened?'

'It wasn't my fault!'

She told the whole story with her face close to Champion's, breathing in his sick marmite smell for support.

She'd thought she'd never see him again. He'd broken her heart, hadn't he? And there'd been no response to the news of her engagement.

'I'd have got over it,' she said dully.

It was one of Eve's tactics (developed to counter her father's more extreme pronouncements) to remain silent when she disagreed. Remembering the subdued girl who'd returned from honeymoon, she was pretty sure Alice didn't believe what she'd just said either.

'Do you believe in destiny?' Alice asked as she stroked Champion's ears with a dreamy look. She made the word sound fresh. Destiny: it sounded like a boat rocking in the waves, waiting to take one to a distant shore. It must be destiny, she told her sister excitedly, if precisely when you were thinking intensely of a particular person, he appeared. (She didn't reason that if the person was always on your mind, the coincidence was a lot less striking.) 'Honestly, it was meant!'

She'd just collected Bailiff from Edgerton.

'You can't imagine how wonderful it was to have him back. I was going crazy here!' She corrected herself. 'I mean, everyone was very nice, but I somehow hadn't thought it was going to be like that.' She examined one of Champion's black ears intently as if it were a piece of embroidery with a missed stitch. 'Do you know what I mean?'

Suddenly the months of planning had been over. The beautiful clothes had been worn, the presents opened, and Alice found herself living away from the family and animals she loved, with a brand new husband she'd discovered she could not.

'I'd have got used to it,' she insisted tonelessly, and straight afterwards – like a denial – bestowed another passionate kiss on Champion.

'Where was I?' she asked, not expecting an answer.

It was October the 31st, just after half past three in the afternoon, and she'd taken Bailiff up to Lamberton Woods. They were going to Edward's parents for dinner and she was dreading it.

'His mother's always looking at me in this creepy way – sort of waiting for me to make a mistake. As for his pa! Imagine if *ours* was such a ditherer! Or droned on and on about how wonderful the slaughterhouse is! Edward says I'm a country girl and I shouldn't be silly.' She bit her lip. It was the first time she'd mentioned her husband.

She'd thought that if she could get in a couple of hours' riding first, she could cope with the formality of Mossbury Park and the ever-present feeling of loss. 'He was part of me,' she muttered, smoothing the blanket where Champion's fourth leg should have been resting.

Eve struggled to understand that betrayal needed justification, and kept her thoughts to herself.

'It had just started raining,' said Alice. Ensconced in her

warm kitchen she could smell the salty wind blowing in from the sea, hear the sound of Bailiff's hooves scuffing the dead leaves on the path and the first hollow spattering of raindrops against the canopy of forest. Something had been about to happen. Destiny.

'I heard another horse,' said Alice with a smile, as if that faint whinny from somewhere in the woods had given it all away.

And suddenly there *he* was, standing with his back to her, facing the horizon.

He could have been anyone: a wiry-legged stranger in faded jeans and a checked yellow Viyella shirt and polished brown jodhpur boots who'd happened on this remote spot and tethered his horse to admire the view. But only one man had black hair that curled around his ears; and threw down his cigarette butt and stamped on it in that impatient dismissive fashion.

She'd almost stopped breathing. For one tiny moment, she'd contemplated quietly pulling Bailiff around and galloping for dear life. Honestly she had! But he'd turned before she could. Destiny!

'I was cool as anything,' she told Eve proudly.

Nor did she even dismount from Bailiff – at first. She sat there, looking down on him, trembling secretly, feeling Bailiff's warm damp flesh against the inside of her thighs, through her jodhpurs.

'There you are then!' was his momentous opening statement (delivered a little sternly). Then he said very gently, 'Hello, boy,' and – smiling at the horse – came close and started to stroke Bailiff's nose with his familiar coarse hands with their bitten nails, making Bailiff whicker with pleasure.

And Alice had asked with innocent wonder, looking down at him: 'What are *you* doing here?'

'He just stared at me. And I knew. And he knew.' She bit her lip as if struggling to crush down the memory of the confusion so swiftly followed by ecstasy. Destiny! 'It was amazing, Eve – just amazing! But when I came home, Ma was here – she'd just turned up, for some reason – and it was really hard trying to act as if nothing had happened.'

Finally Eve spoke. 'Oh, Alice!'

'What?'

'He was waiting for you!'

'How could he have been?'

'He'd been following you for weeks. He *knew* you went up to Lamberton Woods!'

At last Alice met her sister's eyes with her own innocent blue ones. 'Do you really think so?'

How lacking in guile she was! How utterly vulnerable!

'You must have known he was likely to turn up again when it looked as if he'd lost you for good!'

'No.' Suddenly she looked horror-struck. 'If you thought that, you should have warned me! Why didn't you? I would never have got married.'

Eve said nothing.

'He's changed!'

There was another incredibly annoying silence from her sister.

'I know you don't believe me.' She went on in a rush. 'You can't imagine what a relief it is to talk about it! I mean, I feel terrible about everything, but I can't help it. It was meant to be.'

'Oh, destiny!' thought Eve, keeping her lips tight shut.

'Destiny means never having to say you're sorry!'

She asked, 'Does Edward know?'

Alice looked horrified. 'Of course not!'

'He's bound to find out, sooner or later.'

'Why?' asked Alice, genuinely puzzled.

'Look at you!'

A door slammed, and Alice's eyes widened. 'He's here! You won't——?'

Eve shook her head crossly. How could Alice even ask such a question? And there was no time to warn her to be cleverer this time round.

She viewed Edward as a tragic figure now. It made her feel guilty just to look at the too-short hair, the plump thighs, the sheep-like profile.

'Hullo, Eve!' he said with his usual enthusiasm.

He'd brought his mother: weather-beaten Lady Farquhar, once young and pretty, now simmering with unspecified distrust for the luminous-skinned siren who'd captured her son.

'Any chance of a cup of coffee, darling?'

It was the first time Eve had seen Alice operating in good-wife mode. She bustled round agreeably, looking for cake. She stirred something on the stove, looking ravishing. She asked Edward about his morning (spent discussing pigs with his father) and called him 'darling', and he basked in the pleasures of being a husband. It was only when he put an arm around her – poor Edward, who quite rightly saw no reason why he shouldn't – that Alice stiffened, and immediately tried to cover up her reaction. And Eve realized she could only manage to be this nice to her husband with an audience.

Did Lady Farquhar notice? It seemed not.

'We're not having it in here, are we?' she demanded.

She sat with her stout woollen-clad legs wide apart under her pleated tweed skirt, reeking of disapproval.

'If you ask me, that dorg should've bin put down.'

Alice said in her gentle voice that trembled a little, 'We couldn't do that to Champion.'

'Funny looking thing. If you ask me, your father needs to pay attention to his breeding. Hasn't a decent dorg amongst the lot.'

It was at times like this, thought Eve, that, for all his autocratic behaviour and blatant favouritism, she really appreciated her father.

'What's the use of a dorg with only three legs? If you ask me, a dorg wants to pay his way. You're doing him no favours. You're not, you know!'

Eve saw her sister bite her lip.

'Alice loves Champion,' said Edward. 'Don't you, darling?' And Eve felt a surge of affection for him.

'It's not homemade, is it?' demanded Lady Farquhar. It was impossible to tell from her tone whether a cake made by Alice would be more or less welcome than one bought from a shop.

'Well, sort of.' Alice admitted meekly, 'It was a cake mix.'

'Delicious, darling!' said Edward. 'You *are* clever!'

It all made Eve feel that it was she who was the innocent.

Usually, life at Edgerton was nicely predictable. Oxford was broadening her mind each day, as was Seb. They were diminishing the family she'd left behind, dis-empowering them all, even Pa. But, this time, being at home was like hearing beautiful music coming faintly from a locked room. One sensed rapture taken as a right, the blameless being trampled.

'Loathsome old cow,' whispered Alice as she took Eve to the door. Then she said, in a rush, 'We've only talked about me! I'm sorry! And I wanted to ask you about Seb! Is it serious?'

'Very.'

'*And . . . ?*'

Eve nodded, smiling. 'Christmas Eve,' she confirmed.

Alice hugged her with delight. 'About time!' she pronounced a little unfairly. 'He's nice,' she confirmed. 'Different,' she ventured (though she didn't elaborate). Then she giggled happily. 'Marcus can't bear wearing suits, either. Do you think we go for the same type?'

'Alice!' called Edward from the kitchen. 'What are you doing, darling?'

Alice rolled her eyes, made a face; but Eve couldn't help feeling that she quite enjoyed the adoration.

'You won't tell anyone? You promise!' Then a line formed between her eyebrows: evidence of a different worry that would soon need to be properly discussed. 'There's something funny going on with the parents, Eve. Have you noticed?'

Chapter Seven

Like many children brought up in great old houses, the young Chandlers believed in ghosts.

During the Civil War the family had hidden the heir of their greatest friends, the Montagues, in a priest's hole leading off the keeping room. Linked for more than a hundred years, the Chandlers and the Montagues had developed a mutual strategy for safeguarding bloodlines and wealth. When one family was endangered, the eldest son would ride over to seek refuge with the other on the best horse, bearing the family silver. But this time the plan went tragically wrong. The young cavalier, Edward Montague, was betrayed by a servant and shot on the spot, and the Chandlers almost lost Edgerton and were forced to pay a fine that crippled them for years. (The children believed this explained the eerie chill in the keeping room.)

Then, a hundred years later, a scion of Edgerton, a golden boy, had been found dead in his bed in the blue room, for no apparent reason (making it the most unpopular guest room in the house). It was to be expected, perhaps, that a place which had been home to the same family for four hundred years would be steeped in their emotions. What insipid characters they would have been, poor ancestors too, if all they'd left of themselves had crumbled into dust in the graveyard.

Eve reported that one night, when she let the dogs out for a final run before locking them in the stables, they'd growled and refused to follow her past the chapel; and Kathy insisted there was a creepy patch in a corner of the great hall (where she'd been told her great-grandfather had breathed his last, one evening, in his rocking chair). It was a sure way of annoying their father. Ghosts didn't exist, maintained Harry: just children seeking to make themselves more interesting. (Though this didn't stop him from reading aloud the stories of M. R. James by the fire if he was in the right genial mood to terrify.)

But it was Felicity who – on the morning of 29th December – first saw the young woman in black.

She'd awoken suddenly at three o'clock, catching the last shivering resonance of the bell in the tower. She switched on her bedside lamp, and by its dim radiance saw Harry fast asleep beside her in their four-poster, his face slack and creased against the pillow, his mouth slightly open. 'How can I endure it?' she thought, her mind returning to precisely the same miserable track as when sleep had finally overtaken her. 'If – at last – I say something, what will happen? Will it become better, or worse?' And – snatching at the future in an uncharacteristic moment of spite – she wished Harry old and helpless, no longer able to betray her.

Then she heard a faint sound coming from somewhere the other side of the closed door.

Her first thought was that one of her children was ill and looking for her. Immediately she pushed aside the heavy bedclothes, flinching with the cold as she stood in her long nightdress searching for her woollen dressing gown and slippers, feeling the anguish as intensely as if it were a third person.

The lights were out on the long landing and the air was bitter. She could feel snow muffling the house, enclosing it in a freezing dark embrace.

First, she checked on Hugo. He and Carson minor were flung on twin beds on their backs with their mouths open as if they'd lost consciousness simultaneously, mid-conversation. She tucked in their blankets, smoothed Hugo's hair, seized a rare chance to kiss him and, as an afterthought, pressed her lips on Carson minor's damp forehead too.

Kathy was deeply asleep, also, in her pink bedroom striped with beams. Felicity heard a rustling sound and, following it to its source, discovered Kathy had hidden a hedgehog in a cardboard box full of straw. Like a grumpy pincushion, button eyes gleaming with mistrust, it did not appear grateful for being rescued.

But Eve's room was quite empty. It said something about Felicity's attitude to her eldest daughter that it never occurred to her she might be sleeping with her boyfriend. Alice was the one who'd needed careful supervision. If Eve wasn't in her bedroom, there had to be a practical explanation.

A draught swept the whole length of the landing, lifting the old rugs, rattling the panes in their leaded frames. Then, as the wind paused momentarily, she heard a semi-controlled sob as if the person responsible was ashamed of being distressed and struggling for control.

'Eve?'

The sound had come from the end of the corridor, where a faint reflection from a crescent moon gleamed off a copper bowl set on a carved oak chest. As she felt her way along the landing, fingers caressing the gloomy panelling she loved so much, she gradually became aware of a blacker shape against the darkness, the pale impression of a face.

'Darling?'

But it wasn't Eve.

A young woman in black was seated in the recess of the bay window, twisting her hands while glittering tears fell from unblinking eyes that held an expression of frightening resignation. Otherwise, Felicity absorbed no more detail.

She, also, had sat in that window in a state of despair, hidden by its heavy curtains, finding strange comfort in its view of the graveyard.

She was twenty-two when she learnt about Harry's first affair and now the crushed-down memory of how she'd reacted to that knowledge returned with cruel intensity. She'd leant against the rough stones of the window frame, feeling their cold strength through the material of her dress, and wept. Twenty-one years on, Felicity shivered with shame. She remembered that she'd considered, for one moment, easing open the heavy window and leaping out on to the pitted honey-coloured flagstones beneath. She'd been pregnant with Eve. (Sometimes she wondered if Eve, curled inside her, had picked up on that suicidal impulse: it might explain her strange lack of self-worth.)

But, in the end, her younger self had risen wearily from the curved stone seat, leaving innocence behind, and made a solemn resolution never again to allow herself to be so vulnerable to another human being.

'Am I going mad?' thought Felicity, straining her eyes, because a moment later the young woman in black had been absorbed by the darkness as thoroughly as a piece of blotting paper laid in black ink. The whole experience had probably lasted a few seconds. She couldn't even describe what the ghost had looked like or been wearing, only her paradoxical mixture of desperation and acceptance. 'And I know her,' thought Felicity. 'I know that I know her.'

Was her portrait somewhere in the house? Had she been the wife of another faithless Chandler? It was strangely comforting to have a sister in anguish, somewhere in time.

Why had the woman returned? The grief must have diminished; her husband had never left her, because separation and divorce were unrecorded in the family. They would be buried in the same grave somewhere out there, just as she knew she and Harry would be one day – their coffins stacked one above the other in missionary position under a headstone, a brief summary which revealed nothing of the real story of their marriage.

How absurd she was! This had been a trick of the mind provoked by great unhappiness. Harry was right, of course. Ghosts did not exist.

Harry was sitting up in bed when she returned to their room. He was wearing his new nightcap.

'Mmm?' he enquired sleepily.

If she'd known, when she was twenty-two, that her

dangerously attractive husband would one day wear a ridiculous red cotton nightcap that perched in a crumpled heap on his head because Beatrice, in pointed Christmas spirit, had given him the smallest size, she might not have sobbed her heart out.

She couldn't laugh at Harry, of course, but might pass on the joke to Johnny when they lunched the following day. She saw herself talking about Harry in the affectionate though disparaging fashion that was becoming easier each time, and imagined Johnny's nice plump face lighting up with pleasure at proof that she was starting to become her own person. She might tell him about the so-called ghost, because she knew he'd be interested rather than scornful. She could even share the worrying suspicion – which had only just dawned on her (and would not be passed on to Harry) – that her eldest daughter was having her first serious love affair.

But all she said was, 'I thought I heard a noise.'

'Oh?'

'It's started snowing again.'

She took off her dressing gown and re-mounted their four-poster that was like a ship marooned in an Arctic waste, and turned out the light. His warm foot accidentally brushed against her icy one and instantly – as much for his sake as for her own – she pulled away. They lay back to back, feet apart, staring into the darkness.

If she expected him to talk at all, she guessed he'd want to discuss the boy Eve had brought home. After all, he'd seemed fascinated by him at dinner. A nice boy, but not really suitable – though, of course, he was up at Oxford too. However, Eve was looking so pretty and happy that maybe she was wrong to have misgivings. But, in this – as in so much else – Harry disappointed her.

'How's Alice, d'you think?'

'She's looking well,' she replied in her standard cool way. Always Alice! Let him say it first!

'Oh, she's looking extremely well,' he agreed, and she imagined his mouth twisting downwards, saying so much more.

She understood that this was the only way he could ever reveal deep feelings: unobserved, in the dark. There was nobody else he could talk to about his children, and she hugged the privilege to herself.

'She looks, she looks . . .' He sounded bewildered and afraid and proud all at the same time. He couldn't finish.

'She wouldn't do anything silly,' said Felicity, seizing her advantage in uncharacteristic fashion.

A long silence. Then: 'No?' He badly needed reassurance, she could tell.

'No.'

Harry said: 'We did the right thing.'

'I think so.' A pause. 'Alice is a woman now.'

'Oh, yes!' Tenderness clogged his voice. 'She's so impressionable!' He made it sound the greatest of compliments. 'She can't help it if . . .'

'Of course she could!' The bitterness cut through the darkness, surprising her.

'But she'd never . . .' he began, and there was something placatory in his tone.

'Even if . . .?'

'No.'

'How can you be sure?'

'It's not worth it. Ever.' He paused, then said with meaning: 'Alice knows that.'

Thus they communicated with each other – discussing, without accusations or admissions, everything that divided them. Then, suddenly, he turned to face her and, sealing their understanding, made love to her under the usual weight of moth-eaten blankets hemmed with loops of wool and topped by a lumpy quilt.

It was the first time for a month. Feeling his familiar athletic body through layers of nightclothes, the programmed economical moves of a long marriage, Felicity thought, 'If only I could go back to that moment when I saw him as laughable, and Johnny a real escape.'

But he always knew exactly when she was beginning to move away from him. Even so, he never once kissed her, and the absence was bitter.

As she stared over his shoulder into the freezing void, her lips moved silently and a despairing but resigned admission mushroomed into the darkness before evaporating like a ghost.

Chapter Eight

Seb had never eaten pheasant. He'd certainly never thought about how pheasants were killed.

'Oh, by the way,' Eve told him very casually, 'there's a pheasant shoot tomorrow.'

The tips of their cigarettes glowed in the freezing blackness surrounding his bed.

They'd made love for just over forty-five minutes, the bell in the clocktower marking each quarter of an hour before one momentous resonating chime that seemed to burrow into the surrounding stone.

Was it as marvellous for Alice? Being Alice, she used Alice language. The stars exploded and the earth moved every time. 'Honestly, it's amazing – just amazing, Eve!'

Alice couldn't feel like this, Eve decided: not this aching replete surrender. For Alice, she suspected, sex was about vanity and contrariness: conquering the one person who hadn't fallen at her feet like all the others.

'Tell the truth, Evie, I don't fancy bloodsports.'

'It's only pheasant! And we won't be doing the shooting. And it's good fun. And Alice'll be there.'

'Yeah? I thought she loved animals!'

The pheasant shoot two days after Christmas was an Edgerton tradition involving all the staff. It was a way for Harry to entertain friends and neighbours and keep the servants sweet: a chance for employees to mingle with employers and enjoy the brief festive pretence that the balance of power between them was less sharply defined.

As with so much else he'd been shown, Seb found himself strangely captivated; amused when Harry asked him quite seriously if he'd packed a gun. ('My dear fellow! Plenty to go round! What? Never? Good Lord!') He wanted to dislike Harry and all he stood for, but was finding it impossible. Not for the first time, he observed that, in Harry's company, everyone seemed more alive.

By half past eight on the morning of the shoot, the drive was packed with expensive cars and milling with excited dogs. Dress seemed to be uniform but ancient: tweed jackets, corduroy trousers, tweed caps, gumboots clotted with mud. At first, it was hard for Seb to determine who was who. But it was Harry's guests who exchanged noisy small talk as they buckled on cartridge belts and broke open their shotguns to check them, the estate workers who stood quietly at a discreet distance, guns slung around them like employers' luggage.

The whole operation seemed deeply sexist. None of the women would be shooting and only a few were judged capable of flushing out birds under the instruction of the keepers. Most would not be making an appearance until halfway through the day when, led by Felicity, they'd turn up for lunch in the folly.

Hugo was sulking because he wasn't allowed a gun. 'It's not fair. You let me shoot crows.'

'Crows are different,' said Kathy, who, since Alice's departure, had been lobbying hard for the position of resident favourite.

'Exactly,' said her father. 'So stop whingeing.' He was addressing both boys because, predictably, Carson minor's mouth had turned down at the corners too.

'You promised,' moaned Hugo. 'Last year, you said—'

'When I consider you're safe with a gun,' said Harry, 'you can have one. Consider yourselves lucky you're allowed to beat.'

'Yes, consider yourselves,' echoed Kathy smugly. She herself was looking forward to flushing birds out of the undergrowth so they could be shot. Pheasant didn't count. Like Hugo, she'd grown appreciably since last holidays. She'd be eleven soon. She was even starting to enjoy boarding school (though she'd never admit it to the parents).

Alice and Edward arrived with his parents, Lord and Lady Farquhar, and Seb had a chance to reassess her. She was some knockout – the more so, now he knew her secret – and he could almost see the horns sprouting from Edward's sheep-like head. Another couple turned up round about the same time – he solid and rubicund, she red-haired, white-skinned and dressed in green. 'More candidates for the tumbrils,' thought Seb, listening to the affected confident way they spoke, and he watched as the man joined Harry and chatted easily and the wife went into the house to drink coffee with Felicity and the other women until it was time for lunch.

At a quarter to nine, looking handsome and rakish and quite unfazed by the flakes peeling assiduously from a yellow-grey sky, Harry gave his customary pre-shooting speech to his guests who, frosted with falling snow, were looking increasingly spectral.

'You all know our excellent Tommy, of course.' He gestured in the direction of the head gamekeeper, a burly crimson-cheeked man.

'Tommy's in charge, so that means all of us, including the dogs, jump to attention when Tommy and his boys wave their red flags. That's right, isn't it, Tommy?'

'That's right, Sir Harry.'

'And Tommy's word is law. Few words from me about ground game . . . Erm, shortage of woodcock this year so they're out of bounds. We're a few beaters short, too, so take care not to bag one of them.' (Harry paused with his wolfish smile to allow for laughter.) 'On the other hand, if Tommy gives the nod, feel free to shoot foxes. We can sort it out with the hunt later. Jays and magpies are fair game. Grey squirrels count as high-flying game – the more the better. No buzzards or owls. Four drives before we convene at half past one in the folly, where Mrs Briggs will be laying on one of her excellent lunches. Two more after that. Plum cake and sloe gin back at the house depending on when the light's gone – around four.'

Before the day of the pheasant shoot Seb had not ventured far from the house, apart from occasional light walks with Eve and the dogs. Now he began to comprehend not only the magnitude of the estate, but the variations in its landscape. The house was situated in a wide shallow bowl, but beyond the perimeters of that setting there lay deep valleys and high hills and seemingly endless stretches of woodland.

'How many acres does your dad own?' he asked Eve, but of course she didn't know. He was irritated by her vague acceptance of all this, not appreciating her resolution that if she behaved as if privilege were unimportant, it might lessen the divisions he perceived between them.

'Come on, Evie! Is it as far as we can see?'

'Dunno really.'

'How much of it's farmed?' asked Seb, who'd spotted a large herd of indolent cows the colour of horse chestnuts in a meadow; sheep grazing patchily on the hills.

'D'you know, I've never asked,' said Eve.

'How does he pay for it all?'

'Dunno, Seb. Does it matter?'

For the past year, the pheasants had been living happily around wire pens situated on various hills planted with kale. Life had been good. They'd learnt where to come for regular plentiful supplies of maize and become quite plump. True, there was the shock of the occasional marauding fox, but they could always scuttle through the kale and take off in squawking panic for the safety of trees in the dark woods the other side of the valleys. Now, in one day, all this carefully nurtured trust would be shattered.

Shooters and beaters were transported in ex-army jeeps with trembling skirts of mud to the location of the first drive. Junior keepers clung on precariously at the back as the vehicles laboured through heavy snow, occasionally skidding on the icy ruts beneath; inside, squeezed between a forest of legs, the dogs trembled with anticipation.

The shooters were set down in a deep wide valley while other jeeps took the beaters to the base of one of the kale-capped hills enclosing it.

The world had turned white and silent. Each black leafless twig supported a delicate slice of snow, and more and more flakes whirled out of the sky as the beaters stared through soaked lashes at the beautiful barren landscape and stamped their icy feet, in heavy socks and Wellington boots.

They were a mix of Chandlers and friends, reinforced by Tommy's professionals. The amateurs were politely ordered to fan out round the base of the hill at regular intervals. Seb managed to place himself next to Eve; Alice took up position on her other side. There was a lot of waiting around while red flag messages were exchanged between Tommy's men higher up on the hill and down in the valley.

The beaters were forbidden to edge closer to each other while they waited for the signal to move and ordered to keep quiet, so, in the snowbound silence broken only by occasional birdcalls, they developed their own semaphore.

Hugo and his friend Carson minor aimed imaginary shotguns and engaged in competitive blasting at unseen birds whirling across an opaque uncertain sky, and Alice turned to face her sister.

Eve raised a questioning thumb.

Alice nodded ecstatically. She hugged herself and rocked to and fro. She looked like a Tolstoy heroine with her black fur hat and hourglass shape. Then she froze as a deer shot past, heading blindly for a barbed wire fence. Crashing horribly, it appeared simultaneously to effect a vertical take-off. Seconds later it was gone: wounded but free. Alice put a gloved hand to her mouth.

From a distance, Seb had been watching this pantomime with interest. So the affair was going hot and heavy. Somewhere down in the valley was the cuckold, who'd no doubt prove to be an excellent shot. He wondered coldly if the upper classes were more licentious as a species. But the Chandlers were such courteous and generous hosts; the beauty of the house was so overwhelming. He was even warming to Felicity, whose aloofness had originally repelled him. He'd noticed the tender unobtrusive way she mothered timid Carson minor who'd lost his sibling. He perceived great tension in the marriage, without guessing the cause, and instinctively blamed Harry. But he'd been so nice to him: he was so unexpected. They were like Oriental carpet sellers unfolding for him one colourful seductive scene after another – first Christmas with all its contradictions and private jokes, now a shoot – and the fanciful idea occurred to him that, unless something dramatic happened soon, all these gorgeous backdrops would go to waste.

On his other side was one of the professional beaters, plainly used to long patches of inactivity and boredom. Probably had better insulation for his feet, too, thought Seb gloomily. But the cold no longer seemed quite so abominable. He was even coming round to the view that Edgerton *should* be lived in as in the Middle Ages.

Finally, with the distant crack of a frozen red flag, it was time to go, and the beaters started crunching clumsily through the snow in their Wellington boots, circling up towards the brow of the hill. There, they were ordered to stay still for a moment. Then, with the dogs bouncing excitedly ahead of them, they were given the go-ahead to push through kale laden with fresh wet snow and teeming with secret life. Suddenly, a fat pheasant rose, squawking, and more and more followed in a panicky cacophony – and they heard the first shots far down in the valley, as the birds sailed overhead, trying to seek refuge in the trees on the other side.

To his relief, Seb found himself detached from the carnage even though he could hear guns blasting away down below, and even feel occasional light shot peppering the frozen kale around him. Visibility was minimal because of the whirling snowflakes. He couldn't help thinking that, in these circumstances, somebody could easily get killed; and also that anyone else but Harry might have cancelled the shoot. The beauty and strangeness of the scene was offset by extreme discomfort. For the second time in a week he thought he'd never been so cold. His jeans were frozen stiff, as were his woollen gloves.

Now they reached the brim of the valley and, through the blizzard, could make out dark shapes streaming through a fusillade of shots across the chalky disintegrating sky. One bird after another dropped as life ceased instantaneously, or spiralled into flapping free-fall; still others managed to wing it to the woods opposite. And suddenly, with a flash of red against white, silence fell. The first drive was over.

In the jeep, on the way to the second drive, a cautious camaraderie was building up between the opposite social classes of professionals and amateurs. They compared notes on common ground: the ordeal of pushing through snow-laden kale, the revolting presence of the soaking dogs between their icy knees. And Eve started tormenting everyone by visualizing lunch, for which they'd have to wait more than two hours.

'Couple of glasses of gin'll do me just fine,' said the seventeen-year-old son of one of the keepers, and laughed suddenly as if he'd made an impertinent remark. A dog had caught a baby rabbit in the kale and, when he'd heard the squealing, the boy had been seen deftly to wring the rabbit's neck.

Alice said, 'This is one of my favourite days of the year,' and Seb looked at her dreamy blue eyes and delicious soft lips and wondered how she, the protector of animals, could make such a statement, not appreciating that it was round about this time she'd first met Marcus. Now each anniversary of every advance in the relationship was prized, whatever else it held; and all other voices were distracting unless they could be filtered for just one person's interest and amusement. Her eyes narrowed a little as she contemplated telling Marcus about Eve saying, against a background of protesting groans, 'And the crust of Mrs Briggs' steak and kidney pie always has these scrumptious crispy buttery bits round the edge.' She hummed with life, simultaneously guilty and triumphant, and felt as separate from Edward as if he were still in that deep valley and she on a high hill above.

Formal lunch for sixty people had been set out on two long trestle tables in the folly – a hideous Gothic extravaganza erected by Harry's great grandfather and situated in a beech tree glade now hung with ice and snow. In another culture, the folly – separate, secluded – might have served as a mausoleum. Cars were drawn up all round it, and Mrs Briggs, in thick coat and woolly hat, was orchestrating a mini army of warmly-clad girls from the village, who ferried dishes of still-steaming food from the cars and offered them to seated guests in heavy overcoats and hats. (Just as at Edgerton, the meal would be tepid by the time it was eaten.) There were exquisite arrangements of holly and mistletoe by Felicity on the tables, and plenty of bottles – but Seb noticed that although the second table had been provided with just as much alcohol as the first, it had nickel cutlery on it and plain white china rather than the gold-edged transparent-looking stuff arranged on the other.

Outside the folly, the snow whirled down. It added gaiety to the already merry proceedings: shutting off the outside world, masking differences. Maybe, thought Seb, with a few drinks inside them they'd forget about the afternoon's shooting. They'd certainly killed enough game. He could see dozens of red and brown corpses, some with exotic tailfeathers, strung from the back of one of the jeeps, and half a dozen small, drab birds someone had said were partridges. He pulled his right glove off with his teeth so he could hold his glass properly, and felt it grow numb. But there were no complaints from the other guests.

The women had arrived from the house with the children deemed too young and irresponsible to act as beaters. Felicity was chic in a tweed hat and long matching tweed coat: a contrast to most of the other wives. Seb saw her run a critical glance over the tables to check everything had been set out correctly. Beatrice, in an ancient mink coat with a heavy scarf bundled round her head, looked like a moth-eaten potentate. She eyed the morning's bag scornfully. In her time, she'd been a better shot than any of these men. But you couldn't take proper aim from a shooting stick. Arthritis reduced you; the pity was nobody remembered your glory days.

Lady Farquhar was discussing her hunting spaniel. 'Dorg's a wonderful mouth on him. Can't give a dorg a good mouth. Either has it or hasn't. That's what I say.'

'Natural retriever,' confirmed Edward. He was flushed from his morning's successful shooting. (Aim, fire – finish! Why couldn't life be that simple?) Then his gaze shifted to where Alice sat between Eve and Hugo, looking gorgeously pretty in her fur hat. She hadn't even noticed his triumph. His happiness fell away.

Nobody told the estate workers to sit at the second table. They knew where to go – even the young ones, who, in the jeeps, had appeared on equal terms with the Edgerton children and their friends. But they joked with the village girls waiting on them and even sounded suspiciously as if they might be imitating some of those on the other table. As the noise rose, Tommy kept glancing across at Felicity.

'We're over here,' said Lady Farquhar.

'We're on this table,' confirmed her son.

There was steak and kidney pie to eat, baked just as Eve had predicted, and red cabbage that was slightly caramelized and chestnut-coloured roast potatoes. Mrs Briggs wasn't a particularly good cook, but her burnt food was spectacular. Pastry was her pride. There was apple pie for pudding (also exquisitely overdone) and cream from the Edgerton dairy, so rich it was almost solid, and enormous slabs of waxy yellow cheddar, also produced at Edgerton, with the hard rusk-like biscuits that were a speciality of the area.

Afterwards Seb couldn't have said how the girl appeared, or at which stage of the meal. When he reviewed the day, many hours later, he found he'd retained an exact image of Harry's expression – half horrified, half proud and amused – and of the vitality and colour seeping from Felicity's face as dramatically as if someone had passed a sponge across it.

He'd thought Alice was a doll, but even Alice couldn't compare with this kid. She was seriously young – no more than sixteen, he guessed – and her skin had a velvety glowing quality, all the more touching and exquisite because it could not last. She was a blonde, too, with thick hair tumbling down her back; but, unlike Alice, possessed a sly merry expression which made her appear older. He couldn't discern what lay under the heavy coat she wore, but she moved very gracefully as if proud of her body. The effect she had on the men at the second table was astonishing. Instantly the noise level started rising, as they competed for her attention.

Hugo and Carson minor were goggling as if they'd never seen a girl before – while automatically continuing to shovel food into their mouths.

'Hugo!' said Harry sharply, 'watch your manners!' And Hugo and Carson minor fixed him with identical looks of simmering resentment.

'Who's *that*?' asked the red-haired woman in green Seb had noticed earlier.

She levelled the question at Harry, and there was an edge to her voice that made Seb feel uncomfortably alert. He noticed that the other women round Harry were starting to take notice too.

Harry looked elaborately puzzled. He politely cupped an ear with one hand. Couldn't hear, with all the noise, he indicated. (Not going deaf, though, of course.)

The woman raised her voice. 'The pretty little thing over there. Don't tell me you've not noticed her, Harry!'

'Priscilla!' said the red-haired woman's husband.

'Ah, now I see who you mean!' said Harry, with his lethal smile. 'I believe that's the daughter of my head gardener. Excellent man. Been with us for years.'

'She seems to know *you*,' said Priscilla with enjoyment.

'Oh?' Harry sounded very innocent.

'She does,' agreed one of the other women – black-haired, heavily made-up.

'Of course she knows him,' said Beatrice crossly, and Seb saw Felicity look at her mother-in-law for a moment with what seemed like fear. But Beatrice went on. 'Everyone on the estate knows Harry. Pass me some more of that excellent cheddar, will you? Good rind. And a drop of Madeira to go with it. We're going to get snowed in at this rate. Might as well enjoy ourselves.'

Then the girl waved at Harry.

To Seb this didn't seem so extraordinary, because he'd no experience of the hierarchy of a house like Edgerton.

Having servants was wrong, of course – though he certainly enjoyed having his bed turned down at night and ineffectually warmed with a china bottle. But he'd noticed that Mrs Briggs (who, oddly, didn't ever seem to have had a husband) wielded considerable power: the Chandlers all seemed terrified of being late for meals. Because he found himself so unexpectedly charmed by Harry, he strove to think of him as a father figure to his employees, autocratic but generally protective. The girl had probably known him since she was a baby. And hadn't Eve assured him the whole point of the Edgerton shoot was to promote a sense of democracy? It had been Harry, he was informed, who'd started the tradition. Eve said that, for all her eccentricity, her grandmother still disapproved.

But even Seb could see this wasn't a 'greetings, sir, and thank you' sort of wave. The girl had a cheeky knowing expression. It looked more like a 'hello again' kind of gesture, as if the two of them had met in the recent past, perhaps in less crowded circumstances.

'May one know her name?' asked the red-haired woman. Her mouth smeared with scarlet lipstick parodied amusement, her tone was bitter.

'Her name,' Harry repeated.

'She does have a name, I assume?'

'Pam'la.'

It was the girl who'd provided her name. She'd left the other table and come as close to Harry as one of his dogs. She stood beside him as if she were entitled. She glanced at the red-haired woman as incuriously as she might have at any of Harry's middle-aged friends.

'Ah, Pamela!' he said in his rich drawl, with that unforgettable mixture of embarrassment and conceit – and Seb experienced a sense of deep shame for witnessing Felicity's anguish, the secret beneath her chilly façade. He glanced at Eve quickly, but she wouldn't look at him and seemed on the point of tears. Then he felt her gloved hand grip his under the table.

But Alice was still absorbed in her own drama. Seb even saw her smile slightly as she dreamily sipped at her glass. Then he noticed that Edward's seat was empty. 'Gone for a pee, most like,' he remembered thinking afterwards.

'Pam'la!' It was a rosy middle-aged man on the servants' table who'd called her. He sounded sharp and anxious. 'Pam'la, you come right back here, right now!'

But Seb got the feeling that nothing would make the girl leave Harry's side: there was something too determined and also innocent in her whole attitude. She glanced at her father's employer from under her dark lashes; Seb even thought she moved still closer.

Then a deafening shot rang out.

Everyone screamed. Lady Farquhar pushed herself back in her chair so savagely that, but for the quick reaction of Ian Copeland next to her, she might have fractured her skull on the stone flags. Lord Farquhar's terrified little eyes stared into catastrophe; his safe world vanished for ever. Of course the shot had involved Edward: he was the only one missing from the feast.

Even more shocking, though, was the sight of Alice still absorbed in her happy daydreaming.

'Alice!' said Eve, very sharply.

They must have guessed what horror was waiting: a young face obscenely altered, scarlet gore staining white snow, a picture of a death that would stay with them for ever. Even so, they didn't pause as they streamed out of the folly into the blizzard. Seb thought with savagery: 'Poor berk. What did she expect?' He'd learnt over the past few days that the upper classes scorned displays of real emotion. They brushed off disasters, just as – conversely – they exaggerated the pettiest of misfortunes. ('*Nightmare!*' Seb had heard Alice shriek. '*I've got butter on my sleeve!*' And Eve had told him, with pride, about an illustrious ancestor who'd fought in the Crimean war and, after both legs were shot off, calmly propped himself on a cannon and went on firing.) But – as had now been most tragically demonstrated – anger and grief and jealousy gathered force, eventually imploding.

As it turned out, Edward had only shot himself in the calf. Even so, the scene resembled one of the abattoirs his father waxed so enthusiastic about. The colour had drained from his usually ruddy face to blossom – obscenely bright – all around him.

'It's quite all right, Mother,' Edward managed to say, his jaw wobbling with sorrow for himself.

'Eddie, what have you done!' cried Lady Farquhar.

His gun had been sticking all morning, Edward told them. 'Something wrong with it – could feel it all morning.' So he'd come out to check.

'But what were you *doing*?' cried his mother.

'It's a new gun, Eddie!' his father pointed out.

'Brand new,' Edward agreed sadly. 'Only four months old. But there's definitely something wrong – could feel it all morning. Something badly wrong.' He looked at Alice as he said it. And, for the first time that day, she really looked at him.

'Oh, Edward!' She sounded exasperated and disappointed, as if he were a naughty child. 'Don't you know you shouldn't fool around with guns?'

'Now that's not fair and you know it!' All Lady Farquhar's dissatisfaction with her daughter-in-law came steaming out. 'He told you. Gun was sticking. He came out to try and fix it. That's what he said. You heard him.'

'Bad shot,' commented Beatrice who, because of her arthritic hips, was last on the scene.

'What?' exploded Lady Farquhar.

'Not considered safe,' said Hugo in the silly fluting voice that drove his father mad, and he and Carson minor snorted with repressed mirth.

'Minor flesh wound,' pronounced Harry smoothly, even though the extent of Edward's injuries was unknown. 'Might be a good idea to get him to a hospital, all the same.'

They'd have to abandon the remaining two drives – though Seb couldn't shake off the suspicion that Harry might have objected if the snow wasn't forming in drifts. Since the drama had moved in a new direction, he was back in control, master-minding operations to get Edward loaded into one of the jeeps. Alice would accompany her husband to hospital, together with his parents. Seb heard her laughter ring out – 'Pa!' she exclaimed, as if shocked as well as amused – and felt sure the joke had been at Edward's expense.

Without being asked, the same servants who, a moment ago, had been enjoying themselves as guests, started dismantling the tables. They seemed to find it a relief to return to their usual status even though, having drunk too much, they were strangely clumsy. Two crystal glasses slipped from freezing fingers and shattered on stone.

But the girl had vanished as suddenly as she'd appeared; and neither could Seb any longer see the man he'd assumed was her father.

He noticed that Felicity had slipped away too. Had she taken one of the cars and returned to Edgerton on her own? Or perhaps her ingrained courtesy had prompted her to offer a lift to the servant and his daughter? Seb could imagine it easily: the father sitting awkward and unsmiling

in the front, the exquisitely dangerous daughter alone with
her secrets in the back. As she concentrated on the icy road
ahead, Felicity's pale face would be set in a mask, narrow lips
moving as she exchanged dry platitudes about the weather.

'And now I have to go back there too,' thought Seb, and
affected not to notice Eve's anguished looks.

This has nothing to do with me! Eve willed him to pick it up.
Nothing!

Chapter Nine

Johnny said, 'Sure you want to do this?'

'Quite.'

'I warn you, might not be up to much. Out of practice.'

'I'm glad.'

'What?'

'Honestly!'

'Oh, Flick . . .' His breath smelt of peppermint, and it touched her that he'd cared enough to brush his teeth. 'I can't believe my luck!'

'I can't believe I'm here,' thought Felicity.

They were lying close together and naked in Johnny's low single bed. It was four o'clock in the afternoon and, in the red glow of the double-barred electric fire he'd switched on, she could make out a dark chest of drawers, the dull shine of a pair of silver-backed hairbrushes, a trouser press imprisoning a pair of cavalry twills, a pullover neatly folded over the back of a wooden chair. There were no books by the bed. It was obvious that until now this little room had been used only for sleeping, with perhaps the occasional bittersweet dream of a former life.

'You're crying.'

'All that alcohol.'

'Medicine.'

'So kind to me.'

'Just ordinary.'

'Oh, Johnny, you have no idea.'

How lovely she was, he thought: womanly and firm. It was hard to believe she'd given birth four times. He appreciated her body all the more for the peculiarly feminine wars it had endured. He'd tried so valiantly to shut down on memories of intimacy, and briefly ached with pity for his dead wife.

That did it. 'Sorry,' he muttered, mortified.

'It's all right.'

At least, I can do lips and bosoms. He nearly said it out loud. *I can be good at those.* He kissed her very gently on the mouth – no slobber, no tongues – and felt her respond. In the end, he amazed himself: diving down the length of her body to explore, with his lips, the core of her femininity, the sublime scents of women.

'Ah!' Thank the Lord! He looked shy and pleased and anxious, teeth gleaming in the darkness, as he held her very close. 'Now are you quite sure you're sure?'

'Quite.'

In the end, it was unexpectedly successful, by Johnny's standards. He didn't think she'd climaxed, though he heard her sigh deeply. That would have been too much to hope for, the first time. It seemed to him an entirely logical and natural thing they'd done, and he wondered what Felicity was thinking as she lay so quietly beside him, holding his hand.

Felicity was thinking, 'I have a lover! Funny how different it was – but nice. Not threatening at all. I *like* the cuddly chunky different feel of him. He's kind and good. I mustn't hurt him. Mustn't, mustn't, mustn't . . . Oh, God, what have I done?'

'No regrets?' asked Johnny, and she heard the smile in his voice in the dark.

'None.'

'Nor me,' he said, and hugged her close. 'I thought I might feel guilty. Was that very foolish?'

At lunch in the restaurant behind the cathedral in Nether Taunton she'd told him about the pheasant shoot. It was not her style to dramatize but somehow – telling the story in her clipped detached fashion – the shock and humiliation emerged all the more savage. It had been gratifying to see Johnny grow pale with rage.

'That night,' he asked quietly, 'what did you say?'

It had been one of the most miserable dinners she could remember. Eve hostile to both parents in her silent and mutinous way; her friend Seb abstracted, overly polite; Kathy excited and tearful because the events of the day had baffled and frightened her; the boys locked into their maddening world of silly jokes. Only Harry had seemed his usual smooth self, but she noticed the occasional uneasy glance, as if he were trying to guess the extent of her knowledge. It was only Beatrice who kept any sort of conversation going. As usual, it was her own affairs that preoccupied her: a tick lodged in the nether quarters of one of her spaniels (which had bitten a stripe of its own hair out); the escalating cost of poultry feed.

In their enormous bedroom, colder than ever, Harry immediately went on the offensive. 'You weren't very pleasant to Mama.'

'Wasn't I?' she responded coolly. After all, she'd said nothing. She'd sat at the head of the table, eating and drinking sparingly, exhaling the chilly disdain her family was used to.

A moment of silence, then: 'Mama is entitled to respect.'

'So are we all.'

'And what is that supposed to mean?'

Felicity looked tight lipped as she removed her clothes and pulled on a woollen nightdress, whilst contriving not to expose an inch of flesh. Nobody could have guessed that she was struggling to summon up all her courage to confront her husband.

Harry reached under the pillow his side of the bed and attempted, with a serious expression, to fit on the red cotton nightcap Beatrice had given him for Christmas. He pulled it down over one ear and it popped up over the other, finally settling on the crown of his head like one of the ineffectual home-made felt warmers Mrs Briggs kept for boiled eggs.

'Harry, what happened today was unacceptable.'

A beat: one of his famous pauses to give himself a chance to marshal his reactions so as to retain control. Then: 'I agree.'

She could feel her heart start to pound, and her mouth dry up. 'You do?'

'I'm concerned about Alice. I think we should both be. Feller's an idiot.'

She'd gone to the window then and looked out at the white unmarked lawn, the drifts on the lake beyond. She could feel knives of icy wind streaming through cracks in the mullioned windows. There seemed a real possibility, now, that they would become snowed in, and a separate part of her, the good wife, wondered dully about food and fuel supplies.

She imagined him behind her in their bed, confident that she would now engage in a discussion about the shooting accident: could even see his faint fragmented reflection, topped by a blob of scarlet, in the diamond-shaped panes of glass.

'I'm not talking about Edward, Harry.'

Silence. Then in an easy relaxed tone: 'I'm not with you.'

Finally she turned to face him. In that moment, he'd taken off the absurd nightcap. Inside, she raged against him. But looking into his charming face, his empty eyes, all she managed to say, voice nearly a sob, was: 'No!'

He patted her side of the bed. 'You'll get cold,' he said. And, recognizing the familiar meaningful tone, consumed by dread and longing, she thought dully: 'Now I'll have to arm myself against him all over again.'

'She's younger than Alice!'

It was Felicity, rather than Harry, who felt the mortification – crimson hateful shame that made her long to hide, even from Johnny.

'The fool,' he went on with quiet contempt. 'What happens now?'

The question was irrelevant, of course. She and Harry were bound together for life. Harry believed in the family and loved his children and might prize Edgerton even more. In addition, there was the threat of his Lloyds losses. It was all very well for him to continue slinging envelopes into an unopened pile on the table in the great hall. Sooner or later, he'd be forced to settle. Several thousand pounds to be paid now; more of the same soon; debt hanging over them. There'd be less and less money for frivolity, certainly none for divorce.

'I think I'm expected to put up with it.'

For the second time, Felicity saw Johnny's pleasant face stiffen with anger. But all he said was, 'I don't understand.'

'No . . .' But a part of her couldn't help wondering how quickly even Johnny might change if he were suddenly to acquire Harry's charm and opportunities.

She thought, 'What would he say if I told him Harry made love to me that night? His form of comfort!' She shivered.

'Cold?' he asked, instantly solicitous. He stroked her hand, and Felicity, who hated being touched, found herself responding. It seemed that this very ordinary man was capable of magic.

She could see that she was no less attractive to him because her husband had fallen for a much younger woman, and the knowledge boosted her miserable lack of self-worth.

She wasn't at all sure if she found him similarly enticing but, after the second gin and tonic and a whole bottle of Margaux, a drunken woman took the extraordinary decision to go to bed with him. It would be medicinal, like the alcohol. In the car on the way back to his cottage she thought, 'I might have to seduce him,' and couldn't stop a very uncharacteristic giggle.

'Flick?' He smiled as he wove his little car inexpertly through the narrow lanes. He was driving much too fast. It was lucky there was no other traffic; still more so that they didn't meet the local police. 'What's the joke?'

'Oh, nothing, nothing.'

In fact, it was he who suggested with a smile that belied his extreme nervousness: 'How would you feel about going horizontal?'

Just before it happened, she thought, 'If I shut my eyes he could be anyone.'

But it was Johnny, and she was glad of it.

Chapter Ten

Alice and Eve were giving Champion his daily exercise through the pear orchard at Mossbury Park. Snow still clotted the ground, but the black and spiky trees had shed their icing sugar coating. It was bitterly cold and Alice was wearing her black fur hat.

It was amazing how quickly Harry's once favoured dog was adapting to only three legs, and the wound left by the amputation was healing well. He seemed very cheerful as, with tense concentration, he sniffed at a patch of bare earth before urinating dismissively on it.

'Such a clever boy!' crooned Alice.

They'd left Edward lying on the sofa in the drawing room in front of the television. Alice mentioned that he watched it a lot these days, but Eve was about as interested in Edward's apathy as Alice was in her father's daily tirades on vampires.

They were going to talk about love. It was the only area in which Eve felt less clever.

'Alice, what does it mean when a man says he needs space?'

'Is that what he said?'

'It's bad then?' Eve sounded terribly anxious.

'Um, not exactly.' Typically, Alice brought the conversation back to herself. 'I mean, it's what Marcus said, and look what happened! So it doesn't necessarily mean the worst.'

'He said we were too different,' said Eve miserably, 'and he needed to think about it all. Oh, I should never have brought him home for Christmas!'

They'd reached the peak of a low hill that looked down on another great house, a grey porticoed structure Harry had dubbed 'the barracks'. Mossbury Park, adorned with yew trees sculpted into peacocks, hadn't been built to soothe the eye and lift the soul, but perhaps Seb might have found it as daunting as Edgerton. It was a foghorn statement about the continuing importance, through the centuries, of the Farquhar family. The Farquhars had not made the mistake of joining Lloyds – mostly because Lord Farquhar found it extremely difficult to reach decisions. Now he was of the triumphant opinion that Lloyds booty was 'funny money' and the Hurricane Betsy disaster 'served the damn fools right' (having conveniently forgotten that, at his son's wedding, he'd meant to enquire about syndicates).

'You can't help it!' said Alice indignantly. Then she went on, with a tender smile, 'Marcus doesn't mind one bit now. I think it makes me more exciting.'

'It wasn't just that,' said Eve. Even thinking about the girl made her angry and embarrassed. The night of the pheasant shoot, she'd crept into Seb's cold bed, as usual, and he'd made love to her; but she'd been unable to penetrate his shell of misery. (Or the mystery of why he, who didn't even belong to her family, had taken her mother's humiliation so greatly to heart.) What had happened had made him decide to leave Edgerton early – even though Eve argued, swallowing a sob, that there was no real proof, nothing concrete.

'I don't want to talk about it,' said Alice.

'D'you think I do?'

'Then let's not.' But Alice went on almost immediately: 'It's just a silly crush. Something to do with his age.' She paused. 'She *is* pretty.'

'Very.'

'But . . . he'd never actually *do* anything!'

Eve was silent.

'He couldn't, Eve!'

More silence.

'She's younger than us!' Alice sounded panic-stricken. 'What are you saying?'

Eve looked at her. 'I think she likes him.'

'You don't think—' Alice shook her head violently as if to rid it of the disgust. 'He couldn't, Eve!'

Eve said nothing.

Alice muttered, 'It's probably Ma's fault.'

'What?'

'You don't fall for someone else unless something's wrong,' said Alice, adeptly swinging the discussion back to her own predicament.

When Eve failed to respond, she went on crossly, 'Has Ma *said* anything?'

'Of course not!'

Alice thought about her father becoming infatuated with someone even younger than herself. She turned the notion over and over in her mind, trying to come up with a way of looking at it that would make it less repulsive. 'I suppose,' she said slowly, 'that if you've only ever slept with one person in your whole life and then someone else comes along who you can't help falling for, you're bound to take it hard.' (But this romantic picture hardly tallied with the controlling sophisticated person she'd always known.)

'He'd never leave Ma!'

'Wouldn't he?'

Eve stared at her sister. She hadn't even contemplated the break-up of the family.

'I mean,' Alice went on with a dreamy look in her eyes, 'if you really really fall in love with someone else, then it's the only honest thing to do, isn't it?'

'Poor Ma,' said Eve.

'It's terrible. And not fair, is it? I mean, even though Pa's so old, you get the feeling he's still quite attractive to women, don't you? They do adore him! Even though, of course, up to now it's only been flirting. Probably still is. Poor Ma! I mean, even if she wanted to be with someone else, she couldn't.'

'Ma?' said Eve immediately.

Alice snorted with amusement. It was such relief to know some things were set in stone.

Since Edward had shot himself in the leg, it had been far more difficult for Alice to meet Marcus. Consequently, she was not well disposed to her husband, whereas he depended on her more than ever.

'Is that you, Alice?' he called even as they were closing the front door of the house behind them.

Alice didn't answer. She was looking for a towel to pat Champion's three feet dry. 'Here we are, my darling. All nice and cosy.'

'Alice! Are you there?'

'Yes!' Alice shouted crossly. She made a face at her sister and mouthed, 'Nightmare!'

Eve put her head round the door of the drawing room. Edward was lying on the sofa watching some sort of game show. A coal fire glowed intensely and it felt wonderfully warm to Eve. A plump middle-aged woman in mauve was looking confused and excited as an unseen crowd roared at her, 'Open the box!'

'Open the box!' shouted Edward, and smiled self-consciously at Eve. 'Have you seen this before? Awfully jolly.'

Eve shook her head. 'How's your leg?' She noticed that his face seemed to have become even rounder and pinker since the accident.

Edward became serious. 'Doctor Hudson said I was lucky not to lose it.' He was almost bellowing over the noise of the television. 'Did Alice mention if she was making tea?'

'I'll go and find out.'

In the kitchen, Alice was cutting a piece of raw steak into tiny pieces while Champion watched intently with a complacent expression.

Eve put the kettle on herself, made the tea and took it in to Edward, together with a few limp chocolate biscuits.

The game show had finished, and – after consulting a copy of the *Radio Times* – he asked her to switch off the television.

'Boyfriend here?' he enquired.

Eve shook her head curtly. Subject closed. And Edward seemed to accept it, for almost immediately – sounding very casual – he moved on to a rather more interesting one.

'How's your father?'

'Fine,' she replied curtly. 'Your leg's really okay, is it?'

'Getting on, getting on . . . That was a funny old day, wasn't it?'

Eve said nothing.

'Mother's right – it doesn't work treating them like us. Leads to all sorts of complications.'

Eve said nothing.

'How's *your* mother bearing up?'

Eve said: 'I do hope you've had your gun checked, Edward. You wouldn't want it to go off again accidentally, would you? Especially not if someone else was holding it.'

Inside, she was trembling with crossness. Nice man, was he? Serve him right!

After Alice's house, Edgerton seemed colder than ever, as well as lonely, and Eve found herself missing the younger children now they'd gone back to school. She longed for her own term to begin, but had seven more days to sit out.

Though terrible tensions were gathering, it seemed nothing could affect the style and order with which the house was run. As usual, dinner was laid with exquisite arrangements of flowers and candles and linen napkins, as if the most important of guests were about to take their places instead of a reduced and silent family.

As usual, they listened to Mrs Briggs' trolley approaching from a long way off, rumbling along the stone-flagged corridor from the kitchen on its rickety metal wheels, periodically getting snarled up with rugs, clattering with cooling dishes.

As the cook bent over each person in turn, offering over-done vegetables and dried-up game, Eve studied her carefully. Seb had been right: she'd have heard the gossip and would find it hard to hide her contempt.

'Sure that's enough carrots for you, Sir Harry?'

'Plenty, thank you.'

'I've done the bacon nice and crispy just as you prefer it, sir.'

'Nobody does bacon like you, Briggs.'

Beatrice was in a bad mood. She'd been inviting herself to dinner every night since the pheasant shoot, because something was going on. But nobody would enlighten her, and she was becoming crosser and crosser. Her arthritis was playing up, too. She thought, 'I'd like to bang their heads together,' and fretted about Eve, who looked pinched. What was wrong with young men nowadays? They wore the wrong clothes, too: not that anyone had commented on it.

'Hung just right,' said Harry with relish, and raised his glass of claret. He looked more handsome than ever, gleaming with health and bonhomie.

Beatrice and Eve gave him identical looks of scorn, and Eve put down her knife and fork.

'I thought we did well, in the circumstances,' he went on suavely, as if all that had happened on that fateful day was the successful slaughter of a lot of birds in a blizzard. He looked serene and amused. It was almost as if he were deliberately goading the others for his own pleasure.

*

Felicity mused, 'I thought I hated secrets.'

She'd been astonished to discover how easy it was to deceive.

The woman she'd been for most of her adult life sat at the head of her polished exquisitely set table in her freezing dark-green dining room that danced with flickering light, looking pained and eating sparingly. She observed that her eldest daughter's happy glow had fallen away, but appeared only to be offended by her plainness.

The other woman didn't exist here at Edgerton. She bloomed in a cosy thatched cottage a few miles away where she was fed Black Magic chocolates in bed between kisses, made to feel that every crease in her flesh was precious. Johnny never saw her as middle-aged: for him she was for ever Flicky Wapshott, aged seventeen.

'I wonder what will happen?' thought Felicity, and, for the first time since her marriage to Harry, felt that it was she who controlled her destiny. She found she could look at him almost dispassionately now, believed she sensed a growing puzzlement.

For the past week, Harry had indeed been agonizing over a problem. For a change, he was pleased to be interrupted by his mother when she stumped abruptly into his study after dinner.

As usual, he'd made them watch the news in the numbingly cold keeping room – no more natural disasters, thank God, just a royal tour and a rise in the price of petrol – and now he was re-reading another of his favourite books, *A Russian Gentleman* by Sergei Aksakov. It was pleasing to read about a way of life much like his own, while enjoying the advantages of a modern age. He always thought of himself as the luckiest person he knew.

Of all the places in the house he loved, it was here he felt happiest – surrounded by his books and sporting trophies in a room scarcely changed since it had been his father's favourite place too.

'Ah, Mama!' He removed his spectacles. As usual, he rose to his feet when a woman entered a room. 'Glass of Madeira?'

'No no no!'

'Sure?'

Beatrice failed to respond. Eve was very like her, thought Harry with irritation – very. She planted herself in the low lumpy tapestry chair opposite him. From the way she fumbled with a cushion at her back, it was obvious she was uncomfortable. But it wouldn't have occurred to Harry to offer her his own favourite velvet chair. His manners were public school taught. He never thought about what they meant. Anyway, everyone knew that despite her arthritis, his mother was tough as old boots.

'I need your advice, Mama.'

Beatrice stiffened. She'd come in search of her son, determined to do something almost unheard of in their family. Perhaps there there'd be no need, now.

Harry sipped at his drink appreciatively. Moments passed as they listened to the crackle of the fire in the grate, the wind blowing down the narrow chimney. Then he said, 'If Papa had decided to sell a piece of our land . . .'

This was not what Beatrice had been anticipating, but she spat out spiritedly: 'Never!' Next he'd propose selling one of the pictures!

'Pointers' Copse?' Harry suggested lazily, as if she hadn't spoken.

Pointers' Copse was boundary land: a strip of coniferous woodland edging the northern corner of the estate.

'Christmas trees,' said Beatrice dismissively. She added: 'Bartlett'd never want it anyway.'

Bartlett was the farmer whose land lay the other side of the boundary, a dour widower who'd often complained about Harry's dogs trespassing and once threatened to shoot them.

'Cooper's Hill?' Harry continued, seemingly unfazed.

'It's a hill!'

'Parson's Corner, then.'

'We can't sell Parson's Corner!'

Harry made an effort to keep his temper. 'Mama, I've been giving a lot of thought to this.'

'The way you live . . .' said Beatrice, firing a first shot. Once, she'd existed in much the same style, but moving to the dower house far earlier than expected had meant scaling down. Now she had just one live-in servant (who cleaned and tidied round the dogs and cooked for her), and Arthur Stevens' underlings to help sort out her garden. It was a pleasant life and, at the same time, she could complain about all sorts of privations.

For generations, her family had relied on the income from Lloyds, but somebody had to be held responsible for the financial disaster looming over them all. Harry was certainly extravagant.

She said, 'That aeroplane of yours!'

'What?' Harry stared at his mother in amazement. It was true he'd dreamed of soaring over Edgerton, viewing his domain like a bird, and voiced the fantasy more than once. But he'd never even got round to taking flying lessons.

'I don't know what next! I don't!'

Harry said, holding himself under control, 'We're not alone. A lot of people we know are having a bad year, too.' He added, 'Selling off land is one way to raise the money.'

Beatrice scowled.

'Premiums are bound to go up,' Harry went on. 'I can always buy it back later.'

'Your father never had bills like this,' said Beatrice.

'He was lucky.' Harry bared his teeth pleasantly. Underneath he was seething. He supported them all to the hilt, didn't he? It was he who had to take the decisions, in the end. Where was the gratitude, or sympathy?

'We'll have to take out a loan then,' he said briskly.

'We?' asked Beatrice pointedly. It was she, of course, who owned their greatest asset.

'You're going to have to help me on this, Mama,' Harry warned.

'I don't know about *that*!' Beatrice harrumphed.

Harry ignored this. 'It's settled then. I'll talk to the bank.'

They would argue about it later, for hours. But now there was something else Beatrice needed to discuss.

'And another thing . . .' she began.

Harry looked at her over his glass as he sipped his Madeira. What empty eyes he had, she thought. There was never a way of telling what he was really thinking.

Beatrice meant to say it this time — she truly did. However, all that came out (with a burst of saliva) was: 'Man's a fool!'

Harry looked mildly amused.

'Should never have been made to marry him. There's trouble brewing there, you mark my words.'

And with that oblique allusion to another's suspected adultery, Beatrice got up and left the room. In the process, she let out an involuntary loud fart that spoilt her exit and made her even crosser.

Most of all, she was cross with herself. Why did she always end up pretending she was angry with him about something else? It was just like his father all over again. She couldn't be frightened of men, could she? Perish the thought! And she definitely ought to stop eating potatoes.

That night Eve crept into the icy bed Seb and she had shared in the Chinese room across the corridor. He hadn't telephoned; he wouldn't write. They might even meet as strangers when term resumed.

But if she tried very hard, she believed she could conjure up his arms round her as they'd burrowed under the covers, breathing endearments into each other's mouths. How could all of that intensity be over because of one dreadful day?

The last night they spent together in this bed, he'd asked her, 'What's Marcus like?' There was something dead in his voice, as if he already knew the answer.

'Cruel.' She knew it was a mistake, but it was not in her nature to be anything but truthful. 'The worst person Alice could possibly have chosen. And I know he's only going to hurt her all over again.'

Eve remembered miserably how he'd turned away from her at that.

'Gotta get out of here,' she'd heard him mutter. 'Doing my head in.'

And he'd given a deep sigh, as if it was real endurance to have to wait until the morning, when he could leave all this arrogance and rarefied cruelty behind.

Chapter Eleven

Spring came late in 1966 but suddenly. One day the sky turned blue and the air became warm and sticky apple-green leaves began unfurling from black twigs. As always, Edgerton was slow to catch up, its façade glowing with sunlight, its stone interior chill as a prison.

It was the only time Felicity ever felt impatient with the house she loved so greatly. She'd order the servants to fling open the heavy windows, so the sun's rays could finger the rooms, but the house would stubbornly resist. By nightfall, it would be cold as ever.

As Alice approached Edgerton in her silver Mini, her anxious mood was soothed by the sight of it turning from dull gold to bright gold as the sun ducked from behind a mass of cloud. It was so comforting – especially at such a thrilling uneasy moment – to know that this place of extraordinary beauty would always be a constant in her life.

She said to Champion, sitting up in the passenger seat beside her like a person: 'Home.'

The dog looked puzzled but interested.

As always when visitors passed the last great beech tree, the other dogs streamed out of nowhere to surround the car, barking frantically, and Champion remembered exactly where he was and became just as excited.

Alice drew up on the gravel by the porch with its lacy turrets and opened the passenger door so Champion could hop out. The other dogs sniffed round him, pausing without real interest at the gap where his fourth leg should have been. Then they all trotted off purposefully in a pack through the stone arch leading to the back of the house and the big lawn sloping down to the lake.

She sat in her car for a moment, looking up at the window of her old room. Ma had left it just as it was. She imagined its pale-blue walls and white draperies, remembered its faint lavender smell and having her bed to herself for nearly all of her life. She thought of the unmarried girl who'd lived in that room. Now her life seemed to her to be divided into two parts: before Marcus had properly loved her, and afterwards.

She'd deliberately arrived without warning because – right up to the moment of turning into the drive – she'd been thinking, 'I can always go home.' But, as she got out of her car, destiny intervened. Her father emerged from the open front door with a man Alice hadn't seen before: a small suited person carrying a briefcase. Her father looked dapper and trim in a new cardigan and Alice felt suddenly insecure. Why wasn't he in the holey old cashmere thing he'd worn for as long as she could remember?

'Ah, my turtledove!' At least he seemed delighted to see

her. Alice felt very safe in her position as favourite. She'd come to talk to both parents and, though dreading Ma's reaction, knew with certainty she could count on Pa's support.

He said, sounding very aloof, 'I'll be in touch,' before the man disappeared round the back of the house, where tradesmen always parked their cars.

Alice said, 'You're not going out, are you?'

'I was thinking of it,' he admitted with a smile. There was something else different about him. For once, she didn't have his whole attention.

'Where's Ma?'

'Out somewhere.'

'Out?' Alice looked surprised, but her father shrugged lazily.

'She's always going off for lunches.'

'Oh.' Another niggling change. Alice did wonder briefly whom her mother could be lunching with. The other day Eve had pointed out something strange: 'Ma's not good at friendships, is she? She doesn't have a single woman friend.' But then it had occurred to Alice that – apart from Bill Manners – Pa didn't have close male friends, either.

The dogs came trotting back to surround them, but instead of being pleased to see the animal he'd once doted on, Harry looked disgruntled.

'What's he doing here?'

'I thought he might be missing the others.'

'Ugly brute.' He wouldn't look at Champion. He flinched when the dog hopped lopsidedly towards him, wriggling and yelping with ecstasy. He certainly wasn't going to touch him.

Alice opened her mouth to reprimand him, but changed her mind. He might decide to go out, after all.

'Well,' he said cheerfully, 'shall we annoy Briggs by asking her to rustle up some lunch?'

He was meant to be elsewhere. That must be why he looked so abstracted, in spite of his friendliness.

After his initial (presumably apologetic) telephone call, conducted in privacy, there were two incoming ones for him during lunch. Each time, he set off at a run for the great hall (rather than let one of the servants answer), looking a little apprehensive. Alice could hear the faint echo of his voice in the distance as she sat on her own at the table in the dining room, being offered overcooked second helpings by Mrs Briggs.

'A little more onion omelette for you, Miss Alice?'

'I've had loads, thanks,' said Alice, patting her stomach. For some reason, she blushed.

'How's Mr Edward?'

'Um, fine.'

'Sir Harry's lunch will get cold,' warned Mrs Briggs, as if this would be an aberration.

'Here he is.'

Alice could tell Mrs Briggs was cross with him by the way she pressed her lips together and banged out of the dining room.

'One of these days,' he said when she was just within earshot, 'I'm going to find myself a manservant who'll make me paper-thin slices of bread and butter with transparent slices of smoked salmon and wedges of lemon whenever I want.'

'What else, Pa?' asked Alice.

Her father looked delighted. 'He'll be called Rochester and he'll mix me Gibson martinis and smell of eau de cologne.'

'And you'll have your aeroplane by then, of course.'

She was trying to please him, ensure he stayed in a good mood, but the attempt misfired.

He said coldly: 'Not you too.'

Tears pricked at Alice's eyes. She felt so emotional these days. It was foolish to have come. She thought of leaving.

But immediately her father said softly, 'Sorry, turtledove, didn't mean to snap. Lot on my plate just now.' And Alice gave a tremulous smile and thought, 'I *am* the only person he apologizes to – ever.'

'Maybe if you go and smile like that at Briggs, she'll make us some coffee and we can drink it in my study.'

For days, Alice had been thinking exactly how best to explain to the parents. It was Ma's reaction she'd been scared of: perfectionists expected a lot. But, as Alice knew, nothing bored Pa more than people who lived predictably. And he was an old softie where she was concerned. Facing unpalatable facts, it wasn't as if he didn't *know* it was possible to fall for someone else (even though Alice continued to insist to herself that, in his case, it was just a silly crush). It meant he was bound to offer support. It was lucky for her she'd found him alone – destiny, actually.

The trouble was that conversations played out in the privacy of one's mind didn't necessarily follow the same pattern when the real person entered the frame. Also, Alice had somehow forgotten how difficult it had always been to have an intimate discussion with her father. She certainly found it no easier now she was married.

Once Mrs Briggs had shut the door of the study behind her, leaving Nescafé in tiny green gold-rimmed cups, she dived straight in – 'Um, it's about Edward' – and simultaneously remembered beginning another conversation in exactly the same way, not long ago.

'Ah, the cake-wrecker!'

Alice gave a smile like a grimace. Why must he always make jokes? And why did he look so relaxed? He must have guessed there were problems in her marriage. So why couldn't he, for once, make this easier for her?

But he was waiting with his familiar little half smile, and it never even occurred to her that he might be embarrassed and fearful also.

'Um . . .'

He frowned momentarily as he flicked a dog hair off his new cardigan. Alice had never seen him do that before.

'Um, this person I was in love with . . .'

She half expected him – as so often before – to pull her up on her woolly grammar while engaging in elaborate play-acting. 'What? This person here? I don't see him.' But he said nothing.

'The thing is, Pa, I've met him again and I still feel the same and he does too and it's no good with Edward and I should never have done it and I'm sorry but – I *can't* go on with it!' It all came out in a tearful rush, not a bit as she'd planned. But at least she'd said most of it – if not the important part. She couldn't help bursting out like a child: 'It's not my fault!' And then, of course, she started crying properly – unattractive rasping sobs as if all the misery and ecstasy and secrecy of the last few months were finally taking their toll.

'Turtledove . . .' he began with an element of helplessness in his voice, and at that moment Alice knew it wasn't going to be anything like as easy as she'd anticipated. She remembered, too late, that tears distressed him. She also realized to her consternation that he must already know about Marcus.

But what he said next really shocked her. 'Marriage isn't about sex or love.'

Alice stared at him, appalled.

'It's a common misconception,' he went on with a smile. (How dare Pa be amused while saying something so dreadfully cold and cynical?) He ruminated for a moment. 'What marriage is really about is safeguarding property and continuing bloodlines.'

'But—!'

'The trouble comes when people forget it.' He smiled. 'Novels have a lot to answer for.'

'But you don't believe that, Pa!'

'What?'

'You believe in love,' said Alice. It was the most daring and personal thing she'd ever said to him – also the greatest of compliments.

Harry smiled again. 'I think Ma and I both recognize that the most important things to us are all of you and, of course, this place.'

'But it's not enough,' said Alice. 'Is it?' Once more she had the feeling of going to the edge.

'No,' he said, momentarily serious.

'You see?' said Alice triumphantly.

Harry paused. It was as if he were weighing up the desire to help his beloved daughter against the wisdom, or otherwise, of going further. He seemed to make a decision.

'It's separate,' he said. 'Love, or whatever you want to call it. It's perfectly possible to keep it separate.'

'What?'

'As long as you're discreet.'

Alice thought of her father's vulnerable doting expression, like a wound, when he'd looked at the girl at the pheasant shoot; the hateful way her husband and in-laws had referred to it afterwards. She also thought of all the years he'd spent with Ma.

'But, Pa, I thought . . .'

'What?' he asked. There was something very warning in his tone.

Alice continued in a tearful rush: 'If you really really love someone, you want to be with them all the time. Don't you?'

'That's as maybe,' he said, with the same 'keep off' quality in his voice.

'But, Pa, I can't *be* like that!'

Harry said nothing.

'And Edward,' Alice went on. She shuddered. 'I just can't!' She thought of Marcus's beautiful muscular body and the pleasure it gave her; and, very briefly, of Edward's fumbling inadequacy. How could the same act be sublime with one person, so completely repulsive with another?

'So what do you want to do?' asked Harry. He sounded very cold, though still amused. 'You've only been married for – what? – eight months. Do you really want to leave your marriage without a penny to your name for some wastrel who brought you nothing but grief? I assume he's no real money. What would you live on?'

Alice looked at him with her beautiful blue eyes.

'I'd give it five minutes.'

Alice went on staring at him imploringly.

'It's no use looking at me like that, turtledove. I've no spare money at all. I'm being pressed to pay an enormous bill. I'm having to make all sorts of adjustments.'

Alice didn't believe him. Eve had told her about Pa's rantings every time an envelope from Lloyds arrived, but she'd not taken it seriously because she wasn't interested. She didn't understand about money (let alone the concept of unlimited liability). She was too used to wealth. She thought of her wedding day – her beautiful expensive dress and the glorious flowers and the vanloads of delicious food and wine and the music and the extra servants who'd been hired – and of passing through it like a ghost. What lunacy it had been to marry Edward. She hadn't enjoyed one single second of happiness with him. Even their former friendship had vanished.

She said, 'You don't understand – I *have* to leave.'

Her father got up from his comfortable armchair and stabbed at the fire with a poker. It was as if he wanted to punish someone, or make them see sense.

He said, with his back to her: 'Mossbury Park is not – nothing. Of course, it's not a patch on this place but it's not unimpressive. They've almost as much land, and Farquhar's been . . . good with his money.' He dug at the coals. 'He's not going to live for ever. Always huffing and puffing. Got a heart condition unless I'm very much mistaken. Looks a hell of a lot older than fifty or whatever he claims.' He paused before adding, with meaning: 'I'm not saying you have to give up everything.' Another pause. 'Might be an idea to start breeding soon – get it over with, give yourself something to do.' And then in his wheedling honey way, 'I'm only thinking of you, turtledove.'

Alice had never been so shocked in her entire life. She thought of how Pa had always scoffed at stuffy convention, his passion for art and beauty, his never-failing courtesy, the tears when he listened to music, the soppy tremble in his voice when he called her by her special name. That person had vanished, leaving a calculating money-grubbing cynic who only looked and talked like him.

One more matter needed to be discussed – probably right now – but Alice believed she already knew her father's response. She felt a terrible new weariness. She understood that now she was finally in charge of her own destiny; and knew with absolute certainty that, whatever arguments Pa put forward, she was not going to stay with her husband.

As Alice drove away from the house with Champion swaying in the seat beside her, uttering contented wuffs as if still with the other dogs, she met her mother in her grey Morris Minor.

There was no way of avoiding a meeting.

Alice scrubbed at the traces of mascara she was certain were staining her cheeks. There was no time to powder her face or comb her hair or put on lipstick. She knew she looked dreadful, so they'd be off to a bad start.

Ma brought her car to a halt too, switched off the engine and climbed out. She was wearing something Alice had never seen before, a lovely soft blue jumper that enhanced her dark hair and pale skin. For the first time in her life, Alice perceived her mother as an attractive woman. Ma looked rosy-cheeked and relaxed, and she'd done something new to her hair that made it curl becomingly round her face.

'Darling!' said Ma.

Alice allowed herself to be kissed, expecting the usual minute smiling inspection, the standard deference to beauty. But this time Ma just said, 'You weren't looking for me, I hope.' She didn't appear to have noticed her daughter's disarray. It seemed as if all her attention were elsewhere.

Alice said: 'I just had lunch with Pa.'

'He told me he was going out!'

'Well . . .' There was no point in telling Ma what had been said: she'd learn Pa's version soon enough.

'Briggs won't have been pleased.' For a moment, Ma looked quite worried. Then she asked, 'Is everything all right?' But it sounded perfunctory. She seemed more interested in Champion. 'There's a good boy! How's your poor old leg? Did you see your friends, then? Dear old chap!'

Alice said: 'Well, I'd better be getting back.' She felt affronted and cross. She found herself longing for her mother to pick up on her distress and provide what Pa had failed to. She seemed so much more approachable: the kind of person one might be able to talk to, after all.

But Ma just said, 'All right, darling. Another time. Let me know when you're coming, though, and I'll make sure I'm in.'

And then she was gone, chugging up the drive in her car with an abstracted expression. 'She'll be planning the flowers or something,' thought Alice bitterly.

A memory returned: going to look for Ma in the drawing room after telling Pa about Edward's proposal. She'd sat down on the sofa beside her, tearful and unconvinced and ready to be swayed. But then Ma got that familiar preoccupied critical look. She'd risen from her seat to adjust one of the honey silk curtains, tweaking with firm careful precision at its folds so they fell in a perfect long line to the floor.

By the time she'd turned round, ready to give her daughter her whole attention, the room was empty.

Chapter Twelve

'You're so different now,' Johnny had told Felicity.

'Am I?' She'd sat at his kitchen table in her new jumper, enjoying being spoilt.

'You look about seventeen.' He was always saying it. He'd placed a plate of lamb stewed with apricots in front of her. He served himself too, took off a frilly pink apron that must have belonged to his wife, kissed her on the top of her newly waved head, and sat down opposite. 'I cut this out of *The Times*. If it's filthy, say the word, and I'll open a tin – or we could always drive in to our restaurant.'

As he tasted it himself, he looked first apprehensive then proud. Not bad! First a lover, now a cook!

Then Felicity broke an unspoken rule by saying thoughtfully: 'He never notices anything. I don't think it would even occur to him,' and some of the vitality and confidence drained from Johnny's beaming face. When they were together like this, he somehow managed to convince himself it was her only world.

She'd smiled at him happily, not seeing or understanding. She was unused to adoration. There'd been too many years of carefully preserved distance, with always the impenetrable base.

As she turned into the drive, she remembered, without remorse, that she hadn't done the flowers, and dreamily pictured vases of stagnant water ringed with fallen petals on gleaming surfaces all over the house.

How comforting and sweet the day had been.

But after the lovemaking (which got better) and the tea (always too strong) he'd said worriedly – as if recalling a written memorandum – 'How do you see us?'

She'd shrugged, smiling, and waited, stroking his big hand with its clean pruned nails.

'I'm falling a bit in love with you.' He'd stared at her as he said it, willing her to respond in kind, even though – in a vain attempt to protect himself – he'd quantified the terrifying declaration.

'But I can't,' thought Felicity, changing into second gear to cope with the abominable ruts, 'because it would mean agreeing to so much else. And I'm not ready for that yet. And perhaps I never will be.'

It was at this point that, to her surprise, she saw Alice driving towards her from the opposite direction.

And then she remembered that Mr Symonds from the bank had been expected that morning. And now it was almost four o'clock, and she'd been gone since eleven, and Harry was sure to have forgotten about the appointment also.

She felt panic rising. She must get back, as quickly as

possible. But first she was obliged to greet her daughter.

'Darling!'

Alice looked terrible – hair all over the place and no make-up (so important, thought Felicity, to keep on making an effort once you were married). But at the same time she seemed defiant.

'I just had lunch with Pa,' she told her and, wrapped in guilt, Felicity heard condemnation.

'He told me he was going out!'

To cover her confusion, Felicity concentrated on poor old Champion, cast out of Edgerton so Harry needn't be reminded of the cruelty he'd inflicted (whilst passing it off as kindness, of course). As she petted the dog, who was pathetically affectionate in return, she thought: 'Those two are so close. Should I ask? No, better not!'

'Well,' said Alice, sounding tart and dismissive to her mother's ears, 'I'd better be getting back.'

And Felicity looked at her daughter's puffy unmade-up face and thought of Harry waiting inside the house, and more coldness to come, and only wanted to be back with Johnny.

She thought, 'Why couldn't I have told him what he wanted to hear? What meanness of spirit stopped me?'

Harry was waiting for her in the great hall.

'You've just missed Alice.' He sounded very accusing.

'No. I saw her.'

'Ah.'

They circled round each other.

Felicity thought, 'This time, he's going to ask me where I've been, and I can't tell lies. I just can't.'

She made an effort. It came very naturally to be cool and remote now she was back at Edgerton. 'Tea?'

They were so used to restraint as a framework for their marriage that she was shocked when he responded with a drawn and unsmiling face, 'You and I are going to have to have a very serious talk, Felicity.'

The clocktower bonged the quarter hour outside and the doves fluttered up and down and Felicity thought in similar heart-stopping panic, 'Somebody must have seen us together. Somebody must have told him. How ridiculous I am – at my age! What on earth was I thinking of?'

Then Harry said, watching her closely for a reaction, 'I saw him.'

Felicity just managed to say faintly: 'Oh?'

'Nearly went for my gun, I can tell you.'

She didn't dare look at him. Oddly, nothing about this scene struck her as unfair.

'Told me we're going to have to pull in our horns. Bloody nerve of the man!'

'I see!' She felt her whole body relaxing with the relief.

Calmly and competently, Felicity picked up the reins of the house once more, and the memory of her sweet afternoon was put away. 'Let's ask Briggs if there's any fruitcake,' she suggested, 'and then you can tell me all about the meeting with Mr Symonds.'

It wasn't until much later that she asked: 'How did you think Alice was?'

Harry pulled at his jaw. It was almost as if he (of all people) was trying to hasten the natural process of decay.

They were sitting in the drawing room. They never sat in

Harry's study when it was just the two of them, as if an unspoken understanding existed that the room was too personal. A log fire crackled in the enormous fireplace but Felicity had a woollen shawl round her shoulders to counteract the chill. As usual, when they were alone after dinner, she was engaged in mending, using the assortment of reels of cotton and silk and buttons in her blue enamelled sewing box, patterned with pink roses. Tonight, she felt as if she were cobbling up the fabric of her life, restoring it to its former neat shape.

'She didn't look too good to me,' she went on, biting a piece of thread off a button she'd been sewing on one of his shirts. She tweaked at the material around the button to straighten it, picked up another shirt. She'd taught Alice and Eve to sew when they were quite young, just as she'd been shown by her own mother, but hadn't yet got round to Kathy, who was quite uninterested.

Harry said: 'When I think what I spent on her wedding . . .'

'But how were we to know?' Felicity was thinking about the style Lloyds had kept them in for years and years.

'It was very foolish of her to have become involved with that good-for-nothing again,' said Harry. 'It's going to do her no good. None at all.'

Felicity sat quite still, arrested in the act of threading a needle. So there it was. She asked, 'When?'

'Does it matter?' He sounded very weary.

'What did you say to her?'

'I told her that she couldn't abandon her marriage after only eight months.'

'Of course not!' Felicity thought of her daughter's

dazzling beauty, the ambitions she'd had for her. But, like a
hurricane, Marcus had come out of nowhere to jeopardize
her chances and break her heart.

At least half a dozen (mostly eligible) young men had
been eager to console Alice, but Edward was chosen.
Felicity remembered the thoughtful bouquets during that
wretched time of lost appetite and red eyes. 'You're worth
so much,' read the card on one, and she could still hear
Alice's heartfelt, '*Sweet!*'

He must have offered something exceptional then: an
understanding of the pain of rejection which transcended
his conventional upbringing. It had forced Felicity and
Harry into a new appreciation. 'Thank God someone's
putting a smile back on her face,' Harry had said.

For all that, they'd never considered Edward as a suitor
(which was odd considering that every young single man
who came to the house was seen as husband material). But
then, neither had Alice.

'They were always such friends,' said Felicity.

'Indeed . . . Don't let's forget, it was *her* idea to marry
him.'

'We didn't push her into it,' Felicity agreed, honestly
believing it.

But neither of them could sleep that night. The wind
prowled round the eaves and the conversation continued,
off and on, with qualifications added and increasing
sympathy for Alice.

'If it really can't work . . .' Felicity began, staring upwards.
In the darkness she envisaged the belly of the canopy over

their bed: the same tucked embroidered lid that had enclosed generations of married Chandlers, keeping them neatly together.

'I hate to think of her unhappy,' Harry agreed, his voice much softer now.

'Oh yes!'

'But I think she should at least give it another year.'

'She's only eighteen,' Felicity pointed out.

'Plenty of time,' said Harry.

'Mmm.'

'She might even have had a child by then.'

A silence while they both considered this possibility.

'But she can't carry on with . . .' Felicity was unable to finish. 'Not if . . .'

'No.'

He tried to make love to her then. But, to his great astonishment and also hurt, Felicity turned away.

He hid it, of course. As always, he kept his real feelings wrapped tightly round his heart for insulation.

Chapter Thirteen

'I BEG YOU TO COME HOME NOW' the telegram read.

Eve tried to contact Alice, but it was always Edward who answered. In the end, she put aside her essay on Wordsworth and the sublime, climbed into her battered little car and drove to Edgerton.

This time, the roads were dry and firm and the hedgerows and trees alive with leaf. She and Seb were happily back together, as if Christmas had never happened. They'd not discussed her family. It had been easy to forget about them once term began. For all sorts of reasons, she didn't tell him about Alice's distress call. She said she'd forgotten she was expected home for the weekend.

She thought she could guess what had happened. Edward had finally confronted Alice, and she was refusing to give up Marcus. Either that or Alice had decided to leave the marriage but hadn't informed the parents yet. 'Beg' was worrying. There was no argument with 'Now!'

*

'How lovely to see you, darling,' beamed Ma, but she was distracted.

Suddenly Edgerton was alight with sun and – instantly responsive, dressed in her old gardening clothes – Ma was supervising the adornment of the eight enormous stone urns along the terrace. Beside her was a trug piled with moss to be bedded around the pale-green shoots of tulips, eager suddenly to throw up splashes of pink and scarlet and purple, which would be protected with sacking if frost threatened. The camellias were being wheeled into place, too: dark shiny-leaved bushes in enormous tubs, buds like frogs eyes with sleepy slits of creamy pink and pure deep red. Stevens was helping with this important seasonal ritual, and Eve heard him suggest in a hoarse conspiratorial whisper, 'Spot of tender begonia'd make a nice contrast by the paving, Your Ladyship.'

'It might,' Ma agreed, narrowing her eyes as she envisaged a splash of vivid yellow tucked into a background of dull gold. As they bedded in the plants, their hands accidentally touched: his big leathery ones ingrained with dirt; hers soft and white, smeared with precious soil.

Pa wasn't in, which came as no surprise.

It was easy for Eve to slip off to see Alice almost as soon as she arrived. There was no need to invent an excuse.

The meeting place they'd decided on was the Swinging Stone, which was about a mile from the house.

It had always been a favourite place for Chandler children: an enormous boulder set into the side of a hill, which rocked when jumped on. The legend was that if you made a wish while it was in motion, it always came true.

As she crossed the last field, enjoying the sun and a light breeze ruffling the grass, Eve saw Alice in the distance, seated on the stone with a blob of ginger and black beside her. She'd be wishing for happiness, of course. What else? But as she came closer, she saw that Alice's face was pale and puffy with crying.

'What is it?'

Eve put her arms round her sister. Unusually, she could feel the bones in Alice's shoulders. Her blond hair — normally so pale and shiny — was lank and smelt of lard. She was wearing a jersey and a dirty old pair of jeans. She looked as if she hadn't eaten or even bathed properly for days.

'Thank goodness you're here!' She started sobbing, and Champion looked baffled and uneasy.

'Course I am.'

Eve wasn't a natural comforter, but she did her best. Because she didn't know what to say, she held Alice until she calmed down a little, beating her heartily on the back.

'You've got to help me!'

'I've come, haven't I?'

'You're the only one who can!'

'You'd better tell me!'

More desperate sobbing, then: 'He's gone!'

Eve wondered how she could ever have believed in Marcus. She'd met him only once — in the coffee bar in Nether Taunton — and found herself immune to his obvious good looks. He hadn't liked her much either. He hated successful families like theirs. He'd probably encouraged Alice to tell Edward about him and, once maximum damage had been inflicted, taken real pleasure in leaving her to her fate.

She said cautiously, 'I never thought he was right for you.'

'I loved him.' Alice clenched her wet ball of a handkerchief.

'You'll get over it.'

'You don't understand!'

'I think I do,' said Eve slowly, remembering her own despair after Christmas.

Alice sighed very deeply. Then she looked carefully at her sister as if assessing her maturity. 'I'm pregnant.'

Eve stared at Alice, too shocked for words.

'I was so pleased at first . . .' more noisy crying, and Eve took her hand and held it tightly. As she did so, her fingers touched Alice's wedding ring: a glittering twist of gold and platinum. 'He'd gone on and on about how he wanted us to be together and, I mean, I'd made up my mind to leave Edward even though Pa was so awful and said I couldn't. When I told Marcus about the baby, I thought he'd be so pleased too. Our love child!'

'I think I might be pregnant.'

She'd rehearsed the scene a dozen times on her dog: walking the woods and fields, supplying Marcus's responses.

'Just taking Champion for a walk!' she'd shouted at Edward as usual as she slammed the front door, thinking defiantly, 'Maybe, this time, we'll never come back . . .'

But as soon as the confession had faltered out – quite differently from the confident way she'd imagined it – they were in another play. But, then, Marcus had always confounded her. It was part of his attraction.

Why couldn't he love her as other men did? She knew

that the tenderness was there: she felt it in his rough and skilful hands, the touch that made horses whicker.

He understood how to handle women all right, but he'd never trust them. The most she got was hints that, if she played her cards right, she might eventually be permitted the key to comprehension. 'It gets heavy in here,' he'd once confided in an intimate moment, indicating his head with its helmet of wavy black hair. 'Can you cope with it, Alice?' But his inner self stayed maddeningly out of bounds behind the fence of refined cruelty: and innocent much-adored Alice was incapable of seeing that some forms of damage could never be reversed.

'What?' exclaimed Marcus. But he didn't seem particularly surprised.

'October,' said Alice happily, just as in her imaginings – for she was pretty certain he'd just smiled. The reality of her situation was beginning to hit home. A baby had started growing inside her; day by day, it would become bigger. She rushed on. 'Do I *seem* different? I definitely *feel* different!'

'It'll look just like me,' said Marcus. This time, the smile was radiant, unmistakeable: a slow flaunting of even white teeth. But the expression in his black eyes didn't match at all.

'Lovely!' squeaked Alice, and held on to Champion for comfort. She was becoming very frightened.

'For who?'

If Pa was there, Alice couldn't help thinking in her panic, he'd have corrected Marcus: 'For whom?' Why was she thinking of Pa now? She swallowed. 'For me,' she ventured. 'You too, of course . . .'

'You can leave *me* out for a start!' said Marcus, still smiling.

'What are you saying?'

'*Think*, Alice!'

'It was an accident, Eve!'

Eve trembled with sympathy. Every single time she and Seb managed to make love, they courted similar disaster. 'I *hate* these fucking French letters!' he'd complain as they lay in his single bed in the afternoon, after she'd dared to let him smuggle her into St John's; or, lately, with the advent of warmer weather, in the long grass of a secret bank of the Cherwell. 'I can't feel you, Evie. I promise I'll take it out in time. Please!' And each time she'd anger him by refusing. She'd decided to combine this unscheduled visit home with an appointment to see the family GP – Dr Parsons, who adored Pa and had never married and was fiercely emotional. The pill was so new that Eve had insufficient faith in it. She'd expect a lecture, and plead for discretion while being fitted with a Dutch cap.

Alice said piteously, 'He promised he'd be careful.'

'What are you going to do?'

Alice plainly hadn't summoned her sister for advice, because she said immediately: 'I can't have it.'

Even as children they'd known exactly what to wish for, and never deviated thereafter. Alice's ambition seemed far more accessible than Eve's – after all, how many girls like them managed to get to Oxford? Whereas a handsome prince (heir to a house like Edgerton), a menagerie of animals . . . Easy! Not forgetting the children, of course. Harry, Charles, Susannah and Elizabeth.

Eve said slowly, 'Well, you could.'

'D'you think I don't want to?'

'Well, why don't you, then? You'd love a baby.'

Alice looked at her sister with her big blue eyes. They had acquired a terrible new sadness. 'Because there's no way Edward would believe me.' Then she actually smiled and, for a moment, looked just like Pa. 'Unless he believes in immaculate conception!'

Eve suspected it was Marcus's joke: could almost hear his chippy fake rough accent.

Then Alice confessed, 'I haven't slept with him since the honeymoon.' She looked astonished as well as guilty, as if she still couldn't believe that the girl everyone thought of as gentle and malleable could have so wilfully disobeyed her marriage vows. 'I just . . . couldn't.' She shivered. 'And when it started again with Marcus—' She shut her eyes as if trying to forget.

'Poor Edward,' said Eve.

But Alice said with unusual sharpness, 'Not poor anything.'

'If you left him now—' Eve began.

Alice said immediately, 'The parents'd never forgive me!'

'You can't stay,' said Eve.

'No,' Alice agreed. 'But I can't leave *and* have the baby.'

Eve was silent. Alice was right, of course. Girls like them didn't have babies on their own.

'You've got to help me!'

Eve stared at her.

'I don't know where to go.' She started sobbing again. 'I don't even know what it costs, but I thought if I sold my wedding pearls . . .'

'How long?' asked Eve.

'Four weeks.'

Afterwards it occurred to Eve that they'd not used the word once.

That evening at Edgerton, there was a dinner party.

Eve thought of all the dinner parties that had punctuated her growing up. They had about as much to do with real life as the Charades the family indulged in at Christmas: everybody in benign mood, dressed up in fancy clothes, never talking about the matters which really concerned them.

Sometimes she believed her father was happiest being a host. He always had an incandescent slightly surprised look as he sat at the head of his long table in his dark-green dining room, offering his guests a taste of his charmed life.

Even Mrs Briggs would change gear and produce one of her more elaborate party menus: slabs of overdone beef jacketed in trademark burnt pastry, trifle with an encircling palisade of soggy sponge fingers swamped in over-sweet raspberry jam and vivid yellow custard, enlivened with a slug of sherry and smothered in whipped cream with glacé cherries as the final touch.

Eve watched her father as he talked to the woman on his right. Like all women who found themselves in his vicinity, she became both vivacious and compliant, and Eve noticed that her husband was watching expressionlessly from the far end of the table. The woman on Pa's other side – another old family friend – was behaving in exactly the same way, whilst he more or less equally divided his lazy amused attention between them.

His financial problems appeared to have changed

nothing, which was all the more reason why nobody else in the family took them seriously. Tonight there was champagne, as usual, and the finest of wines and, for the first time in her life, Eve wondered what it all cost. If her father were to forego just one dinner like this, there'd be no need for Alice to sell her pearls.

But then, of course, the parents would have to know.

She wondered how they'd react to the news that, by the following Christmas, they could be grandparents. Pa popping open more champagne? Pulling down his face as he deplored this further proof that he was growing old? The two of them relieved but thoughtful as they toasted the young couple?

All of her life, Eve had viewed her father through the distorting lens of the un-favourite. She'd wonder how it must feel to be Alice, and sometimes marvel that they remained such friends. But even Alice believed there'd be no welcome if she abandoned her rich husband and crept home pregnant by a lover who'd deserted her.

It was Ma who cared what people thought, surely? Pa was different. He mocked the stuffiness of his neighbours. To care too much about money was 'mere', he'd say. He didn't believe in birth control for his animals. Wasn't it possible that he'd welcome the bastard child of his favourite daughter?

Eve heard someone ask, 'And how is Alice?'

And watched her father's easy false response: 'Settling in, settling in.'

After dinner she slipped away to telephone her sister. As usual, she could hear canned laughter in the background, a tinny echo of the polite merriment coming from behind the closed doors of the drawing room.

'You can't talk?'

'No.'

'You're still certain?'

'Oh yes!'

'I've got some news.'

'Edward's watching his programme,' said Alice for his benefit, making it sound as if he were engaged in an enterprise requiring concentrated brainpower. 'Hang on a sec . . . I'll take this somewhere else.'

Eve waited for Alice to pick up the telephone in her hall, then heard the tap of high heels on parquet as she returned to her drawing room to make quite sure the extension was put down there. The canned laughter was cut off.

'I phoned Primrose Farringdon,' Eve told her.

'You didn't!' Primrose Farringdon was the daughter of a local earl, notorious for her penchant for lorry drivers.

'I thought if *anyone* knew . . .'

'What did you say?'

'That I had a friend.'

'What?'

'She thinks it's me!'

Alice actually giggled on the other end.

'Anyway, I've got you a name.'

'Fabulous!' Alice whispered.

'He's up in London, of course. Wimpole Street. Primrose says you need letters from two doctors. She says her man can arrange all that. But you'll have to go and see him first.'

'That's easy,' said Alice. 'Liberty's sent the wrong samples for the curtains in the second guest room.'

'And when it actually happens,' said Eve, 'you're going to have to stay the night somewhere.'

'I'll think of something . . . even though you know who watches me *all* the time. Nightmare! Primrose has got a mews house in South Ken, hasn't she, lucky thing?'

'No, Alice,' said Eve sharply.

'Maybe not.' She sounded very languid.

'Well, I'll give you his name and phone number, shall I?'

'Oh Eve!' pleaded Alice. 'You couldn't ring him for me, could you?'

Silence.

'Please please please! It's *so* impossible from here. You do see, don't you? Honestly, I'll be in your everlasting debt!'

As Eve shivered in the great hall at Edgerton the door of the drawing room opened and Ma came out, wearing a chiffon blouse under a shawl, and a long tweed skirt.

'Eve?'

'Got to go,' said Eve.

'Eve? You promise?'

'Who on earth are you talking to, darling?'

'You promise, Eve? You promise!'

Chapter Fourteen

Day by day, Oxford was changing Eve. To have achieved a place at this centre of excellence had to be a compliment, didn't it? Would it really be so arrogant to start believing she deserved it? Foolhardy to hope that this golden time was only the beginning?

After all, she was merely echoing the reaction of other undergraduates. She saw it every day in their shining eyes: the wonder and then the pride in being a part of this ancient, enclosed and magical place. 'And I'm in love,' thought Eve. And, to put the icing on her very special cake, summer would soon be unfurling its gaudy banner.

That day, she remembered – too late – what was happening to Alice. The abortion was scheduled for half past ten. At a quarter to eleven, halfway through a lecture, Eve looked at her watch and felt guilty for having forgotten and, after that, relieved. Whatever Alice had endured (a syringe, Primrose had said ominously), it was over now. The mistake was cancelled.

At half past four, Eve was sitting in the college garden, wearing a thick sweater, eating toast and strawberry jam and drinking Earl Grey and talking about George Eliot. One of the many things she relished about her new life was that all conversations were fascinating, and each new friend seemingly a kindred spirit. They knew they were special, too. 'Crème de la crème?' joked Lorna, as she offered the milk jug.

When she saw her neighbour, Miranda, waving at her, Eve returned the greeting, meaning: 'Come and join us.'

But Miranda was on a mission. 'Your sister's been looking for you. I've just shown her to your room.'

'My sister?'

'She doesn't look very like you, does she?' said Miranda.

And Lorna, with whom she'd been having such an enjoyable discussion, said, 'You've never mentioned a sister!'

She found Alice sitting on her bed, flicking through a book on the Brontës. She put it down immediately. She was dressed as if for a smart lunch, in her pink going-away suit and stiletto heels. But her hair was escaping from her French pleat in wisps, and she was very pale. 'I'm sorry,' she said immediately. But there was a new defiance in her attitude, no real contrition.

'What are you *doing* here?' Eve could hardly get the words out. Alice should be staying with a relative in London. It had all been arranged.

'Don't be angry with me!' Alice's blue imploring gaze was starting to moisten at the edges.

'I'm not!' The truth was, she was thoroughly taken aback. Alice didn't belong in Oxford, or this pleasingly tidy room; and nor did the rest of the family.

'You *have* had it?' (Afterwards, Eve remembered that she'd wished most fervently for Alice to respond 'I couldn't!' But perhaps that was all part of the crazy dreaming: the 'what ifs' and 'if onlys' that would replay themselves for years and years; the cursing of all those failures to speak when – out of inherent stubbornness? – she'd remained silent.)

'Oh yes!' said Alice. She rushed on: 'It was a nightmare, Eve! And I so need to talk! And you're the *only* person! It was ghastly! He had rubber gloves! I think he got a kick out of it! Honestly! I was going to stay with Deirdre Whitby Chandler in her ghastly house in Streatham, but I couldn't face it. Imagine having to talk to dreary Deirdre, pretending nothing had happened! Well, *you* couldn't have, could you? I only just had enough money for the ticket. I couldn't *face* being with anyone else!'

'Poor you!' whispered Eve.

'*And* he had bad breath,' Alice observed as she eased off her shoes.

'You can't stay here!'

'Why not?' demanded Alice pathetically.

'Because it's not allowed.' A hotel room would have to be found and somehow paid for. If they went out now, there was a good chance of arranging it.

'It's not as if I'm a man!' protested Alice. And Eve calmed down a little and remembered that the scout would not be coming in until at least ten o'clock the following morning. Sensing it, Alice started to become her old self.

'Is this it?' she asked wonderingly as she absorbed the small room with its single bed, the linoleum with a striped rug set dead centre, the desk overflowing with books in one corner, the black anglepoise lamp, the wooden chair with Eve's familiar jacket hanging over the back of it. There was an armchair with wooden arms positioned in front of the gas fire, more books on shelves.

'Everyone's is the same,' said Eve, remembering her own first reaction. 'But look here – just look!'

However, though Alice made a pretence of interest in the timeless view of the quadrangle with its scurrying undergraduates, it was obvious her mind was elsewhere.

'She's pretty!' she said wonderingly of Miranda, who had titian hair in ringlets and an hourglass figure, and was reading philosophy, politics and economics. Then: 'Where's Seb? Do you see him every day?'

'He's got to work, too,' said Eve. 'It *is* why we're here.' She looked at her pile of books and felt a little comforted. 'Have you had tea?'

Alice shook her head violently. 'It was a hundred quid!' She sounded outraged.

'Is that all you got?'

'Ninety-five,' admitted Alice. 'I made it up from the housekeeping. They weren't really me, were they?'

Eve thought of Alice on the morning of her wedding, bowing her head as if for an executioner so her father could loop his gift of milky lustrous pearls round her neck and ceremoniously fasten the diamond clasp. The necklace had come from Garrards, where he had an account, and must have cost many hundreds of pounds. 'What's Pa going to say?'

Alice shrugged. The impression conveyed was that she couldn't care less.

'Well, why don't you . . .?' Eve gestured towards her

narrow bed, indicating that Alice could lie down for a while if she wanted to. After that, they'd review the situation.

'I'm fine,' said Alice.

'It must have been horrible,' said Eve, aching for Alice, but flinching away from the pain.

'I'm fine,' Alice repeated.

But, once Eve had lit the gas fire, she lay back with her head on the pillow. And soon after that her eyes closed. Her colour had not returned. She'd got up at six to catch the seven o'clock train from Bellingham, she'd told Eve. Everyone, including Edward, was under the impression she was on a shopping trip.

As usual, Eve had an essay to write. ('Had I met these lines running wild in the deserts of Arabia, I should have instantly screamed "Wordsworth"' – Coleridge to Wordsworth, 10th December 1798). But, instead, like making an apology, she found herself curling up at Alice's feet. Then she took off her spectacles and tucked them under the bed. Just before her eyes closed, she thought of how many times they'd lain like this at Edgerton, she listening to Alice's adventures.

The drawing room was strangely warm, even though Pa was poking violently at the logs in the fireplace. Big red sparks flew up as he hit them. She'd never seen him so angry.

Then Eve awoke, and realized that she was in her little room in St Anne's and morning light was pouring through the un-curtained windows and somebody was knocking on her door.

Instantly, she remembered about Alice. But Alice was gone.

The door opened and Miranda put her head round it.
'What is it?'

Miranda was in study mode. Her red hair was screwed up
in a bun with a pencil stuck at a right angle into it. Her legs,
in black stockings, looked very thin.

'What?'

'Psycho!' There was an edge of hysteria to her voice.

'What?'

'Psycho!'

Without asking more questions, Eve followed Miranda in
the direction of the bathroom. Afterwards, she thought that
she had always known the drama would involve Alice.

Miranda was babbling now. 'See?' she said, and Eve saw
that she had blood on one hand: glistening red blobs on the
fingers as if she'd touched a sticky mass in disbelief.

She was rubbing her hands on her skirt now, a little
strip of beige that was beginning to look like a butcher's
apron. She looked terrified by her intimate connection
with whatever dreadful drama had occurred. Soon she'd
start washing her hands over and over again, and the
sound of running water would, always, for Eve, be
associated with horror and finality.

The bathrooms at Edgerton were bleak, too – but Ma
had made something special and stylish out of each one. So,
even as you convulsively shivered while immersing your
naked body in hot water that almost immediately cooled,
you could admire the lovely colours she'd made the walls,
her comforting dried flower arrangements reminiscent of
summer, the perfectly matched curtains framing frosty
views.

But here there was no style at all. Green walls. Tiled

surfaces. Like a hospital, Eve had thought, with strange prescience. And, even though they were regularly serviced, the baths and basins were always a little grimy, the lavatories stained.

'See?' Miranda was wild-eyed and terrified.

She repeated, 'Psycho!' The shocking impact of Hitchcock's film had yet to fade. If a maniac with a stabbing knife could burst into a shower room, what was to stop him (or her) from doing so in an even more private place?

Blood, rich and stately as a funeral procession, was seeping slowly from under one of the lavatory doors. Even as they watched, it started collecting in a puddle on the grubby white tiles.

Miranda pushed at the door again. 'It's locked!' she shrieked. 'Why's it locked?'

It was Eve who fetched a chair so she herself could look over the top of the cubicle partition. Watching, white and terrified, from a distance, Miranda applauded her courage. But she didn't know that Eve had already guessed what she would see.

Alice was slumped against a wall, blond head on her knees, knickers twined round her ankles, pink skirt bunched about her thighs, the pretty pink wool all dark and sodden.

'Who is it?' Miranda whispered.

'It's my sister,' Eve whispered back.

'The one I talked to yesterday?'

Eve nodded miserably.

'What's happened to her?'

Silence.

'She's not been——?' Staring at Eve, trying to read her expression, Miranda copied her, shaking her head. Eve's pretty sister had not been murdered, after all. She swallowed. 'What's happened to her then?'

Miranda and Eve were friends. They'd liked each other immediately on discovering they were neighbours on the staircase. Eve had told Miranda about her feelings for Seb. Miranda had confessed her own interest in a PPE undergraduate called Piers. 'But he's not my priority for the time being.' She'd confided, with a flicker of self-congratulation, 'I'm expected to get a first.'

Now Eve entrusted her with another secret. 'My sister's had an abortion.'

'An abortion?' Miranda reacted as if Eve had confessed to a crime. 'An abortion!' The word didn't belong in this perfect world. She'd heard about abortions, of course. But they happened to friends of friends.

'We've got to get help!'

Miranda's eyes widened with alarm. Eve was her friend, but now she was seeking to make an accomplice of her. The fear of exposure was already starting to wreathe up like smoke rings.

'If I stay here with her, can you call the nurse?'

Miranda didn't react. She was staring down at a fresh trickle of blood escaping from the cubicle.

'Miranda?'

Miranda nodded without saying a word, and backed away.

Alone with her sister, Eve called down to her, 'Alice! Alice!' and, to her enormous relief, Alice moaned and shifted slightly and, for some reason, said, 'There's no paper.'

'Alice, open the door!'

But Alice seemed not to hear and, soon after that, the nurse arrived.

Miranda was gone for good by then. All she wanted was to escape from the blood and fear, dive back into the safe dry world of Descartes. (And who could blame her?)

'What's all this?' Nurse O'Brien, fortyish, unmarried, prepared to be briskly friendly – for the only minimal information she'd been given by Miranda was, 'There's been an accident!' Eve had visited her once, suffering from flu, and been prescribed aspirin and plenty of hot drinks. Nurse O'Brien had asked what she was studying, and volunteered the information that she'd not been to university herself.

'D'you know who's in there?'

'My sister,' Eve admitted miserably.

'Your sister.' Something in her tone told Eve she was already sniffing scandal, and there could only be hostility (or perhaps that was in retrospect, too).

There followed the commotion of fetching the porter, who brought up a stepladder so he could climb over the cubicle partition; the shocking scene once the door was unlocked; the immediate decision to transport Alice to the nearby Radcliffe Infirmary.

'What's her name?' one of the ambulance men asked. Then: 'Alice? Alice? Can you hear me, Alice?'

Alice's blank eyes opened momentarily, like those of a white china doll whose mechanism was running down.

'Be brave, Alice – going to shift you on to a stretcher now . . . there we go . . .'

Sick with terror for her sister, Eve was sidelined because – by then – the word had been uttered once more. (Why had she damned herself by spelling it out? Eve wondered bleakly, long afterwards. She could so easily have professed ignorance.)

Perhaps it was because of the way Nurse O'Brien had questioned her. 'What's she done to herself?' she'd demanded, already suspicious. (After all, she could see, with her professional eye, the source of the blood.) Coupled with Eve's misplaced guilt, and natural truthfulness, and longing to save Alice, it had been the undoing of her.

Dictionary definition: miscarriage; wilful causing of miscarriage; arrest of development; failure of a project to develop; dwarf or misshapen person.

It was illegal, too. According to Nurse O'Brien, it was murder. Not the removal of a few unformed cells with no real semblance of humanity but the wicked execution of a beautiful little baby. She even said it then and there, in that bloody bathroom.

She *would* be a committed Catholic as well as an hysteric and a vengeful bitch. She even wore a gold crucifix under her white blouse.

It had all come of daring to hope.

The summons came as Harry was sitting alone at breakfast. Unusually, Felicity was away because Hugo was in a different kind of trouble. Harry had seen her off the evening before, driving herself to Windsor in a controlled panic. Nobody else could go, of course. If Hugo had got himself into a mess then he would need understanding (which he was unlikely to receive from his father).

Harry was feeling a little hard done by as he ate a couple of solid fried eggs and four strips of half-burnt bacon in the dining room. Lacking conversation, he'd already done the crossword. He kept on his loathed spectacles to re-read *Anna Karenina*. At nine he heard the bell in the tower bong out the passing hours and – as the last chime shrank back into the stone, having alerted the house clocks – the querulous shrilling of the telephone started up in the distance.

Sitting in the cold dining room over his book, thinking, 'She's tiresome, tiresome, for all her charm,' Harry heard Mrs Briggs' faint voice. 'Her Ladyship's not here, Mr Edward ... Would you like to speak to Sir Harry?' And thought, 'Damn, what does *he* want?'

'You'd better wait in your room.'

'Is she going to be all right?'

But, despite Eve looking so ashen and wretched, nobody would answer her (though some were quite kindly then).

She'd asked one of the ambulance men: 'Is she going to be all right?'

Alone in her room – where she could no longer feel herself flowering, becoming someone else – she could only go over and over his silent reaction, like a person seeking to interpret a painting glimpsed just once. Pity. Because Alice was dying and it must have been obvious to those professionals even then.

But, despite the anguish and terror, she was not allowed to be with anybody, though life went on outside her room. She could hear footsteps, even laughter once.

They'd have phoned the parents by now, and already Eve was terrified of Pa's reaction. He'd keep the grief inside, of course – Pa never revealed vulnerability – but she was in no doubt about where he'd direct the anger.

The interviews would come later. However, with some strange self-destructive instinct (some deep acknowledgement of her own worthlessness?), she'd already admitted to Nurse O'Brien that it was she who'd, in effect, procured the abortion for her sister.

Edward was an invalid himself; he was in no condition for a long car journey. And besides, there'd been too many shocks to absorb.

After those appalling words had been sobbed out over the telephone – 'It's Alice! She's dying!' – Harry had jumped straight into his Daimler, still wearing his backless leather slippers. It was he who should have been alerted first, of course. Edward was an irrelevance and always had been.

He arrived at the Radcliffe at eleven o'clock. (It usually took three and a half hours by car.) He was lucky not to have been killed himself.

All his smooth certainty had vanished. His world was a different place. There could be no more pretence, certainly no escape. Alice was dead. That must be what the doctor even now approaching was about to tell him.

'Mr Farquhar?'

Harry was obliged to put him right – though he could only manage to whisper that he was not the Hon. Edward Farquhar, husband to Alice.

Then he stared at the young dark-haired doctor, eyes dull with pain, face stiff as wood, a speck of egg yolk still clinging to his chin.

'Your daughter's lucky.'

'What?'

'We've managed to stem the bleeding. We've given her two transfusions. She's still very weak, of course . . .'

'She's going to be all right?'

The doctor nodded cautiously, was about to elaborate in the same careful vein, when the girl's father sank on to a chair and started crying convulsively.

'Thank God, thank God!'

The doctor had seen distress before – it was the natural accompaniment of his job – but, even so, was shocked by the nature of this harsh noisy anguish, each racking sob like a terrible admission.

Finally, he put a hand on Harry's shoulder. But by that time Harry had recovered himself. He shrugged, and the doctor took away his hand. He blew his nose very thoroughly with an enormous, beautifully pressed, very white handkerchief. He smoothed his hair. He appeared to notice, for the first time, that he was wearing slippers, and even smiled faintly.

'Can I see her?' he asked coldly.

The girl was limp and pale as a white rag, pierced with a tangle of tubing. A layman might have believed she was dead. But her chest rose and fell very faintly. She'd survive, even if checks must continue to be made every quarter of an hour.

The doctor watched a little curiously through a glass window in the door as the girl's father approached the bed looking tender and troubled and quite unlike the angry though rigidly courteous man who'd been obliged to answer a few questions (whilst managing to ask some himself).

Of course he'd not known his daughter was pregnant. Of course he'd no idea what she'd planned – and neither had her husband. He could say that categorically.

And then he'd told the doctor, with cold distaste, that he

was appalled that his eldest daughter had colluded in – no, he corrected himself, *instigated* – a scheme that had so nearly cost his younger daughter her life.

Inside the room, just the two of them, Harry said softly: 'Turtledove?'

But Alice's eyes stayed tightly closed.

'Turtledove, how could you *do* such a thing to me?'

No change.

'Why didn't you tell me?'

Still no response.

'You know I'd die rather than let my precious turtledove suffer.' His voice shook, and a tear rolled down his cheek. 'I'd give my life for my turtledove without even thinking about it, and that's the truth.'

Alice was deeply unconscious. He was certain of it.

So why did he feel as if every trembling heartfelt word had been coldly measured and discounted?

Chapter Fifteen

As they approached Edgerton, Hugo grew increasingly agitated; but his mother, usually so sensitive to his moods, failed to respond. Mostly, the journey had passed in silence. Her lips twitched as if she was holding a long imaginary conversation with someone; she often sighed, and once actually shook her head and pressed her lips together as if even unspoken diatribes must be censored.

As they bumped slowly along the familiar rutted drive with its central green toothbrush, he picked his nose.

'Don't do that, darling,' his mother said immediately.

Hugo jiggled his leg manically, and his mother laid a soothing hand on his knee.

'I'm starving,' he moaned.

'We're home now.'

As usual, the dogs came racing up to surround them, barking madly, and Hugo's spirits lifted. He exclaimed: 'Bingo's pregnant!'

'What?'

'Look, Ma!'

It was true: Bingo's midriff had thickened like a bulb.

He was surprised by her violent reaction.

'I don't believe it! Really, this is *too* much!'

Hugo knew how fed up his mother got with the dogs – it was becoming impossible to find homes for mongrel pups and, every year, their own pack grew – but, as far as he was concerned, it was something to look forward to.

She'd been fine to begin with, even after the dreaded talk with his housemaster. She wasn't going to tell him she approved of his behaviour, of course, but gave him the usual silent reassurance that she'd continue to love him, no matter what.

He was suspended until further investigation. Even so, he'd been promised chocolate cake at his favourite treats place, the Cockpit, before a leisurely drive home.

But at breakfast, Ma had been called away to the telephone. Then she'd said they must leave for Edgerton straight away. Anxious and guilty as he was, he had the annoying feeling of being upstaged.

But when they finally returned home, Pa wasn't even there to go into one of his terrifying furies, working himself up like a turkey cock, bellowing stuff about standards and shame and failure and having to show an example because they were different.

'Didn't I tell you?' said Ma (who hadn't).

Hugo relaxed slightly even though he knew very well that his ordeal was merely postponed.

As it turned out, once Ma had settled him inside she was off again. She told Mrs Briggs not to prepare lunch or dinner for her or Pa, and she'd phone the next day. Then she kissed him and told him he was to be good (with one of her meaningful looks) and said they'd be home soon. And after that she climbed into her car and chugged back down the drive.

Hugo went in search of Mrs Briggs.

Beyond the swinging green baize door lay another world, where there were delicious smells and warm yeasty treats to eat rather than the tepid soggy ones that turned up in the dining room. Shallow stone steps led down to Mrs Briggs' big kitchen with its tangle of black pipes and tall built-in cupboards stuffed higgledy-piggledy with sugar and flour and bicarbonate of soda and gravy mixtures and custard, and its enormous cooking range that threw out a constant blistering warmth that was so enticing in winter, suffocating and smelly in summer. It had a tiny room leading off it that, all of his childhood, he'd been forbidden to enter. He couldn't see what the problem was. In the course of various clandestine visits, he'd established that it had a table covered in flaking gold oilcloth, an uncomfortable armchair and an old wireless, and smelt very strongly of Mrs Briggs. He assumed this was the place she relaxed, but couldn't imagine such a thing. She must be at least fifty. For an ancient person, she was always on the go. Pa had observed during the Christmas holidays that she was a passionate woman – and she could certainly get jolly cross without actually saying anything.

At least someone at home was waiting for him, seemingly full of pleasure. 'There you are, Master Hugo!'

'Can I have some breakfast please, Briggs?'

'Of course, Master Hugo! Now what would you fancy?'

'Can I please have fried bread and sausages and bacon and tomatoes and mushrooms and three eggs, not runny?'

She wasn't listening. 'Where's Her Ladyship, Master Hugo?'

But now it was Hugo who wasn't paying attention. 'Are these rock cakes?' He picked up a crisp inflated bun studded with burnt currants from a wire tray where a dozen lay cooling.

Mrs Briggs said, questing for information, 'Sir Harry was called away early this morning . . .'

Hugo shrugged.

He crammed a rock cake into his mouth and Mrs Briggs warned, 'You'll spoil your appetite.'

'Starving!'

Beaming, Mrs Briggs took down her heavy black frying pan from the greasy hook where it dangled over her range. There was nothing she liked more, she told Hugo, than cooking for people who enjoyed their food.

'Having a little holiday from school, are we, Master Hugo?'

'Something like that,' said Hugo, with all the smooth superiority of his father.

She punished him by threatening exile to the freezing and lonely dining room. 'I know Her Ladyship'd prefer it.'

He pouted. 'Why can't I eat in here?'

'How's your schoolwork coming along?' she asked casually as she flipped his eggs over in sizzling dark-brown fat.

'Okay.'

'Oh yes?' She cut a thick slice off a spongy white loaf and settled it in the pan. Magically, the fat drained away and the bread turned deep brown.

Hugo conceded. 'It was just a football game.' He added, 'It wasn't my fault some blithering idiot got in the way.'

'Well, just this once,' said Mrs Briggs, setting his heaped plate on her scrubbed table.

Then she sat down with him and drank a cup of tea and, in the course of it, managed to extract the whole story of Hugo's alleged savaging of a fellow pupil.

That still left the mystery of where Sir Harry and Her Ladyship had gone. She'd a feeling that one would be a lot harder to get to the bottom of.

After he'd had his breakfast, Hugo wandered out on to the terrace, burping enjoyably every so often, the pack of dogs shadowing him like adoring fans. He thought of how everyone back at school would be sitting at their desks doing Latin.

It was surprisingly warm, and peaceful, with the sleepy background buzz of insects revving up for spring. A window swung open above and one of the housemaids flung a rug out on to the sill so it could air in the sun: giggly Penny, of the moon face and tree-trunk legs.

Hugo waved very casually, and she waved energetically back, smiling. He was glad of the distance. It meant that, for the time being, he wouldn't have to deal with more questions.

He'd go down to the lake first, he decided. He'd see if there were any moorhen or coot chicks then have a leisurely swing on the rope.

Until his parents returned, the whole of this magical kingdom was his – just as he'd always known it would be one day. He found it strange when people asked what he wanted to be when he was a grown-up – as if, like other boys, he must ponder the respective merits of the law or politics or the city. It was here that he belonged, just as his father had. He couldn't imagine a better life – though he'd definitely install a heated outdoor swimming pool.

But as he approached the lake, he saw that somebody was using the rope. The top of it, where it looped over the pine tree, was swaying violently to and fro. The dogs were looking at him questioningly. He knew they were preparing for the signal to act savage. He'd trained them thoroughly – 'Postman!' was all he had to say, in a fierce whisper.

'Bloody cheek,' he thought. He hastened his step. 'Don't you know this is private property?' He was already forming the words when he realized that the trespasser was the blonde bird he and Carson minor had seen at the pheasant shoot. The rope had slowed down now and she was swinging dreamily to and fro over the water, her head flung back, her long hair streaming out beneath her. She was wearing blue jeans and a tight white T-shirt and thick pale-pink lipstick. The detail struck him – together with her very grown-up bosom – because it looked out of place on someone only slightly older than himself. She had black lines drawn round her eyes, too. But the heavy make-up merely accentuated her beauty. Hugo thought he'd never in his life seen anyone so pretty.

Then she noticed him, and left it too late to regain the bank. Hugo felt very superior. She'd no choice now but to drop into the water, and it would put her at a disadvantage.

Quite unfazed, she said in a soft little voice with a local twang, 'Hugo, isn't it?' and Hugo felt affronted. This was the daughter of a servant. How dared she address him like that?

But, instead of reproving her, he found himself mumbling assent.

'Why aren't you at school?' she asked with a smile.

Hugo gave one of his sulky shrugs.

'Give us a hand, then,' she said and, without even thinking about it, Hugo waded into the water in his woollen school trousers and socks and heavy shoes, took her little soft hand and pulled her back on the rope to the bank.

He muttered: 'Don't be scared of them, they're not really fierce.'

She didn't seem to have heard. 'Soppy things, aren't you?' To his astonishment, the dogs clustered round the girl and responded to her petting as if they'd known her all their lives.

He said eagerly, 'This one's pregnant.'

'Bingo,' she confirmed. 'Well, it's only natural.' There was something very comfortable about her acceptance of the fact.

'My mother's furious!' said Hugo.

'Yeah?' She gave him a swift amused glance followed by a smile so radiant that he found himself forced to look away.

To cover his confusion, he seized the rope and clumsily launched himself from the bank. He felt extraordinarily excited and happy. As usual, whenever he swung over the lake he thought about letting go at the highest point of his trajectory and flying through the air to land on the tiny island. How wonderful it would be if today he could bring off this spectacular feat. But, as always, the opportunity was gone even as he contemplated it and, in plenty of time, he regained the bank, still smiling like an idiot.

He stole a look at the girl to see if she'd noticed the expert way he'd executed the manoeuvre.

It was like pilfering sweets. At school, he was accustomed to skins that shone with grease and erupted in blackheads or disgusting white-headed pimples, bruised by squeezing. But this girl's skin was matt and creamy, without a single flaw. Similarly, each hair on her head gleamed with health, and there seemed to be about four different colours in it, ranging from dark gold to nearly white. But her most disturbing feature was her almond-shaped blue eyes – not on account of their great beauty but because of the mockery he perceived in them.

He surprised himself by offering her the rope, but she said: 'No, ta, I've had enough now.'

'Sure?' he asked, and to his horror his voice did one of its surprise turns, emerging as a mangled squeak.

'It's boring.' She dusted off her little hands and examined her nails, which were painted pale pink to match her lips but bitten, and Hugo suddenly became conscious of his soaking trousers and shoes filled with water and thought he'd never enjoy swinging on the rope again.

'Where's your dad, then?' she asked casually.

It was the first time Hugo had heard anyone from the estate call his father anything but 'Sir Harry'. But such was the girl's effect on him that he merely stammered: 'I don't know.'

She was still looking at him in the same bright inquisitive way, as if she expected him to carry on, so after a moment he added: 'They've both gone off somewhere, as a matter of fact.' He found himself eager to oblige, rather than irritated, and wished he'd been more curious.

Then she said something that astounded him. 'Your dad's going to take me up in his aeroplane.' For the first time she sounded as innocent and trusting as a child. 'I've never been in a aeroplane before.'

Two days later the dogs streamed off up the drive to welcome his mother and father as they returned home in their separate cars.

Trying not to show his nervousness, Hugo waited outside the front door. At least there'd been time for Pa to cool down a bit. 'It wasn't my fault,' he thought, feeling aggrieved. In a minute he'd say it.

Then, to his astonishment, he saw that each of his parents had an unexpected passenger: Eve sitting up straight in the passenger seat of Ma's Morris Minor, Alice reclining like an invalid in the back of Pa's Daimler.

By this time, Mrs Briggs had joined him. It appeared that she'd been forewarned about his sisters coming home.

'Here's Miss Eve,' she said, glancing at him enquiringly. 'And Miss Alice.'

His mother drew up first, and both she and Eve got out of the car. 'There you are, darling,' she said to Hugo. Then, in a businesslike way, 'Ah, Briggs . . . We'll be ready for lunch in ten minutes. Miss Alice will have hers in her room.'

Mrs Briggs hovered, trying to look solicitous rather than curious as they watched Pa lift Alice carefully out of the Daimler. Obviously there'd been some sort of an accident. But that left the mystery as to why she'd been brought here and Edward was nowhere to be seen. Even Hugo, who wasn't observant, noticed Alice was very pale. However, she managed to give him a weak smile like a grimace: a sort of

'What on earth are you doing here too?' look before shutting her eyes in exhaustion.

'Hugo,' said Pa, in acknowledgement, but there was none of the dreaded sternness. He seemed anxious and preoccupied.

Hugo hunched his shoulders and wriggled, as if trying to render himself even more unnoticeable, and Ma said, 'Let's all get inside.'

Nobody ever told him anything.

The phone rang at one point and Mrs Briggs came into the dining room and said apologetically, as if she'd been pressured to interrupt lunch, 'Lady Farquhar's on the telephone, Sir Harry,' and his father put down his knife and fork with a clatter and looked at his mother with a helpless expression Hugo hadn't seen before, and it was she who went to take the call.

As usual, from the distance of the great hall they could hear the flavour of the conversation though not the gist, as they went through the motions of eating. There were long silences while Ma was obviously talked at, but she got in a bit of firm murmuring, too. She came back looking tight-lipped. 'They're coming for tea.'

Pa said nothing, but she must have felt some criticism because she said shortly: 'Insisted. Can't be avoided.'

For some strange reason, both parents were treating Eve with cool disfavour. They didn't seem to like looking at her, and neither did they want to speak to her. At least somebody else was in trouble. But he couldn't help feeling sorry for his sister because she appeared on the point of tears.

As soon as lunch was over, she muttered, 'I'll just go and see if Alice needs anything.'

To Hugo's puzzlement, his father snapped, 'I should have thought you'd done enough,' and, at that, Eve burst out sobbing as she rushed from the room.

Hugo took the very sensible decision to absent himself. He wandered off in the direction of the garden, looking vague but purposeful. He was hoping to bump into the girl again.

Lady Farquhar turned up with Edward at teatime – she looking fierce in a pudding basin hat, he wobbling along on a pair of crutches. (Hugo made a mental note to ask if he could have a go on them himself.) To Hugo's surprise, they'd brought Champion. Alice wasn't there to greet her dog, of course: by then, she was ensconced in her old room above the porch. So, once released, Champion hopped off happily, surrounded by friends.

It was Ma who came out to greet the Farquhars before leading them into the drawing room and shutting all the doors so the servants couldn't eavesdrop.

For Hugo, throwing a ball for the dogs outside, listening incuriously to the occasional rise of Lady Farquhar's voice through the closed French windows – disjointed words like 'disgrace' and 'annulment' – the drama scarcely impinged. But then, most of his life passed in a dream of marking time. Nothing was ever explained to him, therefore why should he bother to be interested? So what if days sometimes passed without Ma and Pa speaking to each other? They went on living at Edgerton, being his parents, didn't they? Nothing changed.

He'd got on okay with his father until quite recently. Now, it seemed, he couldn't do anything right.

He'd known, even as he'd kicked another pupil viciously on the shin as they tackled the same ball, that it would lead to more confrontation with Pa, and terror turned to an odd disappointment when Pa seemed too distracted to remember to be angry. But Alice had always come first. Even though he enjoyed being his mother's favourite, Hugo knew he'd swap places with Alice in a trice. It was a perpetual source of grief that, unlike other fathers, Pa didn't want to do things with him. But instead of trying to please him (as Alice had always done) he found himself behaving in an ever more surly fashion, as if testing to its absolute limit what should be his by right.

At least the dogs noticed him. It was wonderful to have all eleven of them, including Champion, waiting on his slightest move. He pretended to hurl the ball towards the lake and, galvanized by enthusiasm, ten of them dashed off – only to halt, looking idiotic and worried. Hugo did it again and again, and they reacted in exactly the same way. Only Champion continued to stare steadily at Hugo, waiting for him to throw the ball for real. Son of Freckle (part King Charles spaniel, part pointer, with a sprinkling of terrier), he'd been sired by a visiting German Shepherd. He was the most intelligent dog they'd ever owned, and he'd been Hugo's favourite too. But now Hugo thought like his father. He even said it out loud, with only a twinge of shame: 'What's the good of an animal with only three legs?'

Chapter Sixteen

It had been Edward's idea to bring Champion, though he'd come to detest Alice's dog – even more so after being cooped up alone with him for days.

'Swear you'll look after him properly?' she'd extracted from him before departing on her shopping trip. She'd reeked of savage misery, but Edward had refrained from comment. For all she knew, he'd noticed nothing.

She'd left a whole range of home-cooked delicacies in the fridge – minced steak, poached haddock, even a couple of freshly roasted pheasant legs. There was also a selection of TV dinners she'd found in the big new food store which had opened near the garage at Chorley Cross. 'I knew you'd adore them!' she told Edward. 'Look, it's easy peasy. All you have to do is heat them up, then you eat them off a tray. Look, there are dear little packets of sauce too!' Then, as an afterthought: 'You won't forget to warm up *his* meals, will you?'

To add insult to injury, Champion wasn't even grateful

when Edward dutifully set down his food before attending to his own needs. No, he cast a disinterested eye at his tin bowl and went on moping in his basket.

'*Be* like that!' Edward told him crossly. 'Won't get round *me* with your sulks!'

On his second bleak evening, he found himself eating Champion's haddock (which was delicious with a bit of salt and pepper), almost managing to convince himself Alice had taken the trouble for him. (In a spirit of fairness, he did put part of a roast beef TV dinner into Champion's bowl, but he wasn't interested in that either.)

'Swear you'll take him for a walk every day. He adores his walks . . .' It had been hell struggling to manage, what with his crutches. But even when he'd clipped the lead on, the bloody dog had refused to budge! He'd sat on his backside and dug his three legs into the ground. And when, as a last resort, Edward had hissed 'Fox!', the dog had cast him a pitying glance oddly reminiscent of his father-in-law.

'You're ungrateful,' Edward informed him sternly. 'As well as lazy.'

He hadn't been able to concentrate on the television (even though it was *Wagon Train*), because of course he knew she hadn't really gone off shopping – just as he'd realized, in his heart, exactly when the thing with Marcus started all over again. Alice so radiant, skin like porcelain, and humming with secrets . . . Only a fool wouldn't have guessed! But then, he'd always understood he was less than Alice, and lucky to have won her.

Only, Lady Farquhar – being his mother – saw it the other way round.

*

'Nothing but a common whore!' she'd spat on learning about the botched abortion. She pronounced it like 'hoover' without the 'v'. She never used words like that usually. It demonstrated the measure of her outrage.

But the shocking telephone call from the Radcliffe had only shown Edward how very much he still loved Alice. The thought of her lonely courage, her shining vitality draining away in a pool of blood, made him quite faint with horror. Of course, he hadn't been able to manage the journey to Oxford, but it wasn't through lack of feeling. He'd never felt more confused in his short life. His mother kept telling him he must hate Alice. If only he could.

It had been his mother's idea to have a showdown with the Chandlers, and, in anticipation, all her thinly concealed dislike and contempt came spilling out. Harry was an arrogant spendthrift, *and* more, declared Lady Farquhar. 'If you ask me . . .' She didn't finish the sentence because it wasn't done to talk about sex with one's child (just as it was *infra dig.* to discuss politics or religion at mealtimes). No wonder his daughter was a hoo-er. As for Felicity, the woman was obsessed with *that* house – which was pretty, yes (Lady Farquhar sounded very condescending) but a folly when set against the substance of Mossbury Park (no fussy late additions there!). Obsessed to the detriment of everything else, Lady Farquhar added darkly.

'What are you *doing* with that thing?' she'd demanded when she arrived to collect him, only to find Champion waiting patiently, too.

'He's coming with us, Mother.'

'I won't have that dorg messing up the Bentley,' said Lady

Farquhar, even though her hunting spaniels accompanied her everywhere and the car smelt atrocious. But her son's obvious distress must have touched a deep part of her, because she opened a back door for Champion with only her usual grumble: 'If you ask me, that dorg should've bin put down.'

But as soon as they arrived at Edgerton, Champion seized the opportunity to gallop lopsidedly off with the rest of the dogs. ('Oh, do shut up!' bellowed Lady Farquhar). In a trice, he'd disappeared with the over-excited rabble. ('Not a decent dorg amongst the lot of them!')

It was Felicity – alerted as usual by the barking – who came out to greet them, looking tense but elegant. But, then, Edward's mother-in-law believed in standards. She and Lady Farquhar never kissed. 'Pearl,' said Felicity, as if briefly picking up a strange ornament, and Lady Farquhar in her old tweeds, keeping her hat on, gruffly responded: 'Felicity.'

'Edward,' said Felicity. She didn't kiss him either. But she smiled at him: one of her painful little half-smiles. What was she really thinking? Edward had no idea. But, then, he'd always found the Chandlers baffling: utterly charming one minute, subtly unkind the next.

Harry was waiting in the big drawing room, but he was strangely quiet, to Edward's relief. He looked very pale, and Edward noticed that – while tea had been laid out on the big circular silver tray on its collapsible four-legged stool – there was a half-empty glass of whisky at his elbow.

Lady Farquhar started to say her piece, and soon afterwards Harry excused himself. He'd an important appointment, he informed them with his usual courtesy, and Lady Farquhar rolled her eyes under her pudding basin hat.

It didn't stop her, though. Far from it!

Edward couldn't bear to hear his mother saying those dreadful things about Alice at the top of her voice, telling him what he should say and do. In the end, something snapped, a rebellious part of himself he hadn't known existed. He found himself staggering to his feet, saying in a voice which trembled: 'We'll ask *her* then, shall we?'

Next minute, he was grappling with the catch on the French windows and manoeuvring himself out on to the terrace and down the shallow stone steps to the lawn where Hugo was playing with the dogs. He aimed a crutch at the loop of Champion's lead, still trailing from his collar, and skewered it. Then he slotted it over one wrist, wobbled painfully back into the house and set off up the long flight of stairs.

Champion dragged, of course. But then Edward hissed, 'Alice!' and the dog immediately became compliant.

'Where is she?'

Champion stared at him, alert and longing, glancing this way and that, puzzled and anxious.

'Alice!' Edward managed to entice him upstairs and along the whole length of the first big landing. Each time the dog pulled back, suspicious all over again, rucking up the rugs, Edward repeated her name. Then, of course, the dog started catching her scent. By the time they'd reached the little winding staircase leading to her room, he was pulling madly – yapping like a desperate lover, thought Edward with grim humour.

He let go of Champion and was just in time to see him

land on her white bed in a flurry of ecstasy, and Alice's reaction as he covered her with wet kisses.

'Oh, my darling! I've missed you so so much!'

Then Edward saw Alice shoot him a strange look: as if astonished that at such a time, he, of all people, had thought to give her this marvellous present.

She said, a little shyly: 'Hello.'

'Alice.' Then, less formally, almost concerned and friendly, Edward asked, 'How are you feeling?'

'Okay.' She repeated, with a bit more firmness in her voice: 'Okay.' Then: 'How are you?'

'These things are pretty tricky,' he said, nodding at his crutches. 'But I'm getting the hang of them now.'

'Well done,' breathed Alice. But Champion's attentions were becoming a little too ardent. She whacked him gently on the nose. 'Stop it, you silly old sausage! Hey, I'm a human!'

'The thing is . . .'

'Mmm?' Alice lifted her bedcovers for Champion, who'd been waiting impatiently for the invitation.

Edward relinquished his sticks and sat down heavily on her bed.

'I don't want a divorce.'

'Oh, Edward!'

'I don't.' Edward went on, as if still defending himself: 'I don't care what anyone says.'

'What about—?' She couldn't finish the question, just looked at him wonderingly with her blue eyes.

'It's over now, isn't it?'

Silence.

'It is, isn't it, Alice?'

'Yes.' Her voice faltered with the pain of admitting it.

'Well?'

She said slowly, disbelievingly, 'So you'd . . .?'

'Yes.' He sounded very proud of himself.

'Honestly?' She sounded almost dispassionate, as if viewing their dreadful situation from a great distance.

'It's my life.'

Silence.

'That's what I just said downstairs,' he went on, and she noticed that his apathy seemed to have melted away. He looked as young and eager as on the day she'd accepted his marriage proposal.

He leant towards her and she allowed him to take her hand.

'Listen,' he said, 'I know you don't get on with Mother. I know you don't like the house. We could get away from everything, if you like. We could even move to London for a bit if . . .'

'I love the country,' she protested weakly.

'Well, we could move away from Mossbury. Start again properly. You'd like that, wouldn't you?'

'What would they say?' she asked and even managed a shaky smile.

He shrugged with bravado.

A tear rolled down Alice's cheek.

'And I'll never talk about it again,' he said. 'I promise.'

She shook her head, and more tears fell.

'It must have been awful.'

She nodded, unable to speak.

'Listen,' he said (as if she could do otherwise), 'I know I've not been very nice lately, but it was only because I felt so . . .'

'I know,' she said.

'It'll all be different. I promise.'

'It's so kind of you,' she said.

'*Kind?*'

'Yes.' She sounded as if only now did she understand the rarity and value of kindness. But it wasn't enough. In spite of everything she'd been through, Alice found kindness wanting.

'I love you!' he protested, as if kindness had nothing to do with it.

'I know,' she said. 'I'm so sorry, Edward.'

'What are you saying?'

'I can't come back.'

Neither of them spoke for several minutes. Then Edward asked, 'What are you going to do?' His voice was already changing. He'd been rejected twice now, he'd lost all his pride, and misery was starting the slow shift into anger.

(Deep in Alice's bed, dreaming of racing after rabbits on all four legs, Champion felt the movement of her body as she shrugged helplessly.)

Then she said, 'It's all my fault, Edward. I should never ever have married you.'

Chapter Seventeen

It was Beatrice's Emma who revealed to her that three of her grandchildren had unexpectedly arrived at the big house. She measured out the information in seemingly haphazard portions, like Mrs Briggs making one of her cakes.

'Cook says Miss Alice looks white as a sheet.'

She had her back to her employer as she arranged a neat pyramid of paper and wood in the open fireplace for the solitary evening that lay ahead. Minutes ticked past while she balanced logs, and Beatrice's spaniels, slumped on the sofas and chairs, watched through half-closed eyes like bored aristocrats.

'Cook says it's a wonder she's not in the hospital – though Her Other Ladyship keeps saying it's only the flu.'

Beatrice thought her heart would jump from her body with fright. But today's *Times* – open at the crossword page, where she'd paused on nine across ('Suspend break for a substitute' – seven letters) – didn't even rustle on her lap.

She felt her ears prickle with the tension of trying not to miss a word.

'Well! I daresay there's times you only want your mum, aren't there?'

'Mum' indeed! Beatrice stared with hatred at the soles of Emma's feet, stuffed into tartan felt slippers, the thin hair falling over the back of her collar with a spatter of dandruff. She knew perfectly well what Emma meant. 'Times' were the province of young women. Beatrice was straight away convinced that her granddaughter had suffered a miscarriage. Patently, she thought, all the servants knew it too.

She felt angry and uncomfortable. There were no woolly areas, for her, in the relationship between master and servant. But, just for now, she was forced to tolerate the familiarity so as to gather as much as possible.

'As I said to Cook, however much you love your husband there's times you're better off without!' Emma, who'd never been married, cackled with mirth.

'Miss Alice loves Edgerton,' said Beatrice, sounding totally expressionless, and, as revenge for her disappointing lack of reaction, Emma chose to drop another ingredient into the conversation, like a spoonful of flour to confuse the mixing.

'I said to Cook, I daresay Miss Eve's come back from her university to keep her sister company.'

'I expect so,' Beatrice managed with admirable restraint.

'Those two are that close.'

'They are,' Beatrice agreed through stiff lips. It was infuriating to have to sit there quietly boiling, but it was second nature, of course, to hide real feelings.

Then came the final dollop of meddling: 'And if Master Hugo's got himself into a pickle . . . Well! As I said to Cook, it's only high spirits, isn't it?'

Fortunately, Emma, who was not clever, observed merely that her employer assumed a maddening attitude of hauteur (and reminded her to clean up a mess one of the dogs had made). She wasn't the lady of the manor any more, Emma thought dismissively once she'd regained her own quarters. Hadn't been for years now, so there was no call to act all hoity-toity. Gratitude would be more in order, if you thought about it.

Beatrice waited impatiently for the usual morning telephone call from Felicity, but it never came. Neither did her son make contact. So she decided to find out what was going on for herself. The walk would do her hips good, and give her the advantage of surprise. She'd drop in for tea, and stay for supper. After all, she had the right.

It was a beautiful afternoon, and clumps of purple and white crocuses spiked the long grass in the orchard that made the dower house feel so separate and secluded even though it was less than five hundred yards from the big house. As she passed by the lake with its aggressive coots and meek scuttling moorhens she noticed that the moles had returned. There were half a dozen finely sieved piles of black earth heaping the lawn. Harry would be furious. It meant more arsenic and cursing. Beatrice wondered why Stevens hadn't dealt with it.

The pack of dogs trotted into view and Beatrice greeted each one formally while her chosen companion for the trip – Charlie, as usual – pressed jealously close. She noticed that Bingo was pregnant again, and sighed with exasperation. In her day, there'd been no unwanted pups. It was kinder to drown them at birth. But, aged six or thereabouts, Harry had stumbled on an under-gardener carrying out orders. She could still remember the screams. Then there were refusals to eat, bed-wetting – his nanny reported it all. You never knew such a sensitive child! But, unusually, Harry had kept his angry childhood promises. 'When this is *my* house,' he'd shouted in his squeaky little voice, 'I'll do what I like.'

As usual, when Hugo was home he was never far from the dogs, and vice versa. In a moment, he sauntered into view, eating an apple, his heavy fringe flopping over his forehead.

'What's this?' said Beatrice.

'Hullo, Gran.'

'Not at school?'

He looked furtive.

'I'll ask your Pa,' she threatened.

'It's only a suspension,' he admitted sulkily.

'Only!'

'A fracas on the football field,' he said in a silly fluting voice.

What a handsome boy he was. Spoilt, though – and there was nobody but his mother to blame. 'I won't hold with favouritism,' thought Beatrice, who'd managed to give birth to just one child.

'Where *is* Pa?'

Hugo shrugged and looked mutinously into the distance, and Beatrice's mouth tightened. Even at a time like this! No wonder Hugo was playing up, poor lamb.

'And Ma?'

'In the drawing room.'

'Visitors?'

Hugo made a face. 'Edward's mother.'

'Ah.' Come to mourn, no doubt. She couldn't bear Lady Farquhar, whom she considered intolerably opinionated.

'And Edward.' Hugo went on, sounding more interested, 'He's taken Champion upstairs to see Alice.'

'Hmmph! Think I'll go and see her myself.'

She left Hugo languidly tossing his ball for the dogs.

Climbing the long oak staircase with its polished steps, Charlie creeping up alongside, she paused to rest and, at that moment, Edward propelled himself down from the top like a desperate skier, his crutches skidding and slipping as he tried to keep control.

As he passed, she said, 'Edward?'

She heard him gasp for breath, as if he'd been winded; and, because her spectacles were buried in the depths of her handbag, never noticed the tears running down his face.

'Lady C.,' he muttered, and – with a last crash of wood against wood – was gone.

Beatrice managed to negotiate the rest of the stairs. It was some time since she'd been up there, and – once she'd attained the first long landing – she considered it worthwhile to go through the tiresome process of putting on her spectacles. It was no surprise to find her daughter-in-law had made further changes: floor-length curtains of pale-green velvet looped back to frame the great window overlooking the lake. Beatrice had to admit, grudgingly, that they worked. During her own brief custodianship of the house she'd run it in a fairly slapdash way, taking the view that if there was nothing wrong with good quality furnishings that had been around ever since anyone could remember, why bother to change them?

As she approached Alice's eyrie, she heard bright young voices, and felt her spirits lift.

'I feel awful,' Alice was saying – but oddly cheerfully, without conviction.

And after that came Eve's indignant: 'You're eighteen years old!'

Then Beatrice stumped into the room on her shooting stick, and they looked up with identical guilty surprised expressions.

'Gran!' said Alice.

How peaky the child looked! As if every drop of blood had drained from her face.

'What's all this?'

'Flu,' said Eve quickly.

Beatrice noticed that Alice's eyes had filled with easy tears. Her heart ached for her granddaughter, but all she said gruffly, settling herself down on a chair, was, 'Lot of it about.' She thought: 'I should tell her how many times I went through this miserable business myself. I should assure her it all comes right in the end.' Pity and sadness were tempered with relief. A failed pregnancy was a sign that the marriage was not dead. And, because Alice was so very young, there'd be many more chances; indeed, it seemed she'd interrupted Eve telling her so.

Which reminded her. 'What about you, darling? Why aren't you up at Oxford?'

'Holiday,' responded Alice equally speedily.

'Hmmph! But you've only just started your term, haven't you?'

She looked from one innocent young face to the other: the beauty of the family and the brains. But it was getting harder and harder to keep them in the pigeonholes their parents had allocated them. For one thing, they treated each other as equals. Alice was getting sharper by the minute and when Eve left off her glasses, like now, she looked positively pretty.

'I just saw Edward,' said Beatrice, like a fisherman casting a line, and intercepted the brief alarmed look that passed between them. Did they honestly believe that she, who'd lived more than half a century longer than they, knew nothing about life? That amiable fool of a husband had been disappointed, of course, and had tactlessly not thought to hide his feelings. Everyone knew men were emotionally retarded. That was why he'd left in a huff. And now there was fresh division, and one of them – most likely Alice, who'd not been concentrating on her wifely duties – would have to forget stupid pride and make a real effort.

Didn't these girls know how greatly she loved them and always would, no matter what? They ought to, even though it wasn't her way to spell it out.

However, seeing a black snout questing up from beneath Alice's quilt, all she said crossly was, 'That dog shouldn't be in your bed.'

'I know,' said Alice, sounding fond and relieved. 'But he's a darling, and I've missed him so much.'

Beatrice felt a second current pass between the girls. But she decided not to investigate further for the moment, and they giggled with relief. Then they all petted Champion, who made a strange purring sound in his throat, more like a cat.

*

It seemed she was doomed to come in on the end of things. As soon as she'd lop-sidedly descended the stairs and limped through the great hall, there was Lady Farquhar flouncing out to her car, where Edward was already sitting in the passenger seat, staring straight ahead.

'Felicity?'

But her daughter-in-law was her usual dry closed-up self. 'Ah, Mama,' was all she said with one of the resigned looks Beatrice was used to. 'I'll ask Briggs to fetch more hot water.'

'Felicity! What on earth is going on?'

Now Briggs was lurking in the background, all ears.

'Briggs? Is there any chocolate cake for Lady Chandler?'

Once the drawing room doors were closed, Beatrice decided to make it clear to Felicity that she wasn't an idiot.

She said, 'Poor lamb. She'll get over it.'

She observed the extraordinary sight of her daughter-in-law continuing to pour tea from her silver crested teapot into a blue and white Spode cup until it overflowed and flooded the tray.

'A hiccup,' Beatrice went on. 'Happens all the time.'

'Look what I've done,' Felicity whispered. She started mopping at the tea with a napkin.

'Probably for the best. Nature's way. Good chance it was a mongol or suchlike.'

'You're probably right,' agreed her daughter-in-law after a minute.

'No more trying for at least six months . . .' Beatrice went on briskly.

'No.'

'Lots of rest and good food. I'll send up some of my duck eggs. When's she going home?'

'I don't know,' said Felicity after a moment. She looked miles away, twirling a strand of hair round a finger. Now she'd be worrying about her pet, Hugo, thought Beatrice.

She helped herself to a second slice of chocolate cake and went on establishing her right to be kept informed on family matters – even if it wasn't respected. 'After all, a suspension means nothing.'

'What?'

'It's not the end of the world,' she continued authoritatively.

But now her daughter-in-law was staring at her with a strange expression, a mixture of bitter resignation and even amusement. 'Oh, I'm afraid they're taking it very seriously indeed.'

'A fracas on the football field?' exclaimed Beatrice in disbelief, unconsciously borrowing Hugo's affected phrase.

Felicity's startled double take, her consequent clamming up, told her she'd made the mistake of overplaying her hand. Her maddened old mind couldn't work it out. She'd get no more here. She might as well cut her losses and go home and make her peace with Emma. It was Friday, too, which always meant fish – even though there'd not been one rebel mackerel-snapper Chandler in four hundred years.

Chapter Eighteen

As Felicity pulled up outside Johnny's cottage, the door opened. He was delighted to see her, as always, but she could trace the anxiety in his eyes and his eagerness to help her out of her car. She thought: 'It's me who's done that. First I made him feel life was worth living again. Now I'm short-changing him.'

'Sorry I'm late,' she said. 'So sorry.'

'It's all right.'

'It's so difficult to get away . . .'

'I know, I know.'

'. . . especially now the children are home.'

'I do realize.'

'They will ask where I'm going . . .'

'I understand.'

'. . . and I hate telling lies.'

'Of course you do.'

'To the children, I mean.'

'You're here now, aren't you?'

She made a despairing face. 'I'm interviewing a man who cleans tapestry screens.'

He'd fancied he heard her car half a dozen times before it finally arrived, and always gone out to check. 'I'm behaving like a mistress,' he'd thought, grinning at the idea. He revelled in his new-found virility. All he wanted was to sweep her upstairs to bed, but made do – for the time being – with an embrace and a kiss.

'You look as if you need a drink.'

'What a good idea.'

Her discreet stylish touches were all over his little sitting room, fiercely protected against the administrations of his daily. A poem of yellow roses she'd created the last time had been permitted to die publicly, its petals fallen, its leaves dried and curling. ('You don't want those any more, sir.' 'Leave them . . . JUST leave them, please.')

'I'll do you another,' she said, gesturing at the vase – because she noticed it straight away, of course. Then she plumped up the silk cushions she'd bought for him, and patted them into place in a way nobody else seemed capable of.

'No no!' He gestured towards the sofa. 'Just you relax.'

He knew how distracted she was by family troubles, how perpetually short of time.

'Mrs Thing made a stew I can warm up,' he said. 'I think I'm just about capable of that. And I can handle some beans. Yes ma'am!'

'I can't stay long.' Then, seeing his expression, she amended, 'A couple of hours.'

Johnny looked cheerful. It was his speciality. 'So!' he said. 'Tell me what you've been up to?'

'Disaster.' She closed her eyes against the horror of it all, and he thought of her nakedness against his and momentarily shut his eyes too.

'Eve?'

'I've never seen her so miserable.'

'Poor girl.'

Felicity nodded grimly. Indeed. For the sake of pacifying a religious hysteric, a loose cannon, Eve had been sacrificed. Nurse O'Brien had threatened to make the affair public, bring the college into disrepute, if the dons (who were a great deal more liberal) were not seen to do something.

It had been a terrible injustice. But then, Eve had not sought to defend herself in any way. Eve, who'd striven so hard for her place at Oxford, had given it up without so much as a whimper.

'My life is over,' was all she'd said, when the letter arrived telling her of the college's decision. She'd seemed unsurprised. She gave the impression it was only what she deserved.

'I know it was wrong to—'

'Oh, Johnny! It was the most terrible thing imaginable! *And* it's against the law!'

'—but she *was* only trying to help her sister.'

'I don't understand why they didn't tell us!' Felicity sounded genuinely and miserably puzzled.

Johnny stared at her. He knew her as a loving compassionate woman. He'd no picture of her and Harry as a couple.

'Anyway . . .' Felicity sipped at her drink. 'Eve asked if she could invite her boyfriend for the weekend. I said yes.'

'Good idea.'

'Harry doesn't think so.'

'Oh?'

'But as I told him, it's not as if she isn't suffering . . .'

'I agree.' He dared to put a hand on her shoulder. 'And Alice?'

'Alice is all right, I think.' But she bit her lip, as if Alice was worrying her more than she could say. She added resolutely, 'It's *good* to have her home again. It's almost as if she never left.'

'And how's your boy?'

For the first time, Felicity looked genuinely happy. 'Hugo's going back to school next week!'

'Splendid!'

'Oh yes, they're having him back.'

'He'll have to behave himself from now on.'

'He's a good boy,' she said immediately.

'Of course he is,' he said, stroking her hair.

'He's had a shock.'

'He has.'

'He's the cleverest of the lot, you know.'

'Of course he is!'

'If only he'd put his mind to it!'

Then she said tenderly and softly, cutting through the small talk, 'Johnny, this isn't enough for you,' and he felt his heart plummet like a descending lift. Whoosh! Floor after floor after floor.

It was strange, because he'd been steeling himself to say something similar. The wonder was giving way to the first rumblings of anguish. But, instead, he responded valiantly. 'Who says?'

She smiled at him sadly and shook her head. Her dark eyes looked misty.

He beamed. 'I think it's for me to decide.'

'I feel so guilty.' Her voice was a whisper.

'Don't,' he said briskly.

'Not about him.' She laid her head against the back of the sofa and looked at him sideways in a way that made his heart react all over again. 'You're such a darling.'

'And so are you.'

'You deserve better.'

'Let me be the judge of that. Now, are you peckish?'

She smiled. 'I haven't much time. What about you?'

'You know what I want!'

She smiled again and held out her arms. Always before, sex had been a longing that dared not declare itself, lest it was turned against her. But she trusted Johnny. It was so wonderful at last to be able to trust a man. It was more important, in the end, than fulfilment could ever be.

Johnny thought, 'When I'm dying, this will be one of my reasons for having lived.'

He would always consider that he'd enjoyed a happy marriage. Mary had been a brick and a sport, an unfailing support and no whinger. She'd longed for children but, when they never came, had briskly got on with things. She didn't bemoan the unfairness of contracting cancer, or let on how frightened and uncomfortable she was, even at the agonizing end. Nor did she permit Johnny to weep in her embrace.

But it was these very things, he realized in his forty-fourth year, which made for true intimacy.

The odd thing was that Flicky and Mary were very similar. Sometimes he'd look at Flicky when they were out in public having lunch at the bistro behind the cathedral, which had become their place, increasingly wary of discovery since the affair had started. He'd observe with tenderness the controlled way she held herself, the cool dry way she spoke, and think of the secret woman he'd discovered, almost by accident.

Sometimes, when they were very close, he'd fancy Flicky was his wife and always had been. It was because she'd known him before the war, and Mary. It was only logical, he told himself hopefully, that eventually they'd be together. For Flicky, like Mary, was a woman of profound moral character.

Later, as they drank tea, he asked carefully: 'How is Harry?'

Felicity shrugged. What place did her husband have there?

'Do you think he guesses?' As usual, he wanted to believe that this relationship was so important to her that she couldn't help but give herself away.

'Oh no!' said Felicity with a smile, and his spirits plummeted. ('You fool!' he told himself sternly. 'Do you *want* him to turn up with a horsewhip?') She added: 'I don't think it would even occur to him.' She made a face. 'He thinks I'm cold.'

'Not you!'

Felicity smiled delightedly at him and his spirits revived. He adored her!

'Down boy!' he joked, and – for a second – Felicity looked a tiny bit alarmed.

Then he said: 'This young girl . . .'

'Still going on,' said Felicity, 'I assume.' She looked a little tired and untidy, but to him only seemed well loved. 'He's hardly ever there,' she continued. She made a face, and one of her new joking observations: 'The other day he came home with grass on his back!'

Johnny shook his head. It was so shocking, all of it. She'd told him she no longer cared, so long as Harry didn't humiliate her in public again. Equally offensive, to Johnny's mind, was Harry's neglect of his family at a time like this.

He went on: 'You'd think he'd want to be with Alice and Eve . . .'

'Oh no!' Felicity looked surprised that Johnny had failed to grasp something so elementary.

'I don't understand,' said Johnny, who knew very well that, given the chance, he'd have been a most tender and attentive father.

'He can't bear anything that upsets him,' said Felicity.

'But he dotes on Alice!' Even from a distance, Johnny had picked up on this one constant.

Felicity said slowly, as if she still couldn't comprehend it, 'He can't bear to be anywhere near Alice now.' She added, puzzling Johnny: 'It was exactly the same with Champion.'

Chapter Nineteen

'I could have sworn I saw Bailiff in your meadow just now,' Rosemary Pettifer remarked in her affected way, eyes on the dish of over-boiled Brussels sprouts Mrs Briggs was offering.

Harry glanced at her sharply. But she looked very demure.

'You know Alice,' he drawled with a sigh, as if he'd had to be dragooned into accepting her beloved horse. 'Can't move an inch without her menagerie.' As for anyone suspecting he might have sent over one of his own horseboxes to collect Bailiff, together with a case of decent Merlot for Edward, and a note tucked in for his own amusement ('A portentous little vintage with an endearing flaccidity') . . .

The witch on his other side piped up: 'She's still here then?'

'Bad flu,' said Harry, with his serious face. Then he shook his head with eyebrows raised, shrugged as if to convey similar surprise that Alice hadn't yet returned to her husband, helped himself to Brussels sprouts. (And, not for the first time, noted with detached curiosity and some amusement that his cook possessed that mark of true sensuality, the circle of Venus: a single deep line scored around her plump neck.)

The Chandlers were having another dinner party. A starched white apron for sweating Mrs Briggs as she presented one of her upgraded menus, familiar guests, predictable conversation – and a spectacular Chambertin from Berry Brothers (though there seemed to be fewer bottles than Harry remembered ordering up from the cellar).

It was his idea, of course, this comforting ritual of good manners and play-acting. It showed the world he was still a rich man.

The day before, he'd been obliged to make out an enormous cheque to Lloyds.

He'd managed to borrow a comparable sum from the bank after his mother – who owned Edgerton – had provided a written guarantee. The interest would be outrageous; and Beatrice had had to pledge repayment of that, too, if all else failed. But at least this way there'd been no chipping away at the estate, or the house's treasures. His mother would never stop reminding him of the perilous position he'd put her in. But that was another matter.

Before setting his name to the cheque, he put Haydn's Creation Mass on the gramophone. Tears rolled down his cheeks as the music thundered in his ears. Bugger them all! But beauty would remain. And at least in his own dining room he was still the conductor.

In truth, though, being forced to hand over all that money was nothing compared with his other loss.

They hadn't talked once, on the long journey home.

Wrapped in rugs in the back seat, Alice had slept for most of it. He knew because every few minutes he'd check in his rearview mirror on her white face buried in cushions.

It wasn't until he was tenderly lifting her out of his car that she opened her eyes and looked at him. He'd nearly dropped her with the shock. He could find no affection or interest in her azure stare, just what seemed weary disappointment. Then her gaze shifted and she smiled weakly at someone else.

He passed off the moment with his usual nonchalant confidence, of course: she couldn't have guessed his desolation. He carried her upstairs to her bed, kissed her gently on the forehead (her eyes had closed again by then) and let the women in the house take over.

He made one attempt to re-establish their former closeness, seeking her out in her blue and white nest when he knew she'd be alone.

'Turtledove . . .'

She was propped on lacy pillows with a book, and didn't look up. He couldn't remember the last time he'd seen her reading.

He tapped on the door. 'May I come in?' he enquired in a silly voice; and only then did she lift her eyes and close the book, though he noticed she kept a finger in the page. Her expression was blank, patient, unamused.

'This is ridiculous,' he said, with his charming smile.

'Sorry?' she responded with cool politeness.

'Nothing for *you* to be sorry about, my turtledove!' he said expansively.

'No,' she corrected him coldly, 'I meant, what's ridiculous?' But she sounded quite incurious.

'All this.'

She didn't reply.

He let it go, for the time being; also the slight movement he perceived under the covers. (He'd not voiced a single protest about that damned dog moving back in!)

'We haven't talked about everything,' he continued with another pleasant smile. She'd no idea of the courage that was required. To remember the unnatural act she'd inflicted on herself – the butchery and the murder – made him quite ill with horror. She couldn't have devised a more effective torture if she'd tried.

Alice shrugged.

Her world-weary air appalled him, but he went on slickly: 'These things happen,' and straight afterwards thought soberly, 'no.'

How pale and lifeless she looked – almost plain really – but it only increased the love he felt. She was being monstrously unfair. He'd done nothing wrong, he told himself. He'd only tried, for her sake, to make her face reality. And of course, as it turned out, that man of hers had been no good at all, just as he'd always known. It was Marcus – idiotic name – who was the real villain.

'That's not to say it wasn't a foolish and wicked action that could have cost you your life.' A pause here for her to take in the enormity. 'The important thing now is that you're all right, thank God. You're on the road to recovery.' But even to himself his voice sounded hollow, as if there was no longer any centre to him as a man.

There was still no response.

'And if you don't want to go back to your marriage,' he continued magnanimously, 'that's all right. You know Ma and I will support you, whatever you decide.' He should have left it at that, of course, but – stung by Alice's coldness – was unable to resist adding, 'Even if it's not easy for us, at this point.'

Alice bit her lip, as if now she really had to force herself to remain silent.

'What are you reading?'

She didn't respond, and he had to move closer and flip over the book for himself. It was *The Feminine Mystique* by Betty Friedan.

He couldn't help a mocking smile. 'Must be Eve's.' They'd set up the joke between them, of course: they'd known he'd come.

Alice's mouth tightened.

He said gently, 'Shouldn't have thought that was your sort of thing at all, turtledove.'

'It's interesting,' said Alice coldly.

'You don't want to turn into one of the hot-water bottle and cocoa brigade,' he joked, with his marvellous grin. 'Nothing more disagreeable.'

He could hear, in his mind, an echo of her old voice – mock outraged, streaked with tenderness – 'Oh Pa! You're so extreme!' But this time there was no reaction whatever. It was painfully obvious that she couldn't be bothered.

It wasn't his fault, thought Harry bitterly, that she'd suffered a botched abortion. After all, she'd chosen not to tell him about the pregnancy. But he struggled to understand that, in her shock and misery, she needed to blame someone, and he'd always been closest. He showed none of this loving compassion, though – or the hurt.

'On that note,' he said urbanely, 'I must get on.'

He blew her a kiss in overdone courtly manner (it always used to make her laugh; she'd invariably blow one back), but couldn't help observing that even before he left the room, she'd immersed herself in her book once more.

He couldn't resist one last shot: 'Those were very fine pearls, you know.' But outside her bedroom door he pulled down his face and almost wept.

Then an idea occurred to him. Cheered, he decided to give Edward a telephone call straight away.

'So,' began Rosemary, with the smile that could transform a bland English rose into an houri, 'what's been happening?'

'What's been happening?' Harry repeated slowly, as if it had all been far too humdrum to leave an impression. He thought: 'I feel a stranger in my own house.'

Alice should be here, of course: adorning his table, showing up these withered blooms. For her sake, he'd even tolerate Eve.

But instead of his daughters, Felicity had pressed their delinquent son into service. She'd placed him next to her for protection – watching, proud but wary, as, unnaturally neat and clean, he politely fielded questions about school.

She was looking surprisingly pretty, Harry noticed, in something black with an heirloom diamond brooch pinned to her shoulder. As always when they held a dinner party, she was vivacious in her composed fashion. But it would never have occurred to him that she'd taken a lover. Not her thing at all. Hadn't she rejected him, last night in bed? No words had passed – it had all been very civilized – but he'd felt hurt as well as angry. She was his wife, wasn't she?

However, in a secret compartment of his life, hidden away like a jewel, there was always the girl. If he justified this last and most significant adultery (which had caused him to break all his rules) it was along the lines of: 'How could any man have been expected to say no?'

'Would you?' he thought mockingly, as he looked at the sagging blotchy face of Richard Pettifer, a staunch churchgoer. 'Or you?' he wondered, appearing to be charmed by Simon McCorquodale's yellow teeth and boy scout heartiness.

It had started with a succession of delicious, seemingly haphazard meetings, all instigated by her. She'd be waiting for his car at the turn in the drive, dawdling decoratively against a tree trunk where the avenue of beeches swept away from the house. 'Give us a lift?' she'd beg with that half-knowing half-innocent smile that so reminded him of the painting he loved. And, as his Daimler bumped over the long green toothbrush, 'Where are you going, then? Can I come too?'

In all fairness (Harry reminded himself self-righteously), he *had* decided, at the beginning, 'Absolutely not. Whatever happens. Not this time.' He'd grimly totted up the very good reasons why. Her father was a long-time employee (who continued to do wonders for the garden, by the way). Nothing sickened him more than the image of innocence defiled. How would *he* feel if somebody his age took advantage of one of his daughters?

But each day she'd devise some fresh (though hardly subtle) temptation – a skirt so short that he could see her knickers, a top so low he was forced to act as if he was wearing blinkers. And, however hard he tried to retain the mask of charmed but aloof employer, he found the position increasingly absurd.

His mistake was allowing the cheeky flirting to continue, while fooling himself he could stop it at any minute. Inexorably it led to that astonishing moment when he'd realized exactly who, in this case, was the real seducer. Even now, as he relived it – sitting at his dinner party, protected by a starched napkin – he felt his body react, and casually moved closer to the table as if listening attentively to his neighbour on his right.

'Did I see Eve earlier on?' asked Susan McCorquodale and, as he turned towards her with his lazy smile, he thought, 'This damned coven is ganging up on me.'

'You did.' He'd known so many fevered preludes. But this time there was no post-coital distancing, no cool reappraisal, and it was beginning to worry him. Sometimes he believed it was all down to her perfect envelope of flesh that was like no other skin he'd ever touched. Had skin make him break every rule so far? Where, in the end, would skin lead him?

'Isn't she up at Oxford?'

'Was,' admitted Harry, forcing himself back to the present. It was probably time to reveal that Eve had returned home, though – with luck – the collapse of Alice's marriage could be concealed for a little longer.

'Was?' echoed Rosemary Pettifer, on his left, looking surprised and concerned.

'Didn't suit her,' he said airily. He added without compunction, glancing casually in the direction of Felicity to check she wasn't listening, 'Too much like hard work.'

'But all Eve ever wanted was to go to Oxford,' protested Susan, and Harry enjoyed seeing Rosemary's decorous smugness ruffled. He guessed quite correctly that she was wondering if she and Susan McCorquodale had more in common than she'd realized. They did. At least he was still capable of commanding a smidgeon of power somewhere.

In Alice's bedroom, she and Eve were eating dinner party food off a tray while Champion watched each transition from plate to mouth with intense concentration.

'Such a relief to be an outcast.' Alice passed Champion a snippet of roast lamb and he briskly snapped his jaws together, already anticipating the next one.

'You're telling me!'

'I *hate* dinner parties! The only nice thing is the food.'

There was silence from Eve, but only because she was absorbed in Mrs Briggs' profiteroles.

'I had to give two when I was married.' (Alice had already removed her wedding ring.) 'Kipper pâté, chicken supreme and raspberry trifle; prawn cocktail, carbonnade of beef and lemon soufflé. Nightmare! All Edward had to do was choose the wine.'

In a moment, Eve asked, 'Shall I fetch us more pudding?'

'See if you can find any scraps for Champion,' said Alice. 'And more drink.'

They'd already stolen a bottle of Pa's Chambertin, sluicing it down like cough mixture. It had been Alice's idea.

So what if she'd hurt and frightened her father? Look what a hypocrite he'd shown himself to be.

She decided to leave the telltale bottle around for him to find. Then he'd seek her out to reprimand her and she could take pleasure in making him flinch under his confident gloss all over again. She'd been delighted to find Bailiff back at Edgerton, but it hadn't made her any more forgiving.

'I'll get blamed,' said Eve. But in her present state of mind, it was hard to care.

'Well, just pinch anything you can,' said Alice accommodatingly.

She'd not seen the point of alcohol before. But now she drank to forget Marcus, and the destruction of their baby, and her guilt about the punishment that had been meted out to her sister.

Would she have embarked on the affair with Marcus had she been warned of its dreadful repercussions? She only speculated on it once. It was too painful to acknowledge the truth.

With alcohol inside her, though, she could even pretend to be happy. Tonight, she and Eve were putting on an impressive show.

As Eve stole down the long staircase, she could hear the dinner party in the distance: the clink of silver on porcelain, the rise and fall of sedate talk. Her parents became strangers when they entertained, Pa so benign and hospitable, even his laugh was different.

In the enormous mirror at its foot – gilded cherubs prancing round patchy old mercury – she saw a pale sliver of a girl, eyebrows raised as if she would never believe what had happened to her.

'My life is over,' she told herself, feeling the panic start. 'My life is over.'

And for what? Alice's marriage had crashed in a gathering ripple of scandal. What real difference would it have made if she'd returned home pregnant? Eve found herself mourning the lost baby as another strand of her new despair. At least it would have been something to look forward to.

On her way to the kitchen, she passed the closed door of the dining room and the sounds of the dinner party briefly defined themselves. 'I assure you he's not!' protested one of the women, sounding as if she was saying something very much more daring and, in the background, Pa laughed in his genial dinner party way.

With pity, Eve pictured her brother trapped in there, hair slicked down, boiling with boredom in his suit and tie. He'd be shovelling his food, planning an early escape.

Hugo's newly gruff voice fell into a lull in the conversation like a stone chucked in the lake: 'Pa?'

'Mmm.' Harry reluctantly acknowledged his son's presence, thinking, 'No points for trying to curry favour.'

Hugo glanced at his mother for the usual fond reassurance. 'Pa, when are you going to get your aeroplane?'

'An aeroplane!' exclaimed Rosemary Pettifer, looking sly and delighted.

Predictably, Susan McCorquodale entered into competition. 'But, Harry, how thrilling! When?'

Hugo's expression brightened momentarily. See? He wasn't so insignificant, after all. He'd told them something they didn't know, and now the conversation had a chance of becoming interesting.

'It's all nonsense!' There was lazy amusement in Harry's voice, and he'd assumed the contemptuous expression that could move his children to tears. He might as well have drawled, 'My son's an imbecile.'

'But she told me!' Hugo exclaimed, his voice breaking up with indignation and hurt, and he glanced at his mother again.

This time, however, she failed him.

If just one of those round Harry's table had instantly and determinedly begun to talk about the fluctuations of the stock market, say, or the present dearth of woodcock, or the difficulty in finding decent servants, then the danger might have passed. But nobody said a word. It was almost as if they guessed what would come next, and were waiting with patient, even sadistic, curiosity.

So Hugo ploughed on regardless, squeakily outraged, determined to acquit himself. 'That girl at the pheasant shoot! *You* know! The gardener's daughter! She *told* me you were going to take her up in your aeroplane!'

Mrs Briggs had retired to her room, where she was listening to a play on the wireless. As Eve eased open the green baize door that shut off the servants' quarters, she heard an upper-class male voice enquire languidly, 'Spring '54? Shepherds Hotel, Cairo?'

The bowl of profiteroles in the larder wasn't quite empty. Eve envisaged Mrs Briggs listening to pretend people who sounded like her employers and their guests, wiping chocolate and whipped cream from her moustache with a genteel flick of her handkerchief. She was always referring to her sweet tooth.

Most of the wine for the dinner party had been decanted for the dining room, but half a bottle of something called Château Yquem had been left out on the kitchen table and Eve found a crusty looking bottle of sherry in one of the cupboards. She piled it all on to a yellow wickerwork tray lined with glass.

She walked quickly past the door of the dining room.

At the base of the stairs, she paused, set down the tray for a moment and, longing for the illusion of freedom, walked through the great hall.

But the front door was already open, and, to her astonishment, she saw that her mother was standing outside, arms wrapped tightly round herself, gazing up at the cloudy tracings of stars, a crescent moon. She was beautifully dressed in black velvet and her hair was a lacquered shell. As usual, when she gave a dinner party, she smelt of Chanel No. 5.

'Ma!'

'Darling!'

Then Eve noticed that her mother's eyes glittered in the faint light. She instinctively started to move closer, but Ma shook her head slightly in gentle warning.

Eve expected her to come out with an anodyne excuse for her extraordinary action of escaping her guests: something contained but soothing that would do. But instead she said, looking up at the sky, 'Your friend's coming tomorrow, isn't he?'

'Yes,' said Eve, watching her mother anxiously. Her brooch glistened, too.

'That's good,' said Ma, nodding her head several times. Then she asked, 'Are you all right?'

'Yes,' whispered Eve, swallowing hard.

'That's good,' said Ma. 'And Alice?'

'She's fine.'

'That's good,' Ma repeated. 'That's very good indeed.'

Then she gave her daughter a tremulous but determined smile and went back to her dinner party.

Chapter Twenty

After one brief tearful telephone call, Eve had been spirited away.

As his train chugged into tiny Bellingham station, set down in fields of long grass, Seb found her pale anxious face among the knot of people waiting on the platform and thought grimly of the explanation he was owed.

The letter she'd written asking him to come had been almost as brief as her phone call: 'We have to talk. You have to let me explain. You know I can't come to you.' And there was a solemn postscript: 'I swear it'll be okay this time.'

What did 'okay' mean? There'd be no more ritual slaughter of harmless birds to endure? No more blatant adultery from her father and gut-twisting humiliation for her mother? No more feeble but excruciating suicide attempts from her cuckold of a brother-in-law? At least, he told himself, the weather had improved – so there'd be no more bone-melting cold.

At least, too, he knew about the insidious charm of Edgerton and could arrive forearmed.

Eve said, with a break in her voice, 'Thanks for coming,' and Seb found himself muttering a gruff reassurance. She looked terrible, with dark circles under her eyes and a lost, frightened expression he'd never seen before. It wasn't hard to imagine how it might feel to be banished from Oxford, denied a precious degree. He thumped her shoulder, and immediately started searching for his Zippo. Cracking it against his denimed thigh, he lit a fag to steady himself, and – the familiar afterthought – passed it to her.

It was that wonderful optimistic time just before the arrival of real summer and, as Eve steered her little car through sunken narrow lanes trembling with buttercup and campion, he felt soothed despite himself.

He'd no moral objection to abortion; if he blamed anyone, he blamed the law (which, thankfully, was about to change). He'd known of several girls who'd trodden the same lonely path as Alice, but without the horrifying consequences. To his mind, it had to be better than a forced marriage.

But he'd been puzzled and wounded by Eve's failure to let him in on the secret. They were lovers, for Christ's sake! It could only be because she'd colluded with her family. It didn't tally with what he knew of her character. She'd paid, of course. Even so, his real sympathy lay with Alice.

It was down to beauty. He forgot what Eve had told him about Marcus and, remembering the lively captivating girl he'd met at Christmas, decided on his own scenario. That gorgeous bird had dared to prize apart the bars of the cage they'd shut her in. She wouldn't have chosen to destroy a child by the man she loved. No. She'd been coerced: sacrificed for the sake of its own precious reputation by a class he'd always mistrusted and now hated.

Eve told him the truth in the car, drawn into a lay-by. As she put her head in her hands, a tractor clotted with mud cranked past, churning out more chunks of mud, and he received a flash of an amiable concerned face, a similarly puzzled-looking collie perched in the passenger seat.

'Bastard!'

'I told you.'

'How could he have?'

'He's like that.'

'Well, at least she hasn't gone back to that berk of a husband.'

'No.'

'At least she held out against that.'

Eve let him believe it, whilst noting sadly that he hadn't yet enquired how *she* was feeling.

But he did ask, 'What are you going to do now?'

Eve shrugged as if she hadn't even thought, overcome with misery that he could sound so uninvolved.

But, then, the balance between them had shifted; and she couldn't summon up the courage – yet – to ask what it meant for their relationship.

Seb had been prepared for Edgerton but, even so, the house confused him all over again, like a fascinating briefly known woman he'd been struggling to forget.

As they left the avenue of beech trees behind and turned

into the last stretch of the long drive, suddenly there it was: gleaming gold in the sun, with its fantastic lacy turrets, its embroidery of creeper, its extraordinary mixture of patience and peace.

The clocktower boomed once — a brief interruption — like the house clearing its throat.

'We're late,' said Eve anxiously.

Seb smiled faintly. He'd forgotten, of course, what a crime it was, in these circles, to keep staff waiting.

This time, there was no welcome committee at the door.

They left his suitcase in the boot of Eve's car. As they entered the house, he could feel the remembered chill closing in, like a falling shadow, and hear in the distance metal wheels grating on ancient flagstones, the clatter of dishes as the wheels became snarled up in old rugs.

Eve's parents were already in the dining room.

'Ah, there you are,' said Eve's father, looking down his nose, and he took a gold watch out of his cardigan pocket and checked it. The cardigan was new, but he was exactly the same arrogant affected man Seb recalled.

'Sorry,' said Eve breathlessly.

Her father gave one of his lazy toothy smiles, as if that were enough to cancel out the rudeness. But her mother smiled anxiously at Seb as if to say, 'Don't take any notice.' She looked different. It occurred to Seb, for the first time, that she must have been very pretty when she was young.

She and Eve's father did not address each other. So lunch (the same stodgy overcooked tepid food) was mostly silent except for Eve's mother's efforts to engage him in conversation. His train journey had been okay, thanks; and, yes, the weather was wonderful. She carefully avoided the subject of Oxford.

He assumed Alice was still recuperating in her bedroom, but she was not referred to once.

He didn't yet know that she refused to be anywhere near her father.

It would only increase his admiration.

They found her grooming Bailiff in the stables with Champion for company.

They could hear her talking to the horse as they approached across a bed of sticky smelly straw.

She was wearing a pair of old jeans and a flimsy shirt over one of her lacy trousseau bras. Her back was to them as she stretched on tiptoe to draw a brush across Bailiff's chestnut rump.

'Hold still, my darling,' she was saying. 'Hold still.'

Then Champion wuffed quietly in warning, and she turned round.

'Yep,' thought Seb. 'You are one gorgeous bird.'

She looked hot and untidy. She was bare of make-up, her blond hair tied in a knot: quite different from the glossy expensively dressed young wife he'd met at Christmas. He didn't see the raw unhappiness, only a new freedom and recklessness that rendered her even more attractive.

'Dig the kit,' he said, raising his eyebrows with a smile to detract from the impertinence, holding out his hand.

Alice laughed and leant forward and kissed him on the cheek and he was aware of a whiff of scent, a glimpse of damp cleft between her breasts. 'Thank goodness you've come,' she said. Then, to her sister's horror, 'Eve's been desperate.'

There was a half-eaten slab of Cheddar and an apple on a plate balanced on a nearby shelf.

'Lunch,' said Alice, making a face at them both.

'Well, you didn't miss anything,' Eve told her, noting Seb's admiring expression. As usual, though, she passed off any unease by seeking to entertain.

'Pa asked Seb about Oxford – for my benefit, of course. Cue for Ma to burble on about how magnificent the wisteria's going to be this year. Still not talking to him.' Eve gave a passable imitation of her mother: 'Could you please ask your father if he could possibly send down the redcurrant jelly?'

'Barking mad,' said Alice, smiling at Seb. Then she told him, opening her blue eyes wide and nodding grimly: 'Actually he's worse than.'

'I'm not here,' thought Eve.

She could feel her familiar body – bejeaned, like Alice's, but slight and athletic – taking up space. And, less and less frequently, she could hear her voice striving to make an impression on the duet soaring away between the others. The experience brought back painful bewildering feelings of childhood: 'I love her because she's my sister and I can't help it – but I could so easily hate her because, without even realizing it, she blots me out like the sun.'

To make things worse, Alice kept glancing at her happily as if to say: 'Aren't you glad I'm getting on so well with your boyfriend? Isn't this fun?'

They were talking about Socrates and Alcibaides now. Or

rather, Seb was. Alice had abandoned the grooming of Bailiff and she and Seb were sitting on a bale of straw, while she ate her apple.

Alice knew nothing about the classics – and very little about anything else. However, to Eve's astonishment, she heard her questioning Seb about his course, getting away with it as only Alice could.

'Um, how's it all going then?' was all she had to say, fixing him with an earnest blue gaze; then, at regular intervals – as Seb spoke with passion, smiling at her every so often to make sure he still held her interest – '*I* see' (when Eve knew perfectly well, from the dreamy look on her face, that she was really thinking about Marcus).

'And I had to try so hard,' Eve remembered with some bitterness. 'When I first met him, I went to the library and read up on his subjects for days . . .'

She'd ached to see Seb again – convinced that, once she could get him to Edgerton, she could re-establish their old intimacy. But now she could see that, unless something was said soonish, she might become a less and less important part of a threesome.

'Alice?'

'Mmm?' She was brushing her hair at her dressing table, wearing an exquisite mauve silk nightdress. As usual, Champion was reclining on her quilt, waiting, like an impatient husband, for her warm body.

'Can we talk?'

'Course.' Alice finished with her hundred strokes and took a run at her bed, just as she'd done as a child when she was afraid the tiger in Pa's study might be crouching underneath. She lifted the sheet for Champion and – after a brief unconvincing show of disinterest – he burrowed inside.

She asked without curiosity, gobbling iron pills the doctor had prescribed, 'How was dinner?'

'You're going to have to come down soon.'

'Watch me!'

'Gran was there tonight.'

'Uh-huh.'

'You know what she's like . . .'

Then Alice abruptly changed the subject. 'Tell me honestly, what do you think he's feeling?'

'Nothing,' said Eve firmly. It would be unkind to encourage her.

'If I knew he was feeling bad,' Alice went on, with a wheedling note in her voice, 'it'd make it easier.'

'You have to let it go.'

But Alice went on nagging away like a child. 'People don't get away with it, do they, when they've done something dreadful?'

'Only if they've a conscience.'

Eve wondered if Alice thought about Marcus all the time, viewing other people as interruptions, like interference on the wireless. She never talked about the baby – though sometimes, without warning, she'd start sobbing piteously. 'I'll be okay,' she'd insist, when Eve tried to comfort her. On the surface, it seemed as if she'd blotted out the experience – or at least convinced herself she'd suffered a miscarriage as Gran still seemed to believe.

But her body must be grieving, thought Eve, looking at Alice's ripe gleaming breasts bursting out of her nightgown.

She thought of becoming pregnant by Seb – and knew she would not, under any circumstances, be able to undergo what Alice had.

'Oh,' said Alice, as if becoming aware of outside static, 'you wanted to talk.'

'Of course you want to talk!' Alice had exclaimed, horrified by her own lack of tact. 'You won't even see me, I promise!' Then, as an unimportant afterthought: 'He's nice, Eve.'

It was too late. Even though Alice made herself too tired or busy to accompany them on walks or join them for chats, her charisma remained, like an invisible fence; her unhappy situation like a spot Seb kept picking at.

Eve still crept into his bedroom at night, and he'd make love to her, and – for the time it lasted – she'd be convinced everything was mended. But afterwards Seb would distance himself, and Alice would reappear in the conversation, as if Eve hadn't suffered a tragedy just as annihilating.

Chapter Twenty-one

There was a particular spot in the churchyard – facing west towards the lake – which Harry often visited. It was where his crusty self-centred father was buried ('Blessed are the righteous, for they shall be comforted'), and there was an empty space to its left.

When Harry looked at this space, like a plot for the construction of an inverted house, he felt both fearful and comforted. Since the war and his father's unexpected death, he'd been governed by an awareness of mortality; but, on the other hand, he could imagine few more agreeable places to rot. In death, as in life, he'd be surrounded by his own kind. In four hundred years not a single non-Chandler had penetrated this burial ground – no beloved nanny, as in the Hapsburgs' mausoleum in Vienna (though it was rumoured that in the seventeenth century a favourite whippet had managed to slink in). He would be within the sound of the clocktower bell: part of his beloved Edgerton for ever.

His stone would, of course, be made of the same Ham (which was not that suitable for engraving, because of its softness), and he was still enjoyably playing with an inscription. It would probably be from the Apocrypha – either 'Let no flower of the spring pass us by' or 'Let us leave tokens of our joyfulness in every place'.

It wouldn't be for some time, though. It was nearly always accidents (hunting errors like the one which had killed his father) that saw off those Chandlers who failed to complete their three score years and ten. Of course, over the centuries, there'd been numerous deaths in infancy (pathetically small headstones, like milk teeth, with trusting tearful inscriptions). But other stones spoke of a formidable record of longevity. His grandfather had lived to be ninety-three, his great-grandfather to eighty-five, which was really something then.

'Good breeding,' thought Harry complacently. Theirs was a very healthy family – give or take a touch of arthritis here, a protesting liver there. It was something they took for granted. Keep out of trouble and you could live to be a hundred. He was almost reconciled to his fine and private place – though not for a long while yet.

On the second day of Seb's visit, the telephone rang at breakfast time.

It was Mrs Briggs who answered it – interrupted placing a silver salver of scrambled eggs and grilled bacon on the sideboard – and thus, servant to servant, was the very first to learn of the drama.

Unusually, she hurried, rather than toiled, up the long staircase. Excited as she was, she noticed a newly upholstered chair on the landing and thought, 'She never stops, that one.'

She knocked on her employers' bedroom door.

Lady Chandler opened it, neatly dressed and made-up as Mrs Briggs had only ever seen her. Behind her could be seen the four-poster, scarcely rumpled. She looked surprised, but also faintly displeased that Mrs Briggs had taken the unprecedented step of reminding them they were running a few minutes late. After all, how often had they been so inconsiderate as to be truly late for a meal? 'We're on our way now, Briggs. Sir Harry'll be two minutes.'

Mrs Briggs shook her head, put her hand on her heart, which she could feel thumping away with anxiety and the effort of climbing the stairs. She was conscious of the inexorable sweating – worse even than usual. 'There's been a telephone call, Your Ladyship. I'm afraid it's bad news.'

Instantly Lady Chandler's face became stiff as cardboard, paler by the minute, and even Mrs Briggs – who'd never been a mother, never even been married – could guess what was passing through her mind. Bad news by telephone must involve the two children who were not safely under her roof. 'Yes,' she whispered. It could only be Hugo.

'Emma just phoned,' Mrs Briggs began, and saw Lady Chandler close her eyes and let out a faint sigh. ('But then,' as she said later to one of the other servants, 'they never got on, did they?')

Then Sir Harry appeared behind Her Ladyship and she put a hand on his arm and said in her familiar controlled way, 'Harry, I'm so sorry. There's been an accident.'

*

Once the dramatic fact of Beatrice's death had been established, the story was told and retold in copious detail throughout the day.

The postman heard it from Mrs Briggs at the end of his long toil up the drive on his bicycle and the noisy attention of eleven dogs. (There was no way Champion was going to miss out on this enjoyable ritual now he was back at Edgerton.) Unusually, he was given a piece of Mrs Briggs' shortcake with his cup of tea.

Seb and Eve heard it from Felicity in dry précis form when they came down a quarter of an hour late for breakfast.

Alice heard it from Harry, who appeared in the doorway of her room like a spectre and said, without expression, 'I thought you'd want to know that your grandmother is dead,' and left with an image of Alice's shocked face, suddenly come alive.

Just as he'd hoped, it meant that – scared and guilty – Alice initiated a temporary uneasy truce.

The story was that Emma had gone up to Her Ladyship's room with a cup of tea on the dot of a quarter to eight, as always, only to find it empty apart from three snoring spaniels. The bed had been slept in, but old Lady Chandler's skirt and jumper and whatnots were still laid out on a chair – and she wasn't in her bathroom. It had seemed a mystery at first to Emma, who was in a dreadful state, dreadful. Well, it was understandable. She'd been so attached to Her Ladyship, hadn't she?

Then one of the dogs – it could only be Charlie – had scampered downstairs and started scratching at the front door and whining. It wasn't locked, and Emma knew for a fact that she'd locked and bolted it herself. She'd guessed then. She'd thought she was going to faint. And, of course, when she'd opened the door to let Charlie out he'd led her straight to the poultry pen.

Her Ladyship must have thought she'd heard her fox again. It was the only explanation. The way she went on about it! As if that animal had a human intelligence concentrated on making her life a misery. All Emma could say (and she did, over and over again for weeks to come) was that old Lady Chandler had looked that peaceful and happy, lying on the muddy ground just outside the pen, wearing her late husband's blue and white pyjamas. And – wouldn't you know it? – she must have imagined the whole thing, because all her ducks and chickens were accounted for.

Arthur Stevens and three of his underlings conveyed Beatrice into the great house on a door removed from its hinges, and laid her out in the morning room where Felicity usually dealt with her correspondence. Later – after the undertakers had performed their mysterious ceremonies – she was transferred to an upstairs guests' bedroom facing north and known, for some reason, as the grey room (though it had been magnolia for years). There, she was dressed by sobbing Emma in a lacy white cotton nightgown she would have abhorred in life. It was a Chandler family tradition that a body must lie in the house until the funeral to allow friends and family to pay their respects.

A massive stroke, pronounced the doctor, no time even to think – but the servants whispered round the grey room as if there were a real risk of disturbance, and the house began to acquire an eerie hush.

It was all very strange for Seb, who could recall with painful clarity the raging incomprehension surrounding the deaths of his parents. After a tear-drenched funeral, he and his aunts and uncles and grandparents had repaired to the pub that had been his home to commemorate the lives so brutally snatched away with an abundance of alcohol, an ensuing hilarity that seemed as natural as the crying.

But the Chandler parents carried on more or less as if nothing had happened. They ate breakfast (Harry had two eggs and four rashers of bacon, followed by toast and marmalade, while skimming his newspaper which, as usual, he folded up at the crossword page for later). They behaved rather as if there'd been a minor disaster in the house or garden, which needed to be efficiently dealt with.

'You'll ring *The Times*, will you?' was Harry's first reference to the death – flat, without emotion – directed at his wife.

'Of course,' said Felicity, looking cool and competent, as if she'd already composed the obituary notice. ('Chandler, Beatrice Margaret, widow of the late Sir Hugo Chandler. Beloved mother and grandmother. Suddenly at home, Sunday, June 3rd. Flowers welcome. Funeral, Edgerton, June 10th'.)

'And you'll see to Hugo and Kathy?'

'I'm going to ring their schools now.'

Seb thought he could sort of understand Felicity's reaction – after all, she and her mother-in-law hadn't exactly got on, as he'd observed for himself. But he was deeply shocked by Harry's. After all, he'd been an only child. Seb thought he'd never in his life met such a cold man.

The two girls reacted more naturally.

After breakfast, tearful and bewildered, they retreated to the stables, which – since Alice's return – had become their private meeting place.

It transpired this was the first death they'd known, and they seemed to have great difficulty absorbing it. Seb sat on a haybale thinking how fortunate they were, while Eve clutched at his hand, needier than ever.

'We saw her last night!' exclaimed Alice, as if Beatrice had played a malicious trick on them.

'She looked fine!'

'I know!'

'She never stopped talking!' Eve told Seb with an incredulous look.

'I just wish I'd been nicer.'

'Me too.'

'You couldn't tell her anything . . .'

'And even if you had, she never listened . . .'

'No.'

'. . . although she was always trying to find out.'

Silence fell while they both thought about their grandmother and what she'd meant to them.

'But even if someone drives you mad,' said Alice plaintively, 'they can still know you love them, can't they?'

'Oh yes!'

'Honestly? You're sure?'

'Absolutely.'

More silence.

'I did,' said Alice, like a child.

'Me too,' Eve echoed miserably.

'Do we have to see her?'

'They'll expect us to.'

Alice shivered elaborately. 'I've never seen a dead body before.'

'At least it'll seem real then.'

Alice turned to Seb with a sad smile, including him in their tragedy. 'Have *you* ever seen a dead body, Seb?'

It was Harry who paid the first formal visit to Beatrice.

Strangely enough, given his famous squeamishness, he wasn't too upset by the prospect. After all, it was a family ritual, a rule of the house. He'd done it for his dead father also.

He slipped into the grey room about an hour after she'd been left on her own in its cold airlessness. The curtains had been drawn but, as they were unlined, sunlight poured through. All the normal Edgerton comforts had been removed. No ancient paperbacks beside the bed or china chamber pot beneath it, no rusty bottle of tomato juice or silver box of soggy biscuits. Beatrice had been prepared for a future without luxuries or sustenance and, for once, there were no complaints.

'And this is how we all end up,' Harry thought grimly, forcing himself to press his lips respectfully to his mother's marble-like forehead, without wincing. Robbed of the electricity of life, her body resembled a cold shell, a cast-off garment. That had been her argument for the existence of an afterlife: because if a body could change so drastically from one moment to the next, she'd tell the grandchildren, what else had activated it but a soul? And if that soul had left the body, there was more than a sporting chance it had gone elsewhere.

His mother had been a churchgoer, of course: a believer. But Harry (who also regularly prayed in his own chapel, but had seen men die in battle) thought it much more likely that a black and final curtain came down.

He seated himself on a chair beside her that had been provided. She smelt unnaturally of lavender (bags of which had been stuffed under the pillows). He considered touching her hands, which had been clasped piously across her chest, but decided it would be dishonest and also mawkish. They'd never been tactile and, besides, he'd done his duty by dead flesh.

He half expected his mother suddenly to start up a rant about the nightdress, the lavender bags, the isolation, the funeral arrangements. She wouldn't pay attention to anything he said, of course. She'd never listened. Sometimes he'd marvelled at her ability to maintain such an interfering presence in the family.

She'd never told him she loved him. But neither had she, to his face, condemned his adulteries, or more than obliquely referred to them. And yet he'd never doubted that her devotion was as savage as her disapproval. 'People like us don't talk,' thought Harry with a flash of self-knowledge brought on by the emotion of the occasion. But they knew what they meant, all right. People like them had a strange terror of getting too close, coupled with an unswerving faith in standards and certainties.

She'd never told his father she loved him either. He'd appeared, to Harry, to induce in her a mixture of irritation and boredom. But his death had devastated her for a time, and afterwards she'd become even more brusque and mannish, as if mimicking part of his personality was her way of clutching on to his essence.

Harry stared at his mother's bloodless slack face, her closed eyes already beginning to sink into their sockets.

It was his children who'd brought out the sensitive loving side of her nature: once a grandmother, she could at last relax and show it. With him (on whom so many expectations rested), she'd been brisk and strict. She'd sent him off to boarding school at the age of six and refused to take seriously his tear-stained letters begging to come home. When he was twelve and his Labrador attacked a visiting child, she'd had it put down, despite his desperate pleas and her own love of dogs. She'd constantly questioned his decisions regarding the estate, humiliating him.

But now he told himself that she'd done all of these things for the best of reasons.

A tear welled and he let it stay, proud he could feel such sorrow for the loss of his mother.

It was about ten minutes later that he suddenly became very thoughtful. His eyes widened and he pulled at his jaw.

He didn't know why it hadn't occurred to him straight away. It was to his credit, he told himself sentimentally. It meant he'd really loved his mother.

None of them – let alone Beatrice – had envisaged she'd die just yet. She was only seventy. Apart from the arthritis, she'd always been healthy and she, too, came from a family with a record for longevity.

Even so, for some time now – unable any longer to

ignore their financial problems – he'd been pleading with
her to visit the family solicitor (Dodd, Dodd and Hussey,
who'd always taken care of their affairs in not particularly
competent fashion). This Labour Government, thought
Harry, continuing to pull at his jaw. They appeared to loathe
people like him. ('Why?' thought Harry, honestly amazed. It
was people like him who honoured beauty and strove to
preserve it.) For people like him, the basic rate of income
tax was eight and threepence in the pound now, and surtax
meant liabilities fast approaching the 100 per cent mark. As
for death duties . . . They could reach the 80 per cent rate.
But if Beatrice had only arranged for the transfer of
Edgerton five years ago, then this fresh nightmare might
have been avoided, and he could honestly mourn her.

He knew why she'd procrastinated. It was all very well to
let him live in the house and manage the estate. It was even
acceptable – after a lot of disagreeableness – for her to
guarantee a bank loan for him. But making a transfer of
power legal and permanent meant giving up control, and
she'd wanted to hang on to that for as long as possible. It
was typical of her interfering nature. Of course it was
because she'd never listened.

Her death couldn't have come at a worse time. As it was,
he was stretched to the limit, what with these damned
Lloyds losses. But now he might have to sell some of the
land, after all (though prices were terrible). Or a picture,
God forbid. Either that, or take out a crippling mortgage
now Edgerton was finally his.

As he sat there, alternately pulling at his face and blinking
as he stared at his dead mother, an image came to him of
Alice's wedding. His beloved daughter was laughing and

beautiful in white satin, her new pearls glowing at her throat; and he was dancing blithely in the marquee while, all around, the best champagne flowed.

And then he remembered – as if seeing it in slow motion – Felicity's exquisite cake toppling and crashing to the ground.

Chapter Twenty-two

'What's she going to do now?'

'Dunno.' Eve knew very well how sulky and unattractive she must seem. She added briskly, hating the cynical sound of herself: 'I expect she'll get married again.'

'*What?*' Seb whacked at a spray of nettles, and she picked up – for the first time – the unspoken accusation: 'You're as bad as them.'

Armed with walking sticks from the collection kept in the great hall and wearing gumboots, they were exploring one of her favourite places. This was a water garden of great charm, hidden behind the lake, designed by Eve's great-grandmother, who had been a formidable horticulturalist.

But, because the garden was too waterlogged and dark for real flowers (and therefore uninteresting for Stevens and his underlings) it had been allowed to luxuriate in neglect. As summer approached, gunnera plants sprouted enormous stiff canopies, and the garden turned into a dark tunnel, its peace broken only by frogs.

'When I was about eight,' Eve told Seb's back, 'I planned to run away here.' She longed to reach out a hand and touch him but was sensible enough not to.

'Yeah?' He swiped irritably at an insect that had landed on his face.

'I thought I could live under one of these big plants and eat blackberries and hazelnuts.'

But he couldn't have been less interested in this charming anecdote. 'She's an intelligent girl.'

'What?' It came out all wrong. Eve never intended to sound so scornful.

'*I* geddit! Not allowed to be!'

'Seb, Alice didn't get one single O level!'

'Yeah?'

'She only ever wanted to get married!'

'And whose fault was that?'

She couldn't win. It seemed he'd appointed himself Alice's defender against the whole Chandler family, including her.

What he said next wasn't intended to be cruel.

The fact was, he felt powerless in the face of Eve's misery, and alarmed by her new neediness. He was beginning to realize that the relationship wasn't strong enough – on his side – to encompass them. But he'd returned to this unnerving place, hadn't he? He was tolerating her father's hostility, wasn't he? He told himself he'd done it just for her. He was pretty sure, too, that he was only trying to be constructive about Alice. But he didn't know the sisters' secret history and might just as well have aimed his stick at Eve, rather than at a clump of annoying weeds.

'It's not too late for her to get herself a proper education.'

*

Later, Eve sought out Alice in her bedroom once more.

'Alice?'

'Mmm?' This time, she was trying on one of her honeymoon numbers: a crisp confection of pink and white gingham with a frill down the front. 'D'you like this? I never wore it, actually. It's Tuffin and Foale.'

'Can we talk?'

'Course.' Alice turned this way and that in front of her mirror. The dress was very short. It demonstrated what very nice legs she possessed.

'Alice . . .'

'Mmm?' Alice stared at her reflection. She piled her hair up, golden arms like the handles on an exquisite jug. She frowned. (What could she possibly be frowning at?)

'Seb's going tomorrow.'

'I know,' said Alice comfortably. She pouted at herself. 'I'm *sick* of wearing jeans.'

'He's catching the twelve o'clock train . . .' Eve's voice was almost a sob.

This night would be their final one. She would creep into his cold bed, make love to him for the very last time – while pleading passionately but silently, just as she was doing with Alice now. Why couldn't she speak to Alice out loud? Was it for fear of what might be unleashed? An ugly (and unfair) diatribe about being too beautiful and charming? A torrent of vindictiveness about the first love that had been so effortlessly stolen away? Or was it because Alice, who knew her better than anyone in the world, ought to understand her feelings anyway?

'Yup,' said Alice, sounding as if she'd just come to a

satisfactory decision. She nodded briskly at her reflection and started to peel off the dress.

'Don't!' But Eve said it too softly for Alice to catch.

'Mmm?' – she appeared just as lazily unconcerned as before.

Then Eve understood that Alice was set on a course from which nothing could divert her. This dull certainty came from having known her all her life. At the same time, she comprehended that Alice hadn't even recognized it herself yet.

If she spoke out now, she knew exactly what Alice would say. 'What are you *talking* about, Eve? He's *your* boyfriend! He was only being nice!'

Alice would wear her pink and white dress tomorrow and look enchanting. And she would do it in all innocence.

And when the inevitable happened, she would never see it as betrayal.

It would be destiny. And who could argue with that?

Chapter Twenty-three

A week later, Beatrice's body was removed from the grey room. Still dressed in the white lace nightgown but minus her wedding ring (which would be kept for the next Chandler to marry), it was settled into an oak coffin whose lid was screwed down. Then the coffin was laid on the long table in the great hall in readiness for the funeral.

'Ah yes!' said Harry, observing the vases of scented lilies Felicity had arranged all round it.

The weather had turned very warm and consequently the grey room was less icy than usual and, although many more lavender bags were stuffed under the pillows, paying last respects to Beatrice became increasingly fleeting. By the end of the week, visitors breathed through their mouths as they peeped round the door at a pinched dusky-skinned old foreigner with a strangely prominent nose.

'It's not right,' muttered Mrs Briggs, who had been with the family for thirty years. She battled with her uneasiness in her own way, baking all day long, overlaying the sour air with fragrances of deep-brown scones and black-frilled cupcakes.

Alice said unhappily, 'People are meant to *want* to see Gran, aren't they?'

There'd been months to plan Alice's wedding in the chapel and engage a talented organist to play carefully chosen selections from Bach and Handel. But for Beatrice's hastily arranged funeral (when the weather finally broke), the chapel had to make do with Mr Barnes from the village, pumping frantically away as if in training for legging it back to his dank cottage and aggressive wife. It was decided to rely on stalwarts he'd had plenty of practice with: 'Oh Happy Band of Pilgrims', followed by Psalm 15 and 'Jerusalem the Golden', with '*Nunc Dimittis*' to end.

Harry made a mental note to start planning his own funeral now. As he waited for the chapel to fill up, gravely handsome in his dark suit, he pictured Edgerton shuttered and silent, the chapel heaving with the muffled sobs of pretty women in black.

In family tradition, Beatrice's coffin would be carried from the great house to the chapel on the shoulders of Chandler men – in this case, Harry and Hugo (who'd got leave from school) and two strapping young cousins, one of whom was in the navy. 'Small steps,' said Harry, who'd learnt from performing the same service for his father. 'And if you feel it start to slip, for God's sake halt.'

As invitations were never issued for funerals, one could not be sure who would turn up. Besides family and genuinely grieving old friends, there were bound to be some whose main motive was to socialize; plus the odd enemy, self-righteous if not actually gloating (like the master of the hunt whom Beatrice had recently and very publicly chastised for failing to run down her fox).

Felicity thought, admiring her arrangements of laurel and white lilies, 'Now Harry is head of the family,' and longed suddenly for grandchildren to compensate for the missing generation.

But, looking at Alice, seated in the family pew with Eve one side, Kathy the other, she remembered that she was already a grandmother of a sort. She'd never discussed the abortion with Alice, but had privately dwelt on it a great deal. She was confused and upset by her reaction. Alice was grown up, had been married, and would almost certainly marry again and have more children. However, she saw her as irreparably damaged. She loved her no less – perhaps even more – but all her ambition for her beautiful daughter had fallen away.

Not that any of it seemed to affect Alice, who was cheerfully spending most of her time in the stables. She was in far better form than Eve, who seemed even more miserable than when she'd first been sent down from Oxford. 'Beatrice would have tried to find out why,' thought Felicity, pressing her lips together as she remembered her mother-in-law. Beatrice would have asked Eve if she intended to sit around for ever crying over spilt milk, and demanded why that young man of hers wasn't doing more to cheer her up. She might have added, also: 'What's going on between you two? I *won't* have strife among my grandchildren.'

*

Eve exchanged small smiles with Alice as she passed her a hymnbook and thought savagely, 'I hate her, I hate her, I hate her!'

Alice wasn't just guileless, she was tactless to the point of cruelty.

'Do you honestly think Seb meant it – telling me I ought to take my O levels again? He says it's all about confidence. Imagine it! Me!'

And now Pa had told her she could no longer sit around Edgerton all day reading books and depressing everyone (as he'd most forcefully put it). For some reason, marriage didn't enter the picture. He'd decided she must be put on a typing course, with a view to finding herself a suitable job. She'd brought disgrace on the family (though he didn't spell this out). More to the point, her shaming had coincided with his financial problems.

Harry asked: 'Where's the Centipede?'

Hugo looked at him blankly.

'Your cousin Cecil,' said Harry, his irritability only just kept under control. As he recognized some mourners, he flashed his legendary smile.

'Who?'

With his unique gift for managing to appear simultaneously menacing and charming, Harry hissed: 'I have reminded you at least HALF A DOZEN times not to forget about the Centipede.' He caught sight of Alice, sweetly pensive in the front row, and – as usual – felt miserable and bewildered, and consequently even crosser with Hugo. 'It was ALL you were required to do today – besides helping to carry your GRANDMOTHER'S

COFFIN. I shouldn't have thought it was TOO MUCH to ask. Now, WHAT HAVE YOU DONE WITH HIM? I need to know NOW because' – Harry consulted his watch – 'IN LESS THAN FIVE MINUTES THIS FUNERAL IS GOING TO START.'

There was panic in Hugo's eyes.

'WHAT HAVE YOU DONE WITH HIM?' Harry nodded pleasantly at the Farquhars. Good of them to have come, in the circumstances. They'd even brought Edward, he noticed. But, after all, the two families had known each other for years.

Suddenly Hugo looked extraordinarily relieved. He said: 'Oh, I um, actually . . .'

'WHERE IS HE?'

'Downstairs loo,' Hugo admitted, his cheeks dusky pink.

'Go and fetch him – NOW!'

Hugo scuttled off and, a few minutes later, returned – still avoiding his father's eye and clutching a small urn.

'Thank you so very much,' said Harry extremely sarcastically, before tucking it under his arm.

As a member of what Harry always called 'the pretender branch' of the family (who'd hung on to the name through the female line), Cecil Whitby Chandler – otherwise known as the Centipede – had no right, of course, to his own space in Edgerton's cemetery. But, cornered by his widow, Harry had promised that when the next minor burial occurred (i.e. of a woman), the urn and its ashes would be discreetly tucked in, with an aside from the vicar.

As it was, Cousin Cecil had been waiting for a mere six months and – on this solemn occasion – his widow was quietly delighted. It was true that once the gravestone was erected, it would proclaim only Beatrice's life and qualities; Cousin Cecil would be like a lover hiding beneath the sheets. But the important thing was that – when it was too late to matter to him – he'd joined the company of the Edgerton Chandlers.

And now Beatrice lay under an enormous wreath of white roses as extraordinary things were said about her. She'd been a woman of deep faith, who'd lived by her principles and placed supreme importance on the family. She'd been an excellent mother and doting grandmother; a good and generous friend; a fair employer; a lover of nature and animals.

The packed chapel listened as the vicar spoke sonorously, every so often consulting his notes. He was an amiable moron in Harry's opinion. But, then, according to him, the church was a refuge for middle-class dimwits, and the even dimmer went into the armed forces.

The piercing whistle of a hearing aid soared suddenly in a cold and musty pause.

It was the undoing of Eve. One moment, she was sunk in the usual despair. The next, hysteria had descended like hiccups: horribly inappropriate, impossible to shake off. It was catching, too. Within minutes, Alice started trembling and snorting. Each time one of them managed, with a supreme effort, to stop, the other would re-start. It was no longer funny. They were sisters in agony, united once more.

The family had noticed. Not Hugo, of course: he was always in a dream. Kathy was smiling politely like a grown-up, tolerant but puzzled, eager to join in but quite unable to see the joke. Ma was looking very concerned, and Pa was getting pink, which meant he was losing his temper.

'Think of Champion getting hit by the car,' Alice told herself desperately. 'Think of that dreadful day in the woods with Marcus . . .' But none of this was of any help at all.

It was only when — mustering every ounce of gravitas — the vicar paused for an alarmingly long moment, glancing down at her over his spectacles from his pulpit, that Alice finally regained control. And, once she'd stopped laughing, so did Eve.

'Dear Gran,' thought Alice, wiping the tears from her cheeks, 'I'm going to miss her so much.'

Next to her, Eve was crying in earnest now, as if the dreadful laughing had temporarily released all the pain and bitterness and jealousy that had been bottled up these past few weeks.

Tea had been laid on at Edgerton, with some excellent sherry set out in a corner of the great hall for later.

But, feeling the usual post-funeral need to celebrate being alive, the mourners quickly gravitated towards the alcohol, and very soon stopped reminiscing about Beatrice.

Eve tried to look neutral as she listened to endless well-meaning people tell her what a shame it was she'd decided to give up on Oxford. It surely wasn't too late for her to change her mind? 'Do think again!' she was urged, and believed she could see the thought ballooning: 'Remember, you're not beautiful, like Alice.' They promised her she would not regret it and added, as if bringing out an original thought, 'Remember, nobody can ever take your education away from you.'

The old thought it gave pleasure to show an interest. They mistook politeness for deference, and saw confidence where it was in painfully short supply, and missed distress signals. They'd forgotten what being young was all about.

Eve froze suddenly as she listened to Alice, nearby.

'Is your husband here?'

'Over there, by the sandwiches.'

'I see his parents have come too.'

'Yes. But, um, actually we're getting divorced.'

'I beg your pardon?'

'We're getting divorced.'

'That's what I thought you said! But you've only just got married!'

'Mmm . . .'

'Well! I don't know what to say! Except – I'm very sorry.'

'Don't be. It's for the best. It was a huge mistake. I've decided I'm going to try and go to university.'

Harry murmured to Felicity, 'Who's that feller over there?'

'Who?'

'Helping himself to my sherry. Think he's a gate-crasher?'

'Sorry?'

'Keeps looking at *you* . . .'

'Oh, I see where you mean!' exclaimed Felicity very casually. 'That's Johnny Tyson!'

'Who?'

'Johnny Tyson. Don't you remember?'

'No,' said Harry.

'From before we were married. You *must* have met him!'

'No.'

'Well, I hardly know him. But – come and be introduced.'

It had been Johnny's idea to turn up. Though Felicity was taken aback, she'd found it impossible to say so.

'Anyone can come to a funeral,' he'd pointed out.

'I suppose . . .'

'Presumably there'll be lots of people there.'

'Oh yes! Mama was very popular, in the county.'

'I'll be your secret support. And you know I'd love to meet your children.'

He'd seen the funeral as an opportunity to move their relationship on a notch. It was time. They'd been having an affair since the beginning of the year. Besides, she was being very publicly humiliated by her husband. Also, Johnny wanted to see Harry for himself. It was high time he looked into her world.

He'd not anticipated how very unhappy it would make him.

He'd never seen Edgerton before. He'd expected beauty and grandeur, but its magical perfection left him feeling assaulted and almost invisible. It was the most wonderful place he'd ever been in, with an extraordinarily peaceful atmosphere, and he asked himself miserably why anyone – especially Felicity – would ever choose to leave it.

Similarly, he'd not anticipated the full force of Harry's charm. Johnny thought he'd never seen such an attractive man. He watched women bridle and glow as Harry came into their orbit and – although Felicity made real efforts to maintain contact (catching his eye every so often, unobtrusively touching his arm as she effected introductions) – he couldn't help observing with anguish what an intrinsic part of another couple she was.

He thought that he'd never in his life felt so lowly and excluded. And then he reminded himself that Felicity looked glowing and confident because of him. For all his overpowering attraction, Harry had had the reverse effect on her. Feeling a little better, he wondered how Harry could be so blind as not to notice the transformation.

The next moment, he was flung into despair as Harry drawled, 'Felicity makes all the arrangements. Don't you, darling?'

He'd been mad to come here: it might even be the end. She feared it too. He could see it in every discreetly mournful glance.

When Mrs Briggs approached Harry asking for a quiet word, he assumed she wanted to warn him the sherry was running out.

'Plenty more Fino in the pantry, Briggs,' he told her before she could even begin, and was about to turn back to the vicar with the expression (half-closed eyes, fixed smile) he was convinced hid his boredom and impatience.

'No, sir,' said Mrs Briggs. 'Arthur Stevens is here.' She said it quietly, so the vicar wouldn't hear.

Harry looked impatient, almost amused. 'This is my mother's funeral, Briggs!'

'He knows that, sir.'

'Well?'

'He says it won't wait.'

Harry studied Mrs Briggs. There was something sly about her, he decided. For all her anxious obsequiousness, he couldn't help feeling that this old servant knew more than she should.

And there was more to come. Mrs Briggs moved closer to Harry's ear. 'He's gone into your study, sir.'

'What?'

Mrs Briggs stared at him with what certainly appeared to be similar astonishment. 'Said he was going to sit there for ever if need be.' Her protruberant brown eyes were very innocent.

Before Harry could react, he was approached by an excited gaggle of Whitby Chandlers. 'Can we show the children the pictures, Harry?'

'Of course! Feel free!'

He heard their voices fade away as they disappeared in the direction of the big drawing room: 'There's a Reynolds that's quite remarkable in its way, though not top rank . . . It's been in the family since we bought it for a song . . .'

The cheek of it made Harry's lips twitch, even though he was becoming increasingly nervous.

He'd a very good idea what Stevens wanted to talk to him about, why he'd taken the extraordinary step of bursting into his private domain. Harry had tried to put the matter to the back of his mind while the funeral was going on – but it had rumbled away uneasily, which was another reason why he'd been so irritable with Hugo.

He had not mentioned it to Felicity. The thought of doing so was very painful. He hated inflicting pain, he told himself, always had – choosing to forget that, more crucially, he couldn't endure being hurt himself.

He looked for her in the crowd. There she was, talking to that perfectly amiable chap she'd assured him they both knew. Something about their body language made Harry all of a sudden frown. He was like a seasoned hound catching the scent in a place where no fox had ever before been seen.

Felicity said, 'Sorry. This is hateful for you.'

'You're here, aren't you?'

'I think he suspects.'

'How could he?'

'I don't know . . .'

'What?' He moved closer to her, breathing in her perfume. 'I adore you. Do you know that?'

'Mmm.' Anybody watching Felicity might have assumed from her composed reaction that she was discussing her late mother-in-law.

'I'm completely and utterly besotted. I'm your slave. You absolutely have to come and live with me.'

She smiled faintly at him, but said nothing. It was always like this. He'd try and push the relationship on a notch, and she'd clam up. Her way of indicating she wasn't ready yet.

'Nice children,' he backtracked, and was rewarded with a grateful beam. She adored her children. He made a resolution to seek out Hugo and ask him about school. He would make all of them like him.

In the distance, he saw Harry surrounded, smiling languidly.

'How many of his women are here now?'

She always blinked when she was taken aback. 'Some,' she admitted with a social smile for the benefit of anyone watching.

'How many?'

A quick nervous count. 'Six, seven . . .'

'Seven!'

'I *think* so . . .'

'Which means there are probably even more. You know he's a monster.' (But, strangely, it didn't tally with what he could see: Harry attending with infinite courtesy to one woman after another.)

A sweet pursing of her lips was all he received by way of reply. She wouldn't admit it – especially not here.

'*Seven ex-mistresses at his own mother's funeral!*' he insisted, revving himself up.

'Don't, Johnny!' she whispered.

'*Here in your house!*'

'Please don't!'

Immediately, he said, 'I'm sorry.'

'It's all right.'

But he couldn't stop. 'He's making a public fool of you, Flick! How much more are you going to take?'

They were very close to each other now – too close. He could see a tremor start in her left eyelid: evidence, he believed, of terrible turmoil. Johnny thought: 'I should make up her mind for her,' and decided that, in one moment, he'd seize hold of her and kiss her in front of all these people. He would! He'd create a *fait accompli*. And then he'd take care of her, for the rest of her life. As the resolution took hold, he drained his drink, looked round for more, for courage.

'Eve.'

'Edward.'

'Excellent address, I thought.'

'Mmm.'

'She'll be much missed,' said Edward, who was well aware Beatrice had considered him an amiable fool.

He was very pale, thinner, too, as he leant heavily on the stick that had replaced his crutches. Why had he felt it necessary to come? Why had he chosen to inflict more torment on himself?

As Eve looked into his unhappy wandering eyes, she understood it was because the funeral had offered one last chance to see Alice. He couldn't resist, even if it was to overhear her telling people it was their marriage (and not the affair with Marcus) that had been the biggest error of her life.

'Oh well,' he muttered in a helpless hopeless sort of way.

'Yes,' Eve murmured, knowing precisely what was meant.

Then she said, 'Excuse me . . .' because she could no longer bear to be in the company of someone who reminded her so much of herself.

As Harry paced the long hall, on his way to a confrontation with the father of the young girl he'd been having such a scandalous affair with, he felt that, with each step further away from the noise of his guests, he left behind something priceless and fundamental to his happiness.

As if looking into the future, he saw his house stripped of its ancient tapestries and marvellous paintings and precious furniture, and – even worse – all of his family flinching away from him, like Alice.

His legs turned to jelly and his heart started racing so that he was forced to sink on to an ancient carved chest. He tried to breathe evenly, but was quite unable to. His head ached as never before: he felt as if one half of his brain was being rhythmically squeezed.

As he crouched on the chest, lonelier than he'd ever been, he heard the sound of laughter in the distance and the pounding of feet as somebody – one of his children? – ran lightly up the long staircase behind him. None of them, back there celebrating his mother's funeral, was aware of the shadows he could sense closing in all around. Dying must be like this, thought Harry, who had seen enough people die.

Through his own arrogance and folly, he was being brought down: reduced from a rich man to a poor one, in every sense of the word. And here was the final ignominy: one of his servants bursting into his inner sanctum.

'If only I could go back in time,' Harry thought. He knew exactly when it had all started to change and go wrong.

He saw himself, less than a year before, sitting in his study, expecting his beloved turtledove, knowing why she needed to talk to him, and also what she really wished him to say. Why had he failed her? 'Did I *want* her to marry a man she couldn't love?' he thought in a rare and painful moment of self-examination.

'I've been like someone behind glass,' Harry told himself, and knew, with dull certainty, that, now he felt himself to be falling through the glass, he would bleed as never before.

AFTERWARDS

2002

Chapter Twenty-four

She started hearing it when she was halfway down the drive: the sound of many dogs, somewhere in the distance. But the dogs never appeared in the old rampaging gang and the barking continued: spasmodic, oddly hollow.

There were more tricks to come. As she entered the half-open front door and heard the clatter of plates from a faraway kitchen, she once more became a sharp-eyed observer, a baffled spectator of a performance in a foreign tongue. But now the stage had changed and the furniture was scuffed and dull and the flower displays cheerfully haphazard.

She'd asked the taxi driver to drop her at the gates so that, unheralded, she could arrive with an advantage. But she'd forgotten about the weather and failed to pack an umbrella and, to her mortification, she was soaked.

One of these days they'd learn to their cost that they shouldn't leave their doors unlocked. Didn't they know that organized bands of thieves had taken to targeting grand country houses? As for letting their children explore the woods and fields!

'I could be living here,' she thought, and smiled at the fancy. You were ruled by temperament. She hadn't changed.

Right on cue, her mobile sang in the neat confines of her handbag. Voicemail from the one she loved: a promise speeding through space and time that though (naturally) he could not be with her, she was in his thoughts. 'I'll listen to it later,' she decided, because more often than not he disappointed and just now she needed reassurance. Instead, she imagined all the messages in his deep lingering voice that might be waiting for her in that little aluminium oblong: 'I am lost, my darling . . . I cannot live without you . . .'

Cheered, she returned to the present and, setting down her suitcase in the hall, began noting changes. There were discreet night storage heaters everywhere, fraying carpet on the grand staircase. There was a scattering of toys: a skateboard lying on its side, a jumble of Lego on a marble-topped sideboard, a big unfinished crossword puzzle on the floor. She smiled as she saw all this. She thought she was looking forward to the children.

'Alice!'

She'd been taken unawares, after all, and, for a moment, felt very vulnerable.

'I don't believe this!'

Alice shook her head. She didn't either.

It was strange, hugging, as they were expected to. Each felt so different now. Boyish Eve had acquired the texture of a badly inflated lilo; voluptuous Alice was whip-thin.

Pulling away, properly looking, the differences were shocking.

Alice thought, 'That frumpy old dress! And flipflops! But she doesn't seem bothered.'

Eve thought, 'She's still beautiful . . . but changed. I never ever thought Alice could look tough.' She said, making a face, 'Sorry about the rain.'

'Not your fault!' said Alice, touching her hair defensively.

'We'd planned to have the party in the garden . . .'

'And you've got dogs!'

They went on staring at each other.

'You look really well, Eve.'

Eve made a face, thinking, 'I know what "well" means.' But she responded gallantly, 'And you look a million dollars, Alice.'

But the past had started to muscle in on them, and – remembering the circumstances of their long separation – they almost immediately moved away from each other.

'Where is everyone?' murmured Eve, looking everywhere but at Alice. She bellowed at the top of her voice: 'Children!' Then she beamed. Back-up was on its way.

There were four of them.

'This is Joe.'

'Joe,' Alice repeated, smiling at the tall gangly boy in fraying cut-off jeans who ducked his head, not meeting her gaze beyond the first quick curious glance. He had something of his father, she decided: though not enough to have guessed.

'And Milla.'

An earnest little girl in glasses, much like her mother had once been.

'And Alex.'

Alex very much resembled his father. As she stared, fascinated, he turned his head sharply away, like a clockwork toy.

'And this is Milo, my baby!'

Milo was definitely the looker of the family, with reddish curls and sleepy blue eyes. (*None of the grandchildren are like Pa*, Ma had once written. Was there regret or relief that Pa's lethal charisma had vanished for ever?)

'I have some gifts in my bag,' said Alice, and the younger children brightened momentarily before disappointment set in. Alice's handbag was very compact.

Eve asked them: 'Where's Dad?'

'Dad?' echoed Joe, seemingly mystified as to whom she could be referring.

'Dad,' Eve confirmed, making an amused face at her sister. 'Remember how Hugo used to be?' she seemed to be implying.

'Uh, Dad's been trying to, uh, get the music system to work.'

'I hope he's not bust it!' cried Eve in alarm.

'Here's Daddy!' exclaimed Alex.

And here he was at last: anxious and awkward to be meeting his first wife again, after all these years – relying on the family for support, just as Eve had done.

'Welcome,' he told Alice, with a dutiful careful kiss.

It was a triumph to get to eighty, they'd told Felicity.

'But it's ancient!' In the mornings, she'd sit in dismay at her dressing table. Who on earth was that puffy old thing? She'd blot her out with powder, re-write her with lipstick.

'No it isn't!' (They had an answer to everything.) People regularly reached a hundred.

'So why celebrate?' Felicity had countered triumphantly.

Well, okay then – but it would be a wonderful excuse for a party.

'Who would come?' Felicity had asked, with her troubled, mock innocent look.

Everyone!

'Who?'

Neighbours, friends . . . But actually, they said carefully, they'd been thinking more of family.

'Who?' repeated Felicity, looking scared and vulnerable.

Oddly enough, it was Eve who'd brought the name out into the open.

'Alice?' It was like using a new word. Then Felicity had stared anxiously at her eldest child. Never forget: beauty is to be feared as well as idolized.

This time she'd come: the daughter and sister and aunt who'd disappeared one day. Why had she never returned? It was a mystery to the grandchildren. Alice would come from California for her mother's eightieth birthday party, which might be her last (they'd gently pressure her). And, because of the significance, they'd hold it at Mossbury Park. It would be a pleasure to have a real party, as in the old days.

But it wasn't like the old days, of course. There wasn't the staff, or the money. More than anything, there wasn't the confidence.

Edward and Eve were considered lucky to have retained his family home. (Indeed, they often found themselves apologizing for it.) But much ingenuity was needed: bed and breakfasts in the summer months, leasing off land in short-term contracts to the beleaguered local farmers for grazing.

Occasionally, if they were lucky, they got a film. (Only last month, a location manager had turned up on spec. Another television adaptation of *Jane Eyre* was in the pipeline, he'd informed them; and Mossbury Park, with its air of portentous gloom, might do for Thornfield Hall, exteriors only.) But what kept regular money dribbling in was the kennels. You could charge almost ten pounds a day for a large dog, and word got round.

No wonder that, with so many children and no servants, the marble floors were scuffed, and the grand furniture dull. The formal gardens had become a jungle: the sharp lines of Lord Farquhar's topiary grown out like a long-neglected hairstyle. The place was an albatross, a white elephant, a poisoned chalice – you name it. But it had also become something it never was in the grand days: a relaxed family home.

Tea was in the kitchen, where Lord and Lady Farquhar had seldom ventured. But by popular request the green baize door separating the servants' quarters had been retained. The children loved the way it swung furrily to and fro. It was becoming very stained and wobbly.

They ambled around like grazing animals, plucking at a packet of crisps here, a fruit yoghurt there.

'I do wish you'd sit down,' Eve complained. She smiled at Alice.

'Bad for the digestion,' pronounced Edward, tucking into his second flapjack. He, too, had become stout, but it seemed to Alice that age had added distinction and becoming a paterfamilias had removed his dithering edge.

She didn't eat a thing. She'd changed from her elegant

two-piece and high heels into a fuschia tracksuit and trainers, and applied matching lipstick. She intended to go for a run, she informed them all, to try and get rid of the jet lag. The children stole covert curious glances at her as she said it, as shy as if she were famous. Aunt Alice, the lovely luscious star of the photograph albums. Had she really been married to their father? She'd brought a delicious smell into their home: a sexy mix of lemon and musk. Milo muttered, unheard, into his mug: 'Beetle.'

'So,' said Eve, sitting so her shoulder almost touched her husband's. 'How's life over there?'

'Fabulous!' said Alice very enthusiastically. There were crumbs everywhere, she noticed, and dirty finger marks on the doors. 'It has it all!'

Edward and Eve were silent.

Alice said: 'You should come! Do! It's a different life.'

'Depends on the old bat, doesn't it?' said Edward after a thoughtful moment, and Alice would have frowned if the freshly paralysed area above her eyebrows had permitted it.

But Eve smiled as he slapped her on her meaty thigh. It was obvious to Alice that they were content together.

'Maybe,' she said, 'if we can ever get away. But who'd take care of the animals? You must look at our horses, Alice.'

Alice ran in practised athletic fashion down the drive and, with each neat kick of her heels, felt panic building. It was all proving to be far more distressing than she'd envisaged. And somewhere beyond the encircling boundary of woods and fields lay Edgerton. As she thought of it – the tolling bell in the clocktower, the rise and fall of the doves, the battlements turning golden with sun – her heart started racing.

Why had she come? Why? There'd been an excellent excuse – at last – for never ever jumping on a plane again. It wasn't as if she needed more anguish, either. She could feel the composure peeling away. She was so alone. It was unfair, at a time like this.

She looked at the plain Cartier gold watch the one she loved had given her to commemorate a secret anniversary. It was noon back home. And, though she hadn't yet listened to his message, on impulse she dialled his number.

'I'm breaking the rules,' she thought.

He wasn't there, of course, just a recording of his voice. For the first time, Alice noticed the certainty in it. Arrogance, actually.

'This is Scott Farley's voicemail. 'Fraid I'm unable to take your call right now, but please leave your name, number and message and I'll get back to you.'

'It's me,' said Alice in a little voice.

And, as the patient tape waited, six thousand miles away, something snapped.

'I never ever stop being supportive to you. But I need support too. I need it now, Scott. I feel like a prisoner in a box, waiting for you to open it. I have rights too. I do!'

Alice still held her little phone against her ear. She felt dazed, already apprehensive.

But then she remembered the automated female voice that had spoken before the tone.

'If you wish to re-record your message, press "one" at any time. Or press "two" for other options.'

Alice seemed to come to her senses. Did she have options? She thought not. She pressed 'one' on her phone and, after a moment, spoke again – this time sounding positive and upbeat.

'It's Alice! Just to tell you I've arrived safely. It's . . . strange to be back. Lots to tell you, darling. Miss you loads.' As an afterthought, she said: 'Hope your meeting about the merger went well. Longing to hear about it.'

Eve said: 'Who's going to feed the animals?'

'Let's do it together once we've finished here.'

She and Edward were making canapés. Eve had found a good two-for-the-price-of-one deal in smoked salmon at the local Safeway. Edward found it soothing to press cream cheese into spongy slices of brown bread, pat the irregular pieces of salmon into jigsaw squares and finish them off with a squeeze of lemon and a sprinkle of cayenne pepper. He loved the business of family life. He was good at sharing, too.

'How do you think she is?' Eve asked very casually.

'Alice?'

Eve didn't answer, but he was used to her silences.

Finally he pronounced: 'Poor girl's nothing but skin and bone.'

Eve looked at him for a long time before asking: 'Do you think she's happy?'

'Happy,' he echoed as if it were a foreign word.

'I'm so lucky,' Eve thought. 'Lucky lucky lucky! But I haven't the slightest idea what my husband is really thinking. Am I crazy to feel afraid?'

*

'Why am feeling like this?' Even as Alice asked the question, she anticipated the response.

'Why do you think, Alice?'

'I don't know!' It was such relief to talk to somebody who knew her well. She continued rapidly into her phone: 'Of course it's being back after all this time.'

'Thirty years, isn't it?'

'More!' said Alice excitedly. 'Sorry! Is this too early for you?' Her heart was still racing, but talking definitely made it better. So did the cigarette. It was the first time she'd smoked in ten years. For some reason, she'd found herself buying a carton in duty free. 'And being so close to Edgerton! It's bound to be upsetting, isn't it?'

'Oh yes, the past has great power over us . . .'

'It's got to be a bit about Eve and Edward, hasn't it?' Alice leant against a tree and looked down at her smooth brown calves. She was very fit.

'Does it disturb you seeing them together?'

'No!' exploded Alice. After a moment, she went on thoughtfully, 'I'm glad for them. But he seems so different now . . . And I can't help thinking . . .'

The call was very expensive. There was no time for proper reflection.

'It's weird! It was me that wanted a life in the country with lots of children and animals!'

Another costly silence.

'What are you saying?' Alice asked anxiously.

'Nothing, Alice.'

Alice swallowed. 'I've no regrets,' she confirmed. 'I've a wonderful life. It's just that . . .'

'Mmm?'

'Nothing.'

Alice thought of that room six thousand miles away: its beige walls, its comfortable but characterless furniture, its lack of paintings or books, its box of tissues on the table. She thought of the hours and hours of talk, stacked up like piles of box files – the impossibility of ever properly explaining Edgerton and the family.

'We spoke about going back . . .'

'Yes.'

'We decided it would be a good opportunity – at this stage of your analysis – to confront some of the conflicts of your childhood.' As always, a little question in the voice – as if, even after all this time, Alice might be stubbornly withholding a crucial piece of the puzzle.

Alice wondered what Dr Sayre's own childhood had been like. After ten years, she knew very little about her. She was a chunky woman of about forty-five with wiry black hair and no wedding ring. She didn't look as if she could ever have had a father like Pa.

'The children are adorable,' said Alice. 'Really . . .' Her voice tailed away and another long silence fell.

'Remember, Alice, you had the choice.'

'Yes,' Alice agreed. She continued in a lifeless voice: 'It's so tiring going on being angry.'

It was Kathy who'd been detailed to collect Felicity. Eve was busy preparing for the party. Hugo, the son, was not expected to do anything.

As she walked up the overgrown path, wet plants assaulting her new pair of tights, Kathy felt exhausted, as usual, and a little silly. When was the last time she'd dressed herself up and put on lipstick and mascara?

She opened the unlocked front door and winced at an odour coming from the kitchen.

From upstairs, came her mother's quavery old voice: 'Is that you, Kathy?'

Putting it on, thought Kathy affectionately. Ma was tough as old boots. She'd better be.

'Yes, Ma!' she shouted (she suspected her mother was becoming deaf). She thought: 'Only fifteen minutes late! I can't help it if a crisis blew up as I was leaving.'

Then her mother appeared in full party fig, conquering the smell of forgotten food with a blast of Rive Gauche, her tabby Posy twining Salome-like round her ankles. A long loose dark-blue silk jersey dress – a catalogue success – was wrapped with a beautiful gold shawl from the old days. Encircling her tiered neck was a nice silver filigree pendant from Greece: a present from Hugo. She wore unsuitable shoes, with heels, and the wrong coloured foundation applied in a dim light without a magnifying mirror, with a flourish of a clotted old powder puff to set it.

'Just a mo,' said Kathy, dabbing at her mother's earlobes where, for an unaccountable reason, blobs of orange had lodged.

'Oh!' exclaimed Felicity, looking helpless, staring into her daughter's eyes and thinking, 'She looks tired, poor love. I wish I could afford to give her a holiday.'

'It's fine now,' Kathy assured her.

'Is it really?'

'You look beautiful.'

Felicity's eyelids fluttered, pleasure battling disbelief. 'Do I, darling?'

'Smile at me, Ma . . .'

Felicity obediently stretched her lips. Just as Kathy had feared, there was lipstick on her teeth.

'Use this Kleenex,' she ordered, as Felicity rummaged for her best lace handkerchief.

She wasn't finished yet.

'Are those shoes going to be okay?'

'Why ever not?'

'You might trip. Then where'd we all be?'

After a bit of persuasion (and last-minute anxiety about her cat) Felicity set off for the party in her muddy old walking shoes, with her high heels in a Tesco carrier bag.

Hannah and Imogen sat in the back of the car looking embarrassed and brazen and vulnerable, colts in party mode. Imogen was hoping her grandmother wouldn't notice her burgundy highlights.

'What pretty girls!' exclaimed Felicity with pleasure. But it was Hannah, of course, who was the beauty. Darling Imogen was the clever one.

'Watch that chili con carne,' Kathy reminded them sharply. Then she leant across her mother to fasten her safety belt.

Felicity had a surprise for them all. She might be an old crumbly now, as Hugo liked to say, but she could still keep secrets. Oh yes!

Then her heart began to beat faster at the thought of the reunion. She turned in her seat and whispered to the two adolescents as if telling them for the very first time: 'Your grandfather once said that compared with your aunt Alice all the other girls looked like black beetles.'

Chapter Twenty-five

Time made such a stew of things. These days, Felicity could remember the flavours of humiliation and sorrow and happiness, but less and less often their contexts. She'd muddle up who'd said what and when, and increasingly invent, and choose to forget the greatest of traumas.

Thus, the period that had preceded the final surrender of Edgerton was much of a blur now. Perhaps it was a compensation for growing old. But why did it still torment her so? She'd pick over the past, increasingly needing an audience.

'He seemed to think we were invulnerable,' she'd tell her daughters, sounding as wondering as a child.

'He was thoroughly spoilt,' responded Eve, the un-favourite, very sharply.

'I'm talking about the two of us, darling. Pa and me.'

But Eve was right, of course. For four hundred years, Chandlers had dwelt in their golden palace, pampered by servants, taking beauty and peace and prosperity as a right.

'We didn't know about the outside world,' complained Felicity, who, until she was almost fifty years old, had never cleaned a room or cooked a meal or even washed up.

In some confused, nostalgic moods Felicity would even doubt that her one extramarital affair had happened. She must have been truly devoted to Harry: why else had she suffered the humiliation? But if she had loved him so greatly what superman could have caused her to betray him? Then she'd remember kindness – as pure and enriching as beauty; the whiff of peppermint; and once, to her astonishment, a pink frilly apron.

For this formerly most private of women, old age brought cautious indiscretion.

When Eve and Kathy were married, with children of their own, a cosy afternoon prompted the daring confidence: 'I have to tell you, darlings, that, for all his virtues, your father wasn't *always* the most faithful of men.'

'Of course he wasn't!' Eve had spluttered, laughing.

'You knew?'

'Ma!'

'But I never said anything!'

'Oh, Ma!'

'What, darling?' Felicity was honestly puzzled.

'It was so obvious!'

'Not then, surely?'

'When I thought about it afterwards,' said Eve with a shrug.

Kathy had smiled knowingly, too – as if, even as the youngest, she'd been party to her mother's anguish.

Felicity felt mortified all over again.

There was worse to come. 'And there was the gardener's

daughter?' – Eve changing a statement into a question in the same irritating way as her children.

Felicity stared at her eldest daughter, shocked and also imploring.

'I heard Mrs Briggs talking about it once,' Kathy confirmed. She added, making a face, 'Imagine! We had a cook!'

But Ma was gazing into the fire. For all they knew, she hadn't heard a word.

When Arthur Stevens came storming up to the great house on the day of Beatrice's funeral, it was the beginning of the end of Harry's life.

He found his head gardener sitting in stained blue overalls in his sacrosanct green velvet chair in his study, muddy boots resting on the tiger skin.

It was obvious that Stevens was drunk. But Harry didn't admonish him. 'Ah, Stevens!' was all he said, with the familiar lethal courtesy. 'You wanted to see me?' Then he helped himself to a large Amontillado and might even have raised his eyebrows as if humorously dismissing the possibility that Stevens needed one too.

The effect was such that, just for a moment, Stevens looked appalled to find himself taking such liberties. He shook his head in disbelief; even touched his dirty overalls with an earth-ingrained finger.

When the shouting started, faintly in the distance, Johnny and Felicity – standing very close together on the edge of the party – were the first to hear it.

Johnny had a strange look on his face – he was very

flushed, swaying a little as he moved closer and closer to Felicity. But when she glanced at him fearfully, he drew back, becoming grave and attentive.

Felicity had seen Mrs Briggs approach Harry, of course – she'd learnt very early in her marriage to watch him – but knew nothing of his visitor.

Her first thought – confided to Johnny – was that Harry had become ill.

'I'll go,' he volunteered quickly.

'No, Johnny!'

First she found Eve. 'Look after everyone, will you?'

Eve gave her mother a questioning look. Who was this strange man who wouldn't leave Ma's side? And why did he know so much about everyone? It had been awful, being subjected to such meaningful sympathy.

Felicity and Johnny found Mrs Briggs hovering near the study, eyes popping with shock, blatantly eavesdropping. Then they heard the voice: 'You people think you can—!' Not even finished. As if murderous rage had stifled it.

'We're running out of sandwiches, Briggs,' said Felicity very coolly, and waited for her to leave.

Straight after that, there was a scuffle then a crash from within.

When they opened the door, they found a shocking scene: Harry, unconscious on the tiger skin, blood running down his nose and smearing his starched white shirt; his head gardener standing over him, dirty fist still clenched, face distorted with rage.

Johnny said sharply and very loudly (as if Stevens might be deaf as well as violent), 'You stop that! This minute! D'you hear me, now?'

But Felicity enquired, very coolly, 'What on earth do you think you're doing, Stevens?' And it had a far greater effect. Stevens seemed to deflate before their eyes.

Felicity bent to attend to her husband, but not before she'd picked up a piece of Ming imperial porcelain knocked over in the scuffle – an exquisite daffodil-coloured bowl with a blue glaze – carefully checked it was undamaged and replaced it on a Pembroke table.

Harry was moaning by now.

'He'll live,' said Johnny shortly.

Arthur Stevens' eyes filled with tears. He muttered, 'It's not how it looks, Your Ladyship.'

'How can this be anything else except how it looks?' Felicity corrected him, composed but gentle.

Johnny chipped in: 'Look here, you can't just come busting in here aiming punches at people!'

'You don't understand, Your Ladyship.'

'No,' Johnny agreed briskly, 'and she doesn't want to. So I suggest you get out of here sharpish before we call the police.'

Harry tried to sit up, caught sight of Stevens and immediately lay down again.

He looked frightened, Johnny observed with grim satisfaction.

'She's nowt but a baby!' moaned Stevens with terrible passion. 'Apple of my eye,' he managed to bring out between sobs. 'The wife's that upset she'll make herself ill.'

Johnny saw Felicity turn ashen. Once more, he longed to take her in his arms. He came very close to it, in front of Harry.

'Like as if he was doing us a favour!' Stevens ranted on in maudlin fashion. 'Like as if the wife and me'd countenance such a wickedness! But the Lord sees everything. Oh aye!'

'That's quite enough,' said Johnny, glancing anxiously at Felicity.

But she seemed to have pulled herself together. 'Quite,' she agreed in her usual detached fashion.

Soon afterwards, the gardener and his family moved away. The servants whispered that it had cost Sir Harry plenty – and then some – and each conversation began: 'I feel ever so sorry for Her Ladyship . . .'

But now Felicity could deal with these prurient murmurings with real detachment. Finally, she knew she was no longer a woman to be pitied.

If you truly loved – Felicity would tell the grandchildren – then you were powerless. It was because love was all-powerful, like the sea. Its currents could take you in unexpected directions, certainly (she would smile a little ruefully as she said this). But struggle against its force and you risked drowning. And if you betrayed love, you might as well be dead.

However, she sounded as if she was still trying to convince herself.

Felicity went riding on the day she broke the news to Harry.

For one moment she thought wistfully of his fantasy: the aeroplane he'd boasted of buying, and swooping over Edgerton like a bird. But Alice's Bailiff would have to do.

He was a good horse: solid and sweet-natured. 'Don't pull him in too hard, Ma,' Alice cautioned, 'he's not used to it.'

She patted Bailiff on his flank. 'Don't let me down now, darling!'

But it was her mother who worried her. Ma had a desperate look about her. She'd said: 'I just want to take a . . .' Then her voice had tailed away as if she couldn't bear to put it into words.

'Last,' thought Alice, in a panic. ' She was going to say last . . .'

Alice still refused to believe that Edgerton might have to be sold; they all did. But every day now the postman delivered more alarming-looking letters and the telephone rang continuously, always with cool male voices demanding to speak to Pa. He still ranted about blood-suckers and criminals. But since Gran's funeral he seemed diminished. He'd even appeared with a black eye at dinner the same evening (though nobody dared mention it).

And now Ma was going riding (which she disliked, by the way) when she should be sitting in the morning room penning letters in her black handwriting that said nothing – absolutely nothing – about what was really going on.

Alice asked fearfully, 'What's happened now?'

'I just feel like a ride,' said Ma. She smiled at her daughter and stroked her cheek with one finger. 'You've caught the sun,' she said, sounding quite unconcerned.

Felicity estimated that it would take about two hours to encompass the whole estate. First, she decided to ride down the drive away from Edgerton, where horses were never allowed. As Bailiff stirred the gravel with his hooves, she looked back over her shoulder and saw the battlemented front of the house, porch like a prow, the looming clocktower to the right, and thought of all the times she'd come home and felt compensated.

She stopped at the stone gateway marking the end of the first drive, turned Bailiff round, and sat for many minutes while he shifted about trying to lower his head. At exactly that moment, the sun emerged from a bank of cloud, and the house turned molten gold. Felicity sighed. And then she remembered a different season: the house iced with snow, the tree in the great hall rearing up like a dark sword, the fragmented windows all rosy from flaming candles.

She wondered dully: 'What will happen to the Christmas decorations?'

She thought of coming to Edgerton as a young wife, and how shabby and dark the house had seemed. She remembered the resentment of having her life taken over, and then the gradual seduction. She thought of all the changes she'd wrought; the complicity that had grown up between her and the house.

And then she contemplated living in a cottage with a faithful man who loved her.

She and Harry had not properly talked since the day of the funeral.

It was Johnny who'd taken Stevens home; she who'd indicated to the guests with impassive courtesy that it was time to leave.

Harry had stayed in his study until everyone was gone.

And then – despite his black eye – he'd eaten a substantial dinner and behaved as if nothing untoward had happened. (Though, every so often, she caught him staring at her thoughtfully.)

It was extraordinary the power he maintained over them all – even Mrs Briggs, who must have known or guessed a great deal.

At one point, Alice had tentatively begun: 'Pa?'

'Mmm.' It was the first time since she'd come home that Alice had addressed him directly, but he didn't even lift his eyes from his plate.

'Nothing.'

In their bedroom, later on, Felicity had suggested to him in her old distant thin-lipped way: 'You'd better put something on that bruise.'

'Mmm?'

She'd fetched a flannel soaked in cold water, but instead of laying it on his forehead, had merely handed it to him.

He'd looked pathetic, though also dignified. But once in bed, Felicity had turned her back. 'I simply will not feel sorry for him,' she thought steadfastly.

Felicity said: 'You mustn't be too hard on your father.' But she'd come to relish being the one who was approved of. Whilst seeming to defend Harry, she'd allow the myth to be besmirched. It happened with the grandchildren, too. They'd never known Harry, but understood he'd been an ogre of sorts. Who else had lost them Edgerton?

She and Eve and Kathy were eating chocolates in her little sitting room. A fire had been lit. Eve had brought caramels; Kathy (who had the day off work) had arrived with a box of violet creams. In Felicity's lap, Posy chattered and twitched, dreaming of birds. The children were at school. It was a rare moment.

*

Harry sold the pictures first, but – faced with his enormous debts – the money made scarcely a dent. He might have been able to keep the house – for a while longer at least – if he'd agreed to sell off his land. But nobody wanted the few less desirable bits he was prepared to part with and he couldn't bear the thought of splitting the estate and so he procrastinated; and the debts piled up until, one day, there was no choice left but to sell everything. Edgerton would pass to its next owner beautiful and complete, like a virgin bride.

'I often think,' said Felicity, 'that Edgerton was your father's only true love.'

'It's easy to love a house,' sniffed Eve.

'It's people who are hard,' added Kathy, with some bitterness.

'I do sometimes wonder if your father ever really loved me.'

'Oh, Ma!'

'We've been over this,' Kathy pointed out reasonably and she and Eve exchanged looks.

'Face it, Ma,' said Eve, 'he was a bastard.'

And Kathy said censoriously, 'I don't understand how you could have let him treat you like that.'

'I couldn't leave you children!' protested Felicity.

'You should have told *him* to go!' said Kathy, who'd done just that to her own husband. 'I'd *never* let a man treat me like that!'

Nettled, Felicity proceeded to reveal far more than she meant to. 'He wasn't the only one who was unfaithful.'

The effect was astounding – and satisfactory.

'Gobsmacked,' she thought, borrowing one of Joe's favourite words.

'Only one love affair,' she qualified, in a quavery apologetic old voice. 'What did your father expect?'

'I must remember the way that all of the land frames this place,' thought Felicity. 'I must remember the way the woods line the edge of the bowl the house sits in, I must remember its exact colour and the perfection of its symmetry . . .' But, even as she tried to fix the pictures, they slipped away.

In the end, she handed Bailiff back to Alice, marched straight into Harry's study (without appreciating the wood carving on the staircase on the way) and announced: 'I'm leaving you.'

He'd been re-reading another old favourite: *Great Expectations*. He was already bathed and changed for dinner – sleek and smelling of lemons – and stared at his hot untidy wife, still in her jodhpurs, with a sort of fastidious disbelief.

At that moment the bell in the clocktower boomed seven times, as if speaking for him. Mrs Briggs would be serving dinner, as usual, of course, at a quarter to eight.

'Did you hear me, Harry?'

'What?' He'd swiftly removed his spectacles. Now he put down his book. 'I'm not with you.' His familiar phrase when he needed to give himself time.

'I'm sorry, but I can't live with you any longer.' ('And why do I apologize?' she wondered, even as she said it.)

Harry was clever. He also believed he knew her better than anyone else did. She waited with dull curiosity for how he'd play it next.

'This is a fine display of loyalty,' he said, his face starting to twitch into rage.

'That's amusing,' responded Felicity coldly, 'coming from you.'

'For richer, for poorer,' he went on sanctimoniously as if she hadn't spoken, at the same time raising his eyebrows quizzically.

'Forsaking all others,' Felicity amended. Afterwards there was a feeling of elation.

There was a short silence during which his expression seemed to be readjusting itself, then he said in a wheedling tone, 'I know how much you love this place . . .'

'This isn't about Edgerton.'

'I appreciate it,' he went on smoothly, as if he'd not heard. He added formally, as if a little embarrassed, 'No man could have asked for a better wife.'

Felicity said nothing.

Harry said: 'It might not happen, you know.'

'What?'

'Lot of huffing and puffing,' he pronounced. 'You know what banks are like. They're trained to put the wind up people. And Lloyds could pick up – easily. One good year, that's all we need . . . *And* this government's cooking its goose. If the Tories get in again . . .'

Felicity thought: 'Should I admire or deplore his failure to face things? And why, even now, am I reluctant to hurt him?' She steeled herself. 'I'm going to live with someone else.'

She could not bring herself to meet his eyes. Instead, she looked down at a rug Harry's father had brought back from Turkey. She'd always adored its muted but daring blend of

golds and blues and reds. Johnny had beige wool carpet
fitted throughout his cottage. It made it very snug.

'Your father wasn't a bad man.' A minute stress on the word
'bad': the girls could read into it what they liked.

Eve said nothing.

'I blame Beatrice,' said Felicity, with a cold edge to her
voice.

More maddening silence.

'Think of it. Never enough love. Constantly being told to
pull himself together. All those expectations. His father was
just as hard on him.'

'Oh bless!' said Kathy. 'Think of living in a council house
all your life! Think of trying to manage on benefit!'

'And another thing,' said Eve. 'Why didn't Pa ever try and
get a job?'

'Wait a minute!' Harry exclaimed, and at last she looked up.
What had she expected? Shock? Pain? He was pulling at his
jaw thoughtfully. 'Not the feller who gatecrashed Mama's
funeral! The one throwing his weight around in my study!'

Felicity's face gave her away.

'Well, well!' He seemed astonished, even a little amused.
'Fine thing, barging into my house at such a time!'

'He came as my guest.'

'Fine thing!' Harry repeated. He was wrinkling his brow
incredulously. 'Pop-eyed? Balding? Little feller like a bullfrog?'

'He's a good man,' said Felicity stoutly. But she could feel
the strength and resolution drain out of her.

'Ah!' It was amazing how much sarcasm he managed to
pack into it.

'He's very good to me.'

'Ah!'

'He loves me, Harry.'

'And do you love him?' He wore a little smile. The question was ridiculous, of course.

'You mustn't forget,' said Felicity, 'that – underneath – your father was a deeply sensitive and vulnerable person.'

'Ever heard of a mimophant, Ma?' enquired Kathy.

'You don't understand, darling. When he realized I might be leaving him . . .'

'Oh, Ma! You got that far!'

And Felicity thought, alarmed: 'Something's happening to me! I never mean to say these things . . .'

Felicity had often seen Harry cry over a favourite piece of music: the quartet from *Fidelio* would produce a stream of sniffles, for instance. She'd never regarded it as a sign of weakness; instead found it touching to discover such reverence for beauty in a man.

Now she heard him exclaim in disbelief: 'You're leaving me, then?'

He rose from his chair and seemed to stumble. 'What will happen?' He sat down again heavily. His book crashed to the floor.

'Harry—' Felicity began. Now he had his head in his hands.

'I know, I know . . .' He sounded exhausted. When he finally looked up, she saw with horror that his eyes were full of tears. He said: 'It's all over with her, you know.'

'This is too late, Harry.'

He put his head in his hands once more. 'You're right, it was criminal.'

'And the others?' She even managed a little smile.

He shook his head violently, as if forbidding her, even for one second, to take that army of other women seriously.

'Why, then?'

He shrugged.

'Other men manage to say no . . .'

'I didn't realize it hurt you so much.'

'That's not true!'

'I don't recognize you, Felicity!' he cried.

'No,' she agreed icily.

Felicity told Eve and Kathy with pride: 'He told me he'd assumed I'd always known . . . '

Tears poured down his cheeks. He kissed her hands as he made the terrifying admission, over and over again, forcing her to listen. His tone was abject, as fearful as if he'd handed her a dagger. He didn't promise to be faithful, though – he knew himself far too well – and, oddly, that respect for truth impressed her. But he said: 'I swear to you, Felicity, no other woman has ever mattered to me. Nor ever will.'

'Well, he would say that, wouldn't he?'

'I don't like that tone of voice, Eve!'

'There was that nice man, waiting to rescue you . . .' Kathy began eagerly.

'A dear man,' Felicity agreed. 'He was there when I needed him.'

'What about us?'

'Oh, he'd have taken all of you.'

'Really?' Kathy was impressed.

'In time,' said Felicity. 'I told your father that, of course.'

'Was he attractive?'

Felicity lowered her eyes. Let them think what they wished.

'And you gave him up for Pa?'

'What else could I do? Pa needed me!'

'Oh, Ma! You could have!'

'Darlings, he was about to lose everything.'

'Exactly.' Marriage had softened Eve. But she remained unable to forgive her father. Suddenly she looked distracted, pensive. 'He wasn't at Gran's funeral, by any chance?'

'Of course not!' said Felicity with a fine display of innocence.

'So what happened to him?' asked Kathy.

Felicity tried to look stoical. 'He married someone else, in the end.'

'Oh, Ma!'

'Well! He was much too dear to be on his own for long. He needed love – just like us all.'

'When?'

'A year or so after we left Edgerton . . . I believe he had children: two little boys . . . And now I want you both to promise me faithfully, darlings, that you'll forget we ever had this conversation.'

'But if he'd only waited . . .'

'One simply cannot think about those things,' said Felicity firmly.

It wasn't true, of course. Regret seeped into one's

dreams, just as time made princes out of frogs. She thought: 'Once I was truly and faithfully loved. And – however senile I may become (and I'm increasingly afraid of it now) – the flavour of those sweet afternoons is indelible, and one of the main reasons I am thankful for having lived.'

Chapter Twenty-six

Kathy turned into the imposing gateway of Mossbury Park where pinned-up clusters of coloured balloons danced, and Felicity shrank into her coat.

'Cold?' Kathy murmured against the heater roaring away, making conversation impossible.

'Did you say something, darling?'

'Are you cold, Ma?' Kathy bellowed at the top of her voice, and the two girls in the back exchanged appalled little smiles over the tray of chili con carne balanced precariously between them.

'I'm warm as toast, thank you, my treasure.'

It was always the same when she entered the radius of Edgerton: abiding sorrow mixed with rising panic. It was like going to a party and knowing that the great love of one's life, never seen since, was lurking in an adjoining room. Should one march in and challenge the cruel gap between memory and reality? Confrontation had never been Felicity's style, though sometimes she'd tease a conversation in the direction of Edgerton like a wistful 'Does he still think of me?'

She'd heard the rumours, of course. Inevitably there were neighbours and leftover acquaintances from the past who took pleasure in passing on stories about that legendarily beautiful house. Felicity had developed a glazed smile, a distant look in the eye, selective deafness (and in the process been labelled 'uppity' and, less respectfully, 'flaky'). Inside, she'd be concentrating on images carefully stored: the sun stealing through mullioned windows like a lover coaxing a frigid princess; the liquorice secrecy of the lake at sundown, with its swirls of coot and moorhen.

But tonight, of course, there was a piece of the past that must be squarely faced. As much as she ached to see Alice, she feared the stirring up of an old sludge of anger and grief. 'I'm too old,' she groaned inwardly.

The dogs were unsettled, too, what with all the cars, and – like Alice, earlier on – Felicity found herself disorientated. Then Imogen informed them excitedly, 'Joe says they've twenty-five!' and Felicity remembered about the kennels and looked scared and wary, as if the others had read her confusion.

As Kathy brought the car to a halt on the drive, lining it up behind Hugo's old Vauxhall, Felicity noticed a litter of toys that had not been cleared away. As she stared thoughtfully at the ragged yews, she remembered Lord Farquhar's pride in his topiary, the neat lawns of old.

Eve had the kennels to run as well as her family. Hugo's latest career move had been to become a double-glazing salesman and Kathy was a primary school teacher. They were always exhausted and Felicity continued to be useful to them. This was to be welcomed, in one's eightieth year, she told herself resolutely. One might be dropping with fatigue, but at least one kept spry. Occasionally, though, she'd feel a sense of bewilderment that other people's children seemed to have far easier and more successful lives.

Edward came out to welcome them, and Felicity felt comforted by his solid predictable presence. It was less and less often, these days, that she remembered he'd been Alice's husband first. Certainly, she never reflected on the irony that it was Eve who'd turned out to be the wife of a peer, the mistress of a great house.

'I do come up to town occasionally,' Edward told Eve at the memorial service in Nether Taunton in the winter of 1984 for Pa's old friend and alibi, Bill Manners.

'Do you?' she responded politely, but without real interest. Edward received the impression that she disliked London. After all, she'd made the long journey down to the West Country to remember a man she admitted she'd hardly known and hadn't seen for years. But then, he reflected, though he'd always lived locally, he'd been acquainted with Bill Manners even less.

'Mostly to see my bank manager.' He made a face, and unconsciously borrowed Alice's old expression: 'Nightmare!'

He saw Eve's eyelids flutter involuntarily, as if she'd been threatened with a blow.

How lifeless she seemed, he thought, remembering the laughing clever girl. She'd be pushing forty or thereabouts. Why had she never married?

'We must have dinner . . .' It was what men like him said:

men who rose to their feet when a woman entered a room, and bathed and shaved before taking her out, and expected to pay the whole bill with never a thought of a quid pro quo.

But there *had* been an ulterior motive, of course. Probably Eve understood that was why he followed up the meeting at the memorial service with an invitation to dinner at his father's old club, the Travellers.

'How is Alice?' But not until the second course was on the table – pheasant in Madeira sauce – and the waiter had departed. Dry mouth as he said it, but voice kept admirably steady and toneless.

'She's still in America,' Eve replied, with the exact same absence of emotion – adding so quietly that he almost missed it, 'so I believe.'

'I see.'

'Not married any more' – Eve saying thank you, in her fashion, for the generous dinner and being momentarily removed from the sad humdrumness of her life.

It cheered him, absurdly, to know Alice was single again. And now that was out of the way, he could properly concentrate on Eve.

He smiled at her across the table, noting, with real concern, her pallor, her quietness, her dull dark clothes.

He could have asked her more anodyne questions about her job – working as a secretary in a law firm. He could have carefully enquired about Hugo and Kathy and Felicity. But instead – with one of those unexpected flashes of empathy that had caused Alice to consider him as a suitor – he said gently, 'You must miss studying. You always loved it so much, didn't you?'

*

The second marriage had been starkly different from the first: a registry office union attended by immediate family only (minus Alice, of course). 'I have grave misgivings,' Felicity had confided to Hugo at the time. She'd longed not to perceive Eve and Edward as two lonely people approaching middle-age, still bleeding from wounds administered by the same person. But just as something fundamental to her being could not accept that Eve would be better loved, in the end, than beautiful Alice, neither could she accept that Edward was a faithful man.

And now? Felicity stared at genial overweight Edward imploringly. Men were restless and impressionable. Who knew it better than she?

Eve joined him and Felicity felt a rush of exasperation. Nobody could fault Eve as a mother – an astonishingly late one, too (Milo had been almost a miracle). But why didn't she get herself a proper haircut and, while she was at it, do something about her grey hairs? Why hadn't she invested in a pretty new dress for this most significant of occasions? It struck Felicity that her eldest child was becoming more and more like Beatrice.

She felt the same impatience with Eve's attitude to her surroundings. Mossbury Park had never been a patch on Edgerton, of course. The barracks, Harry had called it. But, given a bit of thought and effort, and not too much expense, it might still look marvellous. As she frowned at a square of cardboard covering a pane of broken glass (the victim of Alex's golf practice), the stained sofas, the curtains drooping from rails, Felicity's hands would twitch – like those of an artist who'd long ago laid down her brush. It was a mercy, really, that her sight was dimming.

Then she'd notice how the place hummed with fun and life. There was always a child shrieking with laughter somewhere, music pulsating in an upstairs bedroom; and sometimes an abandoned infant animal being bottle-fed in the kitchen. It was so cheerful after the tomb-like silence of her cottage. She'd forget it was close to Edgerton. To be with Eve's youngest children was such pleasure. She'd only to murmur, 'Would one of you be a love and fetch my handbag?' and they'd compete for the privilege. It was like having the most attentive of servants, but with welcome intimacy. 'Why do you smell of baked beans, Grammy?' Milo would murmur, lover-like, into her hair.

Felicity was already regretting the surprise she'd planned. When rattled, she became scatty and infirm. So immediately after Edward kissed her, she mislaid her stick and left her beautiful gold shawl trapped in a sleeve of her coat and forgot she'd brought smart shoes for changing into. It was Kathy who put all this right: adjusting her mother as if tending to a small child. And, while it was going on, a slender over-tanned woman in a neat black suit watched apprehensively from the sidelines.

'Where's Alice?' Felicity faltered.

'Right here, Ma.' Her voice was still gentle and high, but with a strange new twang.

There was just one second – 'Alice?' – when Felicity thought, 'It cannot be!' She felt so hard! She smelt different too, of peppermint and money. Then, as Felicity pulled back and studied the long-missed face, the lens readjusted and, within an extraordinarily short time, the handsome middle-aged woman and the creamy young beauty had somehow fused. The same blond hair (cropped now), the same blue eyes and oval shape of the face, the same endearingly short upper lip ... Felicity beamed at her daughter and looked about her as if to say 'See!' She wouldn't have been a bit surprised to find the old queue of suitors.

Alice thought soberly, 'How must she see *me*?' When she'd left England, Ma had been active and strong, bearing up under her great losses. Now, seeing her so frail and childlike, Alice felt even more guilty.

It was such a shock to have the years telescoped: to see them all so changed and old, with none of the gradual softening up. But it was Hugo who saddened her most. He should, of course, have been living at Edgerton. He should be married to an old-fashioned stoical woman who'd tolerate the odd indiscretion. Instead, he found himself in a box with Lily, his strong-minded wife. Forced to take one stultifying inadequately paid job after another, he was like a man tumbling down a ladder. And of what use were hereditary titles now?

'Any Scotch about?' he murmured as Joe offered a jug of dark-red liquid crowded with chunks of apple and orange.

'Punch.'

'There's fifty pee in it for you.'

'A quid,' Joe bargained briskly, before setting off in search.

There was a problem with alcohol. Alice could see it in the tracing of veins on her brother's cheeks, the trembling hand before the first gulp soothed.

Dinner was laid out on the far side of the great hall. It was to be buffet-style. Kathy's cling-filmed chili con carne had been plonked down next to Lily's Basque chicken and

Eve's lasagne and a variety of pâtés. The little children had stuck home-made flags into them. There were pâtés made of mackerel (misspelt and crossed out) and chicken liver, and a selection of cheeses.

'Jolly relieved you decided against the makerl,' said Hugo.

So nobody could be a martyr about the washing up, a decision had been taken to buy plastic plates and plastic cutlery and blue paper napkins. There were salads of rice and beans and cabbage, made well in advance to accommodate busy lives. Eve would add garlic bread and baked potatoes. They could smell them cooking, in the distance.

'It would be nice to sit down,' Felicity murmured, trying not to sound too disappointed about the loss of the real dinner party she'd been anticipating. (All of her children maintained they loathed dinner parties, and it genuinely puzzled her.)

Once she was settled in a corner, Alice brought up a chair next to hers.

'Darling,' said Felicity.

'Ma.'

They stared at each other. From upstairs, in the minstrels' gallery, came one snatch of music after another as the children squabbled over CDs and the old 78s and 33s that had survived the move from Edgerton.

Felicity had tears in her eyes. 'I'm so glad you've come.'

'Well, eighty!' Alice responded. She touched her mother's hand briefly as 'All You Need is Love' struck up.

Moments passed. Then Felicity exclaimed: 'And you've got a good job!'

'Yes,' Alice agreed like a surprised and obedient little girl.

Felicity shook her head in wonder. 'You're here for a few days?'

'Yes, Ma. A whole week.' Alice was appalled by her mother's look of terrible sadness. She continued briskly: 'I'm here, aren't I?'

'But why?' Ma repeated. 'Why now?'

Alice had known it was cruel to break it then. But misery made for selfishness. And now that the dreadfulness of Pa's funeral had been endured, she longed only to start again. It meant she wouldn't complete her university course, after all; a taste of education would have to do. But she'd been led to believe that, in a country like America, the lack of proper qualifications wouldn't matter. What counted was energy. 'And I'll get mine back,' thought Alice wearily.

'It's for the best, Ma. Eve—'

Ma shut her up with a look. Alice knew what she was thinking; understood that she was blamed for her selfishness, as Eve was pitied for her misery. Ma had watched the chasm develop between her elder daughters, but she would never side with one child against another, nor would she intervene. Unlike Pa, she'd made a point of fairness, in her fashion. Besides, thought Alice, Ma had suffered enough upset. Pa's death had knocked all the energy out of her, too.

Alice watched as Ma folded Pa's clothes and stacked them in one of many cardboard boxes. Black wasn't her colour. It made her look green and old.

'What are you going to do with them?' asked Alice, without real interest.

'Oxfam.' The local charity shops had done well out of

the Chandlers, in recent years. A china garland of yellow and white roses from one of the guest bedrooms was still pinned up in a shop in Nether Taunton. It was no longer for sale. It was part of the decor.

'Wait!' said Alice. 'Can I have this?'

'This?' Ma looked down at the old beige cardigan, darned at the elbows, falling to bits. 'I was going to throw it out.'

'I want it,' said Alice, the soft cashmere already against her face. It smelt of lemons and brilliantine, with a smoky hint of toast.

'She made him buy a new one,' said Ma with a bitter little smile – and Alice thought she couldn't have heard right.

Though she didn't know it, even then Ma had started the long process of trying to understand her old life with its extraordinary mixture of fulfilment and misery.

Hugo joined them, wearing a mask of joviality: part of his family hat.

'So,' he said, 'I gather you've got a business.'

'Yes,' Alice agreed meekly. 'I sell real estate.'

'Oh, an estate agent,' Hugo corrected her with a knowing smirk.

Alice was silent.

'How is the land of the free?'

'I love it,' said Alice immediately. She was remembering the dreamy child with the charm and confidence of his father and the dark good looks of his mother.

'With that autistic gorilla in charge?' Hugo tossed back his Scotch, glanced round casually for Joe while keeping a wary lookout for Lily.

'He's only trying to protect us.'

'What?' Hugo's expression was a mixture of genuine astonishment and growing amusement. 'I could lose my job tomorrow because of what he's doing to the economy.'

'We can't just . . . let some dictator ride roughshod over us.'

'Exactly.' Hugo seemed delighted. 'So how come you've turned into such a Republican? *Cherchez l'homme*, I assume?' He might have been his father, the way he drawled it out, the sneering all lathered in charm so it would have seemed aggressive to be rude back.

Alice was trembling. At fifty-six, and a successful businesswoman, she'd been made to feel exactly as she had at eighteen: a pretty little thing who'd no business to be bothering her head about important issues.

Felicity had missed most of this, but not Hugo's tone, or Alice's distress. 'I won't have dissension at my birthday party,' she grumbled gently.

Hugo sulked. 'I didn't start it.' He glared at Alice, eyes burning with unhappiness. 'Sorry,' he muttered, flashing his teeth as fiercely as Pa's old tiger.

The music situation was deteriorating. Now the children were playing 'A Whiter Shade of Pale'. 'I can't hear myself think,' murmured Felicity.

Alice thought of Lord and Lady Farquhar's pride in their heritage. Lord Farquhar had suffered a massive heart attack while shooting a stag – 'a good death', his heartbroken widow had deemed it. She was in a residential home with dementia now. Eve had said old Lady F. could no longer recognize her only son. And who could blame her? He was so very different.

*

Alice was sitting on her sunny terrace drinking peach juice and decaffeinated coffee when the letter arrived.

The most extraordinary news about Eve . . . Ma wrote regularly, keeping her up to date with family news – ignoring the schism. Not nearly often enough, Alice wrote back (and correctly guessed that, in turn, Ma relayed her minimal accounts of life in California to the others).

. . . I was at Bill's memorial service myself, of course. A horrid death – cancer of the liver – but a lovely service . . . I'd no idea Eve was fond of the old thing . . .

('Of course she'd go,' Alice thought. 'She could never say goodbye, like I could.')

I saw them talking – but I'd no idea they were seeing each other . . . You know what Eve's like . . .

('Yes,' thought Alice, feeling the ever-present guilt. Had Ma really expected Eve to confide in her? Ma had *never* asked about her children's private lives; and, if she sensed suffering, couldn't bear to have it confirmed).

I can't imagine Eve married, after all this time! She does seem to be happy, but you know what Eve's like. It is *rather extraordinary, if you think about it . . .*

And that was the furthest Ma went on the subject of the strange symmetry of her eldest daughter's marriage.

Alice didn't write to Eve because any expression of goodwill might have seemed hypocritical. But, later that week, she mentioned it to Dr Sayre's predecessor, Dr Henderson.

There needed to be a speech, of course. Hugo had scribbled a few key words on a bit of old envelope.

At the moment, though, he was immersed in argument with Joe.

'We can't be a party to carpet-bombing everything in sight,' said Joe wearily.

'Why not? They asked for it.'

'We're talking about invading a sovereign country, Uncle Huge! Where's the justification for that?'

'Because we can!' said Hugo triumphantly. He repeated it slowly and loudly, looking round for an audience. 'Because – we – CAN!' Then he caught Alice's eye and, to his credit, gave a sheepish grin.

Eve said to Alice: 'Bonkers!'

'He's very confrontational, isn't he?'

'You can say that again!' It was passing off all right, she thought, just as Edward had said.

By now, Hugo had turned his attention to his mother: 'What's up, Ma?' As always, his tone was intimate and flirtatious, like a lover's.

'Nothing.'

'Now now! *I've* seen you glancing at the door!'

Felicity retreated into child-like vagueness. 'Am I, darling?'

'You know perfectly well you are, you old crumbly! We're *here* now!'

Lily banged a glass with a fork to subdue the hubbub. She was very protective of Hugo.

'We're here tonight to pay tribute to an extraordinary woman,' Hugo began. He paused (just as his father might have) and, in the silence, everyone heard a childish treble: 'What's he talkin' about?'

Hugo waited for the laughter to subside. 'I'm talking about your Grammy, young Milo. And in a minute, I'll tell you why she's so special. But first I'd like to say how delighted I am – how pleased we all are – that on this most special of occasions, the family is complete.'

All eyes turned to Alice.

'I don't know why my sister stayed away so long,' said Hugo, and once again he paused.

Standing very close together, smiling brightly, Eve and Edward groped blindly for each other's hands.

'But I know it means everything to Ma that she's come back to help us celebrate this special birthday. And I hope this'll be the first of many visits, Alice.' For once, Hugo sounded genuinely friendly, even emotional.

Alice looked down at the scuffed and stained marble and waited for everyone to stop staring at her.

Hugo glanced at his bit of envelope, where he'd scribbled words like 'style' and 'perfectionist'. He wouldn't mention Edgerton by name: it wasn't necessary. After all, he was a rare breed of survivor, speaking to others. They'd lived in peace and beauty, only to be cast out. They would never forgive Pa, whom they held responsible. But Ma was exonerated even though it was she, with the great talents Hugo mentioned, who'd rendered the beauty almost unbearable.

'So I'd like you all to drink to Ma's health,' Hugo concluded, after thanking Edward and Eve for their hospitality, and the family reached for their glasses of punch or fizzy white wine or, in the case of Hugo, Scotch.

Hugo was trying to catch Lily's eye – 'All right?' he was mouthing, with a confident smile – when the front door swung open to reveal someone they had all, with every reason, believed they would never see again.

Hugo's jaw sagged; Kathy frowned; Alice found herself

gasping something like 'Ah!' Eve exchanged horrified looks with her husband. Even the children looked frightened: after all, they knew the photograph albums by heart.

The reaction was far greater than Felicity had anticipated – because, as she herself had discovered, once the man opened his mouth, everything changed.

'Ever so sorry, Felicity,' he told her in a soft Devon burr. 'Alternator's gone for a burton. We been limping for ten miles.' Then they saw that he was not alone. There was a small blonde woman hovering in his wake.

'It's quite all right,' said Felicity. 'Very glad you've managed to come.'

Then she felt for her stick, rose shakily from her chair, went over to the man and kissed him on both cheeks.

Her voice trembled a little as she made the introduction. 'Eve, Alice, Hugo, Kathy' – it was as if she were counting her children off on her fingers, delaying the moment until the very last – 'I'd like you to meet your half-brother.'

He was called Arthur, after the man who'd stood in for his real father. He was thirty-five years old. He was married to his childhood sweetheart, Sue, and they had two small children, Nicola and Mark. He worked as a mechanic in a garage twenty miles away.

It was he who'd made contact with Felicity, not the other way round.

'So it wasn't my fault,' thought Felicity, already expecting trouble.

Chapter Twenty-seven

It was so lonely, being old. There'd been solitude before, but never this aching silence no amount of chatter from Radio 4 could fill. Nobody had warned Felicity that the loss would be unremitting: prosperity, Edgerton, Harry, her beautiful daughter, and finally health. She'd no female friends: there'd been too many instances of intimacy leading to betrayal. The great compensation was grandchildren. She was lucky to have so many close by.

In old age, she'd shrunk to fit her house – but it was obvious to occasional visitors (who might not know) that her few bits of good furniture had belonged to another era. The Chippendale desk, almost unobtrusive in the morning room at Edgerton, was now wedged into the only possible corner of her little sitting room (or drawing room, as it must always be called). The Oriental lamps which had once held court either side of the Elizabethan fireplace in Edgerton's grandest room now perched on much too spindly tables – and, as a direct result, were both cracked (which was lucky really, Felicity told herself, otherwise they, too, might have had to be sold). And the honey silk curtains with big fussy pelmets, which had framed the enormous French windows and their matchless views of the terrace and the lake, now hung, quartered and fraying at the ends, at a low bay window overlooking a small soggy lawn studded with dandelions.

But even in these straitened circumstances, Felicity found that her flickering energy could be recharged by the pleasure derived from the look of things. The pale yellow of the walls (paints were quite marvellous these days, and washable); the perfect blend of soft blues and turquoises and terracottas in the famille rose plates that hung like elegant twin clocks above the door; an apparently artless arrangement of sprigs of flowering hawthorn in a porcelain bowl of palest grey.

Unfortunately, the room was dominated by an enormous purple sofa. Eve had bought it in a sale. Two years later, it still upset Felicity every day, but she hated to offend Eve. 'The colour is very bold,' she'd assured her daughter with a fragile smile. But she continued to ask the grandchildren in a vague worried way, 'It's not *too* big is it?'

'Grammy, it's mega!' (That was exactly what was brill about it. Five of them could sit in it easily, when watching the telly. And – unlike the armchairs, which sagged and threw up impertinent bony springs – it was extremely comfortable.)

But then, thought Felicity, the poor darlings had been deprived of the chance to develop a proper aesthetic sense.

The sofa was a boil-like eruption, as striking in its lack of beauty as the television set – but at least that could be concealed behind an exquisite, though sadly flaking, Chinese screen. You had a duty to learn what was going on in the world, Felicity would say, even if it scared you witless.

She could never learn to live without beauty. She'd adapted to the loss of a husband. She'd learnt how to manage her little house and half-acre of garden with only occasional help from other dispossessed locals: Serbian Galina (who was anxious to improve her English), and Galina's husband Daniel (who flymoed her precious shrubs and left the lavatory seat up). She'd learnt that you could no longer expect to find a butcher, a greengrocer and a baker, each of whom would welcome you respectfully into his domain. Instead, for a pound, you bought the hire of a metal trolley to trundle round the supermarket. It was as entertaining as the cinema, and miraculous to find star fruit from Africa and bresaola from Italy and lobsters from Thailand all under the same roof. Too bad you couldn't afford them. Today, if you wanted a treat, you had to make do with salmon and avocado pears (which you could remember being luxuries).

These days, she'd note with wonder how often the word 'love' was used. 'Love you,' Eve would sign off after a mundane telephone reminder to Edward about the needs of horses or dogs; 'Love you,' said the grandchildren at the end of a day at her cottage. It was catching. 'I love you, too, darlings . . .' The admission made her eyes sting. Did they appreciate how lucky they were?

In the old days, formality had governed their lives. It explained why, until her marriage was on the point of collapse, she'd never taxed Harry with his infidelities. And why, even as the furniture was being removed, she was planting out the herbaceous borders. Stevens had gone by then, of course, and all his boys, and she was forced to do the digging and hoeing herself. But it never occurred to her not to carry on with the seasonal traditions. The service was for Edgerton. No matter that strangers would reap the benefits.

That dark and rainy afternoon, when she heard a car turn into her little drive, she'd assumed it was either Kathy or Eve, who often dropped in. Her mood had lifted. It was always a depressing time of day – the sun going down, too late for a walk, too early for a drink and the news. And she enjoyed being chivvied by the girls (as she would think of them for ever). Kathy had drawn up a set of rules for remaining tolerated by the young. 'Always wear your spectacles in your kitchen,' it began; 'have at least one bath every day; keep a magnifying mirror on your dressing table . . .'

Then the knocker sounded (a bronze eagle saved from Edgerton and over-large), and Felicity sighed. It was probably her nearest neighbour, a farm manager (who also knew the door was never locked, but quite rightly observed the courtesies). He was pleasant enough, and very obliging.

'I'm coming, I'm coming,' she grumbled to Posy, as, stick in hand, she negotiated the bumpy tiled floor in the hall. Her hair was neatly done, as usual; and she always applied make-up, even though days sometimes passed without seeing another human being.

What did she think in those first extraordinary seconds when the door swung open?

There was no security light to point up the differences, and he didn't speak. It was because, however many times he'd rehearsed his speech, he was still unsure how to begin.

So it was Harry she saw, and knew he'd come to explain, in his unforgettable drawl, what all of it had really meant.

Felicity fainted. Luckily Arthur caught her before she did any damage to herself. He was very strong, just like his father.

When she came to, she was alone. She was lying on the purple sofa in her little drawing room with her shoes off, watching fire gobble at a wigwam of logs newly erected in the deep mound of ash in the grate. She could hear sounds of activity coming from the kitchen and, without much guilt, remembered last night's dishes still lying on the table.

When he returned he was carrying a tray bearing her silver teapot engraved with the Chandler entwined doves, and all that remained of her precious blue and white Spode set. There was fruitcake, too (he must have found the old Crawfords biscuit tin). 'The cup that cheers,' he said with a shy grin. He added, sounding a little worried, 'They do say brandy's the business.'

'I'm perfectly fine,' Felicity assured him, struggling to her feet, adjusting her hair, moving to one of the armchairs. 'And it's far too early for brandy.'

She indicated, with a smile, where he should put the tray – on a table she'd earlier polished with beeswax (Felicity never minded that sort of housework, especially as very occasional Galina would cheat with Pledge).

He was so apologetic – about causing her to faint, and taking liberties like removing her shoes and searching her cupboards for the makings of tea (though he didn't mention encountering mouse droppings). He even poured for her, after first measuring out the milk. (He didn't reveal that –

looking for something to keep the pot warm – he'd found an old shepherd's pie heaving with maggots on a counter. It explained the smell that had hit him as soon as she opened the front door. 'Unwanted visitors,' he'd murmured to himself while decanting them into a plastic carrier bag he stowed in the boot of his car for burning later. He'd been shocked by the state of the kitchen.)

Felicity couldn't stop staring at him. He was the identical height, with the same slender but muscular physique and liquid grace. His thick blond hair waved around his ears. Did it smell of Bronnley lemons too? Only the clothes were different. Harry would never have teamed a dark-blue blazer with a scarlet tie and tan slacks.

'You must forgive me for staring . . .'

He gave his sweet smile – Harry's, but without the curling downturn, the threat of cruelty. It was her house, he seemed to be indicating: she was entitled to do as she pleased.

'You're so very like my husband.'

'So I been told.' A statement of fact, seemingly delivered without side or recrimination.

'I always knew you'd come,' said Felicity, and realized to her astonishment that it was true.

'Of course,' said Felicity, sounding like her old reserved self, 'you never saw Edgerton, did you? Unless . . .'

'I seen pictures of the old place.'

'Really?'

'Grandpa took a mass of pictures of the gardens and that.'

Of course. What finer reference could there be for future employers?

'I'd love to see them, some time.'

Arthur nodded with shy pleasure. She knew what he was thinking – so this meeting would not be a one-off.

Felicity searched for the comfort of beauty – the gloss on her scratched old furniture, the perfect shape of a bowl, the delicate blue and green traceries on her Oriental lamps – though, as always, her soul flinched away from the enormous purple sofa Arthur had settled into (Posy following soon afterwards to knead his thigh with her sharp claws). 'I don't know where to begin . . .'

A diffident grin. 'You fire away, Lady Chandler.'

'Please,' she said, 'call me Felicity,' and simultaneously remembered (with a frisson) that he was the illegitimate grandson of a servant.

'Felicity . . .'

She was silent for a moment. It was because she was treasuring the sound. It was like a caress. Harry's voice in timbre, but two syllables instead of his languid four and so strangely hesitant and sweet.

'You must meet my children.' She was warding off until the last moment the revelations that must come, the knife in the heart the past surely still held in store.

That was how the surprise started.

It was easier than explaining.

And why shouldn't her children, too, enjoy the marvellous but momentary illusion that miracles could happen?

Chapter Twenty-eight

'He seems nice.' Eve sounded a little surprised.

Alice said nothing. She was still staring at Arthur with an odd expression.

By then, Arthur had introduced them to Sue, who appeared to be very pleasant too, though shy. And he'd told them, all over again, what had happened to his car to make them so late. Each time, he used their names, as if familiarizing himself with these new relationships.

'Well!' said Hugo, raising his eyebrows. (*Sir* Hugo, actually – as Arthur had nervously reminded him.)

From where the three of them stood, they could observe Arthur and Sue, huddled side by side with plates of food on their laps, earnestly talking to Kathy. Arthur held his knife like a pen, they noticed. As they watched, he put his plate on the floor (where it was instantly investigated by a wandering cat) and started searching an inner pocket.

'I *like* having a brother.' Though Hugo didn't resemble his father, he had many of his mannerisms (whereas Arthur,

who was an almost exact copy, appeared to have none).
Harry had curled his lip, too, when he was being ironic.
'Anyone guess?'

'Never. I mean, I suppose if I had, I might have
assumed . . .' But Eve couldn't finish the sentence – not with
Alice there. It occurred to her that neither Hugo nor Kathy
knew about Alice's abortion. Though Eve was good friends
with Kathy, they would never be as close as she and Alice
had once been.

'Can't think why not,' Hugo went on. 'There must have
been talk.'

'Only among the servants,' said Eve, making a face.

'She was the prettiest girl I've ever seen,' said Alice. She
smiled suddenly, and – like watching a flickering old reel of
film – they caught a glimpse of another ravishing young
woman.

'No real blame, then.' Hugo gave his twisted smile,
remembering a perfect summer's day long ago, and his first
delicious taste of infatuation.

'*Your family*!' Lily – bursting into the frame, trying to force
a position in the knot of siblings. She was big and red-haired
and clever and the best thing that had happened to Hugo
since he'd become an adult. Lily had a good career as an
accountant. She'd never known Harry – or Edgerton – but
hadn't forgiven him either.

Alice was thinking, 'I'll have to find out his birthday.' And
suddenly it became the only thing she wanted to know.

For years, she'd scarcely thought about her abortion.
After all, back then there'd been no choice. Oh, everyone
harped on about the sixties, and freedom and love – but ask
those who were there! For girls like her, reputation had been

crucial. Afterwards, she'd appreciated that the abortion meant freedom to pursue education and, as a result, a proper career. But all that happened before the longing that seemed to come out of nowhere, growing like a cancer.

Increasingly, it had become her habit to notice men and women of a certain age. But the sight of this man of about thirty-five was uniquely painful. 'He could have been mine,' thought Alice quite illogically, the anger blossoming like a fresh wound.

Trust Pa to carry on hurting her from the grave. He'd shown himself to be a hypocrite about her passion for Marcus. Not a romantic, as he liked to make out, but a calculating cynic. So when the gardener's family decamped in a flurry of whispers, she'd assumed the same double standard had applied. Ma had finally put her foot down; and instead of resisting, holding out for love, Pa had complied, whilst probably heaving a sigh of relief.

Now that she understood the real reason for the family's disappearance, she found it hard to believe Ma had not known too.

Arthur was very affable. Meeting his half-brother and half-sisters for the first time, he seemed to want to dismiss the wrong that had been done. He preferred to compare notes on young children, or discuss the work that living in an enormous place like Mossbury Park entailed (a labour of love, he said, as if coining the cliché afresh), or even the weather. (Something was happening to the climate, he told them earnestly; they should hear his grandfather on the subject!)

He didn't yet know Hugo.

'So,' Hugo began with all the deadly charm of his father.

Arthur responded with his sweet open smile. 'Yes, Hugo?'

'I must confess, we're all a little puzzled.' His father's laconic drawl.

'Pardon?'

'As you know, my mother's eighty now.' As Hugo said it, he saw an expression of dismay flit across Arthur's face. (He couldn't know that, in the stress of being late, Arthur had just remembered about Lady Chandler's birthday present: a padded tea cosy in the shape of a sitting hen. He would retrieve it from his car as soon as Hugo had finished whatever he wanted to say.)

'She's told us a bit about things . . .' Which was a very inadequate explanation for Ma's patchy and increasingly contradictory version of the past. 'Obviously, at the time, this whole business was enormously embarrassing for my father and, indeed, my whole family. As it was, erm, for yours too, of course, erm, naturally . . . With respect, one can understand why everyone wanted to sweep it under the carpet, to use a cliché.' (Hugo was quite unable not to stress the last phrase.) 'I imagine after you left Edgerton that was it. End of contact.'

'Grandpa wouldn't have it, would he?' said Arthur with his innocent smile.

'I'm not with you.' His father's phrase exactly.

Arthur was looking a little mystified. After all, he and Lady Chandler – or Felicity, as he strove to think of her – had spent more than two hours talking. She'd described for him the scene in the study at Edgerton, when his grandfather had punched his father. He'd been able to fill in gaps. Why, then, hadn't she relayed the whole sorry tale to her children? But there was no time to ponder on the strangeness of this. He'd have to tell his story all over again.

'He wanted to take me, didn't he, Hugo?' he said, watching Felicity on the other side of the room as she talked to her grandchildren.

'Uh?'

'Yes. He wanted to take me for his own.' There was pride as well as disbelief in his tone. 'As if they'd have allowed it, Hugo!' His father's smile again: but incredulous, purely sweet. 'I'd die before I'd give up Nicola or Mark!'

Hugo spoke very slowly, as if he needed to get this exactly right. 'You mean, he wanted you to live at Edgerton with us?'

'Or not, as it happened,' Eve interposed quietly.

'We used to joke about it when I was raised,' said Arthur, smiling fondly. 'My Nan'd say, "If it wasn't for us, you'd be a proper gentleman."' Then he looked troubled, lest they misunderstood. 'Mind, I'd not change my childhood for the world. Not for the world.'

'I can see it was happy,' said Alice very gently. It was true. Then she asked: 'Do you know if my father ever tried to see you before he . . .?'

'They done right,' Arthur told them very seriously. 'It'd only have led to confusion.' He elaborated. 'At the end of the day, I had a father, to all intents and purposes, in a manner of speaking, didn't I, Alice?'

'So he did try?' She sounded as if it was very important to her.

Arthur shrugged. 'We never wanted for nothing, Alice. I can't fault him there.' And he explained to them (just as he had to Felicity) about the trust fund set up for him by his real father.

Hugo was smiling in the same way that had once warned people to keep clear of Harry. He was thinking of the mortifications he'd endured as a young adult: the ignominy of being removed from Eton and enrolled in a comprehensive; the failure to get a scholarship to Christ Church, his father's old college; the bleakness of the campus university in the north where he'd struggled on a pitiful allowance before leaving without completing his degree to get the first paid job he could find.

'Ma must have known,' said Eve, sounding almost as grim as Hugo looked. She was thinking of another trust fund her father had set up before the money went for good: this time to aid Alice's education. So far as Eve was concerned, it had been sheer sadism: most certainly intended as punishment.

No wonder none of them had been able to forgive Pa.

They could see Ma on the other side of the room, talking to Milla and Imogen. She looked terribly frail and vulnerable. As they watched, Milla produced a parcel from behind her back and handed it to her grandmother, who appeared to be pretending she'd never seen a present before. Milla undid the ribbon for her. Salmon pink bath salt crystals. Felicity sniffed at the packet ecstatically.

'When did the old place go, then?' asked Arthur. He was only trying to be friendly. But, coming out of what looked uncannily like Pa's mouth, his flippancy was insufferable. Suddenly, he was no longer almost one of them; wasn't even on a par with the Whitby Chandlers.

'November the fifteenth, nineteen sixty-eight,' said Eve

very coolly. She did it for all of them. She longed for Edward to breeze into the group and change the subject. She wished they hadn't decided to hold this wretched birthday party in the first place. More than anything, she wished Alice had never returned. And now there were these ghastly complications Ma had set in motion! Of course, it wouldn't be she who'd have to deal with them.

Then Arthur said softly, 'Forgive me, Eve. Shouldn't have put it like that, should I?'

'It's okay, Arthur.' His combination of humility and candour was as irresistible as Pa's charm had once been. 'But we hate talking about Edgerton.'

'I understand.'

'Do you?' asked Alice. Again, that tender sympathetic tone, like one of Edgerton's doves.

'I think so, Alice. Mum's always told us it was the nearest thing to paradise.'

'Did she really?'

'Must have broken your hearts . . .'

None of them replied. How could they, to such an understatement?

They were reliving walking through empty echoing rooms, colder than ever, piling into Ma's Morris Minor (the only car that remained), wondering if they dared take a final backward look at the golden battlements.

Eve shrank away from contact with Alice, crammed next door. She feared Alice now, as well as hated her. Hugo was on her other side, staring blankly out at the rain; Kathy was sitting on Ma in the front, shamelessly sucking at La-la (her old toy lamb rediscovered during packing up).

Only Alice bloomed with energy and excitement. Eve knew why. She was beginning to believe she had a brain, after all: walking towards a future previously not envisaged, like a person entering a newly discovered room. Eve suspected she had a new love, too, though – understandably – the joy was packed away for now like an unwrapped present. As Alice steadied Champion on her lap, Eve saw her turn round as the car reached the stone gateway and give a secret smile, as if saying goodbye to her own unhappiness, rather than Edgerton.

But Eve – who could not look – knew she would never again dare to look forward to anything. All hope was dead, just like the thirteen other dogs including Bingo's pups Pa had told them it was kinder to shoot rather than try to find homes for. (Naturally, he hadn't done it himself; it was the head gamekeeper, Tommy, who'd been charged with the dreadful task.)

Pa seemed in a trance. He hadn't that long to live. Perhaps he knew it even then.

'How is your mother?' asked Hugo formally. If Arthur had known him better, he'd have understood he wasn't really interested at all.

'Very well, thank you, Hugo.' He felt in his pockets again. It seemed he'd donned a hidden lining of photographs under his navy off-the-peg suit. 'I took this in June. No – I tell a lie – July.'

They were looking at a picture of a smiling middle-aged woman. She was good-looking certainly, with traces of the sixties in her long hair, which was still defiantly blond, like Alice's. She looked happy, with sunburst laugh lines. But there was no trace left of the beauty that had stopped conversation, broken codes, caused a scandal that was still reverberating, almost forty years later.

'Is she . . .? Have you . . .?'

'I think what my sister means,' Eve explained with a smile, 'is did your mother marry? Have you brothers and sisters? I mean, more of them?'

'Not that I know of,' said Arthur. If he'd had more of Harry in him, the joke would have slid out, honey-like and probably amused. As it was, they reacted blankly, a little taken aback.

'Did she marry?' Eve repeated.

'No.' Then, as if in gentle rebuke for what they might be thinking, he told them, 'Mum's always said as I was the best thing ever happened to her.'

Alice coaxed with that strange coo in her voice: 'Tell us more.'

'She's an artist, isn't she.'

It was so unexpected that none of them knew how to react.

'I never hated my father,' Arthur explained earnestly, and repeated it just as sincerely in case they hadn't got the point. 'I never hated him 'cos that wouldn't have been right. Wouldn't have been right at all.' He added shyly, 'And Mum's always told me it was him as taught her how to look at things.'

'Really?' said Hugo faintly.

'Oh yes!' Arthur seemed very anxious they should appreciate there'd been poetry in that scandalous liaison. 'Took her off in his Daimler to show her the sights, didn't he.' The local countryside had inspired a multitude of landscapes, he told them solemnly. She did seascapes too. She sold very well to the grockles – tourists, he corrected himself with a smile.

Eve had an odd expression on her face. She was remembering being twenty and having lunch in the dining room at Edgerton and all of a sudden noticing Pa had grass clinging to his back. Nobody said anything. The blades had trembled on the fine wool of his new cardigan as he controlled the conversation, as usual. Mrs Briggs must have seen them too, as she served vegetables.

Arthur had brought photos of some of his mother's pictures, too.

The Chandlers pored over brightly coloured depictions of the beaches they'd loved as children. They knew they were the same ones because the pictures had titles: 'Fun at Burton Bay', 'Crabbing at Combe Regis'. They remembered crunching through pebbles in oilskins and gumboots, vengeful rollers chasing them up the shingle. But in these pictures there were flat golden sands where chubby toddlers in sun hats toyed with nets in sunlit shallows as friendly seagulls swooped overhead. And the sea wasn't slate coloured, as they remembered, but a brilliant Mediterranean azure.

'Monkton Beacon,' said Eve faintly.

'Yes,' Arthur agreed, with his wonderful smile. Wasn't his mother talented?

The heather-capped crag their father had loved to climb was now a friendly mauve hill. It looked as if, at any moment, smiling little folk might peep out from its sun-drenched crevices, carolling jolly troll songs. Around its treacherous base, the rocks had been excised, replaced by gently lapping waves.

'Why did she want to paint that?' asked Alice, sounding as miserably perplexed as a child.

'Sorry, Alice, I'm not with you.' Arthur's open trusting expression sat so strangely on their father's face, they thought they'd never get used to it.

'You must know what happened, don't you?' Hugo told him slowly. Like his father, he made a practice of deflecting a conversation if it threatened to turn serious, taking refuge in mockery and, very occasionally, sentimentality.

But there could be no dodging away from this one – more was the pity.

Death was inescapable; but – as all of them had discovered – suicide carried its own dreadful legacy.

Chapter Twenty-nine

When Hugo was removed from Eton, he understood, finally, that his world had changed for ever. Only then did he appreciate how much the school – with its infuriating hierarchy, its incomprehensible language, its artificial austerity – had really meant to him.

At Eton, amongst his own, he'd known exactly who he was. At the local comprehensive he was sent to, he understood only how he was perceived. 'Ewe-gow!' the boys would taunt (none of them had names like that). They'd mock his accent, his bobbing up on autopilot whenever a woman entered the scene (he made himself stop that pretty quick), the different way he held his knife and fork.

They called him Lord Snooty, after the character in the *Beano*. The only way to cope with it all was to become a cartoon character himself: smile inanely at the taunts, adopt a silly voice, and develop a sly wit. He never explained why he was so different – or took the risk of attempting to make new friends.

He imagined it was much the same for Kathy, who'd also been torn from a smart school, but never discussed it with her. After the first storms of sobbing, the angry threats to run away, Kathy had developed her own shell. They were like frightened foreigners, dumped in an alien world, forced to learn a new language at speed. Hugo envied his older sisters, who'd both moved away by then.

Suddenly, there was no structure to life, no web of agreeable pursuits to while away the cushioned time. Space had shrunk to fit like a box. Beauty had vanished, along with certainty.

If Hugo had been asked to name the dominant flavour of his childhood, he might have replied: 'terror'. It was fear that had seasoned the bland perfection of life at Edgerton. All of them except Alice had been afraid of Pa, who had controlled them so effortlessly.

But now . . . Pa would appear for breakfast, silent and grey, his familiar clothes hanging off him. When they first moved into the new house, he'd try out one chair after another, never satisfied. It wasn't for ages that Hugo realized what he was searching for. All his life, Pa had been greeted by sunlight. But the cottage faced north, so there was never any sun in the mornings.

The family would sit at the round table from the morning room at Edgerton, which only just fitted into the new dining room. Hugo remembered a deep gloss with, always, the reflection of flowers. Now the table was covered in green felt and, over that, a white cloth, and there was no longer money for flowers.

It was Ma who cooked for them these days: poor Ma, who was doing her best. But meals were always late. And even though Ma used one of Mrs Briggs' old recipe books (*Cookery in Colour*), the food never tasted the same.

They lived off Ma's modest marriage settlement, or dowry (which Lloyds could not touch), the trust having been freed by concerned executors. Pa could have tried to get a job, of course. But, for reasons Hugo didn't understand, this was never an option. And what employer would put up with Pa's moodiness, anyway?

And now there was a new kind of tension between the parents. Hugo couldn't work it out. It was as if a secret conversation was being held behind the mundane queries and responses – Ma's attempts to impose a structure – that began once breakfast was finished with.

'Are you going to sit there all day?' Sounding brisk and pleasant – but Hugo knew she'd never have dared say it before.

'Am I?' Pa would respond very courteously. It was as if he were playing a game of handing Ma something. And then he'd start shaking with laughter – but with a frightening savagery, as if really he was mocking himself.

'There's wood to be fetched,' Ma would continue in the same energetic reasonable way, ignoring the laughter. Then she'd add, 'Darling', as if she'd just remembered to.

'Ah!' said Pa, raising his eyebrows. Then, as an afterthought, he too would tack on an endearment. 'My love,' he'd say expressionlessly.

'. . . and shopping to be done.'

Hugo approved of the newly confident way Ma spoke to Pa, although, at the same time, he couldn't help feeling it didn't become her. Ma had always been a very feminine kind of woman – though he'd sensed a power there all right.

But Pa never did fetch the wood or do the shopping, and Ma would only mention it once. So Hugo fetched the wood, before leaving for school. He did as much as he could for Ma, who managed everything else. Her hands were changing, he noticed: becoming red and chapped. But she still wore her nice clothes from before, and at the end of the day, after cooking another revolting meal, would change into smarter clothes to eat it, though she no longer smelt of Chanel No. 5.

Pa never read now, or even did the crossword. He wouldn't listen to music, either. Once, after Ma had been catching up on the news, Fauré's *Requiem* came spilling out of the old wireless, bathing the dingy room in sweetness. But Pa snapped the sound off immediately, as if it were dangerous.

Hugo wondered what he thought about, as he sat staring into space. Sometimes he'd mutter strange things – 'don't!' he said once, very urgently; and, on another occasion, with terrible weariness, what sounded like 'skin!' Hugo never made any sense of it. He wondered if Ma could. Sometimes he'd catch her looking very afraid. But then – as he picked up the anxiety – Ma would smile at him. It was all right really, she was telling him. He felt very close to her these days.

But, for all Ma's gentle nagging, Hugo noticed that Pa did have his own secret agenda. An hour or so after breakfast, he'd put on his walking shoes and his tweed cap and tuck his corduroy trousers into his socks. Then he'd set off through the sagging wooden gate and down the tiny lane leading to their new home.

He'd be absent for hours. He'd return not spruce and

jaunty, as in the old days, but more silent than ever. Hugo never knew where he went. Edgerton was at least thirty miles away. Even so, he would picture his father creeping close enough to their old home to hear the bonging of the clocktower and the fluttering of the doves. Pa would be trying to fool himself he could reverse time. Hugo knew, because it was what he himself never stopped dreaming of doing.

Every so often, Eve would come back for a weekend. Hugo noticed that she didn't seem happy either – but at least she'd escaped. She didn't have to put up with life in this minuscule house, despising Pa a little more each day. Eve was lodging in Streatham in London with one of the pretenders. Having been put on a typing course by Pa, she'd found herself a secretarial job working for a firm of chartered accountants. But she never talked about work. She wasn't fun any more. She didn't even look the same, in her neat dark clothes, with her hair cut short.

Alice was in London, too. For her, it was different – but then, it always had been, thought Hugo bitterly. Alice who seldom came home if she could help it and wouldn't even look at Pa if she spoke to him. His parents never stopped reminding him they were no longer rich but, mysteriously, there was money for Alice. Alice had somehow been able to afford to share a flat with two girls – 'A hoot!' she told them; and, unlike Eve (whom she never seemed to see any more), was free to pursue her dreams.

All his life, Hugo had perceived Alice as silly. He'd been encouraged to believe it was part of her charm. But – with help from a crammer – Alice had retaken her O levels and passed all six. She was doing A levels now. Her sights were set on one of the new universities. 'You'll be ancient!' mocked Hugo. 'So what?' retaliated Alice. She hinted at a mysterious but richly rewarding private life. (Soon she'd shock them with news of a second marriage.)

It was such fun. She said so lots of times, her face lively and rosy. Being Alice, she'd even persuaded Ma to take Champion. This was a bonus for Hugo, who rediscovered all his old love and admiration for the dog. Not so Pa, who still flinched away from Champion as if he were the devil.

It might have gone on like that for ever: Pa getting older and more resigned, and, with increasing frailty, disappearing less and less often. And then one Saturday, just over a year after they'd left Edgerton, Mrs Briggs made contact.

Hugo heard his mother on the telephone (there was only one, just as there'd been at Edgerton). 'Briggs!' she exclaimed, thoroughly taken aback. 'How nice!' she went on, trying to compensate for the discourtesy.

Hugo watched his father become strangely alert, like when Champion smelt a fox.

'Well, yes,' said Ma. 'Why don't you come at four o'clock? That would be lovely!' And then they heard her give Mrs Briggs elaborate instructions on how to find the cottage.

'Briggs?' enquired Pa, when Ma had put the phone down.

'She's been visiting her niece,' said Ma. 'She's agreed to drive her over, apparently. They're only five miles away.'

'Briggs?' said Kathy in a little high voice, as if awakened from a dream of childhood.

Then Ma started faffing about what to give Mrs Briggs and the niece for tea. There was no time to go to the village shop, she told them; still less to work out how to cook scones. In the bread bin, there was half a sadly sunken chocolate cake she'd made two days ago and two flabby ginger biscuits. Then she had an inspiration: 'Honey sandwiches!'

'Is that wise?' asked Pa with his old harshness.

Then Hugo saw Ma bite her lip, one hand to her forehead. She looked suddenly appalled. Hugo was puzzled. How could it be unwise to make Briggs and her niece honey sandwiches? He was looking forward to them himself. But actually, he was hoping against hope that Briggs would roll up her sleeves and magically produce a rack of warm and yeasty black-frilled buns.

Mrs Briggs had put on a lot of weight. She still smelt powerfully of sweat, though. Hugo stared at her plump face with its popping brown eyes, the familiar deep line – like a cut – round her fat neck.

She seemed very pleased to see them all, though strangely rattled. By contrast, her niece – a dark bird of about thirty, caked with make-up – seemed pretty confident.

They all sat in the drawing room, and Hugo had to fetch two wooden chairs from the dining room. He saw Mrs Briggs' pop-eyes return again and again to the Oriental lamps each side of the tiny fireplace, as if she were trying to get her bearings.

'Cosy,' said the niece, and Hugo saw his father raise his eyebrows and smile faintly.

'It gets nice and warm in the evenings, with the fire,' Ma agreed. Hugo loved her dignity. It struck him that nobody possessed enough power to take away that.

Then Champion trotted in on his three legs. 'Remember Champion?' said Ma. She excused herself and left the room.

'How old is he now?' asked Mrs Briggs as if she couldn't think what else to say. (Pa was being very silent.)

'Seventy-seven,' Hugo told her.

'Seventy-seven?' repeated Mrs Briggs, very puzzled.

'Dog years,' Hugo explained airily.

Ma came back with the heavy tray of tea and immediately Mrs Briggs rose and would have taken it from her, only her niece caught her by the sleeve, smiling, and pulled her down again. 'Be-ryl!' she said, and rolled her eyes ceilingwards.

Hugo offered round the honey sandwiches, which looked very lumpy and inelegant against one of Ma's old blue and white plates.

'Thank you, Hugo,' said Mrs Briggs with a smile.

Soon afterwards Pa got up and left the room.

It took Hugo a whole day to work out what was wrong with that sentence.

A week later, it was obvious where Pa had gone on his mysterious expeditions. Monkton Beacon was fifteen miles away – nothing for a man as athletic as he. It had always been a favourite spot of his – a natural watchtower from which to survey the lesser world; and, from the apex of its great height, it was even possible to locate the honey speck of Edgerton. It must have brought back memories, too, of the first scent of a new love affair, more delicious and dangerous than all the rest.

They found him sprawled and broken on the rocks at its foot. In its own savage way, the act had beauty as well as logic. Years later, Hugo understood that, for Pa, choosing to die in such a fashion must have perfectly encapsulated his fall from grace.

Chapter Thirty

'I guess you'll be throwing this pâté?'

The visitors had gone and Alice and Eve were alone together in Mossbury Park's great hall, slinging smeared paper plates into black plastic bags, picking up torn wrapping paper and ribbon from the floor.

'God no, Alice! That's for tomorrow's lunch.'

As they straightened chairs, Alice discovered that Ma had left one of her presents behind. It was the hen tea cosy Arthur had retrieved from his car. It had a scarlet head, staring purple eyes and brilliant yellow wings painted with emerald feathers to match its yellow beak. It would be very useful: Ma's tea was always lukewarm. Eve said as much to Alice: 'She forgets everything, these days.'

'What in heaven possessed her?' Alice separated out each word, as if still in shock.

'When he came in . . .' Eve shivered.

'Soon as I saw his tie . . .'

'He was wearing Brut,' Eve recalled with a wry smile.

After a bit, she went on, voice flat, 'Wonder what he'd be like now . . .'

The shell of a log settled noisily in the enormous fireplace, joining a mass of glowing embers: all that was left of the splendid blaze Edward had created earlier.

'Not attractive any more . . . Not active . . .'

'He'd have *hated* it.'

'That's what I've had to keep on telling myself,' Alice said quietly.

The old intimacy had crept up on them: dreaded and longed for, as inevitable as being pounced on when playing grandmother's footsteps.

Edward put his head over the banisters. 'Got Milo to sleep!' he told Eve triumphantly before starting to descend the grand staircase. Thump, thump, thump. He was a big man now with shelves of flesh under his chin and a football midriff. Alice also noticed how frayed the carpet was. It couldn't have been good quality in the first place.

'*Think* that was a success . . .' Now he and Eve could hold an enjoyable autopsy on the evening. No reason why the unnerving presence of his first wife should interfere.

'Oh yes!' Alice assured him brightly. 'Ma had a wonderful time.'

He examined the bottles that were left, found himself a cleanish glass, measured out some dregs of supermarket plonk and tasted them in exactly in the same pernickety way Alice remembered from their marriage. He frowned slightly, caught her watching him, waved a bottle a little uneasily in her direction.

'Funny fellow,' he pronounced as he fell back into a flaking leather armchair like a big stuffed doll.

'Mmm?' Eve murmured as if thinking of something else.

'Oh, very agreeable!' he assured her quickly. Nobody could accuse him, these days, of being a snob. No, what he'd really meant was funny *business*. He sipped at his glass again, as if taking medicine. 'Looked a lot like your father.'

'What?' exclaimed Eve.

He was honestly astonished. 'Didn't you notice?'

'Darling,' said Eve sharply. 'Go to bed.'

'What?'

'It's past midnight.'

'But I've only just . . .'

'Alice and I can manage here,' Eve told him firmly. 'We'll talk about it all tomorrow.'

He stared at her, puzzled, a little hurt. Alice guessed that, if she hadn't been there, he'd have objected. But, in that case, the conversation might have been quite different.

'Righty ho,' he agreed surprisingly amiably. The Bulgarian Merlot had left maroon crescents, like crudely crayoned smile lines either side of his upper lip. Eve licked a paper napkin and rubbed them off before letting him kiss her. 'See you very soon, my darling,' he said, turning it into a plaintive enquiry. As an afterthought, he gave Alice a peck on the cheek too, but couldn't resist asking, 'How long are you with us?'

'As long as she likes,' said Eve.

'Till tomorrow afternoon, if that's okay, Edward,' said Alice with a smile. 'Then I'm going to Ma for a few days.'

After he'd left, Alice didn't look at her sister, but Eve wouldn't have noticed anyway because she was absorbed in rubbing at a mark on her skirt.

'I'm glad he came,' she said.

'Me too,' Alice agreed, understanding precisely. It was as if the interruption had never occurred.

'Interesting for the kids to have more cousins.'

'Mmm. I must try and meet them, before I go.'

Eve said, 'Now *he* was good.'

'Seemed so.'

'Decent and kind.'

'Not exactly scintillating, though,' said Alice, glancing at Eve.

'Not exactly.'

'Not that it matters,' Alice amended too quickly.

Eve said nothing. Her face in repose was old and full of worry.

'If Pa had been given more tenderness . . .' Alice began eagerly.

Eve smiled faintly. 'Gran was kind to *us*.'

'That was different.'

They'd finished clearing the long table where the buffet had been laid out. Alice wiped it over with a damp cloth, noticing the scratches and rings, remembering a dark mirror skimmed by white mats, as fathomless as Edgerton's lake with its floating water lilies.

'Tea?' Eve offered.

'Love some.'

Alice followed her sister into the big un-modernized kitchen, leaning against a cupboard and watching as she plugged in an electric kettle, found teabags, opened the enormous refrigerator to search for a matching-sized carton of milk. Little magnetic strips were scattered over it: fridge poetry constructed without real thought or effort, 'hunt a golden queen with monkeys . . . spray dreams after diamond highs . . .'

Alice spelt out in similar fashion: 'pale arms snatch solace in daffodil tempo.' She said: 'They give you odd words, don't they? Tempo . . . And how often do daffodils actually come into a conversation?'

'Not yours. More like bougainvillea, shouldn't wonder.'

'Yes, I've bougainvillea in my yard.'

'Yard!' scoffed Eve. 'Won't find *that* here!'

The enormous house was quiet now though it creaked occasionally, just as Edgerton had done: old floorboards flexing back into shape after the punishing trampling of the day, beams groaning under the weight of an ancient lead roof.

'Where is he?' asked Alice. She'd forgotten the wonder of being able to communicate like this, in private shorthand born from an intimate history. But there was apprehension in her voice too. Did she truly want to know?

'Library,' Eve responded immediately. When Alice raised her eyebrows, she went on. 'Ma wanted it.'

'The barracks?'

'He *hated* the cottage.'

'All this time!'

'When the people who bought Edgerton said no,' Eve explained, 'nobody seemed able to make a decision. I think Ma's totally forgotten about it.'

'It suits her to forget,' said Alice. It was probably the most critical thing she'd ever said about her mother.

After a moment, she looked at her sister, eyes gleaming. Her voice rose a little with excitement, just as it used to. 'Eve, you're going to think I'm crazy!'

'No,' said Eve immediately and very firmly.

'Why not?' demanded Alice.

'Because,' said Eve, as if talking to one of the smaller children.

'If it's Ma you're worrying about –'

'Not really.'

'– she's not even going to notice. You just said so!'

The two middle-aged women looked at each other and a silent smiling argument took place. They might have been back at Edgerton in the old days, planning an escapade. Eve had been frightened of their father then; Alice, the favourite, had nearly always managed to win her round.

Eve warned, 'You'll get a shock.'

'I'm prepared.'

'Sometimes it's best to leave things be.'

'Oh, Eve,' said Alice with passion, 'that's where you're *so* wrong!'

In the unlikely event that Edward would wake up, they left a note on the kitchen table. 'Gone for drive,' it said. 'Don't worry, back soon.'

Outside, the rain was threatening to start again – a faint peppering of fine drops – and Eve cast a worried look at the sky. Heavy rain, of the sort they'd been getting increasing amounts of lately, meant further saucepans in the attic. Yesterday, she'd had to crawl through spiders and dust to reclaim one before she could boil up kidney beans for a salad. The roof was constantly in the back of her mind, putting a damper on plans for holidays and new clothes. Sooner or later that problem would have to be faced. But then so, too, would the long boundary wall which had collapsed last winter, and the guttering on the south side of the house knocked awry by rampant Virginia creeper.

They took old Lady Farquhar's Volvo that stank of dog and had served the family faithfully for ten years now.

'Should we fasten his seatbelt?' Alice asked her sister before she got into the front beside her.

The joke brought home the reality. Pa was behind them in the darkness, silent while they talked. Pa was surely gathering up the reins of his old power with every wobbly metre of road examined by their rain-spotted headlights. At one point, Alice actually turned in her seat, as if expecting to see him leaning lazily back in his beige cashmere cardigan laced with moth bites, wavy hair sleek and smelling of lemons, lips twitching at some naughty secret; even caught herself wondering, a little sadly, 'How would he see me now?' But there was only the dull glimmer of pewter tucked into a dog blanket.

They started justifying themselves.

'I know he'd want this.'

'Oh yes!' Eve sounded very confident.

'Mean of those people.'

'No skin off their backs.'

'Ma would want this, too.'

'I think so.' But Eve thought: 'I'll never tell Ma – unless she asks, which she won't. Or Kathy. Or Hugo. I'll have to decide about Edward.'

Alice was remembering taking this same drive to break the news to her parents that she was leaving her husband for another man. Each turn of the road brought back the pain of being young and scared and in love.

When she'd found Pa alone, she'd believed it was fate. There was nobody she respected more, or strove harder to please. But now, for the first time, they'd talk as equals. She was going to break it to Pa that she was a romantic, just like him. It wasn't her fault. It was her nature, and it would be another bond.

Pa's reaction had marked the true end of innocence. Nearly forty years later, the memory of it brought tears to her eyes; and, not for the first time, she wondered if her own tragedy could have been avoided, had Ma been present. Pa would never have dared talk in front of Ma in that detached cynical way; Ma might even have guessed about the pregnancy. With a strange wistfulness, middle-aged Alice lingered on the scenario that had never happened. Then she recollected meeting Ma halfway down the drive. Returning from her own lunch, Ma had seemed just as self-absorbed as Pa (and probably only thinking about flowers or suchlike).

'Oh, you won't believe this,' said Eve, as if reading her sister's thoughts yet again. '*Ma had an affair!*' Then she bit her lip, conscious of a lack of tact. But the fact was, for all his terrifying power and legendary charisma, Pa was reduced to a heap of old ash in a metal jar.

In more than thirty years, the public roads had changed a lot: smooth tarmac, efficient signs and complicated white lines and cats' eyes. Even after living in the United States for so long, Alice had perversely expected everything in England to stay the same.

'It's not far away at all as the crow flies,' said Eve. 'Do they fly straighter than buzzards, do you think?'

Signs loomed up: they should prepare for a lay-by, a Happy Eater, a hotel with forty bedrooms.

Alice said: 'It can't be true!'

'Mmm?'

'We'd have noticed something!'

'It is! She told Kathy and me all about it.'

'She's made it up,' said Alice very definitely, as if she needed to believe this.

'You weren't there, Alice!'

'At least *we* won't have to invent men!'

Eve glanced at her sister in the dark, and experienced a wave of intense affection. The sweet profile had scarcely altered with the years. 'She's the only person I never have to explain to,' she thought.

'*Don't say you've forgotten!*' It was as if a third person spoke out loud in a harsh sardonic tone. Eve heard the voice in her head, even as she felt the still presence of Pa in the seat behind her. '*You cannot possibly have forgotten!*'

The car swerved, and Alice glanced anxiously at her sister.

They couldn't have arrived, even though Eve had slowed for turning, because a sign on a new gateway made of yellow cement informed them that this was the Monkton Glen Hotel.

Still, Eve did not reply. Cruelly, it seemed, she let realization dawn on Alice. The green toothbrush down the centre of the road had been excised – it was smooth as a main road now – and the beeches either side pollarded so they could no longer exchange decorous embraces. But each turn in the avenue was familiar. It felt like crawling towards a light.

Eve drove on, stubbornly choosing not to respond to Alice's imploring expression, or stop so as to allow her to recover herself. But she slowed the car right down just before they rounded the last corner.

Reason told Eve the house couldn't have been altered too

much: it would not have been allowed. But beauty and order vanished. That much she'd learnt.

She was confounded. The house delivered the exact same punch to the gut as it always had, however many times they'd returned to it: the same magical composition of golden stone and lacy turrets and mullioned honeycomb-like glass; the same graceful grouping around it of clocktower and chapel. She heard Alice sigh; and then she stopped the car – but at a distance, tucking it discreetly on to a dark verge.

They were silent for a few moments, and then Alice whispered: 'Why's it all lit up?'

At last Eve responded. 'Hotels never turn their lights off.'

They tiptoed over the gravel in their party shoes, noting changes. There was hidden lighting, too, that illuminated each leaf on every neat shrub, the faint stripes on the shaved lawns. They were two women in late middle-age. Surely nobody would take them for burglars?

'D'you think they've got CCTV?' asked Alice nervously.

'These are probably just for show. Anyway, everyone's asleep by now.'

At least there were no dogs, thought Alice; and remembered, with a pang, the old fiercely protective mob. It was very late. She glanced at her gold watch and waited, mouth already dry, for the bell in the tower to mark the second hour past midnight. The sound was as crucial a part of Edgerton as its smell compounded of beeswax and dried flowers and over-boiled vegetables.

But nothing happened.

With her excellent long sight that only improved with age, she focused on the clock face (another pale moon in the darkness), and saw the big minute hand inch past the hour hand.

'Did you know?' She could scarcely speak.

'No,' said Eve. 'I knew they'd sold it for a hotel. I told you, this is the first time I've been back, too.'

'But why?'

'Imagine paying to come here and expecting to sleep!'

'There are no doves!' Alice sounded utterly disconsolate at the lack of rustling and settling, the flashes of white feathers.

'Milla *never* cleans out her budgie,' observed Eve for some reason.

But Alice was noticing a new sound. The house hissed, as if expelling its breath: a constant low 'ssss'. She looked anxiously at Eve.

'They had to put in central heating, of course.'

Alice shivered with distaste. Standing outside, staring at the house's exquisite unchanged façade, she pictured walking through its long corridors in light clothing; and, with unreasonable melancholy, remembered the deadly chill in the bedrooms, the ancient Turkish carpets lifting with the draughts.

'What about the panelling?'

Eve shrugged.

'Pa would be furious!'

All this time, Alice had been holding him. (By unspoken agreement, it had been she who removed the urn from the car, just as he'd once infinitely tenderly lifted her out of another.)

It was Eve who carried the trowel.

They were reminded of the real purpose of their visit.

*

At first they believed they'd gone a little crazy. Or maybe they were in one of those recurring dreams that seemed to happen as often in California as in the west of England.

They knew exactly where the graveyard was: more than thirty years on, they could have drawn detailed maps of Edgerton and the estate. Besides, the graveyard was positioned exactly where one might expect it to be: at the back of the exquisite Ham stone chapel.

Except that behind the chapel they could find only level asphalt, with dozens of expensive very clean cars parked on it.

Alice shot Eve a look of panic. Where was terrifying old Grandpa, whom she believed she just remembered? And great-Grandpa, who'd met his maker in a rocking chair in a corner of the great hall? And the legions of other Chandlers who'd lived in the sure knowledge that they were entitled to fetch up in this beautiful exclusive spot? What had been done with their leaning headstones and rotting coffins? And what had happened to all the urns, like cousin Cecil's, tucked in at the last minute, like gatecrashers slipping into parties?

'There's no law to say you can't do away with graveyards,' said Eve slowly.

As one they turned and looked at the chapel. They remembered an exquisite rood screen, a pulpit of dark wood carved into leaves.

And then they became aware of the same hiss exhaled by the house, and a sign in gothic lettering proclaiming: 'Annexe'.

'*There are people in there too!*' Eve whispered. She found it unbearable to envisage warm space sliced into bedrooms and bathrooms and perhaps even kitchenettes. Instead, she thought resolutely of sleeping bodies bandaged with motheaten hemmed blankets and arranged head to toe along mahogany pews, breaths cloudy against the incense-tinged darkness.

'Pa would be furious!' Alice repeated. Then she asked pitifully, 'What shall we do now?'

A week ago, Eve would have urged Alice to abandon her plan – pointing out how foolhardy and perhaps even unseemly it had been in the first place. But, since meeting Arthur, there'd been a crucial sea change in her. She found, to her astonishment, that she could not bear to inflict any more disappointment on her father.

She noticed that Alice was stroking the urn as if to soothe whatever was inside. She asked, 'Do you remember where it was?'

'Of course!'

'D'you think we could find it?'

But Alice was already off.

A cloud freed the moon, and by its full chilly light they replaced the cars with plots and gravestones.

'Uncle Hector,' said Eve, pausing by a gleaming mud-free Land Rover with a bull guard across its radiator. She murmured under her breath: 'Blessed are they which do hunger and thirst after righteousness.'

'And here's Gran,' Alice called softly, as she stood by a green BMW with a personalized number plate parked near the west wall.

Eve joined her and they silently shared the horror of their first funeral: Beatrice hidden in a bewilderingly small coffin, they being encouraged by the grown-ups to throw handfuls of earth on to her.

'Somebody must have told Ma,' said Alice, as they went on searching the car park.

'They probably did ... She wouldn't have wanted to know.'

'Where have they *gone*?'

Eve shrugged. 'I expect we could find out.'

'Pa would be furious!'

Eve thought: 'More likely, having the last laugh. As it turned out, he was the only one *not* to be dug up by bulldozers and carted off to some unknown destination.'

'But actually ...' Alice began, as the same thought occurred to her.

Hugo is being simply wonderful, Ma wrote during the months following Pa's terrible funeral – and, thousands of miles away by now, Alice winced at the implied criticism.

She had seen her dreamy little brother turn into someone else: watched him being jerked into the real world as violently as if he'd been slapped. He was expected to be the man of the house now. His voice was no longer a boy's, and it had become strangely rough and classless, as if Hugo was very determined not to sound like Pa.

He will keep on calling them usurpers, but I'm sure they're perfectly nice people, Ma wrote of the rich family who'd bought Edgerton but refused to allow Pa burial in the family graveyard.

She explained to Alice in her letter that these same nice people – who had six children – had just denied her request for Pa's ashes to be interred there. ('So he can't even sneak in like a pretender,' thought Alice.)

I think it must be because they're mackerel-snappers, Ma wrote, borrowing the expression from her late mother-in-law (and resisting pointing out that, in four hundred years, there'd never been Catholics at Edgerton). *Hugo says that if I won't make a fuss, he will . . . But of course, I'll let him do no such thing . . .*

'Usurpers!' thought Alice contemptuously. At Edgerton, of course, Pa's body would have lain in the house for a week (though probably not in an open coffin) before it was buried in the space he'd long marked out for himself.

But in the family's changed circumstances it had been deemed prudent for Pa to remain at the undertakers; understood, too, that – failing burial at Edgerton – cremation was the sensible option.

Ma still agonized about that decision, in her fashion.

Besides . . . she'd begun, before neatly excising it: the closest she came to spelling out what they all knew – that Pa had been horribly broken on the rocks as well as disfigured by the sea.

Far far away, Alice reflected once more that none of the Edgerton Chandlers had ever been cremated.

But then, none of them had endured exile.

Alice still believed in destiny (though she called it karma now). So when they found an empty space at the exact site they'd been searching for, facing west towards the lake, under the bay window where Ma used to sit, she smiled at Eve – her unchanged seductive smile radiating excitement and triumph: 'You see?'

It was the only empty space in the graveyard, and it had a silver Mercedes one side, a black Volkswagen Golf the other.

Alice set down the urn on the asphalt, and they crouched

each side as if waiting for Pa to tell them what to do next. Eve felt her bad hip click.

'Some form of words as we do it?' asked Alice.

'Let's just think about him first.'

The moon went in again as Alice tried to summon up the father she'd blamed for more than half her life. But it was no good. The selfish charmer who'd haunted two psychoanalysts' rooms had vanished as thoroughly as the inhabitants of the graveyard. She could find only pity for him now, and sorrow for the waste.

'It was my fault, not his, that I married a man I couldn't love,' thought Alice soberly. 'My choice alone to destroy a child I've never stopped mourning. After that, I appropriated my sister's happiness, as well as her education, only to toss them away like broken toys . . . And everything since, except my precious career, has been disaster. Three marriages have failed, and now I am on my own. But none of it was really Pa's fault. Finally, I have to face that. Pa loved me as much as he was able.'

Something of this inner turmoil must have shown in her face, in the moonlight.

Eve said, 'You've not told me about your life, Alice.'

And Alice thought with anguish: 'How am I going to be able to leave her?' But she said with a forced smile, 'We're meant to be thinking about him . . .'

'Tell me . . .'

Alice shrugged and then reeled off in a flat voice, unaware that she was blinking rapidly (just as her mother used to, when she was fazed): 'I have a wonderful life. I adore living in California. I've a marvellous job, masses of friends . . .'

'And love?'

'Oh, that!'

'Yes. That.'

'There's someone special,' Alice admitted. It was the most economical of explanations for Scott, who was married with three grown-up children and would never ever leave his wife; even Alice didn't believe it any more.

'And is that . . .?'

'What?'

'Something that might lead somewhere?'

'Eve, I'm fifty-six!'

'So?'

'It's . . . not what I want any more!'

'Isn't it?' asked Eve very gently, and – in the dark – more tears of self-pity welled up in Alice's eyes. Damn her sister! She felt the stoicism, layer upon layer, start flaking away. Perhaps Eve was right. Why shouldn't she wish for more?

'You're still a beautiful woman.'

'Don't!' said Alice, flapping away the absurdity, very pleased.

'You've always been able to have anyone you want.'

So there it was at last. A statement of fact. More crucially, a charge made more than thirty years late: an airing – finally – of the anguish and despair that had stifled a passionate hopeful youth, and led to hatred.

Alice stared at her sister, the tears beginning to overflow. *I'm so sorry*. She meant it from the depths of her being, but didn't – couldn't – utter the words. But then she'd never apologized, at the time, for taking Seb away from Eve. And nor had she apologized to her sister when – after that brief but formalized mismatch (which should never have happened) – she'd moved on to the next man. Throughout, she'd presented a bright brittle façade that must have appeared utterly heartless. She wasn't without empathy or shame: she understood very well what she'd done to Eve. But it had been easier to remove herself six thousand miles away than face the consequences of saying sorry.

It had seemed like punishment when, on her third marriage, eager at last to have children, she'd found herself incapable. Even so, in her heart – and most unfairly – she'd occasionally blamed Eve for not talking her out of the abortion. ('I was a child myself . . . And she was the eldest!') And now Eve had four children! Fertile Eve, who'd wrested her last, Milo, from the tumult of menopause!

Anger and jealousy had not been allowed, in their world. Pa had never taxed his mother with neglect and unkindness, just as Ma had not upbraided him for his infidelities. Denied release, the outrage had festered; but, of course, because of the secret language of families, everyone knew about it anyway. That was the thing about families. You dared not confront because there was no getting away from those people ('wrong!' thought Alice). You believed it diplomatic to keep quiet.

Only Pa – for once, not mocking or evasive – had dared speak out about the rules protecting the all-important structure, with the result that his favourite child, the one woman he truly loved, turned her back on him for ever. Small wonder that, when Edgerton was lost too, he saw little point in going on living. Pa, who'd used women so mercilessly, perceived himself finally at their mercy, and found it unbearable.

'Oh, Eve!' was all Alice said, but with a depth of sadness and regret her sister had never heard before.

It was enough.

Eve reached out a hand and – over all that remained of their father – touched Alice's briefly.

Long moments passed before she said softly, 'I envy you.'

Alice stared at her, thankful for the darkness. Was Eve trying, out of innate kindness, to play down the momentousness of what had just occurred? Or could she be speaking from the heart?

'I never thought it'd be like this!'

Alice became suddenly alert, waiting for the despair to pour out. This time there must be no holding back, because all of them had changed. The world they'd grown up in was lost for ever. What had replaced their Eden might be ugly and dangerous, but it had also brought liberty.

'Lady F. in her castle,' said Eve with a sharp edge to her voice. 'Isn't it ironic? I feel like Alex's gerbil.'

'What?'

'Running round in circles.' Eve pulled a heap of blue lavatory paper from a pocket and blew her nose very thoroughly. 'Always pinching and saving, never getting anywhere, no time for myself . . . Oh, if you only knew how I long for that!'

Water gushed from a pipe beneath the skirts of the house and Alice imagined a guest – like a ghost – rising comatose from a warm and comfortable bed and stumbling into an en-suite bathroom.

'And Mossbury Park!' Eve went on. 'It's like old Lady F. Nothing's ever ever enough.'

'I thought . . .' Alice began.

'Well, now you know.' Her old tight-lipped way: the misery tamped down, bottled.

Alice said cautiously, 'You don't have to live there.'

Eve said nothing.

'Pa was right. It's a hideous old barracks. It's not worth it!'

Eve didn't agree or disagree.

'Eve,' said Alice, putting out an impulsive hand, 'you can always come to me.'

Silence.

'For as long as you want,' Alice rushed on, thinking, 'I've done it! I've shaken off the handcuffs of the past.' It was an axiom of Dr Sayre's. Alice could picture the analyst's approval: not a smile, of course – never that – but a satisfied compression of the lips, followed by a lift of a wiry black eyebrow to indicate they could move on.

The moon emerged from the clouds once more. Eve was about to speak – Alice saw her lips part – but, then, for some unknown reason, was impelled to glance up at the house.

Somebody was sitting in the softly lit bay window, looking down on them.

Eve's immediate reaction was anxiety: they were, after all, trespassing. But there was something in the attitude of the watcher – a quality of stillness and resignation – that told her this should be her least concern.

It was a young woman in black. By contrast, her face was very white, set in a mask of anguish. As Eve stared back, straining to comprehend a wierd sense of recognition – she *knew* this person! – the woman twisted her pale hands together, as if some frightful idea had occurred to her.

Eve glanced fearfully at Alice but, during the brief moment she looked away, the woman vanished. When Eve searched for her once more, she found only an empty space, bisected by fussy looped curtains of a kind their mother would never have chosen.

Alice heard her sister sigh, and knew she'd been right to say what she had, and thought of the peace of her spacious sunny apartment in San Diego with its early morning view of sleeping seals on the beach. It would be a blessing, not an interruption, to have Eve there: a chance, at last, to expunge the guilt.

'Oh well,' said Eve, her voice flat, 'let's get on with it.'

'Eve?'

'Don't mind me . . .'

'Honestly?'

'Honestly.' Eve smiled at her sister in the moonlight. It definitely was a smile, thought Alice. 'If I can't let off steam to you,' Eve went on, 'who *can* I let it off to?'

'You don't have to live there,' Alice repeated.

Eve seemed honestly astounded. 'Of course I do!'

'I know but—'

'I couldn't do that to Edward!'

Alice stared at her.

'Mossbury means everything to him!'

Alice thought of her sister moistening a paper napkin with her own saliva, wiping the wine marks from her husband's mouth, kissing it.

'And the children adore it so. They're such lovely children, all of them. I'm so lucky.' Eve was speaking very rapidly. 'Hundreds of people'd give their eyeteeth to be living in a place like that. And there are the animals. I'm so lucky. It's *wicked* to complain!'

Moments passed. Then Alice said: 'Okay, let's do it.'

'Okay,' Eve agreed, very businesslike now.

'Let's open it here, where it would have been,' said Alice, 'and then . . . ' she left the sentence unfinished.

Then the wind could lift Pa over the great lawn, where he'd so often tried and failed to train his rabble of dogs, and waft him on to the lake, where he'd loved to sit and contemplate the pattern of his water lilies. It could spiral him up to the top of the silenced clocktower, where his doves had once murmured and rustled; and even blow him down the long avenue in search of new adventures. He would leave his secret mark on every part of Edgerton for ever.

Alice unscrewed the urn and, watched closely by Eve, upended it and shook it gently.

In the end, it was very undramatic: just a heap of old grey stuff pouring on to the tarmac. The slow drift of dispersal would come later.

Alice said: 'What do you think it was really like?'

'Sorry?'

For the first time, Alice was forced to translate – as if Eve were a stranger rather than the beloved sister she'd never stopped missing. 'Pa and Ma. I've always wondered. What do you think it was really like?'

'I think it worked,' pronounced Eve, after due consideration. 'In its own peculiar way.'